Fireflies in the Mist

a novel

D1322098

QURRATULAIN HYDER

Transcreated from the original Urdu by the author

INTRODUCTION BY AAMER HUSSEIN

women
UNLIMITED
an associate of
kali for women

SPEAKING
TIGER

WOMEN UNLIMITED
(an associate of Kali for Women)
7/10, Sarvapriya Vihar, First Floor
New Delhi – 110016, India

SPEAKING TIGER PUBLISHING PVT. LTD
4281/4 Ansari Road, Daryaganj,
New Delhi—110002, India

First published in English by Women Unlimited, an associate of
Kali for Women 2008
This edition jointly published in paperback by Speaking Tiger and
Women Unlimited 2018

ISBN: 978-81-88965-52-6
eISBN: 978-93-88070-84-3

10 9 8 7 6 5 4 3 2 1

Printed at Gopsons Papers Ltd.

Contents

Part III

"I am like that little bird which foolishly puts up its claws, hoping that it will stop the sky from falling."

That Little Bird:
Remembering Qurratulain Hyder

1: Annie Khala

In 1986, my sister rang to tell me that Qurratulain Hyder, along with some other Indian writers with whom she'd attended the Frankfurt Book Fair, would be reading at the Commonwealth Institute in London. Would I like to go along with her? She was our mother's friend, but we hadn't seen her for sixteen years; she might not even recognise us.

My mother called her Annie. I was the first among us to meet her, in 1968. I was thirteen. I didn't think that being a writer was that special—I'd met a few. Passing through Bombay on my way to school in Ooty, I'd been taken to visit her at her flat and, on learning that I was an inveterate reader, she arranged for copies of *Imprint*, the magazine for which she worked, to be sent all the way to the Nilgiris so that I could have my literary fix, since it published condensed versions of novels. (The novels I best remember reading in the journal were one by Aubrey Menen about the wives of Alexander of Macedonia—I think it was called *Conspiracy of Witches*—and *Rosemary's Baby*. Then Annie Khala, as I called her, switched jobs. Issues of the *Illustrated Weekly* began to arrive. I remember the Ghalib issue, which she must have edited. My Urdu wasn't very good—once I'd started to study Hindi after my move to India, I'd forgotten most of the little Urdu I'd known—but to this day I can recall the excitement of reading, in English, about the life of this man whose words I'd been listening to and singing all my life, in the context of his troubled times. (I now have a beautiful little book which contains Qurratulain Hyder's writings about, and translations of, Ghalib.) Another issue had an extensive coverage of the life and times of the actor Balgandharva; it made me aware of indigenous theatrical traditions that I, who had only ever seen bits of the odd nautanki at the Gwalior fair, wouldn't even have guessed existed. (Indian theatre is a constant motif in Hyder's fiction, and I am convinced she must have masterminded that issue.) Another focussed on Balasaraswati, grande dame of Bharatanatyam. So, in a way, she was my mentor at that time, even from a distance, connecting me, in English, to the sort of local vernacular traditions, high and low, that the urban bourgeoisie tended to marginalise or forget.

Then, in 1970, the time came for us to leave for London, and we were in Bombay again. Annie Khala invited my two sisters and me along with our mother to tea, and took us to a café nearby. That day, as we walked along the seafront, she talked about Nirad Chaudhuri's *Continent of Circe* and his theories of ancient India; I think she brought in Naipaul, too, of whom I'd never heard. Along with the erudition, the curiosity and the resources of knowledge, were phrases from her vocabulary that I picked up: 'male chauvinist pig', 'LMC' (lower middle class was an aesthetic, not an economic, judgement with her); and there was the hospitality of the send-off she'd arranged for a friend's brood of teenaged children—so casual, and yet so thoughtful and warm.

I'd forgotten so much about my two years in India, but never her. I suppose she was, in one way, the kind of person I was used to: my Karachi milieu was full of women who worked in the arts, journalism and the media, including at least one of her cousins. (In London in the early '50s, she'd worked for the *Telegraph*. Later, in Karachi, she had had a high position in the Ministry of Film and Information, and still later worked for the Pakistan High Commission in England.) But unlike most of them she was a single woman living on her own and entirely independent. Much later, I'd realise that leaving the relative affluence of her Pakistani life for well over a decade of near-anonymity before she achieved true recognition in India, was the price she'd chosen to pay for literary freedom. She was, somehow, one of the most modern people I knew, not in the ultra-chic anglophone Karachi way we were familiar with, but in a manner all her own, which combined tradition and innovation in equal measure. Even at that early age I could see how strangely innovative it was of her to live in Bombay alone, without a family, far from her U.P. roots. At the time I first met her, she must have just received an award—the Sahitya Akademi—for *Patjhar ki Awaaz*, the collection of stories she'd recently published, and between 1966 and 1967, more than twenty chapters of her work in progress, *Aakhir-i-Shab ke Hamsafar* (a novel about East Bengal which would, in its final incarnation become *Fireflies in the Mist*), had appeared in the Urdu journal, *Guftogu*.

Over the years, my mother made regular trips to India to visit her mother and siblings, and would bring back news of Annie. My picture of the intellectual journalist gained new dimensions when I learnt that her *Aag ka Darya* was not only the most famous novel in Urdu, but that she was meant to have left Pakistan, where she'd lived and worked on and off for 12 years, soon after the book was released over some controversy connected with it. (Today it's said that as a civil servant she wasn't allowed to publish without permission; she did, and her book was seen to be overly critical of the regime and the raison d'etre of Pakistan. Annie Khala herself would say, *"Arre nahin saab, aisi koi baat nahin thi. Bas chale gaye ham."* (No, nothing like that. I just left.) My mother and she exchanged letters regularly. In 1980, my mother brought back a signed copy of *Aakhir-i-Shab ke Hamsafar* that had been published a few months earlier. (I have that very copy beside me as I write this.) That, and *Kar-i-Jahan Daraaz Hai*, her two-volume memoir of her family—her parents were the pioneering Turcophile, Sajjad Hyder 'Yildirim' and Nazar Sajjad Hyder, the most popular novelist of her time—silenced forever the people who'd thought that Hyder was a one-book wonder, and that Urdu in India was in its dying throes. I was studying Persian and Urdu then, and delighted to find an essay about her early work in an Italian textbook; but we weren't given any of her stories to read in our courses, though we read some by her older contemporaries, Manto, Krishen Chander and Ismat Chughtai. My mother wanted me to read *Aakhir-i-Shab*, which I started but soon abandoned, because I found its first few pages with their meticulous description of an empty room (oddly enough) too western, and too unlike the robust Progressives I was used to.

In 1981, my mother was in India again, but her mother died before she could see her and for several years, six or seven, I think, she didn't go back. In the meantime, Annie Khala moved to Delhi, letters crossed, addresses were misplaced and they were, for a couple of years at least, out of touch. Now, finally, after all these years, she was in London. My sister and I made our way to the CWI.

"The emaciated old man in the threadbare, shiny suit..." the story Annie Khala read, in English, at the CWI was "Memories of an Indian Childhood." I had just begun to write myself, and it had everything I looked for in a story about childhood: memory, music, something poignant, something elliptical. (A little over a year later I wrote my "Little Tales", a story about children, inspired by "Memories". It was set in Karachi. Somehow, I'd learned more than I'd realised from her about the intimate connection between place, fiction and memory. When it was published in 1990, Annie Khala wanted to translate it into Urdu, but it never happened: Fahmida Riaz got there before her. The last time I saw her in early 2006 she said, with some regret, that it was one of those things she'd left undone. I pointed out the irony of her translating something that was so obviously influenced by her, because

I'd written it as if her hand were guiding my pen. She blushed, smiled, but didn't make one of her usual self-deprecating and dismissive remarks. (That last time I met her was in a Delhi winter. I was on my way to Ajmer with my mother, who was trying to call her, but found that dialling codes for Noida had changed. At lunch with Githa Hariharan at the Jawaharlal Nehru University campus, I mentioned we hadn't been able to get through to her; Githa rang up Ritu Menon on her mobile and said, Aamer Hussein is looking for his Annie Khala, and Ritu, who'd never met me, immediately rang back with the number. A day or two later Annie Khala sent her driver, Haldar, all the way from Noida to Friends Colony to pick us up and bring us to her. I went back to London and classes soon after that, but my mother saw a lot of her on that trip.)

Over the years, at least two other stories by Annie Khala would have a similar effect on me: "Exiles", that astonishing evocation of post-Partition expatriation, and "The Sound of Falling Leaves", with its laconic first-person account of a woman's existential crisis of bad faith and inauthenticity. I read both those in Urdu first, and it wasn't till 1994, and *Fireflies*, that she would become and remain my favourite writer.

At the end of the reading my sister spoke to Annie Khala. "You won't recognise me," she said, "I'm…" "Of course I do," replied Annie Khala, "Shahrukh."

She'd been in her early forties when we last saw her; now she was nearly sixty. She hadn't changed a bit herself, but I certainly had: I was thirty-one, but she remembered me well. A few days later, when she'd spoken to Mother and met her as if the intervening five or six years counted for nothing, she brought over a few things and moved into the guest room in my parents' flat. Life in Delhi, it was obvious, suited her more than Bombay had ever done. There wasn't going to be as long a gap between novels as there had with *Aag* and *Aakhir-i-Shab*. She'd been productive in the last few years and was working on what seemed to be a hugely ambitious polyphonic novel. In the mornings, dressed in neat western clothes and looking like any international postgraduate student, she'd take off for the India Office Library; in the evenings she'd come back and discuss her research, literature, the world. She must have been doing the final bits of research on *Gardish-i-Rang-i-Chaman*, because the next year, when she was back in London, she had an advance copy of the book and was giving public readings from it in libraries, community centres, the Urdu Markaz and the School of Oriental and African Studies, where she was introduced by the then octogenarian Mulk Raj Anand. She created a furore in the Urdu literary community; when asked about *Aag ka Darya* she'd display boredom and say, "Let's talk about today"; and about her departure from Pakistan she'd respond that she left because she wanted to live in India, not because of any controversy. She stayed with us again, probably for a month, and this time she gave me a sheaf of her stories to read in translation: this was most of the manuscript that would become the English collection, *The Street Singers of Lucknow*. I remember the picaresque magic of "Catherine Bolton", the surrealism of "St Flora", the Gothic of "Pali Hill". (I realise now what I didn't then: the minute I started publishing, she treated me as a fellow-writer. No, as soon as she knew I wrote. Intellectually. On another level I'd always be a youngster, to be treated with indulgent affection. And my barrier of respect would never, ever be lowered.)

She had, she told us, just completed a translation of *Aakhir-i-Shab*. An editor at Cape had expressed an interest in it and, it seemed, one of the most powerful agents in town was going to represent her. She showed me only a part of the manuscript: a section entitled "Caledonia", which she said wasn't in the original Urdu edition, and it foregrounded the colonial connection between Britain and Bengal. Something went wrong and the book never appeared in England. I was writing professionally by then and frequented literary circles; I often discussed world literature and politics with her. I think she was here in 1988 again, and by that time Ismat

Chughtai—in particular, for her novel *Terhi Lakeer* and her novella, *Dil ki Duniya*—had become my favourite South Asian writer. We had friendly arguments about that: Annie Khala preferred Manto's style.

The late '80s and early '90s were a prolific time for Annie Khala: *Chandni Begum* came out only three years after *Gardish*; and in 1989 she was awarded the Jnanpith. During the Gulf War she was in London and we would talk about the Muslim world, past, present and future. The bombing of Iraq made her think of the fall of Baghdad, and then of Grenada, Istanbul and the Delhi of 1857 which she'd written about in *Gardish-i-Rang-i-Chaman*. History was an obsession with her; she saw time as a continuum.

Annie Khala's intellectual influence on me was growing. I began to research the modern Urdu short story in the late summer of that year of '91, with the idea of publishing an anthology of translations. I read more in a few months than many people do over three or four years of postgraduate research. We talked about what I might include, about the world of Urdu and Pakistani fiction which I was discovering like a child in the Simsim cave. We explored the possibility that I might translate one of her stories: she suggested "Makalma", a surreal dialogue between two Pakistanis, written in the Fifties. Later, she translated it herself as "Point, Counterpoint", but didn't give it to me for my book because she hadn't been a Pakistani writer for more than three decades. It must have been about then that I read her collection, *Patjhar ki Awaaz*, which bowled me over and knocked me out, to put it crudely. (Annie Khala would enjoy this: she loved using slang when she spoke and wrote in English.) It had first appeared in the mid-Sixties: how could people ever have said that after *Aag* she had written herself out? I hadn't read most of her novels then, so I couldn't have said with the same degree of conviction as I do now, that the collection consists of some of her best and most representative work, including the short novel, *Housing Society*, which is the greatest ever evocation, in fiction or non-fiction, of upward mobility, shifting or assumed identity, financial scams and political repression in post-independence Pakistan.

In 1991 or '92 I was commissioned to write an entry on her for *Contemporary Foreign Writers*. Little by her, besides a handful of stories, was available in English and it was then that I read her work in Urdu. Her use of first-person narration, in particular, changed my way of writing in English. Her memoirs taught me more about the history of modern Urdu prose than any textbook, and filled in the gaps in my knowledge of social history. Even when she avoided specific queries about her texts, she was very willing to answer my questions, and when I talked about one story would often lead me to another. We discussed genre and gender. She had never, she said, made a great distinction between long and short fiction, her stories had novelistic elements, particularly in their chronology, and her novels often framed short stories. Did I, she asked, believe there was a difference between male and female writers? Tentatively, I said I felt there was. Her response was quiet, reflective and astonishingly simple: for a long time she hadn't thought about women's writing as a separate category, and then she'd realised that she saw the world as a woman and that that probably made her fiction different from her male contemporaries'.

One afternoon, she was sharing a platform with the redoubtable Gopichand Narang at SOAS. The Urdu establishment continued to be fascinated by whether she had or hadn't been the first to import the influence of Proust and Woolf and the techniques of modernism—streams of consciousness, interior monologue—into Urdu. None of that had much relevance to what she was doing now; technique was merely a vehicle for her ideas. She'd ceased to try to conceal her boredom at such questions, but Narang used updated terminology. Did you understand what he meant, she asked as we walked away from the lecture theatre, by *pas-jadeed* and *sakhtiyat?* Postmodern and structuralism, I said, and she, who'd wanted to have a laugh with me about the pretentiousness of imported theoretical terminology, was instead mildly amused that I'd bothered to learn these arcane terms in Urdu. (It occurs to me now that critics, if they hadn't had recourse to French theorists, would have had to invent such terminology in order to deal with much of her work.)

Some years later, she'd tell me it was Elizabeth Bowen, not Virginia Woolf, who'd influenced her. Bloomsbury was an influence she had soon outgrown; as for Proust, well, in her introduction to her memoirs she actually refers to them as *gumshuda zamanon ki talaash*—a direct translation of Proust's original French title, *A la Recherche du Temps Perdu*—so she may well have felt some affinity with his method and approach to memory. Then, in 1992, she published her translation of Hasan Shah's eighteenth-century memoir, which she reclaimed as the first modern Indian novel. The text probably proved her point about gender, because one of the most compelling features of her translation, introduction and notes to Hasan Shah's book is their foregrounding of the female protagonist, Khanum Jan's, voice and perspective. I wrote a long review of the book for the TLS; the second time, probably, that I had written about her. When I asked her to sign the book for me I addressed her, for the first time, as Annie Apa: many of her younger friends did, and at thirty-seven I was approaching middle age. She grimaced and said: "*Lo, ab main khala se apa ho gayi? Yeh bacche!*" (So now I've become your sister? These children!) The next time she phoned she said, "*Khala bol rahi hun tumhari.*" (This is your aunt speaking.) That was that. Henceforth all her messages, in Urdu and English, would be signed "Annie Khala", and I never referred to her as anything else. When I wrote about her work I kept a distance from our connection: in fact, I was more stern in my writing than I might have been with other writers I admired as much, if they'd been strangers. Sometimes I look at her handwriting below the crossed-out name on the title page and try to remember when—paradoxically, imperceptibly—the grande dame of Urdu literature and the witty, articulate and hugely affectionate family friend, ceased to be two and became one person in my mind: it seems as if

I'd always known that her public persona was only one dimension of this multifaceted woman, and that everything she was went into her writing, and all her writing, past and present, was there in her conversation and her presence.

2: Fireflies and Fellow-Travellers

In 1994, I was commissioned by the TLS to review *Fireflies in the Mist*. That "lost" translation of *Aakhir-i-Shab* had finally surfaced. I read it, entranced. Though it had many of the features of her stories there were, of course, significant differences: the complex intricacy of its structure, the long poetic passages that punctuate the criss-crossing narratives that are both taut and sprawling, the huge canvas, the sheer ambition of the work. What also remains from that first reading is the brilliance of some of the English prose. Some readers have found that her writing in English isn't that of a native speaker and doesn't quite match up to the fluency of the Seths and the Roys; it is valuable only because it conveys the content of her writing to readers denied access to her native language. In tandem, many admirers of her Urdu claim that the author has made changes to the extent that her English versions are reworkings rather than translations. Does she or any writer (e.g., Nabokov) have the right to edit her or his own texts? And if she does, is it more acute if a linguistic bridge is being crossed, and what are the contingent implications for translators?

Two of her best works, *The Sound of Falling Leaves* and *Housing Society*, had been translated by others, but she'd done "Memories of an Indian Childhood" and "Exiles" herself and proved that, had she wanted to, she could have beaten many of the Anglophones at their game. Even if you didn't like her use of the language, you had to admit that as far as dissecting subcontinental modernity went, Hyder was light years ahead of her contemporaries in any South Asian language at the time. "Exiles", published in book form in the early '50s in Pakistan, prompted visiting J.T. Farrell to say:

"At that age if she had appeared in a major western language, she would have won greater acclaim than Françoise Sagan", which made people in Karachi call her, quite mistakenly, the local Françoise Sagan for a while.

Fireflies in the Mist had new lessons for the writer who was trying to capture landscape—its short, sharp, lyrical fragments, evocative of Kalidasa, could switch from celebration to lament in the space of as few beats. Harvest superimposed itself on drought, drought on harvest. I had spent the winter of 1993, just after publishing my own first collection, in Dhaka, and that, of course, affected my reading of the Hyder text; I could see Dhaka as I read, and the voices of Bangladeshi friends and acquaintances echoed much of what she had written about the East Pakistan years and the creation of Bangladesh.

I was hugely impressed by the range and scope of the novel, and realised that there are, after all, things a novelist can do in one book that aren't really possible, except in miniature, in a short story. (The splendid "Exiles" remains a structural and stylistic precursor of Hyder's major novels.) What I also remember about that first reading is the power of the book's seeming randomness and its set pieces: the long evocations of the East Bengali landscape, of folk and classical poetry, and lengthy episodes that focused on a peripheral character, the expatriate Yasmin Belmont. Reading it again, and looking at the review I wrote then, I find my views have changed little; *Fireflies* is still one of my favourite Hyder books, but coming to it now, all these years later and after reading so many other works by her, I see a continuity: how consistent her world-view is, and yet how varied her style within the political and philosophical frameworks she constructs. As in *My Temples, Too* and "Exiles", she brings together a group of idealistic intellectuals against the background of a changing world, and then switches the backdrop with such dexterity that it takes her characters— and the reader—time to realise that they have suddenly been placed by the scene-changer on a set they didn't even know existed. In this respect, at least, Hyder's vision is remarkably close to that of the Marxist Faiz: in fact, she took the title of the Urdu version from a verse in one of his famous ghazals which casts light not only on *Fireflies*, but on her entire oeuvre until that point:

> *Aakhir-i-shab ke hamsafar, Faiz, na jaane kya hue*
> *Reh gayi kis jagah saba subah kidhar nikal gayi*

> (Those fellow-travellers of the night's last hours, Faiz—
> Who knows what became of them?/Where did they leave
> the morning breeze, what direction did the dawn take?)

Hyder was later to be accused of pessimism, for this novel in particular. But her project is evident in her first novel, and reiterated at various points in her work. A and B, the talking heads of "Point, Counterpoint" say, at one point of their abstract, surreal dialogue: "We are the culprits because we allowed our dreams to be lost." And Hyder herself, in her introduction to *The Sound of Falling Leaves*, the collection she published the year after *Fireflies*, writes: "Humanism has failed. Still, one must not despair, must not give up the fight."

In several of Hyder's works, an idealistic but very slightly doubtful heroine is left clinging to the wreckage of her hopes—the firefly illusion—while her companions (mostly male) are either martyred or join the oppressive system of capital and exploitation. Often, too, a vulnerable woman, sometimes a poet or a painter, allows men to exploit her— indeed, occasionally feels she is exploiting them—before she undoes herself or merely fades into anonymity. *Fireflies* retains these features, but imbues them with a tragic darkness that is perhaps more suffocating here than in any other of her works, with only the faint gleam of hope that the English title suggests, at a remote and future distance.

Urdu critic Neelam Farzana, in her wide-ranging study of Hyder's major fictions, sees the remarkable continuity of Hyder's vision in her work, but maintains that *Fireflies* is more plot-driven and, in spite of its constantly shifting points of view, a more cohesive narrative than her earlier fiction. I would argue that *Sitaharan* and *Housing Society*, though they are of course much shorter, are at least as cohesive; but I do agree that *Fireflies* is more accessible than the early Hyder works because the author has, to a large extent, learnt to dramatise her philosophical and political concerns in the service of a taut, sinewy narrative mode. There is also a careful tying up of loose ends at the novel's conclusion which may seem to some to hark back to nineteenth-century English models, but actually has more in common with early Urdu novels such as *Umrao Jan Ada* and, indeed, those of her own mother; it also has, in fact, in its use of masks, disguises and gradual revelations of identity, similarities to the traditional dastan, a genre from which Hyder, with her disdain for spurious exoticism, usually distanced herself, except in the use of its tropes as pastiche in some of her fictions. Whether this similarity is intentional or not is up to the reader to decide, but I find it endlessly tempting to speculate that she quite consciously and deliberately adapted techniques from our indigenous brand of magic realism to her own subversive post-modernist purpose. (It helps to remember that a mere eight years later Hyder was to publish *Gardish-i-Rang-i-Chaman*, with its princesses and courtesans and its painstaking reconstruction of 1857 and its aftermath, part of which is set at the very moment when the dastan would be rendered obsolete, and the bourgeois novel introduced under the auspices of Sir Syed Ahmad Khan's reformist disciples.)

Another major departure for Hyder is, of course, the very different geography of the novel: whereas in her stories Hyder ranged far and wide, her novels tended to focus on her native U.P. and on Pakistan, very often using the diaspora of 1947 and after as a deliberate ellipse in the narrative to signal the rupture caused by Partition in her characters' lives. *Fireflies* is almost entirely located in a territory (today's Bangladesh) scarcely mapped by Anglophone fiction. (Hyder had written about what was then East Pakistan before, in the playful "Tea Gardens of Sylhet", but that relatively slight work, though it does in Hyder's characteristic manner juxtapose the private and public spheres—continuing cross-border migration in Bengal and Assam—doesn't aspire to the range of the later work.) Ambitious, subtle and intricately structured, *Fireflies* spans nearly four decades from 1939 to 1979; its memories occasionally flash even further back, reliving East Bengal's history from a multiplicity of perspectives. Hyder's many characters witness the uprising of 1857, the dawn of nationalism, the partition of India and the creation of the two Pakistans, and the restless aftermath of the bloody struggle for an independent Bangladesh. While I was writing the early part of this piece, I discussed the novel with writer, Ananya Jahanara Kabir, who is a Bengali Muslim with familial roots in Faridpur. There had been, I said, some criticism of Hyder for venturing away from her familiar terrain of Awadh (and Karachi) into a land she knew less well. Was this justified? And were her aristocratic Bengalis perhaps too close to her U.P. aristocrats, in their effortless use of Urdu and their frequent recourse to the words of Amir Khusrau along with those of Lalan Shah and Nazrul?

"I was astonished at the accuracy of her portrayal," Ananya responded immediately by email. "The Bengali Muslims were really close to home, really authentic. And that amount of Urdu was inevitable at the time."

Fireflies can be interpreted as another chapter in Hyder's epic history of the Muslim presence in the subcontinent, and particularly in the era of the Raj. *My Temples, Too* chronicles Awadh; *River of Fire* and more than a couple of the novellas and stories take us to newfound Pakistan and, to quote Faiz again, the "stained light, the night-bitten dawn" of post-Partition; *Fireflies* adds the saga of East Pakistan and Bangladesh (ironically, history overtook Hyder while she was writing the novel, which bravely articulates the rupture in its architecture). But the Muslim narrative of *Fireflies*, though crucial to its weave, is merely one among many. Never bound to a single ideology or perspective, Hyder articulates one viewpoint only to contradict it in another voice. Colonial officers, native Christians, feminists, fishermen, artists, the victor, the vanquished, the exiled and the dispossessed, all take the platform to recount their stories, or to be represented, in a collage composed of omniscient third-person narration, letters, diary entries, extended exchanges of dialogue, dream-sequences, interior monologue, bone-spare chronicle, and oral history. Lyrical descriptions of East Bengal's landscape in snatches of folk-poetry are echoed by Hyder's own prose which combines sound and vision: "Farmers have put on their conical straw hats as they stand in knee-deep water, planting rice ... The fishermen's nets are filled with a silvery haul ... Famine stalks the land. Allah give us rain ... Allah ... Allah."

At the shifting centre of this many-centred novel stand Deepali Sarkar, a young Hindu attracted to the extreme left wing of the nationalist movement, and Rehan Ahmed, a Muslim radical of Marxist inclinations who introduces her to the life of the rural deprived. Their common political engagement draws them into a quietly doomed love affair. Through their relationship, Hyder explores the growth of tension between Bengal's Hindus and Muslims who had once shared a culture and a history. The secular Rehan dispassionately senses the need for a separate Muslim homeland, though not with the same vigour as his ageing aristocratic uncle who voices the pro-Pakistan ideology of the Muslim League to Deepali, with conviction. Both, however, lay claim to the syncretism of Bengali culture by articulating the enormous, and unacknowledged, contribution made to it by Muslims: Sufis, poets, musicians. What may have been interpreted as a special plea for the case of the East Bengali Muslim is deftly subverted, however, by Hyder's use of Deepali's sceptical Kayastha perspective.

Like a hero from a dastan, Rehan is not quite what he seems: he is, we discover, linked through his mother to the aristocratic world he despises; after the massacre of his relatives during the war for Bangladesh he returns to take his place as the rightful heir to the family's fortune. Here, dark fable combines with critical realism in a metaphor of post-national compromise; for *Fireflies in the Mist* is a post-nationalist epic that details the fervours of nationalist ideologies only to dissolve them in interlocking litanies of lost homes, blighted destinies and bitter civil wars. Deepali resigns herself to an expatriate married life in the Caribbean after Partition. Richard Barlow, a staunch imperialist, never ceases to long for an India lost to him; his son turns to diluted Oriental spiritualism. Yasmin Majid, an emblematic diasporic character of the sort that Bharati Mukherjee would later write about, leaves her strict Muslim background in search of love and art in Europe. Abandoned by her homosexual English husband, she drifts from job to degrading job, only to find herself shunned by her erstwhile compatriots when Pakistan changes shape in 1971. She writes of her double dispossession: "Going back to Hamburg. Now the river and the sea meet the ice. I tremble like a low-down bitch... My heart is the Harlot's Alley of Sonagachi. My wishes and regrets, all garishly made up, stand against the dirty walls, hoping that the next man may bring salvation. All doors are locked." Dying, she longs for the solace of Muslim prayer. But posthumous consolation will come in another shape: Yasmin's recognition as a great Bengali artist. Hyder neatly ties up ends by having Yasmin's diary delivered to Deepali; this will ultimately be the reason for the latter's visit home. (Homecomings, of course, don't really happen in Hyder's universe: the past, as Hartley said, is a foreign country.) The tying up is too neat, perhaps, but plausible within the economy of Hyder's fiction: it's worth remembering that this great and epic novel with its realistic surface texture is also, with its voyages and crossings and discoveries, its lost loves and recovered identities, the closest thing we have to a modern dastan.

Rehan defects, yes. But on second reading, situated as we are in the cynical post-nationalist world of the 21st century, his defection doesn't seem so terrible. In the short span between the establishment of Bangladesh as an independent nation-state and Deepali's first visit to her homeland, corruption is rife and identities once again in flux and in question. But the heritage of a lost generation is revived in Rehan's niece, Nadira, who kills a man in 1971 and is left traumatized by the senseless rape and carnage of war, but remains committed to the struggle for justice. "History," Hyder writes, "is another name for humanity's inability to learn its lesson."

3. An Emigrant and Gypsy of Narrative Structure

"Who is Pramoedya Ananta Toer?" Annie Khala asked me. "Some Sri Lankan writer?"

Writing about *Fireflies* I'd mentioned the Indonesian novelist's name in connection with hers, as a writer from Asia in the front rank of that amorphous category, World Class Literature, who, like her, deserved to be better known. But several works of his were available in English translation in international editions, whereas *Fireflies* was the first of hers to reach England.

English translations did, however, augur a new phase in her career, and an important aspect of this phase was growing recognition as a major literary force in India. Several of her books would appear in translation, beginning with *The Sound of Falling Leaves*, which collected all the stories from her classic collection, *Patjhar ki Awaaz*, and included an additional few. These two books drew the writer Amit Chaudhuri, who, aware of her legendary reputation but largely unacquainted with her work, read them in 1997. (I gave him a copy of the former, and lent him my only copy of the latter: this cemented our growing friendship, and today our admiration for Qurratulain Hyder is one of our many abiding mutual interests.) After much deliberation, he chose the story "Memories of an Indian Childhood" for inclusion in his anthology, *The Picador Book of Modern Indian Literature*. He has described her voice as "detached, quirky, fragile, nervous, by turns melancholy and extremely funny, pretending to hold a social conversation with the life whose passing spectacles it has no real control over". His analysis of her unique qualities continues:

> It is the responsibility of choice, located in the generation and political history she comes from, that occasionally gives her writing its haunting, existential quality. The restlessness and movement that have marked her itineraries in life characterised her writing as well; she is never happy inhabiting one point of view, but must flit startlingly from point to point and make transitions that we did not know the narrative was capable of; she is an emigrant and gypsy of narrative structure, which for her is always a point of departure rather than a resting place.

Chaudhuri, a great admirer of Manto and Masud, sees Hyder, along with them, as one of Urdu's greatest writers, but, speaking on the telephone from Calcutta, he also calls her one of India's best, lauds an experimentalism that crosses the conventional boundaries of the term, and expresses an intention to write more about her work. He points out that her unique qualities are evident not only in her novels, but in her short fiction and in novellas such as *Housing Society* as well. Hyder is also the only one of the writers mentioned whom he can read in her own words, and his admiration for her work rests on her English prose.

The publication of *Aag ka Darya* as *River of Fire* in English, again in her own translation, not only consolidated Chaudhuri's view, but brought critics such as Pankaj Mishra (in the *New York Review of Books*) and, only a few months before her death, Hirsh Sawhney (in the *Guardian*) into the orbit of her admiring critics. She was often seen as challenging prevalent notions of what the Indian novel (which had, until then, meant the Indian novel in English) could do. My own comparison in the TLS in 1998 of her status to that of Marquez and Kundera, her exact contemporaries, and of *Aag ka Darya*'s position in the Urdu canon to that of *A Hundred Years of Solitude* (which appeared a decade later) was to enter the idiom of Indian journalese, with Hyder regularly being referred to as Urdu's, and even India's, Marquez. This had not been my intention. (She didn't ask me who Marquez was, but she never, I think, read him.) More importantly, the publication of the book's Indian edition is a landmark in publishing history, raising questions of literary location, as a novel first published in Urdu, in Pakistan, now officially reincarnated as an Indian English novel which could be reclaimed by a younger generation of Anglophone readers, just as its protagonists reappear in different eras of Indian history.

With *River of Fire* Hyder became visible on the world stage. The novel was launched in London at the Nehru Centre, with the acclaimed doyenne of English poetry, Kathleen Raine, presiding over the ceremony. At Annie Khala's behest, I read from the book to the audience: a section set in London, as well the opening passages (the only time she ever admitted a liking for something she'd written).

The American edition was published in 1999, with an accompanying array of reviews. Finally, Hyder was recognised as a major literary figure in India; the availability of more of her work in English would make sustained and comparative analysis possible, and ensure an all-India canonical status. *Seasons of Betrayals* presented representative shorter fiction translated by other hands. *My Temples, Too* would be Hyder's last published translation of her own fiction into English, closing the circle of her work in a paradox: it's the first, and the last, of her novels. It's also an exquisite rendition of a time, a place and the sensibility of her mother tongue.

Ill health—which started with a stroke in 1994—and failing eyesight prevented her from writing more; but when I last saw her on the cusp of 2006–07, in her Delhi house, she mentioned that she'd been dictating the third volume of her memoirs in Urdu. She also mentioned an English version of the first volume. Where are these works? Were her last words to be found in Urdu, or English? I prefer to believe that she kept faith with her first language: though she loved English, she inhabited it the way she visited London, joyfully, but with a sense of transience and inevitable, if regetful, departure.

These short forays into her second language have left us, however, with a range of works in English which may not encompass the entirety of her canon, but are enough to ensure her reputation in that language; and what she did choose to translate is evidently what she wanted, at the time, to give of herself to the world.

Her international reputation will continue to grow. Many years ago, she wrote to me of a "proverbial slender volume" of her short fiction in Danish; I believe there are translations into German; and two of her works, *Aag ka Darya* and *Sitaharan*, are being translated into Italian. Valerio Pietrangelo, the translator of *Sitaharan*, wrote his M.A. dissertation on *River of Fire*, and remembers meeting Hyder twice in Delhi. He was overawed. When she died he wrote a tribute, regretting the fact that she was as yet unknown in Italy. She was, he holds, "an odd mixture of scholarship, novelty and inspiration; the Grande Dame of Urdu literature, she has no real equivalent in the panorama of 'western' literature". He also defines her work in English in Sukanta Chaudhuri's terms as "cultural or annotational translation", addressed primarily to the South Asian reader.

With her death in 2007, Annie Khala broke the mould. Hers is an impossible craft for successors to master; but in her production there are shards of knowledge for younger writers to pick up and preserve, and wonderful artefacts from which to take inspiration. Speaking of an eminence grise of Urdu literature the last time I met her, she said in Urdu: "These writers have such confidence, such arrogance. You write, I write: so what?"

Attempting to translate her words into English, I'm faced with the difficulty of nuance: I've rendered one word, *zaum*, with two; whereas it's impossible to capture the ironies of *ham bhi likh lete hain, tum bhi likh lete ho*, which diminishes and deconstructs the melodrama that some litterateurs make of writing. That space between our two languages is where I often find myself.

And at her best, that space was one she crossed with grace and ease. Perhaps the abiding metaphor of her work is the transience and resilience of hope, which she approached in so many ways, from so many directions, in both her languages. It emerges in a few lines at the conclusion of "Exiles", that story she rewrote in English as a young woman in Pakistan. These lines encapsulate the entire story and, in characteristic Hyder fashion, became the metaphor of many works to come.

In the stillness of night only the footsteps of death were audible, inscrutable death which suddenly appeared and accosted us. But we will bypass it and move on, laughing. Listen! We have complete faith and the conviction born of that love that some even call treason. This treason or treachery is nothing but a longing for the fragrance of jasmine blossoms.

AAMER HUSSEIN

London
January–February, 2008

Part I

Part 1

I
Caledonia

T HE Ganges is young and sparkling when it comes out of the snow-covered Himalayas. It grows muddy and middle-aged as it traverses the hot and dusty plains of Uttar Pradesh and Bihar. By the time it crosses half of Bengal and reaches Narayan Gunj near Dacca, it becomes world-weary and is called Boorhi or Old Ganga. There it is also known as Padma or Lotus River, celebrated in folk music and boatmen's songs. It is a busy waterway, overcrowded with cargo ships, tugs, barges, steamers and all manner of country-craft. The city of Dacca, once known as Jehangir Nagar, used to be the provincial capital of Mughal Viceroys. When Bengal became independent of Delhi, it was ruled over by the Nawab-Nazims of Murshidabad. The last Nawab-Nazim of Bengal, the heroic Siraj ud Daulah, lost out to Lord Clive in the Battle of Plassey in 1757. The administration of Bengal passed into the hands of the English East India Company. The French, Dutch and Danish traders and their armies also could not hold out against the English. Calcutta became the second largest city of the British Empire and a kind of poor man's London. Dacca, in East Bengal, remained a neglected provincial town, important only for its river-port of Narayan Gunj which handled the jute trade of the hinterland.

Muslims were in a majority in East Bengal, and some of their nobility and the titular Nawabs of Dacca continued to live in this dreamy old town surrounded by broad rivers. The city had many splendid houses, built during the days of the Dutch and English East India Companies.

Identical colonial mansions had come up around the same time in the southern plantations of far-away America. The Mississippi and its paddle boats, and the rivers of Bengal and their gleaming steamers evoked a similar atmosphere of romance, of long, song-filled voyages, high winds and lonely sunsets.

Caledonia was also a planter's house, built in Dacca by a Scotsman called MacDonnel Saheb. It was not as large nor as imposing as Joost House, next door, which belonged to a Dutchman and also faced the Old Ganga. In bright sunshine the waves of the river reflected on the outer walls of Caledonia like the undulating scale of Vangala Raga, or it was time playing upon time. The silent, visual music struck no discordant note because Georgian architecture had long been a part of Bengal's landscape. People like the ruddy-faced and jovial MacDonnel Saheb and his family had been around since the days when they rowed inland on their barges in order to trade in European goods. Slowly and subtly they had taken over as the river-country's blustering new masters. They had come to stay.

William Makepeace Thackeray's grandfather had traded in elephants in Sylhet. Malcolm MacDonnel also followed the upcountry trail, dealing in tuskers and tea and jute. He would have added indigo to his tiny empire, but the competition had become fairly tough. Young men from a not very prosperous Scotland were coming out in droves, and they were thrifty and hard-working.

MacDonnel Saheb did not return to the craggy shores of Auld Scotia. He lived frugally in Caledonia, died of old age and was buried in the European Cemetery in Dacca.

Young Angus MacDonnel took over his father's vast business. But Dacca bored him. After some years he left his Bengali mistress and half-caste children in Caledonia, entrusted the Narayan Gunj office to his Armenian and Jewish staff, and shifted to Calcutta. Once in a while he came back to settle his natural offspring. He sent his sons to various regimental bands, and his daughter to a Scotch Mission Boarding School for Females. The girl later became a governess to the grandchildren of the eminent Bengal Civilian, Sir Edward Barlow.

In late middle age Angus MacDonnel decided to marry a bonnie lass and return home. His natural children were embittered because he gave them no share in Caledonia. Before going back to Glasgow he sold the house to a dreamy-eyed baboo of Mymensingh. The fact was that now the baboos were slowly and subtly taking over. The swarthy MacDonnels gradually merged into the large population of Calcutta Eurasians, and were never heard of again.

Romesh Baboo, the new owner of Caledonia, did not have an aristocratic hyphenated name like Roy-Chowdhry. He was merely a Sarkar, a member of the middling Kayastha caste of scribes. The Kayasthas had mostly worked in the departments of revenue and civil administration from the time of the early medieval Afghan Sultans, the Mughals and the Nawab-Nazims of Bengal. They were an adaptable and diligent people, and had become proficient in English with the same ease with which they had mastered Persian in earlier centuries. Romesh Chandra Sarkar's family owned a small estate along the Brahmaputra in the district of Mymensingh. It had been given to his forefathers for services rendered to the East India Company after the Battle of Plassey.

When his father died, young Romesh Chandra decided to leave the backwaters of East Bengal and live in Dacca. He wished to be in touch with modern times. After purchasing Caledonia in 1889, he added a high-walled courtyard at the back for his womenfolk and set about purifying the house. The drunken, beef-eating Whites had gambolled and caroused in it for far too long. Brahmin priests chanted their reverberating mantras to dispel all unclean influences. With much beating of tom-toms and blowing of conches, a tiny black idol of Kali, the mother goddess, was installed in the erstwhile ballroom. While Caledonia was being washed with gallons of holy Ganga water, Romesh Baboo came across eight sooty little niches in a dank and gloomy ante-chamber. The niches looked sadly empty and forlorn. The new owner was informed that this was the room in which Angus

MacDonnel's low-caste Hindu concubine had performed her daily puja. Her children had removed her eight goddesses, along with their burnt offerings, after she died of smallpox. The half-caste MacDonnels had been baptised in the Scotch Kirk; their mother had remained faithful to her deities, as was the wont of most Indian mistresses of the Sahebs. They usually remained steadfast in their own religions. Not that it made any difference to anything.

Those were stirring times. The upper and middle classes of Bengal had been anglicised for quite some time. In 1945 the titular Nawab-Nazim of Murshidabad had three enormous wedding-cakes made for himself. Each of them was three feet high and eighteen feet in circumference. Cakes notwithstanding, most Muslims continued to sulk after their traumatic defeat at Plassey in 1757, and lagged behind.

Western education led to a Hindu cultural revival in Bengal. Romesh Baboo had passed his F.A. in Mymensingh. He began subscribing to English and Bengali newspapers and journals, and as a gesture to the new revivalism, he changed the name of the house from Caledonia to Chandrakunj—Luna's Grove.

Like most Bengalis, Romesh Baboo was interested in music and poetry. While the Muslims continued to write poetry in Bengali and Urdu, the bhadralok—westernised Hindus—went in for versification in English. They lived in neo-Georgian houses and composed poems in heroic couplets. The Hindu Zamindar class was created by the British after the Permanent Settlement. The new landed gentry and the merchant princes of Calcutta lived in the style of the former Nawabs of Murshidabad, but had also modernised themselves. Romesh Baboo began to follow the same trend, which was also prevalent in Dacca.

It was summer time. He was in the process of settling down in his new house and was being inspired by its picturesque setting. One evening as he strolled in his garden, delicately smelling a bunch of jasmines, it suddenly came to him—

Mango-birds' ode to Goddess Laxmi

Winged songstresses in the Garden of Moon,
Trill they and lilt in mellifluous June:
Lady of the Lustrous Lotus River,
O Padma, Bountiful Ma, Prime Giver—

Not quite satisfied, he began again

O flighty singer of emerald June,
Trilling and lilting while the limpid moon...

The Muse was rudely disturbed by the coachman's child, Abdul Qadir. Instead of Chandravati, the Moon-Maiden, he had materialised like a mischievous little imp, holding a big, fat book in his grubby hands.

He gave the master a toothy smile and said, "Huzoor, I was cleaning out MacDonnel Saheb's landau when I found this lying under the seat. Bootiful pictures of Mem-log and Saheb-log and Nawab-log! Look—!"

2
The Golden Album

It was a morocco-bound, gold-rimmed volume containing small photographs in sepia. On the fly-leaf there was inscribed—

Syed Ahmed Ali, 36 Kensington Park Gardens, July 1st, 1870.

Inside, buff pages displayed the lords and ladies of Albion, and Indian dignitaries residing in Calcutta. The pictures were all of one size. Apparently Mr. Ahmed Ali (obviously some Nawab) had taken a ride in the MacDonnels' landau and forgotten his album in it. These illuminating illustrations of illustrious luminaries, as Romesh Baboo would have put it, more or less changed his lifestyle and indirectly affected the lives of his descendants.

That aromatic evening in June, 1890, he postponed composing his lyric in English and perused the album by gaslight.

He recognised the Barlow family. Edward Barlow, ICS, his wife, son James, daughters Mabel, Maud and Matilda. Dog. As divisional commissioner, Mr. Barlow had recently come to Mymensingh. Romesh Baboo and his father had put on their formal robes and caps and attended the Big Saheb's durbar, which had all the trappings of a Mughal court.

They had to take off their shoes when they were ushered into the Presence, whenever they went to meet a high-ranking English official.

This album revealed a different kind of set-up. It opened before the Zamindar a glittering world of high fashion, high society, and everything that was high and mighty. A graphic panorama of the contemporary upper-crust social scene.

What was he doing in backward, benighted Dacca? The entire world was waiting to be discovered. But first of all he ought to return this album to its owner.

He scrutinized each picture and was fascinated. Embossed cameos of charming damsels and fair maidens. Little girls. Young women. Matrons. Gorgeous gowns. Jaunty hats. Fantastic hair-dos. All so poised and glamorous. Elegant English and European men. Calcutta Nawabs in full regalia.

Except for the Barlow family, Romesh Baboo could not recognise a single face. How could he? He was living in Caledonia but didn't belong to that society, had never even been to Calcutta.

Here was this lady, autographed Gertrude Leighten, photo by the London Stereoscopic and Photographic Co. of Regent Street.

H.H. Muggeridge, bewhiskered and bright-faced. Smiling. Photo by Sawyer & Bird of Regent Street.

Amy M. Pollock, Oct. 8, 1868. Robinson and Cherill, Tonbridge Wells.

Ah, this was young Ahmed Ali himself. Top hat and suit, posing at the Stabilimento Fotografico Antonio Perini, Piazza S. Marco, Venezia.

Annie Bart, coloured by H.G. Gent of 448 Edgware Road.

George Gascoyen, July 8, 1870, by Gemar Frères, Brussels.

A handsome, dignified gentleman, bearded, double-breasted long, black coat, Turkish cap. Brompton.

Who were all these people?

Ahmed Ali on board a ship. Photo by Emile Bondomnean of 10 Blvd. Montmartre, 1866.

Ahmed Ali on a Queen Anne chair, velvet robe over *nari* shoes. Lucknow-style pearl-studded cap; photo by Mayall of Regent Street.

Lord Mayo, Viceroy and Governor-General of India, photographed by Clarkington of Regent Street. "Given to Nawab Ahmed Ali by Mayo. Nov. 4, 1868." He had signed his name in Urdu as well. Four years later he was assassinated by another Indian Muslim called Sher Ali.

There was a lot of difference between the lives and attitudes of Ahmed Ali and Sher Ali, but both of them were Mussalmans of India! Amazing, come to think of it.

Romesh Baboo gazed pensively at the little photograph. Lord Mayo was youthful and good-looking, quite a dandy, in fact. Checked trousers, polka-dotted scarf. Top hat in hand; cleanshaven.

In 1872, while he was inspecting the penal settlement at Port Blair, Andaman Islands, in the Bay of Bengal, this fellow, Sher Ali, killed him. The penal settlement, Romesh Baboo recalled, had been established originally for the Muslim rebels who had waged war against the Sahebs in 1857. Those of them who had not been hanged were sent there as lifers.

The Zamindar closed the album and pondered. This was perhaps after a considerable time that an Indian had killed an Englishman, and that, too, H.E. the Viceroy, no less. As a staunch loyalist, it upset Romesh Chandra Sarkar. Would Indians and Englishmen start killing one another all over again? God forbid. He shuddered to think of the consequences.

After a while he returned to the golden book. Ever yours, Adella Holland.

Annie Holland, by Pierre Petit, Paris.

Truly, S.G. Holland.

S. MacPherson. Severe-looking lady, by Hills & Saunders of Eton and Oxford. Must be some professor's wife.

Ahmed Ali with foreign wife and infant son, Yusuf Ali, Calcutta. Beautiful, European-looking children, Yusuf Ali, Fatima, Ahmedi. Photographed in England, France and Germany. The little boy always wore a Turkish cap.

Emily K. Carloyed, May 31, 1870, photographed at Llandudno. The world was certainly full of strange places.

Florence M. Edwards, July 1870. Exeter. A ravishing beauty. No signature. Renttinger of Paris.

Georgie S. Frazer, July 9, 1875, Paris.

Another beauty, photographed at 8, Boulevard de Italiens. The Nawab was certainly having the time of his life in Europe.

A. Symson, lovely lady in riding dress, Dublin.

Susan Terry, Brighton, October 19, 1871.

A gentleman at Bath Place, Worthing.

Amy Meid by Frank Brigg, St. Johns Wood School of Photography. Syed Ahmed Ali, in nawabi dress, by Schwartzchild, Calcutta.

A descendant of Tipu Sultan, wearing the same kind of broad-brimmed hat his glorious ancestor wore.

Syed Ahmed Ali again. This picture was called the Rembrandt Effect.

An Egyptian pasha, by Monsieur Hubert of Westbourne Grove.

A gentleman of Lima, in London.

So, this was the international set.

Two Burmese princes by Garricks of Calcutta (*for taking photos of Hindu and Mohammedan ladies at their residence, Mrs Garrick will charge double the price.*)

Cecilia Bond at Ipswich.

Annabella Thark at Wincanton, by E. Goodfellow (*they photographed country villas, all kinds of animals and interiors.*)

Mary Webb, London. Lillie Webb.

This gentleman looked exactly like Charles Swinburne writing at his desk. Perhaps he was Charles Swinburne writing at his desk. Perhaps, when this picture was taken, he was composing—*Night, a black hound, follows the fawn white day.*

A Muslim gentleman, probably from Bihar, for he wore a boat-shaped Vasco da Gama cap, introduced in those regions by early Portuguese traders.

Alice Harvey. Stunning beauty. At Firenze, wherever that was.

Nawab Diler Jung, Calcutta.

Some princes of the House of Tipu, exiled in Calcutta.

It occurred to Romesh Baboo that Nawab Nurul Zaman Chowdhry of Arjumand Manzil must be acquainted with a fellow Muslim aristocrat of South Bengal. The album should be handed over to him.

The following morning he ordered his syce to get the phaeton

ready. He put on his formal robe and cap and told Abdul
Qadir's father to drive him to Arjumand Manzil, Ramna.

After his arrival in the city he had called on Nawab Nurul
Zaman and some other notables who had made return calls.
Nawab Nurul Zaman had also told him that he had once
employed old Malcolm MacDonnel to catch a rogue elephant
on his estate, in the district of Faridpur. "His son turned out
to be a bit of a rogue himself," said the Nawab, "It seems that
he has abandoned a woman in every river-port of Bengal. I
am glad that you have bought that house. Keep in touch."

The baron was in his elegant library, reading a book of
Persian poetry. Romesh Chandra Sarkar was ushered in.

When the slightly rustic landlord showed him the album,
the Nawab was taken aback. "Yes," said he, puffing at his
silver hookah, "it does belong to a friend of mine, Syed
Ahmed Ali, Nawab of Chitpur. Have you heard of him,
Sarkar Baboo? He is the great-grandson of Mohammed Reza
Khan Muzzaffer Jung, Deputy Nawab of Bengal, Bihar and
Orissa. Warren Hastings had pensioned him off. Nawab
Ahmed Ali's wife is Earl Roberts' younger sister, Margaret.
She has been re-named Ashraf-un-Nissa Begum. In fact, their
son Yusuf Ali is a close friend of my brother, Fakhrul Zaman."

"They don't have to take off their shoes when they meet
the Big Sahebs?"

"On the contrary, the Sahebs take great pride in meeting
people like Nawab Ahmed Ali. Do you know that when the
Maharani of Cooch Bihar goes to London, she dances in the
royal ballroom with all the dukes and earls of the realm? And
the Queen Empress calls the Indian princes her 'beloved
sons'! It's all a matter of how much wealth and status and
pedigree you have. Mind you, mere pedigree has no value.
The other two things are essential."

The finest of Mughal delicacies would have been served
to the visitor, but the Nawab asked first if the young Baboo
had become modern enough, like the Brahmos, to dine with
Muslims and Christians.

Romesh Baboo thought for a few seconds and smiled awkwardly,

"Never mind! We respect your taboos just you as respect ours. Have you met my brother, Sarkar Baboo? No? He has become quite well-known as a patron of theatre and classical music. Same age as you. I'll take you to meet him presently. Oh, I know how this album came to be found in Caledonia!"

"Chandrakunj, Sir,"

"Sorry, Chandrakunj. The Ahmed Alis had come here, MacDonnel took them to Sylhet on a Kheda trip. Margaret wanted to see how the tuskers were trapped. They must have brought this album with them to put in an elephant or two, and left it behind. I'll ask my brother to take it back to Calcutta. He always stays there at Ahmed Ali's residence, Bamboo Villa. Come along, let's go to the playhouse."

The Nawab's younger brother, Fakhrul Zaman, was in his *jalsaghar* or private theatre hall, situated at the back of Arjumand Manzil. He was reclining on a Grecian couch, engrossed in the rehearsal of an Urdu melodrama. Musicians were busy tuning their instruments. Professional actresses and actors sat around on the carpet, enthralled by the silky voice of their debonair, almond-eyed patron.

All, including the Nawabzada, rose to their feet and lowered their gaze deferentially when Nawab Nurul Zaman entered the concert hall. The Nawab introduced the Zamindar to his brother and strode back to his library.

Fakhrul Zaman Chowdhry and Romesh Chandra Sarkar became good friends. They shared a passion for music and dance. The young Nawabzada seemed to have stepped out of Nawab Ahmed Ali's gold album. He was a very special person, warm-hearted, genial and talented. While Romesh Baboo was given to bouts of romantic melancholy, Fakhrul Zaman was full of the sheer joy of living. He exuded bonhomie and good cheer, and he knew so much about so many things. French and Mughal cuisine. Hindustani classical music. The intricacies and subtle differences between the Lucknow, Banaras and Jaipur schools of Kathak. He wrote plays and composed songs. It was indeed a privilege and a pleasure, an aesthetic experience, to know someone like Fakhrul Zaman Chowdhry. In fact, he was too good to be true.

On his part, the Nawabzada discovered that the young Zamindar from Mymensingh sang well. Fakhrul Zaman invited him to take part in musical soirees and operettas.

Romesh Baboo made the Nawabs of Arjumand Manzil his models of gracious living. However, they owned a very large estate and he really couldn't emulate them unless he mortgaged his lands, which gradually he began to do.

His requirements increased. He had to have a new wardrobe. Chandrakunj had to be renovated. He sent for catalogues from the best Calcutta shops for the latest western fashions in men's wear, as well as in interior decoration. The Age of Victoria was all-pervasive. Russian counts living in their remote birch and pine forests had acquired the same kind of furniture which was found in American homes and in the bungalows of the British Indian Empire. The trends of the Gay Nineties were being followed around the world. P & O liners, passing through the recently opened Suez Canal, held regular fashion parades. White and Brown Sahebs driving their buggies on India's Mall Roads sported the latest Bond Street styles.

On formal occasions Romesh Baboo began to wear English suits. He discarded Malcolm MacDonnel's Regency furniture and antiquated wall and table gerandoles. Chandrakunj was furnished anew. He also bought a new phaeton for himself and a closed carriage for his womenfolk. They remained in seclusion, but he made them wear frilled and bulky Victorian blouses with their saris when they went out to attend "purdah parties".

He started entertaining at Chandrakunj.

Mr. R.C. Sarkar was now all set for his next round of enjoyment in Brighton.

He went to Calcutta and met Nawab Ahmed Ali at his famous Bamboo Villa. The Nawab's son, Yusuf Ali, was getting married to a daughter of Wajid Ali Shah, deposed King of Oudh. A great-granddaughter of Tipu, the vanquished and slain King of Mysore, was married to another great-grandson of the deposed Muzzaffer Jung. Romesh Baboo accompanied Yusuf Ali's wedding party to Matia Burj in Garden Reach, where the last King of Oudh had been interned in 1856. He had passed away a few years ago. The last Mughal King of Delhi had died in exile in Rangoon. The Sahebs had also got rid of the King of Burma and packed him off to far-away Ratnagiri on the west coast of India. And Nawab Ahmed Ali's own brother-in-law, Field Marshal Lord Roberts, was being hailed as the Conqueror of Afghanistan.

Romesh Baboo wondered just how many kings the Sahebs had dethroned while they were about it. Now there were no more kings left to be toppled, except perhaps the Shah of Persia and the Sultan of Turkey.

It saddened him. The alliance between two dispossessed families was celebrated with much pomp and ceremony. There was something wrong somewhere in this entire set-up, he didn't quite fathom what it was but he found it strangely depressing. The sight of ex-royalty making merry and entertaining their conquerors seemed rather tragic. In order to cheer himself up he attended the opening night of an Urdu play in which India's prima donna, the half-Jewish courtesan, Gohar Jan, sang in seven languages, including French, English and Arabic.

Before sailing for Tilbury Docks, Sarkar requested Nawab Ahmed Ali to write letters of introduction to his friends in London. (The ones whose photographs he had seen in the album.)

The nobleman courteously obliged the young Zamindar.

When he returned to Dacca he referred to Chandrakunj as his "town house" and his village home as his "country seat". Nevertheless, he remained orthodox in his religion and didn't take to the newfangled Brahmo faith whose followers sat on chairs while they worshipped the unseen one god, Brahma. They even called their religion "The Church of New Dispensation". That was carrying things a bit too far. He would never exchange his colourful gods and goddesses for the plain emblem of Om, which was placed like a Cross upon the Brahmo altar. He also didn't approve of some aspects of the new reform movement launched by Brahmo leaders. Therefore, he married his daughter, Bhavtarni Debi, into a wealthy family of Faridpur when she had just turned twelve. Unfortunately, she became a widow at eighteen. Brahmo reformers were screaming their heads off that widows should be remarried. Nonsense.

Poor Bhavtarni Debi was childless. Her father called her back from Faridpur and entrusted to her the management of Chandrakunj. His wife had died earlier. He continued to indulge in his pastimes of music, dance and drama.

His friend, Fakhrul Zaman, had fiercely burnt his candles at both ends and died at the age of forty-seven. The Zamindar was heartbroken. In order to cheer himself up again, he began patronising some of the most expensive actresses and singing women the Nawabzada had left behind as his "legacy".

Romesh Baboo also had the practical streak of a Kayastha. He sent his sons, Benoy and Dinesh, to the best schools and colleges in Dacca and Calcutta, and decided that they would take up the professions.

As a reaction to their father's decadence, the boys had become exceptionally spartan and studious. Benoy joined the medical college. Being the older son, his father got him a wife while he was still a student.

Romesh Baboo was hoping to see his grandson before he died, but was sorely disappointed when a daughter was born. Soon, however, he began doting on her and called her Deepali, Light of the Lamp. He celebrated her third birthday with much fanfare, and died the following week, a fairly contented man.

3
Lotus River

DIRE misfortunes befell Romesh Baboo's survivors. His sons were horrified to discover that he had left behind a mountain of debts. Most of the land had been mortgaged, and for the last many years they had been living on borrowed money.

In Calcutta, as their sister Bhavtarni Debi put it, the boys had got into bad company and taken to violent and non-violent politics. Dinesh, the younger one, became a terrorist, and was tried and hanged in Alipur Jail. As further punishment, the remaining Sarkar lands in Mymensingh were confiscated. Older brother Benoy had qualified as a doctor. He became a follower of Gandhiji, took part in the non-cooperation movement in the 1920s, and courted arrest. After he came out of jail, his practice did not pick up. His wife died of cancer.

By 1939, the once resplendent Chandrakunj had turned into a semi-ruin. Its expensive furniture had long been sold off. The ceiling leaked during the rains, the Venetians sagged. The garden had gradually turned into a dense jungle. Thieves and intruders sneaked in and out at will through the surrounding foliage and half-broken doors and windows. The house had been burgled several times, while there were still some valuables left in its dank and gloomy rooms.

Benoy Chandra, elder son of Romesh Chandra Sarkar, treated the poor free of charge and made his family live in penury. The fact that the Sarkars of Chandrakunj had come down rather badly in the world, was well known in Dacca. Now they had very few friends.

The good doctor had converted part of the colonnaded front verandah into his clinic and used his wife's old saris as its curtains. The drawing room was almost bare. A folding harmonium stood in a corner. The walls were also bare, except for two large portraits. Adorned with garlands of tarnished, artificial gold ribbon, they gave the sunless room the air of an unfrequented shrine. Half-hidden behind the garlands, a woman and a man faced each other across the brick floor. The lady was dressed in the fashion of the 1920s and looked a bit like Pola Negri, as she gazed dreamily into the camera. The young man sat by a vase full of roses and solemnly read a book. The same volume was placed on the cornice underneath. The strange, ghostly chemistry which fades the photographs of the dead, had already worked on these portraits.

The ballroom which once served as Romesh Baboo's *jalsaghar*, had become roofless and turned into a quadrangle. Kali had been transferred to a side-room. Part of the dining hall was now used as a dormitory, cluttered with three string cots, ink-stained desks, tin trunks, canvas shoes and school books.

A small room facing the courtyard contained a brass bedstead and a cane stool. A hand mirror, a bottle of coconut hair-oil and a chocolate box, full of glass bangles and trinkets, stood in a neat row on a broad window-sill. College books lay scattered over a reed mat. A trunk covered with a printed bedcover served as a chair.

Songbirds lived in a broken-down carriage which stood in Chandrakunj's little jungle. On moonlit nights it looked like Cinderella's coach lying abandoned in an enchanted forest.

The coachman had died long ago. His son, Abdul Qadir, lived in the servants' quarter with his wife and seven half-starved children. The stable now housed his own horses and rickety carriage which he plied as a *gharry-wallah*.

Chandrakunj's desolation and decay were quite incredible.

It was heart-rending, therefore, that such a miserable household should be burgled again. For, that December evening of 1939, the last of the rare heirlooms were stolen from Chandrakunj's storeroom.

The burglar was Dr. Benoy Chandra Sarkar's nineteen-year-old daughter, Deepali.

Dr. Sarkar had closed his clinic at six o'clock in the evening and gone out for his long walk by the river. His three sons, nicknamed Khokhu, Tonu and Shonu, had not returned from the football grounds. The sound of running water emanating from one of the cave-like bathrooms indicated that the doctor's widowed sister, Bhavtarni Debi, was getting ready for her evening devotions.

Dr. Sarkar's talented daughter, Deepali, used to practise her singing in a lonely turret upstairs. At 6.30 she peeped down through a skylight and saw her aunt shuffling out of the bathroom. Deepali picked up her lantern and came down. There was no one in the courtyard except a crow sitting on the clothesline. It eyed her balefully and flew away. Deepali went inside and posted herself behind the half-open door of the puja room.

Bhavtarni Debi had finished burning her joss-sticks. She closed her eyes and mumbled her shlokas. Presently, she worked herself up into a trance, her plump, broad back to the door.

Deepali picked up the lantern and hurried across to the store-room. In the evenings, aunt and niece were always alone in the house. They were too poor to employ servants and hardly had any visitors. The coast was clear for at least another hour. The girl unlocked the box-room and went in. Bolting the door behind her, she straightened her back and felt suffocated. Nervously, she opened the Chinese camphor box. It contained the Sarkar "left-overs". Twice a year Bhavtarni Debi took out the expensive clothes, aired them, lined them with fresh neem leaves and put them back, sighing.

Gingerly Deepali took out a pair of Kashmiri shawls and Banaras silks. At last she found the proudest of the Sarkar possessions—three "Balucher bootedar" saris. They were a hundred years old but looked as though they had just come off the looms of Murshidabad. Despite the extreme precariousness of the situation, Deepali gaped at the woven designs. The broad end of a purple sari had a row of stylised profiles of a Nawab-Nazim. He sat in a howdah on an elephant. A John Company Englishman in a canoe was repeated on the ends of a sunset orange sari. The turquoise sari displayed a Nawab Begum of Bengal delicately smelling a rose. Time seemed to have stood still as it got entangled in the rich silks woven by the Muslim craftsmen of old Bengal.

Deepali wrapped the three saris in a yellowing piece of Dacca muslin. A cat jumped off a wood-apple tree near the stairs, a hansom clip-clopped past the front gate. Deepali came out with her "loot" and locked the godown.

Bhavtarni Debi continued to pray.

A young man with a bicycle lurked in the thicket outside waiting for Deepali Sarkar.

In the back room of a house in the old city, a group of young men huddled together, talking in undertones. Deepali came in and reverently placed the bundle in front of them. "Sorry," she whispered apologetically, "I didn't have anything more expensive than this."

One of the boys opened the package. "Balucher saris!" he exclaimed. The others craned their necks and stared at the rare antiques. "I told you about these," she said modestly.

"Yes," answered one of them. "But how did your aunt give them to you? Did you say you wanted them for a fancy-dress party or something?"

"I stole them."

"What? Did I hear right?"

"First I pinched the keys."

"You did what?"

"My aunt was fast asleep in the afternoon. I untied the keys from the corner of her sari."

"Nimble-fingered, aren't you?"

"I do a lot of *petit point* embroidery and cross-stitch."

"Look, I didn't mean that you steal your own heirlooms."

"I should have stolen somebody else's?"

There was a short silence.

The girl began to cry. "You said it was absolutely imperative that you get five hundred rupees by this evening, that it was a matter of life and death."

There was another silence.

"I know a person who might purchase these for Calcutta Museum. Thank you, Deepali." Their leader picked up the bundle.

Nine o'clock. Bhavtarni Debi was pottering about in the kitchen. Dr. Sarkar had come home and was tuning his radio set to hear the news.

The boys came back, noisily discussing the evening's football match. After the BBC news had been relayed by AIR Delhi, Dr. Sarkar went into the dining room and called his daughter.

"Don't bring the roof down, Benoy," said his sister.

"Good news, Didi, good news!"

"You hardly ever have good news for us. What it is? Found a nice boy for her?"

Deepali breezed in, panting.

"What happened?" the doctor asked with parental concern.

"Nothing, Baba. I had gone to see Rosie. On the way back near the pond I met this huge buffalo, so I ran for my life." She giggled nervously.

"You came back alone from Lily Cottage?"

"No, Baba, Joseph saw me home." She sat down in her chair and wiped her face, getting ready to be cross-examined by her sharp-tongued aunt.

"You went off to see Rosie without telling me? Did you imagine I was dead? And I thought little Miss Muffet was *upstairs*, singing."

"You were meditating, Pishi Ma. How could I disturb you? Rosie sent this urgent message through Joseph about some homework, so I rushed."

"Well, don't do it again," said her father gently. "Listen, I have some good news today. I had gone to see Aujit Babu. His brother-in-law, Shuniti Babu, has come from Calcutta. He has heard you over AIR and would like to record your songs…"

Deepali looked at him in disbelief. "My records? Are you sure?"

"Hurray!" her youngest brother, Tonu, shouted excitedly. "Didi is going to be rich and famous like Juthika Roy and Kanan Debi rolled into one."

"Her pictures in all the papers!"

"She will go about in a Rolls Royce!"

"Have you ever seen a Rolls even in your dreams?" said Bhavtarni Debi bitterly. She had never been able to forget the glorious days of their past.

Shonu, the quiet one, bent his head over his plate and said, "At least she will buy me a new football, won't she?"

"All the money she gets for her radio programmes she spends on you vagabonds," Bhavtarni Debi snapped. "She won't become a millionairess by cutting a few discs. And if she does earn a little, she ought to start making her trousseau."

Deepali blushed and looked out. One of Abdul Qadir's horses was grazing sullenly under the window. Perhaps he hadn't got his oats. Instead of sleeping after the day's hard work, the poor animal was fending for himself in the weedy patch of grass.

We are like you, Brother Horse, we also make do. The thought filled her with immense sadness, and also reminded her of the terrible deed of the evening. Guiltily, she began eating her fish-and-rice.

Her father asked her, "When can you see Shuniti Babu?"

"She who?"

"Shuniti Babu, who else? The gramophone man," her aunt replied. "How many important people do you see every day?"

"Oh, Pishi Ma, please. Yes, Baba, I can see him tomorrow morning. Will you come with me?"

"Strike the iron while it is hot," the aunt commented archly.

Deepali realised that poverty and frustration had made Bhavtarni Debi cantankerous. Often the children quarrelled with her like slum-dwellers. Economic conditions governed people's behaviour pattern, she had recently learned in the underground study circle run by her new friends.

"You'll have to cut your classes again," said her father.

The boys made a dash for the pantry. Each of them wanted to be the first to reach the massive Shanks wash-basin, imported from Scotland by Angus MacDonnel in days gone by.

"Must grab this gramophone offer." She waited for her brothers to march out of earshot, and added, "I didn't return the new radio contract at the cost of my studies because I have worn out my saris. I saved the last three months' radio fees to make clothes for the boys."

Dr. Sarkar bent his head and remained silent. After a few seconds, he stood up and left the dining room.

Deepali bit her tongue and felt sorry. Bhavtarni Debi glowered at her. "That's a modern daughter for you, making her father feel small and rubbing salt into his wounds. All my life, as God is my witness, I never once raised my eyes in the presence of my father, leave alone talked back to him."

Deepali got up, sighing. This was an evening of disasters. Silently she picked up the lantern and made her way to her private nook upstairs.

The turret had served as an observation post for the MacDonnels. On clear days they sat there drinking whiskey, and through the binoculars spotted their cargo boats sailing in. Deepali had turned the little tower into her music-room. She was not afraid of ghosts and stayed there till late at night, singing.

She came up, placed the lantern on the cornice and began practising for her gramophone recording.

At such a time if someone had looked at Chandrakunj from the banks of the Padma, the house would have presented a charming view. A young woman singing atop the old colonial mansion in the stillness of a winter night, while the Lotus River flowed on. Such was the kind of stuff that the romance of Bengal was made of.

4
Song of the Padma Boatman

"Abani Ganguli."

"Present."

"Molina Ghoshal."

"Present."

"Rosie Bannerjee."

"Present."

"Jehan Ara Chowdhry."

"Present."

"Deepali Sarkar."

"Absent."

Miss Karuna Bose, lecturer in civics, shot an angry glance at the empty chair next to Rosie Bannerjee and Jehan Ara Chowdhry. "Deepali is absent again," she growled.

"Must have caught a chill," said Jehan Ara loyally, "singing as she does in her ice-cold tower at night."

"Girls," Miss Bose addressed the class gloomily. "The annual examinations are round the corner and all of you are going to fail."

"Yes, Karuna-di," Jehan Ara said obediently.

The lecturer turned to her. "And you, princess. You should have been doing your B.A. final. Your father sends you off to Aligarh and calls you back and wastes your academic years, all because of his whims."

"Aligarh's climate didn't suit me, Karuna-di," Jehan Ara defended her father. "That's why he had to call me back."

"And you, Miss Bannerjee, and your singing crony, Deepali Sarkar, are both of you planning to become cinema actresses?"

"No, Karuna-di."

"Join the New Theatre, perhaps, in Calcutta?"

"No, Karuna-di."

"I happened to look at the Common Room notice-board this morning. How many plays do you stage during term? Both of you got the lowest marks in the last test."

Rosie tried to look appropriately contrite.

"Mind you, I have been very lenient with you. Thank your lucky stars that Miss Uma Roy had already left for England when your batch joined this college. She would have made you feel sorry for the day you were born. But she has come back and will start teaching you from July this year, in case you manage to get through your Intermediate Examination."

The class sat very still, eyes glued to their textbooks.

Miss Bose resumed her roll-call. After closing the register she said in her dry, classroom-voice. "Kindly open page 218, Government of India Act, 1935."

Forty minutes later the students swarmed out of the lecture hall in noisy bunches. Some of them made a beeline for the tuckshop. Jehan Ara and Rosie met their friends at the tea-counter.

"Let's have lemonade to celebrate Miss Roy's home-coming," said one of the girls in a sepulchral voice.

"So Typhoon Uma has hit peaceful Dacca again. Why wasn't her ship torpedoed by the Germans?" asked Laila Rahim.

"Shh—be careful," said Jehan Ara, giggling. "The other day a tongawallah was arrested in Lucknow because he was yelling to his horse—'Show us Hitler's lightning speed, son, show us Hitler's gallop, sonny!'"

The girls laughed uproariously.

"Uma Debi taught my sister six years ago," said Laila Rahim. "Apa used to come home laughing her sides out. She would tell us—'Today Uma-di called us the Amazons of Old Ganges,' or, 'Today she addressed us as Valorous Eves of Lady Eden's Garden.'"

"I don't believe you," Jehan Ara sounded incredulous.

"Ask my Apa. But that was when Uma Roy was inspired by Qazi Nazrul Islam. Then she met a budding economist and became utterly prosaic under his influence."

"Uma Roy is potty," said Abani Ganguli. "My brother once told me that in order to assert her independence, she cut her hair very short. Shingle bob, you know. But when she began smoking, her mother put her little foot down. She continued to smoke on the sly and referred to her cigarette as the Torch of Liberty."

The girls doubled up with laughter.

A college ayah approached Rosie and Jehan Ara. "Baba," she said, showing them a slip. "Deepali-baba's brother."

"Omigosh! Hope she is all right."

"He wants to see her."

"Can't be her brother if she's at home."

"I took this to the office. They said tell Rosie or Jehan Ara-baba."

Rosie saw the chit.

Visitor's name: A. Sarkar.

Relationship: Cousin-brother.

Business: Personal.

"What's the matter? Shall I go and see him?" asked Jehan Ara.

"Don't worry, I'll go," said Rosie hastily and slipped out of the canteen.

Shubir Ghosh, the lad who had taken Deepali from Chandrakunj to Nawabpura the previous evening, stood under a tree. He was glowing like Mercury, messenger of the gods.

"Absent," Rosie told him quietly.

"I know. I went to her house, pretending to be a fellow from AIR. Her aunt told me that she had gone with her father to meet some gramophone chap from Calcutta. She's going places, isn't she? Now, look. She'll be at the radio station for her broadcast tomorrow evening. Surendra-da would like to see her urgently. Please ask her to meet him at seven o'clock sharp behind the radio station."

"Why can't she go to Nawabpura to see him?"
"Please do not question me."

Recess was over. Rosie rushed back to the classroom. Miss Gladys Jenkins, a native of Wales and a dedicated teacher of English Literature, opened her *Golden Treasury*.

The college was awash in a buzzing silence. The Royal Family, Lord Linlithgow the Viceroy, and the Governor of Bengal, all grimly supervised the scene from classroom walls. Row after row of Bengali girls of different faiths, Hindu, Muslim, Christian and Buddhist, sat behind their desks, concentrating on Dryden and Alexander Pope. The girls' forefathers had fought for or against Lord Clive and Major Adams in the battlefields of 18th century Bengal.

Robert Clive and Warren Hastings' century had been India's Time of Troubles, her High Tide of Misery. The present one was only slightly better. Troubles came and receded and came again, like the ebb and flow of the sea around Bengal's coastline.

Theatres of war kept shifting. More science and technology had turned the battles of 20th century Europe into world wars. The present war was also being fought on the wavelengths of German and British broadcasting systems.

Radio had been introduced to India a few years earlier. The network was called AIR, short for All India Radio. Since September '39, its importance had increased as a medium of war propaganda, especially because many Indians had started listening to German broadcasts.

The Dacca station of AIR had been opened a year earlier, in a baroque kothi rented from a Zamindar. Radio had come as a boon to the singers and musicians of the intensely musical country of East Bengal.

Deepali Sarkar had become a frequent broadcaster.

On the evening of December 8, as she came out of a studio at a quarter to seven, she ran into her father's old friend, Professor Murtaza Hussain, an eminent linguist who taught at Rabindranath Tagore's Santineketan. He was in Dacca to broadcast a talk. He peered at her through his thick glasses and exclaimed, "Deepali! How are you? How is Benoy Babu?"

"He is fine, sir, thank you," she replied hurriedly. "How are you, sir?" She had once informed her friend Rosie that Professor Hussain knew the Lord's Prayer in thirty-six languages, promised that the next time he came to Dacca she would take him to Lily Cottage to meet Rosie's father, Rev. Bannerjee.

Right now she had a much more important promise to keep. Rosie had told her to meet an underground courier behind the radio station at 7 p.m. She was trying to sneak out unnoticed, but the good Professor was bent upon delaying her.

"And your venerable aunt?"

"She's fine, too."

"Last time I met your father, I asked him to send you to our university."

"Yes, sir. He is sending me there for my B.A."

"That's very good. I'm glad."

She saw the electric clock glowing at the end of the soundproof corridor.

"What is the matter with you, child? You look agitated. That's Abbasuddin Ahmed singing. Let's sit down here somewhere, and listen to him. You told me last time that you were his student."

"Yes, sir."

Inside, in one of the studios the famous singer of East Bengal had started a *bhatiali*—

A long-haired intellectual stopped by. He had also come, like the Professor, to broadcast a Third Programme kind of talk. "Sir," he said eagerly, "how would you compare the Song of the Volga Boatman with a *bhatiali*, say, the famous one in which our rower says, 'I saw her at sundown as I sailed past her red hut.' I think, sir, we are all sailing past one another—"

"Yes, indeed, and in Unsafe Boats," replied the Professor.

The conversation seemed bizzare and unreal. Here she was, being awaited at the gate for some urgent cloak-and-dagger business. Further delay of a few minutes could even cost someone his life—

Quarter past seven. The intellectual uttered some more profundities and dived into a studio. Deepali hoped fervently that the good Professor would not come out with her into the verandah.

He did.

"Excuse me, sir, one of my brothers has come to fetch me. May I go now?"

"Don't they send you home in the radio station's car? That's the rule. If they don't, I shall speak to the station director."

"They always do, but tonight I have to meet a relative. Goodbye, sir."

What a well-bred child, Dr. Hussain thought admiringly. And so obedient. The Professor knew that being of zamindari stock, Dr. Sarkar was still quite conservative about his daughter.

Outside, in the silent dimly-lit street, the courier gave her an envelope. "Rehan-da—," he whispered, "wants you to take this to Miss Uma Roy. At the earliest."

"Uma Roy? I don't know her."

"That doesn't matter. Listen. Her D.I.G. uncle is staying at Woodland, so the place is full of policemen. Only you can manage to go straight to her room."

"And if the letter is intercepted at the gate? The other day they arrested a tongawallah in Lucknow."

He began to laugh. "Nobody would suspect you. And in any case, you have to take a risk. Are you afraid?"

"No, of course not."

"Fine. Those saris fetched exactly five hundred rupees."

"I'm glad." She tried to swallow the sudden lump in her throat.

Abruptly, he disappeared in the mist.

Deepali walked quickly to Adbul Qadir's battered carriage. One of the horses turned his head towards her and neighed, as though he disapproved of her clandestine activities. O, Brother Horse, she whispered, sighing. Look at your condition. We are doing it for you, too, since you animals do not have a political movement.

She opened the creaky door and climbed in. Luckily, being transmission time, there was no one around. Abdul Qadir dozed on his coach-box, probably transmitting his prayerful programme On High. Once upon a time he used to be a little boy who played with young Benoy and Dinesh. His father worked as Romesh Baboo's liveried coachman. Ever since the Sarkars fell on bad days and sold their horses, they had allowed Abdul Qadir to stay on in the outhouse and ply his own carriage. In return he took Bhavtarni Debi and Deepali wherever they had to go. Under-nourishment had aged him fast. Abdul Qadir and his horses had become one, mystically-speaking. Just as the Padma Boatman and his Song and his Canoe were one.

Deepali pushed up the Venetian shutter of a window and called out, "Wake up, Uncle. Let's go home."

The carriage began to move.

5
Typhoon Uma

In the "morning room" of sprawling Woodland, a pudgy, bespectacled woman sat in the bay-window, writing a letter. An Alsatian dozed by the fireplace. The room could have been in any upper middle-class English home, except that the silver-framed women on the escritoire and side-tables wore crêpe de chine saris, and solemn, pince-nezed men and children in sailor suits and frocks had Bengali, instead of Anglo-Saxon, features. Constable's landscapes, a picture of Lord Byron, and a monochrome of Aubrey Beardsley's "Salome" adorned the walls.

Abruptly, the lady stopped writing. It had occurred to her that the letter would be heavily censored. She was known for her Communist leanings and the addressee, a Jewish professor at the London School of Economics, was a famous Leftist. She picked up the unfinished letter and threw it in the fire. Caesar looked at her and went back to sleep. She lay back on the antique Cleopatra couch and closed her eyes.

When Pritish Kumar Roy, Barrister-at-Law, named his house Woodland, he was merely following contemporary fashion, according to which many well-to-do Indians called their homes Shamrock, Wildflower Hall, and Rose Villa. The Maharajah of Cooch Bihar's residence in Calcutta was also known as Woodland. Barrister Roy was a Brahmo. His grandfather had joined the Brahmo Samaj, whose founder, Raja Ram Mohun Roy, had first begun his Hindu Reformation Movement by writing a book in Persian. It was entitled *Tuhfatul Movahhidin* or "Gift of the Monotheists".

The Brahmos shunned idol worship and polytheism, and had also been influenced by Unitarian Christianity. The Tagores were Brahmos, too. Brahmo Samaj and modernism had almost become synonymous in Bengal.

The Roys' son, Nirmalendu, was a confirmed bachelor who spent most of his time in the club or at the race course. Their daughter, Uma, was thirty and a Bolshevik. Before going to England she had taught at a girls' college, taken up with the local revolutionaries, and was called "The Typhoon". In London she got involved with Krishna Menon's India League and Rajni Palme Dutt's Communist Party of Great Britain. She had returned home a few days earlier, more short-tempered and strong-willed than ever.

Thirty-five years ago when he was a law student in London, Barrister Roy had acquired the attitudes of 19th century Liberalism. But he was also a loyal British subject and did not relish the idea of his daughter shouting "Long Live the Revolution" in the streets of Dacca. Specially now, in 1939, when a war was raging in Europe and the Communist Party of India had been banned by the government. Barrister Roy's brother-in-law, Dhirendra, was a high-ranking police officer and had warned him of possible danger if Uma retained her Party affiliations. Mrs. Roy had been awarded the Kaiser-i-Hind medal. Mr. Roy was being tipped for a knighthood. Their son, Nirmalendu, dealt in jute. Uma's flirtation with Communism could be disastrous for the entire Roy family.

She put on her glasses and looked out of the window. Now she could clearly see the bunch of policemen who stood about on the driveway. Her Uncle Dhirendra had come from his Range to attend an official meeting at his headquarters in Dacca.

Uma suffered from migraine. The family had a garden house on a lush island in the river Padma, fifty miles from the steamer-station of Narayan Gunj. Uncle Dhirendra had asked her to go there to rest for a few days as the voyage seemed to have tired her. He probably wanted her to be away from Dacca when he rounded up her comrades.

Was this a kind of house arrest? Resignedly, she sat back in the window and watched the sunset...

6
Woodland

Aʙᴅᴜʟ Qadir shouted at his horses and turned in the direction of Ramna, the pleasant area where the Mughals had once laid out their gardens, and where important people still lived in their beautiful houses.

Coconut palms swayed in the breeze. Dim lights came on in the bungalows. Street lamps had also been shaded because of a war which was being fought in faraway Europe. Somebody was playing a Jeanette MacDonald record in the Circuit House. Strains of western music rose from vast drawing rooms where anxious Britons sat listening to BBC news.

Abdul Qadir muttered under his breath. He had enough anxieties of his own. The prices of essential commodities had gone up, the bazaar was rife with wild stories of Hitler's conquests. A maulvi had declared that perhaps the German dictator was the One-Eyed Dajjal who, according to Muslim belief, would appear before the second coming of Christ. A pundit had told Abdul Qadir that the Russians were coming. Every time England was in trouble, the Russians decided to invade India. And since they spoke Sanskrit in Russia, everybody should learn that ancient language. Another pundit had said that the Germans also spoke a kind of Sanskrit. Look at the Swastika which they had adopted.

Abdul Qadir was also very upset about his late-lamented Master's granddaughter. Of late she was going about with a worried expression on her face. Right now she had told him to just drop her at Woodland and go away. Said she was going there to request Miss Uma Roy to write an article for her college magazine.

Deepali looked out of the carriage window. Her friend Jehan Ara's rococo mansion, Arjumand Manzil, stood at the end of the avenue. Jehan Ara existed on the last page of the story whose Mughal authors had founded Jehangir Nagar four centuries ago. On the same avenue there lived Mr. William Cantwell, in his picturesque bungalow. Cantwell was an almighty character in the story whose authors had conquered the Nawab-Nazims' Bengal. A furlong away from his house lived the Roys. Their forefathers had served as the Hon'ble John Company's agents and clerks and helped the English in setting up their regime.

Deepali was happy she was going to participate in the new play whose authors would shake the very foundations of Arjumand Manzil, Cloudland and Woodland, all in one stroke. In her excitement she had not been able to sleep the previous night. The mastermind, the great invisible Comrade Rehan Ahmed himself had entrusted her with the dangerous task of carrying his message to Comrade Uma Roy. Which meant that an important leader like Rehan Ahmed had inducted a small fry, a humble sympathiser like Deepali Sarkar into the inner circle. She was so excited she wished she could reach Woodland in an instant.

A police constable at the gate! She clutched her bag securely and told him she was a former student of Miss Roy and had come to see her. The constable nodded and let her in. Obviously there was no reason for anybody to suspect her.

She told Abdul Qadir to leave. As the carriage disappeared behind the trees, she felt strangely alone and unsafe. Two police officers, one of them an Englishman, were strolling on the lawn. She approached the porch nervously. Caesar barked at her. An orderly accosted her. She repeated the password: a former student of Uma Miss Saheb, come to pay her respects.

The man went in. After a few minutes a snooty, liveried bearer appeared on the verandah. He nodded solemnly to indicate that she follow him. Deepali entered the gallery and passed a row of glass-eyed antlers, an Italian Pan and massive sofas. She recalled the bazaar gossip that Barrister Pritish

Roy's clients paid him in gold coins, and that Mrs. Archana Roy wore diamonds on her shoes.

Karim Khan, the bearer, beckoned her to wait. He treated visitors according to their social status—Deepali Sarkar was so obviously a poor student. He didn't deign to speak to nonentities like her, unless it was absolutely necessary.

He disappeared behind heavy velvet curtains. Deepali sank into a sofa. Her earlier elation at meeting Uma Roy had given way to depression. How could there be such terrible differences between the lives of fellow Indians? She thought of Abdul Qadir's hovel, and of her own bleak and dreary house in whose clinic her poor father must, at this very moment, be waiting stoically for patients who hardly ever came. There were countless dimly-lit, dingy houses and bamboo huts in Dacca, and in all other towns and villages of Bengal, in the entire country. There was such poverty and such unhappiness in India.

The thought suddenly gave her new energy. She got up and looked around. The Revolution is about to come! We are going to change all this. It's the triumph of the Cause that a rich woman like Uma Roy has joined the Mainstream. Like Jawaharlal Nehru, brought up in the luxuries of his father's mansion, Anand Bhavan, Allahabad ....

The bearer returned and spoke:

"You can go in. Miss Saheb shall receive you."

"Where?"

"In the morning room—there, to the left."

She couldn't quite understand. At sundown, if Miss Saheb is in the "morning room", shouldn't it be called the "evening room"?

Karim Khan lifted the curtains and coughed a little. Timidly, Deepali went in and found herself in a pleasant, cosy room with many windows and doors opening into the rose-garden. Miss Uma Roy lay on a couch, smelling Vapex. Her eyes were closed. Twilight filled the room.

So this is the famous Typhoon Uma, plain, plump and prosaic. Deepali was disappointed. The next instant she scolded herself for her bourgeois romanticism. Shouldn't have expected to meet a glamour girl. Uma Debi is not a parasite, she is the New Woman of Modern India...

The lady opened her eyes and looked up rather dramatically. The room was full of amber light and seemed part of the rose-garden. Everything was still and wondering and expectant.

"Good evening, Uma Didi," she said respectfully, like a schoolgirl greeting her new headmistress.

"Hello. Come. Sit down." Uma fixed her glasses on her pug nose.

"How are you, Uma Didi?"

"What did you tell the servant your name was?"

"Deepali Sarkar."

"Did I teach you before leaving for England? Which year? Which class?" Peering at Deepali myopically she added, "Sorry, can't recognise you."

"Uma-di...I...Surendra-da has sent me. Surendra Talukdar."

"Oh..." Uma became alert, as she stretched her hand and switched on the Cupid-and-Psyche table-lamp.

Twilight vanished in the sudden glare.

Uma was looking at her. "Who are you?" she asked sombrely.

"Deepali Sarkar. How are you, Uma-di? Got a head-cold?"

"Come to the point. Is there any message?"

"Yes. I am studying in Second Year Arts. My father Dr. Benoy Chandra Sarkar is a private practitioner. We live at..."

"What is the message?"

"Rehan-da has sent you a sealed envelope."

"Rehan..." Uma Roy sat up. "You've brought Rehan's letter! Why did you waste so much time talking nonsense? Give it to me."

Deepali opened her handbag.

Right then another doughty lady appeared from behind the Chinese lacquered screen. "How are you, Uma?" she asked without bothering to look at the nonentity visitor.

"Fine," Uma replied in a bored voice. "This is an old student of mine."

Deepali stood up and joined her palms in a "nomashkar".

"Hello," the lady said casually and continued, "Did you take the mixture?"

"Mother…" Uma interrupted her sharply. "Listen, I'm fine. I don't know why I can't be left in peace."

Mrs. Roy ignored her rudeness and said, "Your father and I are going to the Club for dinner. Eat at the proper time and don't forget your vitamins."

Uma kept quiet. Mrs. Roy stood in the middle of the room for a few seconds, then left.

"Oh… Parents…!" Uma exclaimed, and smiled for the first time. "Are your parents also so tiresome?"

Deepali was pleased to see the change in her strange hostess's mood. She smiled back.

"All right. To work. To England, to England to buy a fat hog, Home again, home again, jiggety-jog."

She is quite mad, decided Deepali.

"How old are you?"

"I'll be nineteen in April."

"Just nineteen!"

"Ask my aunt. She thinks I've become an old maid."

Uma frowned and tore the envelope open.

Karim Khan brought tea and padded back in his white socks. Uma began to read the long, mysterious letter.

Deepali got up to look at the paintings. She stopped in front of "Lord Byron Landing on the Shore of Greece". Next to him were the Turners. The monochrome of Salome with the severed head attracted her attention. She looked at the picture for some moments then returned to her chair.

Uma finished reading the letter and closed her eyes again. It had become dark outside. Laburnum leaves rustled against the window. Caesar barked somewhere in the deep garden. Uma opened her eyes and looked at the girl thoughtfully.

"Whose picture is that, Uma-di?"

"Which one?"

"That one...next to the English landscape."

"You don't know? You are in Inter Arts Final. Aren't they teaching you English Literature the way they did in my time?"

Deepali smiled apologetically.

"That," said Uma Roy, "is Oscar Wilde's Salome."

"What is she doing, Uma-di?"

Uma Debi sat up. "Either you are very naive or pretend to be." *How I detest these giggly, stupid college girls!* She added aloud, "Can't you see what that blasted woman is doing?"

"What was her story, Uma Didi?" Deepali asked sweetly.

"Damn her story! Look here, I have no time to discuss decadent Western paintings with damn fools like you. There is important work to do."

"Yes, Uma-di," Deepali said dutifully.

The girl is pretty and foolish and therefore she can create problems. Uma held the letter tight in her fist. But one must take all kinds of risks. "Now, listen carefully."

Why is she bullying me? Because she is rich? Deepali said boldly, "Uma Debi, I am going to listen to you, but before that I would like to ask you a little question."

"Yes?"

"You are so wealthy. Why don't you secretly help the Party?"

"Good question. All these years I was away in London, I have just come back and fallen ill. This is the first time after my return that the comrades have contacted me through you. And for an extremely urgent matter."

"I'm sorry, Uma-di."

"Now I'm going to ask you a few questions, answer carefully. You are going to undertake a perilous mission. The slightest mistake can mean long terms in jail. The Communists of the area are going to be rounded up pretty soon. Comrade

Rehan has sought your help in finding the government orders pertaining to the forthcoming arrests."

"My help?" Deepali repeated, astonished. "How can I find out? And Rehan-da doesn't even know me. He has never met me. And anyway, what can I do—? And how—?"

"He has explained the modus operandi to me in this letter. Now, tell me. Can you speak English fluently?"

"Yes."

"When English people speak among themselves can you follow them?"

"Yes. Miss Jenkins teaches us the language, and we have a lot of Englishwomen on the college staff."

"Yes, of course. Now when you came here—apart from Karim Khan and my mother, who else saw you?"

"A constable and a peon."

"Can you recognise my uncle, the Deputy Inspector General of Police?"

"Perhaps he was pacing the lawn with an Englishman."

"Right. That was Alfred Haig, of Special Armed Constabulary. And there are also a number of plainclothesmen hanging about. Now read that with the utmost attention."

Deepali moved her chair near the table-lamp.

After she had read the letter, she remained very still.

Uma glanced at her. "I am surprised, too, but he knows best. It is obvious that he is familiar with you and is sure that you can do the job."

"What do you mean he is familiar with me? I have never met him, haven't even seen his photograph. And nobody can be familiar with me."

"I am sure he is not treating you like a gangster's moll."

"I beg your pardon?"

"I am positive he—"

"Listen, Miss Roy, both you and the Great Comrade are sadly mistaken about me. He has certainly mistaken me for somebody else. Please let me go." She got up angrily.

"Calm down. You can't work for the Revolution if you are so prickly. And you are not going to tell me or Rehan how to work for the Underground. I am aware of the fact that all the college girls of Bengal are in love with him, but they forget that he is not a matinee idol. He is a practical, down-to-earth revolutionary and he knows damn well what he is doing. All the college girls of Bengal," she repeated in a flat, strong voice, "are in love with him, but only I happen to be his real friend. Nobody knows him as well as I do. We have known each other for a long time. Here at the University of Dacca. At the London School of Economics. Together we worked for the Communist Party of Great Britain. We might have even died together in Spain—fighting for the Cause…"

She would have gone on and on, but Deepali cut her short. "Listen, Uma Debi, kindly understand. I do not know your charismatic Rehan Ahmed from Adam, nor am I in love with him. Please come to the point."

"He can obviously recognise you even if he has not met you formally. There is absolutely no need for you to recognise him. But before we get down to work, you must tell me about yourself."

"Class background? Middle—actually, lower-middle-class."

Uma assumed the expression of a doctor listening to a patient's case history.

"I was twelve when my mother died—of cancer. My widowed aunt lives with us. She also fell ill, so I had to leave school for a couple of years in order to look after my kid brothers."

"Go on."

"Baba adored my mother. After her death he sort of gave up the world."

"Poor man."

"My father," she said with fondness and pride, "is a remarkably handsome man. And my uncle—my uncle was even handsomer—" Her voice choked.

"Kindly do not indulge in mushy sentimentality. You can't work for the Revolution if you are weepy. What happened to your uncle?"

"He was hanged," Deepali said flatly.

"I am sorry. What was his name?"

"Dinesh Chandra Sarkar."

"Good God! Don't tell me you are D.C. Sarkar's niece?"

"He was my father's younger brother. In 1931 when Ma lay dying in the Radium Hospital at Patna, Uncle Dinesh was arrested in the famous terrorist case. Baba went to Mymensingh and sold off our remaining lands to engage the best barrister he could get—" Baba, she recalled, wanted to engage Mr. Pritish Roy but could not afford to pay his exorbitant fees. "The case went on for some time. Eventually Uncle Dinesh was executed, five months after my mother's death."

"Do you remember him?"

"Very well. It happened only six years ago. I was fifteen." She wiped her tears. "After Uncle Dinesh was gone, Baba lost all interest in the world. Unlike my late uncle, he believes in Gandhian non-violence. After his brother's execution he had a strange sort of reaction."

"Began to hate politics?"

"Yes. As he is not socially visible, he doesn't get rich patients. He earns just enough to feed his dependants."

"You said something about lands."

"My grandpa was a Zamindar who squandered his wealth on…"

"…wine and women," Uma put in helpfully. "The old feudal order clashed with British merchant capitalism and the new Indian bourgeoisie and lost—"

Deepali looked at her wide-eyed. What erudition!

"Grandpa died when I was three. My father had to pay off his debts by selling everything except the house. Suddenly we became so poor that, once, we had no money to buy kerosene oil for the lamps. But hope kept us alive, that after we gain independence every home in India would light up with prosperity and well-being—these are actually my late uncle's words."

"Do you have a large joint family?"

"No. A first cousin of my father migrated to some far-off placed called Port-of-Spain."

"How did you join the Movement?"

She started giggling.

"Again!" Uma glared at her, and noticed the change in her mood.

"Uma-di...it happened like this...." She tried to suppress her happy laughter. "One fine evening...."

"Cut out unnecessary details. How did you join up?"

"One fine evening last year...I was standing in the front verandah waiting for my brothers. My father had come back after his walk and was taking his bath. Suddenly I saw this Baul fakir hovering near the statue of Diana the Huntress. In Luna's Grove."

"Are you writing a short story? What on earth are you talking about?"

"See, Uma-di my grandpa called his garden Luna's Grove. Now it has overgrown into a dense jungle. Actually *our* house should be called Woodland! In order to attract my attention the fakir struck his lute and broke into a lively Baul song. My aunt keeps giving handfuls of rice to all these mendicants...Muslim singing-fakirs and Vaishnava bairagis and so on, you know. So, I called out to him to go round to the kitchen door. When he heard me, lo and behold, he rushes forward and leaps onto the verandah. Says he would like to see Dr. Sarkar. Something caught his attention. The drawing room door was open. He dived right in. Just like that. I followed him. There he stood before Uncle Dinesh's portrait, looking at it intently.

"He swung around and said he would like to have a copy of the portrait. 'Are you Dinesh Sarkar's daughter?' he asked.

" 'His niece. He wasn't married,' I replied.

"Father was still in the bathroom. I ran out and shouted: 'Baba, come quick. A most peculiar kind of Muslim mendicant has barged in and has made himself at home in the *baithak khana.*'

"Father came out and followed me to the sitting room. The fakir stood up and began talking in an undertone to father. He told me he had called Bazlur Rehman Mian and that his hospice was situated in Barisal. You know, he explained, we Muslims have our hospices attached to our saints' shrines.

"I was more confused when he said he edited a Bengali weekly, and was going to bring out a special number on my Uncle Dinesh. And he had come to collect some material for that. Old photographs, unpublished articles. Letters written from the death cell, et cetera. His beard was so funny."

"What happened next?" asked Uma. She was all attention.

"Baba told him to come again after a couple of days, and promised to unlock old boxes and things and unearth the stuff. Right then my noisy brothers returned home. I went out to shoo them away under some pretext. When I returned the fakir was not there. Must have jumped out of a side window.

"Two days later he materialised again, after sunset. Baba had gone out to see a patient but had given me the stuff to hand over to the unusual editor. Perhaps the fakir found out the timings of my brothers' football game. He strode in casually and sat down." Deepali began to giggle again.

"Why do you laugh so much?" Uma Roy asked irritably.

"Sorry, Uma-di."

"You have suffered so much and yet you are so happy."

"Sorry." She tried to look ashamed of her happiness.

"Proceed."

"I gave him the file. He said, 'Tell me whatever you remember about your uncle.' I broke down. He was very upset. Childhood memories are very sharp, you know. He took notes as I spoke and asked him about his journal. He said it was a radical sort of magazine, and added that the following week they were going to set up a study circle at a certain place in the old town. 'Try to attend it whenever you can', he said. I asked him to teach me a Baul song. Abbasuddin Ahmed had taught me a lot of Baul songs, but I had never heard the one he sang that first evening.

"He said it was getting late, but he could come the next evening. I was very pleased."

"So he came again."

"He did. The whole thing was so strange. Baba was out, my aunt was in her puja room. The fakir taught me a Baul song and asked me to sing a *bhatiali* for him. Said whenever he could, he listened to my broadcasts. He was a very sweet fakir, Uma-di—I mean, Mr. Bazlur Rehman. He was so *cute.*"

"So I gather," Uma remarked dryly.

"When Baba returned home, I told him that Mian had come and taught me a song. Suddenly Baba became very pensive. 'Deepa,' he said, 'I have lost my dearly beloved brother. Do you also want to follow the same dangerous path?' I crossed my fingers and said, "No, Baba, I have absolutely no intention of getting mixed up with any kind of politics, violent or non-violent. Singing is my only vocation.' He was satisfied.

"Mian came once again, late at night. Just to tell us that he was going away. Didn't say where. I started visiting the study circle in Nawabpura. Never saw him there. When I asked about him, the comrades said they didn't know what I was talking about. I, too, picked up the techniques of the Underground. I would tell my father that I was going to visit my friend, Rosie. First I would go to her house, she would tell her parents we were going to the college club for our rehearsals, then both of us would run off to Nawabpura under cover of darkness. The study circle used to meet every week at night.

"Since then I have been working as a sympathiser.

"Last month I was informed that the police had locked up their small handpress and confiscated all its stock. Their leader, Rehan Ahmed, and his comrades had to decamp from their present hide-out. For that they needed two thousand rupees at once. They had already managed fifteen hundred but were short of six hundred. So I stole my mother's Balucher saris. They have set up their handpress in some distant village."

Uma lay back on the couch and looked very glum. After a while she said, "You are temperamental, and I gather from this letter that you are also reckless and a daredevil. A sheltered girl like you—from where did you get this streak?"

"From my grandfather and uncle, I suppose."

"You are very young. Watch your step."

"They were also young when they started on their..."

"On their road to ruin, in different directions of course!"

"You ask me to be careful, and also expect me to undertake this dangerous mission!"

"This thing has to be done. There is no time to lose. Think soberly about it and give me your answer—Yes or No—in fifteen minutes flat."

"Yes."

"That was only fifteen seconds. All right, come here. Bolt that door and bring the chair closer. Even walls have ears."

Gosh, she is an awful bore. Now she'll say a stitch in time saves nine. Deepali sighed.

"Tell me—is there anything you are afraid of?"

"Yes."

"What is it?"

"Lizards."

"This Rosie Bannerjee. Is she dependable?"

"Absolutely."

"All right. Go and stand before that mirror."

Deepali obeyed. Uma scanned her from head to toe.

"Speak in your Mymensingh dialect."

She spoke a few words.

"Jolly good. Now come here and listen carefully."

"So there are you are," said Uma Roy after she had finished speaking in an undertone. "R. informs me that you are an excellent actress, you'll do it."

Deepali remained silent. How on earth was she going to pull it off? But she must. And how did he know that she could act? He must have seen some of her college plays, too.

"What is your name?"

"My name...my name Kulsum Bano."

"Your native district?"

"I am belonging to Ghaffar Gaon, Mem-Saheb."

"Do you have any certificates, chits, you know, from your previous employers?"

"No, Mem-Saheb. My uncle, he cook for Nawab Saheb of Bogra...He send me."

"Well done! But don't say 'Nawab Saheb of Bogra!' He is a well-known man," Uma said, and laughed for the first time. "I'll think up something else. Please proceed."

"That's fine. Will do. R. is right, you can act. Do you have a muslin veil?"

"I'll borrow one from our coachman, Abdul Qadir's wife."

"Jolly good. Fine. Goodness! It's so late—what will you tell your father?"

"That I asked you a lot of questions about England, therefore it got late. He doesn't mind if I go home late from Rosie or Jehan Ara's place. I don't go anywhere else socially."

Uma pressed the bell, saying, "It's fortunate that my people have gone off to the club."

Karim Khan appeared. "Call the driver."

The bearer went out.

As Deepali left the room, she quite unconsciously threw a glance at the picture of Salome with the head of John the Baptist. Uma came with her upto the porch. "Get off at a little distance from your house," she whispered before saying goodbye. The car came out on the avenue and gathered speed. Woodland lights vanished in the frosty darkness. Deepali leaned forward and said to the chauffeur, "Please, take me first to the Mission Compound."

7
The Rev. Paul Mathew Bannerjee

THE annual all-India conference of "native" evangelists was
going to be held during the X'mas week. Delegates from
Allahabad, Seetapur, Shahjehanpur, Agra, Ludhiana, Ambala,
Lahore and other important missionary centres of north
India had started arriving at the Mission Compound, and
were being put up in a camp. Carol singers were fervently
practising their hymns inside the church. It was the evening
of December 20th. The Rev. Paul Mathew Bannerjee sat in
his study, writing the Christmas sermon. The Parsonage,
known as Lily Cottage, had been beautifully decorated. Mrs.
Esther Bannerjee squatted on the kitchen floor, cleaning dry
fruit for her Christmas cake. Outside, camp inmates were
busy preparing a colourful Nativity tableau.

All of a sudden the choir from Ludhiana burst into a
Punjabi carol, a literal translation of "Silent Night".

Rev. Bannerjee placed his pen on the ebony inkstand
and looked around. Everything was in order. The almirahs
were neatly stacked with logbooks and registers. Fresh flowers
had been arranged in a vase made of painted gourd. The
plain black Cross had been varnished. Hymns were being
sung in the chapel. The Compound's little orphans and
blind children laughed happily as they rehearsed the arrival
of the Three Kings.

All was calm. All was bright. Holy Mother and the Child
were being decked up in the shed. God was showering His
mercy on mankind. Well, not on all mankind perhaps, but
still—

Rev. Bannerjee was hardly ever assailed by Doubts,
otherwise he would not have been sitting in his warm and
cosy little cottage. Like some of his fellow Bengalis he would
have been plotting and scheming to overthrow the lawful

Government of India. But the parson was God's good man, a true Christian and a gentle preacher of the gospel. Tonight he surveyed, through his office window, the little island of peace and serenity he presided over, and thanked the good Shepherd for His loving care.

After a few minutes he pulled out a bulky file from a revolving almirah. Instead of writing the sermon, he decided to first complete the annual report of missionary work.

Of late, there had been a marked decline in conversions. The nationalist press attributed it to the fact that a famine had not occurred for some time, therefore no "rice Christians". There was Hindu revivalism, also, to cope with, and unfortunately, the priests and nuns from Europe had succeeded in converting entire tribal belts to Popery.

Muslims were a dead loss, anyway. Extremely few could be won over, being an arrogant and self-righteous lot. It was useless to argue with Mohammedan fanatics.

The Hindus were becoming increasingly conceited about their ancient philosophy and spiritualism and so on. Acquired a holier-than-thou attitude, overlooking the fact that British and German Orientalists had rediscovered their cultural heritage for them. They seemed to have forgotten that Christian missionaries like Bishop Heber, William Yates, Carey and Marshman had enabled them to become modern.

Must talk about Bishop Heber in the sermon, he was a real friend of this country. He came out to 'green Bengal's palmy groves', spread the good tidings about Christ, and died so tragically young.

Rev. Bannerjee took out *The Heroes of the Indian Empire* and opened the relevant chapter... "When he spoke of the evening walk after his boat was moored: when amid the scent of night-blowing flowers, the soft whisper of waving palms and the warbling of the nightingale, watching the fireflies floating, rising and sinking in the bamboo woods, and gazing on the mighty river with a tropical moon sleeping on its surface, 'I felt in my heart it is good to be here.'"

The Reverend stopped reading and closed his eyes. He found himself in a remote village in the northern district of Rangpur, where nightingales sang in the temple garden, and he accompanied his devout mother to worship the terrifying image of Kali.

Ma. You remained engulfed in the darkness of polytheism and idolatory till your last breath. Alas, that you died a heathen, a lost, unredeemed soul. Where must you be at this moment? In which darkness of eternity? Alas...alas....

Sorrowfully he returned to his facts and figures which were to be presented in the annual report. Human beings who had been saved or lost. And how had he been saved? Was it merely chance? The Hindus call it Karma, the Mohammedans, Kismet. We Christians would say...the Grace of God! Nevertheless, it was amazing, he told himself, how like a fast-flowing river, life could suddenly change its course. An individual takes one step in a certain direction and the future of his subsequent generations becomes totally different.

It had happened forty years ago. Seventeen-year old Monmohun Bannerjee had appeared for his matriculation examination from the centre in Lalmunir Haat. He was returning to his village, and on board the steamer he met an English missionary. During the long, slow voyage on the Brahmaputra, the White man began telling him about Jesus. He wrote down his address on the fly-leaf of the Bible he presented to the youngster. When Monmohun reached home he found his beloved mother dying of an infectious disease. His father had called the Brahmin priest and the witch-doctor to appease some local "goddess" whose wrath the poor woman was supposed to have incurred. Monmohun was horrified. Barefoot, he ran to the nearest village where the Lutheran Germans had opened a dispensary, but by the time he brought the German missionary doctor back, his mother had succumbed to her illness.

And, behold! Her idols could not save her. It was a traumatic experience for the young lad. He did not know which way to turn for solace and reassurance. At a time of crisis his culture and his society were found wanting. And then he remembered the Bible...

It changed his life.

Therefore, I ask the question, was it Karma or blind chance? Nay! It was part of God's plan—Providence—that I met that kindly missionary on the Brahmaputra, and eventually found my own Brahmaputra—Son of God! The Reverend was rather pleased with the unintended pun, and smiled piously.

The choir from Ludhiana had started singing "Come, Let Us Adore Him" in Punjabi.

The Good Book and the hymns had been translated into all Indian languages and tribal dialects. What erudition, what diligence on the part of the ardent, blue-eyed European men and single-minded single women (another good phrase!) They had been coming out to India for the last two-hundred-and-fifty years, and they had popularised the printed book in this country. A few of the men had donned the Hindu sadhus' ochre robes in order to identify with local traditions. Mostly they belonged to India's exclusive European society.

They had trained the "black preacher". Socially, he was not admitted to their fraternity. In fact, he belonged neither here nor there, as he stood, Bible in hand, in between two milieus, European and Indian, fully accepted by neither. Undaunted, he carried on like the black parson of America.

The Serampore Baptist Mission had set up colleges, hospitals and printing presses. Unfortunately, they also published obnoxious literature attacking Indian religions. Lord Minto had once informed the East India Company's Board of Directors in London, that Serampore literature was proving to be highly inflammatory for the Hindus. To which the famous Serampore missionary, Dr. Marshman, had replied that the Indians were stupid, anyway, and their weakness of character could not be cured even by Christianity.

But, Dr. Marshman had added, to live under Pax Britannica was a blessing of God for them. Therefore, whichever Hindu or Mohammedan became a Christian, he would automatically be intensely loyal to Britain because his very existence depended on the might and expansion of the Empire.

After 1857, Christianity received official patronage. One of the reasons for the uprising had been the virulent attacks on Hinduism and Islam by White missionaries. The latter religion had been maligned since the time of the Crusades; "the strange gods" of the Gentoos were a comparatively recent discovery. After 1857 the missionaries entered into polemics with both maulvis and pundits and drew large crowds. The dates and times of the debates were publicised in advance, and the events became a kind of public entertainment.

Bannerjee recalled how, when he visited Delhi once, he was present on one such occasion. The Fountain at Chandni Chowk had turned into a kind of Hyde Park Corner, where verbal duels were fought. That day, an English doctor of divinity from Agra was taking on a maulana and a pundit— the two had ganged up temporarily to confront the foreigner. Whenever one of the Indians scored a point, the huge audience roared its hearty approval and cheered triumphantly. For the young and sensitive curate from Bengal it was a sad spectacle. Here was a representative of the victorious nation attacking his subject peoples' faiths from his position of advantage. Bannerjee felt a certain sympathy for the learned Muslim and Hindu scholars who were both giving a hard time to the Angrez Padri Saheb. Bannerjee felt uncomfortable. Disturbing thoughts came to his mind. How much hatred, prejudice and ill-will had religion generated in mankind! Doesn't each person think his own religion and culture to be the best and the finest? Why was he, Monmohun Bannerjee, wasting his time in this futile exchange? Shouldn't he go back to Rangpur and start teaching mathematics, a subject he loved, in a school?

His doubts were short-lived. Better minds than mine, people like Michael Madhusudan Dutt and the Rev. Krishna Mohan

Bannerjee, had given up their ancient beliefs and adopted the Westerners' faith. Surujkumar Chukkerburty went to London to study medicine and had himself baptised. He became the first *native* to be taken into the Hon'ble John Company's Covenanted Services. Bholunath Das was assistant surgeon to the Company's forces in the Battle of Sutlej. Later he became Civil Surgeon, Dacca. There were hundreds and thousands of young men and women like them who became Christian. Was it only because they wanted good jobs that they embraced the ruling class's dominant faith? Nay! It was also intellectual discontent! The creed was associated with White races who were advancing the frontiers of knowledge and had made all the progress in the modern world.

Once he said this to his friend, Nawab Qamrul Zaman Chowdhry of Arjumand Manzil. The baron puffed at his silver hookah, smiled and answered, "Monmohun Babu, the West's national memories are woefully short and selective. Today the Nazis have forgotten that the Jews are the co-architects of what is known as the Western Christian Civilisation. It is also overlooked by the West that a thousand years ago, Arab scholars and scientists were the leading lights of Europe."

"Ah, but…"

"And that the scientists and scholars and artists and mystics of Islam were the products of Arab Enlightenment."

"Yes, but—"

"Sufi missionaries followed the Turki and Afghan flags into 13th century India. The evangelists have arrived with European and English banners. It's merely history repeating itself. Besides, the subject people often adopt the manners and customs of their rulers, sometimes even their religion. The Bengali Baboo has come to symbolise the modern enlightened Indian. The English resent and ridicule him."

In his *Twenty-one Days in India, being the Tour of Sir Alibaba K.C.B.*, published about sixty years ago, satirist George Aberigh-Mackay had written: "However much we may desire to diffuse babooism over the Empire we must all agree that the Baboo itself is subject for tears. The other day I was strolling down the Mall, I met the Bengali Baboo. It was returning from the office. I asked if it had a soul, it replied that it had not, but some day it hoped to pass the matriculation examination of Calcutta University...

"It is the future of Baboodom I tremble for. When they wax fat with new religions, music, painting, Comedie Anglaise, scientific discoveries, they may kick with those developed legs of theirs until we shall have to think that they are something more than a joke... The fear is that their tendencies may infect others. The patent leather shoes, the silk umbrellas, the ten-thousand horse-power English words and phrases and the loose shadows of English thought which are now so many Aunt Sallies for all the world to fling a jeer at, might among other races pass into dummy soldiers and from dummy soldiers into trampling, hope-bestirring crowds and so on...

"It is this possibility that leads Sir Ashley Eden to advise the Baboo to revert to its original type. But it is not so easy to become homogeneous after you have been diluted by the physical scientists and stirred about by positivists and missionaries..."

Qamrul Zaman Chowdhry had once lent this book to Bannerjee. "Read this, Monmohun Babu," he had said, "and marvel at the amazing arrogance of our rulers."

Whenever he visited Arjumand Manzil, he found the Nawab and his friends discussing politics. The subject did not interest him. As a native Christian he was sincerely loyal to the British Government.

He disliked "Sir Alibaba" laughing at the baboos, but he reminded himself: Nawab Qamrul Zaman was as much a Bengali as Pritish Roy, yet he was not a baboo. And that again led back to the abominable Hindu-Muslim squabbles which had resulted in the Partition of Bengal in 1905, its annulment and subsequent troubles.

Rev. Bannerjee hated all politics, be it of Woodland or of Arjumand Manzil.

And yet, wasn't it one of the mysteries of the Divine Plan that he found his dearly beloved wife, Esther Giribala, through Arjumand Manzil, and precisely because of the Hindu-Muslim Question?

Her father was a Brahmin priest who belonged to Nawab Sir Nurul Zaman Chowdhry's estate in Faridpur. She had been married at the age of four and lost her child-husband at the age of six, while she was still living with her parents. She was nine when a devastating flood carried away her entire family. She survived, clinging to a strong tree. (A miracle, and according to the Almighty's Plans, Rev. Bannerjee always maintained.) Her parents-in-law reluctantly took her in and made her life miserable.

Hindu widows of Bengal were considered inauspicious. Their heads were shaved and they were not allowed to re-marry. Many went off to the sacred towns of Hardwar, Mathura and Banaras in north India, where they became mendicant nuns. Some changed their religion. Some ended up in brothels. A few were rescued by social reformers.

Little Giribala also suffered in silence till she was fourteen when she ran away. She had heard that her feudal lord and lady were a benevolent couple. Traditionally, Indian peasants addressed their landlords as "Mai-Baap", mother-father. She decided to seek her Mai-Baap's protection in Dacca, and managed to get into a country-craft. She could have been picked up by a tout and sold to a madam in Calcutta, but luckily, at the bustling wharf of Narayan Gunj, she was recognised by a servant from Arjumand Manzil. He had seen her on the estate in Faridpur. Giribala was good-looking and men didn't easily forget her face.

The servant had also heard about her plight. He took her straight to the safety of Arjumand Manzil's zenana. Lady Chowdhry employed her as a housemaid. Poor Giribala's troubles were not over. Young Qamrul Zaman began to bother her. Lady Chowdhry decided to marry her off (if she agreed) to the bachelor cook. As a Brahmin widow she could not be remarried, even to a fellow Brahmin. Since she had run away and "cut the noses" of her own high-caste village community, she could not be sent back. It was a tricky situation.

"The best thing," said Lady Chowdhry to her husband, "would be to quietly wed her to our Akram."

It was 1906. Bengal had just been partitioned against the wishes of Bengali Hindus. Dacca had become the capital of the new Muslim majority province of East Bengal. Hindu-Muslim tension was at its peak.

"At such a time if we convert a runaway, widowed daughter of a Brahmin, marry her to our Muslim servant, and the event is reported by the anti-partition Hindu press, think of the scandal... even riots," Sir Nurul Zaman's younger brother Fakhrul Zaman pointed out.

"Christian missionaries," retorted Sir Nurul, "are converting Brahmins and Hindus of all castes in droves. That doesn't lead to Hindu-Christian riots, because the missionaries belong to the ruling class!"

"Idea!" exclaimed Fakhrul Zaman cheerfully. "Give her to the missionaries!"

The Right-Reverend Kenneth Walford-Brown was a friend of Sir Nurul. Lady Chowdhry asked the bishop's wife to take charge of Giribala Chattopadhya, and Mrs. Walford gladly did so. She took the girl home and had her admitted to the Mission Girls' High School. Bishop Brown baptised her as Esther Marion.

From Giribala, Daughter of the Mountains, goddess Parvati, wife of Shiva, she became an Old Testament figure. How easy and simple it all was!

After his baptism in Rangpur, Monmohun had changed into Paul Mathew. Bursting with the zeal of the convert, he had studied at a seminary, taken the cloth and become an itinerant preacher. Later he was posted to various native churches. Esther Marion Giribala Chatterjee passed her eighth class, and Bishop Walford married her to the native clergyman. He was fifteen years older, but she was immensely happy. For the first time in her life she had found respect and comfort, and a home of her own. And her dear Paul was such a considerate husband. They had a lovely daughter, Rosie Shrila. For the last few years, Rev. Bannerjee had been in charge of the Mission Compound in Dacca.

He watched his reflection in the window-pane, and tried to recollect the various phases of his life. The indigent Brahmin lad of Rangpur. The solemn, black-suited young preacher who toured the countryside on his bicycle. He remembered: whenever he strayed into a Muslim locality, he was jeered at by the street urchins, ha, ha, ha, here comes the Black Padre. Hello, Imitation Englishman, did you get all sooty when you fell into the Black Sea on your way to India?

Once he visited a small town in U.P. and the urchins shouted, "Hey, Mule Padre—Angrez-log will never accept you as an equal even after you acquire their religion." Meekly he bore these insults for the sake of sweet Jesus.

The evangelists were still called Mule Padres by the Muslims of north India, because in earlier times they used to go about on mules and donkeys. And the Muslims called all Christian clergymen "Padre" even if they were Protestant, because the earliest missionaries who arrived in Mughal times were Portuguese.

In north India, low-caste converts were often jeeringly referred to as Chamresians—cobblers—to rhyme with Eurasians. They were also called Black Englishmen, since they usually adopted English surnames. They didn't mind the ridicule and didn't care, because conversion brought about a sea-change in their lives. They were educated by the missions, provided with jobs and their lifestyle became much better.

Muslims didn't have an in-built system of untouchability in their society, but they, too, considered sweepers and scavengers as untouchable outcastes. Sweepers became Christian *en masse*, mostly in the U.P. and Punjab.

Of late, Esther had become worried about the marriage prospects of their daughter, Rosie. She had been earnestly praying to the Lord to send a "good-family" Christian boy for their beloved child. The Reverend was sure that the Lord would hear her prayer. On the whole he had much to be grateful for, and tonight as he faced himself in the window-pane, he saw a venerable parson, loved and respected by his parish, well-liked by the English ecclesiastical hierarchy as well as civil authorities, a man with few regrets... He took off his glasses and touched his moist eyelashes. Dear Lord, You have given me everything. A devout flock. A loving, obedient wife. A dutiful daughter, and a contented heart. I can't thank You enough. He dipped his pen in the inkpot and began writing his Christmas sermon: "Rejoice..."

8
A Sari for Virgin Mary

So another Christmas and another splendid sari for the Virgin from Arjumand Manzil! Rosie sat down resignedly on her bed and began stitching a gold border on a length of indigo-blue Banares tissue. She had got both these as usual from Nawab Qamrul Zaman Chowdhry's eldest daughter, Jehan Ara. It had become an annual routine. Arjumand Manzil's wardrobes overflowed with such fineries. Rosie could pick and choose, and Jehan Ara suggested all manner of designs to be worked into the tiny sari.

"Bibi Maryam is our Prophet Isa's virgin mother," she always added pleasantly, as a footnote. "Of course, you People of the Book tampered a bit here and there with the text of the holy Engeel, but what is an alteration or two between friends!"

They laughed cheerily, and Rosie promised to send the Christmas pudding which her Mamma made with special ingredients to Begum Qamrul Zaman. She also received a Christmas present from Jehan Ara. It was always great fun going to Arjumand Manzil and enjoying their lavish hospitality. All that had suddenly changed for her two years ago. Rosie had gone to Lalmunir Haat, where for the first time in her life she heard the entire story of her mother's life. Her father's sister, Flora, rather viciously narrated to her the trials and tribulations of Giribala Chattopadhya in careful detail. Rosie was stunned. Nobody in her school or college had known about it. It had happened long, long ago. The Chowdhrys of Arjumand Manzil, and even their servants, were too civilised to have ever hinted to her about her mother's unhappy past. After learning the sad truth that her dear Mamma had once worked as a housemaid in Arjumand Manzil, Rosie Bannerjee acquired a strange kind of complex.

Now she felt acutely embarrassed whenever she visited Arjumand Manzil, and avoided going there as much as she could.

The revelation affected her social attitudes. She began to dislike Hindu society. Didn't they get little Giribala married at the age of four and persecute her as a child-widow? She started hating the Muslims. They were a lecherous lot. Aunt Flora had hinted darkly that Qamrul Zaman had more or less seduced poor Giribala who had become a ward of his own parents. On the other hand, the English had given her education and self-confidence and a neat and respectable home of her own.

Flora did not point out that the Zaman Chowdhrys could have married her to their lowly cook, or to their Hindu gardener. Instead, they had entrusted her to Bishop Brown.

For nearly a year young Rosie secretly wallowed in self-pity as she also realised the slightly ambiguous position of her own social set-up. Neither fish nor fowl, as it were.

At twenty Rosie Shrila Bannerjee was terribly confused. Ever since her friend Deepali had acquired some mysterious new friends, she had got interested in politics and had seen a way out of her dilemma. This entire *system* must be changed. A system which allowed such atrocities as were perpetrated on her own mother. Now she also wanted to identify with Indian culture and nationalism. Her own "native Christian" society had been created by the British and was generally loyal to its founders. Rosie's saintly father had resolved the dilemma long ago and was happy in his situation. She could not explain her problem to him, he wouldn't understand. Despite her conversion, Esther Giribala was still basically a Bengali Brahmin housewife, uninterested in the problems of cultural identity.

Like most South Indian Christians, the converts of Bengal had retained a watered-down caste system. The paradox baffled Rosie. Her friends, Deepali Sarkar and Jehan Ara Chowdhry, represented two strands of the same Bengali culture of which all of them were intensely proud. In her college she learned how Ireland's Sinn Fein, Russia's Social Democrats and Mazzini's Young Italy had influenced Indian radicals. The terrorists had said: We know we can't get freedom by killing a few Englishmen. We only wish to prove to our rulers that we have the guts to kill and get killed. There were girl-terrorists too. On April 22, 1930, when the government armoury in Chittagong was attacked, one of the girls, Kalpana Dutta, was arrested. Pritilata Wadedar led the attack on Chittagong's European Club. Before she could be handcuffed, she killed herself. Two young girls, Shanti and Suniti, were transported to the Andaman Islands for life. They had assassinated the English district magistrate of Comilla. Beena Das shot at the Governor of Bengal. A number of high-ranking English officials of the province were murdered.

Now Rosie daydreamed: Can't I also become a national heroine like them and atone for the servility of my community?

During the last few years the Terrorists had become Communists. A number of young and brilliant comrades had appeared on the scene. Last winter Deepali had said to Rosie, "Listen, dope. Yesterday I went to a top-secret study circle. You also come along next week. We learn a lot of important stuff which clears the cobwebs of our winds. *We study Marxism.*"

"You are a goonk," Rosie had replied. "If Papa gets to know he'll skin me alive."

"Goof. Tell him you are coming to my place to study for the exams."

The following Sunday Rosie accompanied Deepali to a crumbling old house inside the old city. The girls were welcomed by the host, a myopic, deadly serious young man called Mahmoodul Haque. He worked as a proof-reader in a newspaper office.

Rosie started attending their meetings, and found the answers to many questions which had been bothering her about her own situation. Britain had turned India into a raw-material producing colony. That led to hunger, unrest, unemployment and Hindu-Muslim clashes. The situation also gave the White missionaries ample opportunity to convert the starving Indians.

Apart from being womanisers, the Muslims were fanatics and toadies. She was, therefore, surprised to find so many of them among the Leftists.

Once she said to one of them, called Mushir, "I'm so glad that you all have also joined us."

"And pray who are *you* and who are *us?*" he asked.

"I mean, the Mohammedans are such loyalists."

"Miss Bannerjee," Mushir replied in a huff, "our ancestors started fighting the aliens nearly two hundred years ago…"

"Kings and queens, trying to save their thrones…"

"No. Peasants and artisans who also waged a class war. But you perhaps do not even know about the modern revolutionaries."

"Of course, I do! Madanlal Dhingra. He killed Sir William Curzon-Wylie in London in 1909. Bhagat Singh, who shot Police Officer Saunders in Lahore. Hanged in 1931…"

"Talking of the earliest London-based Indian radicals we tend to forget Khudadad Khan, Hyder Reza and Zafar Ali…"

"Comrade, don't turn it into a communal question," Mahmood admonished Mushir.

"We are here to discuss, analyse and correct our inherited prejudices, aren't we? And we acquired these prejudices only during the last century," Mushir countered. "Our Rosie only knows about playboys like Nawab Ahmed Ali of Bamboo Villa and Nawab Fakhrul Zaman of Arjumand Manzil. Forty years ago in Paris the Russian Nihilists taught the Indian student, Mirza Abbas, how to make bombs. Give me one good reason why our Rosie has not heard of Mirza Abbas. Because our contribution to the struggle for freedom is ignored. Nobody even remembers Umar Sobhani, the cotton king of Bombay. The British reduced the price of cotton and made him bankrupt overnight because he financed the Indian National Congress."

"You are talking like Nawab Qamrul Zaman Chowdhry, you ought to join his Muslim League," Mahmood remarked dryly.

Mushir rattled off some more names. "Ali Ahmed Siddiqui and Mujtaba Hussain of U.P. Syed Rehmat Ali Shah of Punjab. Cassim Mansour of Bombay, all hanged in 1915. Ashfaqullah Khan of U.P., executed in 1927. And lots more hanged, shot down, died in prison. Does anybody talk about them?"

Rosie tried to make amends. "My best friend," she said politely, "is a Muslim, Jehan Ara Chowdhry."

Mushir groaned.

After some minutes she boldly asked Mushir, "Tell me, are you a Bengali first or a Muslim?"

"Both."

"If you believe in dialectical materialism, you can't call yourself a Mohammedan," she retorted.

"Historically and culturally, I am. Look, the trouble is when a Hindu glories in his traditions, it is Indian culture and Indian philosophy. When a Muslim mentions his own heritage he is a communalist. We must correct these attitudes before it is too late. Or else, comrades, this country will break up when the British leave."

"We are all human beings, and Indians," Mahmood tried to solve the thorny problem.

Jyoti had been beaming at them through his horn-rimmed glasses. He turned to Rosie. "And what are you, Rosie?" It sounded like a cross-examination.

"A Bengali and a Chris...." she checked herself.

"Rosie, who was Lord Reading?" Mushir grilled her.

"Viceroy of India. Rash Behari Bose threw a bomb at him in Delhi, in 1912."

"Silly, that was Lord Hardinge," Deepali corrected her.

"Lord Reading?" Mushir repeated the question.

"He was also a Viceroy of India."

"He was a Jew and a Briton, both."

"Really? I thought all Englishmen were Christians. All this is very confusing," she confessed after a pause.

"The great Lenin has solved the question of nationalities beautifully," Mahmood began, lighting his pipe. The comrades always said 'the great Lenin,' 'the great Stalin'.

"When Maulana Barkatullah met the great Lenin..." Mushir interrupted him.

"Who was Maulana Barkatullah?" Rosie asked timidly.

"One of the founders of the Ghadar Party of America, and also of the Government of Free India set up in Kabul in 1916.

"Our revolutionaries were hounded from country to country. Many of them lived and died in great poverty. Maulvi Barkatullah published a radical magazine from Tokyo. It was banned by the Japanese government. He died penniless and forgotten in America.

"They were indomitable men. Sardar Ajit Singh. He lived in Paris, also in utter poverty, disguised as a Russian Muslim, 'Mirza Hasan Khanov.'

"So many Indian Muslims went to Russia from Kabul and came back as staunch Communists. Ferozuddin Mansur, Fazal Ilahi Qurban, Shaukat Usmani, Mian Afzal Shah. Amir Hyder Khan became a member of the Communist Party of the US, they sent him to Moscow for training."

"Fascinating men, those..." remarked Jyoti. "Sarojini Naidu's brother, Virendranath Chattopadhyaya, carried a price of ten thousand pounds on his head. He was a linguist and an expert at quick disguise like our Comrade Rehan Ahmed. In no time he could change his dress, appearance and voice. Comrade Rehan always reminds me of him. And also Comrade Shunil..."

"Whatever happened to him?"

"To Rehan Ahmed?"

"No, Shunil."

"Disappeared in Russia."

"Must have been done in," Rosie put in quietly.

Deepali glared at her.

Mushir resumed his narration: "P.G. Pingle was a Maharashtrian. Posed as Shyamlal, a Bengali, and Ganpat

Singh, a Punjabi. What an excellent actor he must have been! The South Indian Aiyer lived in Cairo as an Egyptian dervish! How on earth did he change his Tamilian accent? Now Sufi Amba Parshad was from U.P., and he was also a scholar of Arabic and Persian. He lived in Shiraz as an Iranian maulvi till the British agents got him. He killed himself in his cell.

"Maulana Mahmoodul Hasan was the Rector of the Theological University of Deoband, and an active radical. The Kabul Conspirators sent letters to the Czar of Russia, the Sultan of Turkey, etc. The letters were written on yellow silk stitched inside the couriers' coats. They sent one to Maulana Mahmoodul Hasan. The Arabs betrayed him and he was exiled to Malta where he was tortured.

"Maulana Obeidullah Sindhi founded a terrorist group in Delhi in 1913. He headed the Free India Government-in-exile at Kabul. Now when the Maulana went to Germany he..."

Rosie cut him short. "Funny, so many Muslim maulvis became revolutionaries. I thought all of them were narrow-minded zealots."

"Rosie, are all Indian Christian and Eurasian girls, tramps?"

"Most certainly not."

"So, don't generalise."

Rosie Bannerjee's education in the study circle was progressing satisfactorily when the Second World War broke out. The comrades told her the California-based Indian patriots had planned a mutiny in India in 1915, that's why they called their movement Ghadar or Mutiny Party, in remembrance of 1857. They chartered a Japanese ship and came home. Before they could land in Calcutta a traitor informed the Government—forty-two of them were hanged.

"That plan seems to have been a bit of tomfoolery," opined Rosie. "Schoolboy adventure."

"It was not. Treason has always ruined us, from the time of Siraj and Tipu. Anyway, the point is that we must now take advantage of the Imperialists' present troubles in Europe. We must start a civil war in India and pave the way for the Red Revolution. The Government has imposed press censorship. Our underground press is going to publish tracts in order to educate the masses."

"The masses are lovable," Rosie repeated the phrase she had heard frequently at the study circle.

"As a sympathiser you must work for us."

"Of course."

"Does the Padre Saheb know where you go on Sunday evenings?"

"He hasn't the foggiest."

"Good. Be very careful. We have difficult times ahead."

A few days earlier the cell had broken up. The comrades went underground. Deepali became tight-lipped and stopped confiding in Rosie.

Perhaps they don't trust me because I belong to a loyalist family, she thought ruefully. Perhaps I was too outspoken. They also know that William Cantwell is very fond of Papa. Mrs Cantwell sometimes visits Lily Cottage. I can never prove my loyalty to the Party, they will always suspect me. Rosie knew that Deepali was in touch with the Underground, but never said a word to her. This attitude had broken poor Rosie's heart.

She finished stitching the gold border on Saint Mary's sari and closed her mother's workbox, after which she made for the shed where working-class Christian women were devoutly preparing the Manger. She joined them and dressed up the tiny plaster-of-paris figurine of the Virgin.

How was this shed different from the pavilions decorated for Durga Puja? she wondered. Hadn't Mary merely replaced the eight-armed goddess for these simple women? Don't we Christians indulge in idolatry? So why are the Hindus heathens and lost souls? If God can come down as a dove, why can't he also incarnate as a fish and a tortoise and a boar, as the Hindus believe? And why should there have been only one

Incarnation in all human history? Who stopped him from coming down off and on as the Hindu *avtars* did?

In the study circle she discovered a historical explanation for superstition. The dogma of the Trinity, for instance, had been adopted by the casting vote of an emperor of Byzantium. The Chinese concept of the Son of Heaven and the ancient Egyptian cult of the mother-goddess and her divine child had also influenced the early Christians.

The irrational beliefs of all religions could be explained in the light of the sociology and economic history of their respective societies. My poor Papa, he certainly wasted his life. He could have become a noted mathematician.

Rosie was fast losing her Faith, and it was a painful process.

Dutifully she put the finishing touches to the tableau of the Nativity and got up. Now she must go and see if the Ludhiana Choir needed anything.

On the way to the small Gothic church she spotted a tiny, pathetic-looking figure at the entrance of the corridor. She went closer and found that it was little Ruth, the blind orphan from Chittagong. She sat on the cold brick floor, facing the wall and knitting a piece of light blue wool. Earlier in the day Ruth had told Rosie that she was knitting a blanket for the Holy Infant. Rosie stopped near her and felt a lump rising her throat. The sightless twelve-year-old lifted her peaceful face when she heard Rosie's footfall. She turned round and gave Rosie an almost beatific smile.

Inside the church the delegates from Ludhiana were singing their Punjabi hymns. The Lord God is King. The Lord God is the King of Glory. Raise your voice and sing. The King of Life and Glory has come.

Young Luther Biswas, son of Rev. Henry Biswas of Ludhiana Mission, was fervently playing the harmonium. O Lord, show Thy true path to Thy creatures, the choir continued. Luther saw Rosie and rose nervously to his feet. The choir-girls, all dressed in white shalwar-kamiz and bright red cardigans, stopped singing and giggled. Mr. Luther Biswas grinned bashfully.

These simple souls belonged to another sphere, a world so different from the Marxist study circle of Nawabpura. Rosie smiled politely and said, "Sorry, I didn't mean to disturb you all. Please carry on."

"Do sit down, Rosie sister," a Punjabi girl offered her a stool.

Thanks, but I have a lot of things to attend to. Must run along. Goodnight."

Turning towards the vestry door she noticed with alarm that Mr. Luther Biswas's eyes were following her devotedly. She had also seen him blush.

O, my God. She hastened out of the church. Her father's silhouette appeared on the window-pane of his office room in Lily Cottage. She walked across and peeped in. Rev. Bannerjee's head was bent over his papers. His rimless glasses had slipped down to the tip of his nose. His pen moved swiftly on the yellow paper. Rosie felt a surge of love for her poor father. God, keep him alive and happy, she prayed earnestly and went in.

The parson was too engrossed in his work to look up. Good old Papa and his annual Christmas sermons! She tiptoed behind the chair and read: Our Lord gave His life for your redemption. Blessed are they who are baptised in the Holy Spirit... For He died for us and was buried and was resurrected. God's only Begotten son whose Birth we celebrate today... We thank the Good Shepherd that we live in peace and security under a benevolent government, and prosper under the banner of St. George...

"Didi," a compound urchin whispered from the doorway. Quickly she left the room. The boy mumbled, "A big black motor car at the gate. Deepali Didi is sitting in it. Wants to see you. Urgent."

Deepali in a motor car? Rosie looked around furtively and ran towards the gate.

Miss Uma Roy's motor car was parked under a dark banyan at a little distance from the Compound. Deepali looked out of the window and said nervously, "Gosh, Rosie! Your place is all lit up and full of people. I didn't realise. Come over to my place tomorrow, early in the morning. We have to discuss the college play for Christmas. Start, driver."

The car vanished in the dark night. It was all too sudden and dramatic.

Another Punjabi hymn rose from the church... O Lord, give peace to my heart, steady my mind so that I keep fearing Thee...

Luther Biswas's voice was loud and clear: Praise the Lord, Come let us praise the Lord... Let us sing with the choir of the truthful... Sing out the praise of the Master. God is the King. He is the King of Glory... Lord, show the right path to Thy creatures...

9
The New Testament

RIGHT after breakfast Deepali went up to her little tower and waited. The moment she saw Rosie cycling down through Luna's Grove she came downstairs.

Without uttering a word she led her friend to her room, bolted the door, and took down the Bible from her bookshelf. (Rosie's dear father had given it to Deepali on her fourteenth birthday.) Dramatically she shoved the scripture into Rosie's hand. "Close your eyes, Rosie," she intoned.

Bewildered, Rosie obeyed.

"Say—I take the oath of undying loyalty to my motherland, and my nation. I swear on God the Father, God the Son and God the Holy Ghost..."

Rosie opened one eye and objected: "Dope. Miss Jenkins told us only the other day not to stress 'h' in ghost."

"All right, all right. God the Holy Gost—now repeat after me."

Rosie opened both eyes and said, "Are you sure my Papa won't get into trouble because of me? He's growing old and is a good, kindly man. He doesn't deserve this..."

Deepali kept quiet. She didn't know the answer. In fact, she hardly knew the answer to anything. "I", she faltered, "what can I say about the future? But Rosie, aren't you a true Indian?" she asked after a pause.

"Yes," replied Roise grimly. Is patriotism a monopoly of the Hindus? Why are they so patronising? Bah.

Deepali was staring at her expectantly. Suppose Rosie refuses? She felt as though the entire future of India's independence movement hung on Rosie's "Yes" or "No".

All of a sudden Rosie knelt down. Quietly she took the oath on the Bible, forgetting that she had recently become an atheist. "So help me God," she added, rising to her feet.

Deepali Sarkar heaved a sigh of relief and sat down on her trunk which served as a chair.

"Come here, Rosie," she ordered. Now she was the leader, the guru, and Rosie her follower.

"Rosie," Deepali continued stiffly, "you told me once that one of your Compound women worked as a lady's maid at Cantwell's bungalow. Is she still there?"

"Yes, Leelabati. Mamma sent her there."

"Does she belong to Dacca?"

"No, but Mamma brought her up in the Compound. She is an orphan. Her grandmother lives in Narsingdi."

Deepali thought for a few moments, then picked up a postcard and fountain-pen from the window-sill.

"I am writing on behalf of this very useful grandmother. The letter will be addressed to your Mamma. I'll write: 'Granny is seriously ill. Please send Leelabati to Narsingdi for at least a week.' Today my brother Khokhu will travel to Narsingdi and mail this letter from there. Now, is your watchman a reliable fellow?"

"Deepali, you've known poor old Joseph for years."

"Fine. After your Mamma receives this letter, Joseph will take it to Cantwell's house and give it to Leelabati. He will also tell her that he has already arranged for another ayah to replace her for a week. Now, this Leela of yours will ask Mrs. Cantwell to grant her seven days' leave. What kind of person is Mrs. Cantwell?"

"She's all right, quite a nice person, in fact," Rosie replied, perturbed. I know Mrs. Cantwell, I keep meeting her. And now I'm going to deceive her so horribly. But look back at history, at how her people deceived our kings. "She is all right," Rosie repeated uncomfortably.

"Good. The same evening a veiled Muslim ayah, Kulsum Bano, will arrive at Cantwell's house as Leela's replacement. First I thought that you should take this postcard to Mrs. Cantwell and ask her personally to let Leelabati go home. Then I decided against it. Why should I get you into trouble?"

"Why, indeed?" Rosie snapped angrily. "In that case why did you make me take the oath? The fact is, you don't trust me."

"Good heavens, Rosie, how can you say that? Would you go to Cloudland yourself?"

"Where is that? Darjeeling?"

"Sorry, that's our code for Cantwell's bungalow."

"Of course, I'll go myself."

"Wonderful! Thank you."

"Why thank me? I'm not doing you a favour, I'm also working for my country as much as you are."

"Good God, Rosie, what's the matter with you?"

"Never mind. But tell me, what are you up to? I hope you're not going to throw a bomb at Mr. Cantwell."

"Rosie, you know very well we are not Terrorists."

The way Deepali said "we", greatly impressed Rosie. She was also part of the Club, the Inner Circle. Suddenly, she said, "But Deeps, there's a big loophole in your plan. Where will poor Leela go for a week? The letter is fake."

"A minor problem. She'll go to Narsingdi all right, to meet her granny. Now listen. Today is the 20th of December. Kulsum Bano must reach Cloudland before the 23rd, she simply must."

"But why?"

"That, I am afraid, I can't tell you."

"Why?"

"Rosie Bannerjee, you have sworn to work for the Underground. Now learn to hold your tongue and stop asking questions."

"Deeps, you've become a hell of a dictator."

"Tut, tut. A clergyman's daughter swearing! Jehan Ara once told me that in her convent school the geography nun always said Amster-bless. And she never mentioned Rotterdam, Always said—that place in Holland!"

"Ha, ha, ha... Jehan Ara must have made it up! She's a great waffler, like Laila Rahim. But I wonder what she would say if she ever came to know about our underground activities."

"She wouldn't have time to say anything, she'd just faint!" Deepali sat down on the trunk and began writing a letter on behalf of Leelabati's grandmother.

On the morning of December 22nd, Rosie squatted on the brick floor of Lily Cottage's verandah, unpacking Christmas gifts. The boxes contained toys and warm clothes for the Compound's orphan children, sent by the District Magistrate and the Bishop of Dacca. A postman brought the morning mail. It included a postcard from Narsingdi. Rosie paled a little as she read it. For a few minutes she thought hard. Even now there was time to destroy the card and forget about the whole thing. The conference delegates' camp was bustling with happy activity. She saw her mother rushing from tent to tent calling the guests to come for breakfast. Every year they would turn the large garden shed into a make-shift dining hall for the delegates. After a few minutes Mrs. Bannerjee returned to the cottage. Rosie blurted out, "Mamma— Mamma—poor Leelabati's granny is very ill. She has written to you."

"Father God, have mercy. What happened to her?"

"Dunno, Mamma. These illiterate villagers always make a single statement: *I am about to die. Come home at once.*"

"Rosie, you go right now to Mrs. Cantwell and show her this letter. Leela told me she wanted to go home for Christmas, but her Mem Saheb won't let her go during X'mas week."

"Why? Leela doesn't have much work."

"They are going to have house-guests from Calcutta."

"How do you know, Mamma?"

"Mrs. Cantwell told me," Mrs. Bannerjee said a little importantly. "She told me last week when I went to invite her to open the Boxing Day Charity Bazaar."

"Who are the guests, Mamma?"

"How do I know that, child? I am not so informal with Mrs. Cantwell as to ask her about her house-guests and all.

Must be some big, big Sahebs from Calcutta." With that Mrs. Bannerjee hurried towards her kitchen.

Rosie carried the gift packages inside and piled them near the Christmas tree. Unconsciously she looked up at the picture of Jesus Christ, which she always did before going out. She took out her bicycle from a side-room and set out for Ramna.

10
Cloudland

An English home in India, especially if it was of neo-classical design, looked like a Greek temple inhabited by radiant offspring of the Sun God. That was what the aboriginal tribes thought when they first saw tall, golden-haired White men and women who seemed to have suddenly descended, apparently from the clouds.

Every district town had its own Olympus, called the "civil lines". Their landscape differed from province to province, for the Public Works Department had adapted and modified the regional styles of architecture for residential as well as public buildings. The most common was the "Portuguese-colonial" with flat or tiled roofs, high-vaulted rooms, long, spacious verandahs and Moorish arches. Airy houses with sloping, thatched roofs resembled Bengali bamboo huts, and had come to be called "bungalows", for they were first built by European traders in Bengal.

The Civil Lines homes usually had a low, round platform in the front garden, a portico, and a well. The drawing-room was known as *gol kamra*. As the Hindi word *gol* indicated, it used to be circular originally. The kitchen, or *bavarchi khana*, and the servants' quarters were situated at a great distance from the main house.

Children were usually sent away to England for schooling. The Sahebs' bungalows and gardens remained engulfed in a silence which was almost sacrosanct, broken only by birdsong, the dogs' barks and strains of European music.

Military cantonments had a similar kind of enchanted atmosphere.

A kothi was slightly different from a bungalow. Originally, kothi meant an indigenous commercial house, and European traders' kothis later developed into elegant Georgian homes. Such houses were also popularised by the Anglicised Nawabs of Oudh. Many upper-class Indians and members of provincial civil services came out of their Indo-Saracenic havelis and took up residence in the Civil Lines, but the Whites had no social contact with their Indian neighbours.

The Civil Lines' quiet avenues led to the Mall, which was the Sahebs' shopping centre in larger towns. It included a branch of Whiteways, a wine shop owned by an ancient Parsi, and an English cinema hall. Some "stations" also had a convent school run by European priests and nuns. The Indian elite proudly sent their children to these schools because of their excellent education, and also because of the snob value attached to being "convent-educated". The hill-stations were famous for their English public schools and convents.

The railways colony, the Post & Telegraph quarters and the Police Lines were the domain of the Eurasians. Once, an English satirist had commented in London's *Vanity Fair*, "For the Whites a Eurasian, however fair, was *bete noire*, and Mrs Ellenborough Higgins was always setting or pointing out towards black blood. Towards the natives, the Eurasian was cold and haughty and formal, an attitude repaid in scorn and hatred."

On Sunday morning White families attended the European church, and spent their evenings in exclusive clubs. In summer-time they went to the hills. This pattern of life had continued for the last two hundred years. Of late, "pictures" had become part of their entertainment, which still included fancy-dress balls and amateur theatricals.

The Sahebs' domestic staff was the legacy of a not very distant Mughal past. Many districts still did not have electricity. The *mashalchi*—Turki for torch-bearer—lighted gas lamps and lanterns. The coolie—Turki *quli,* for servant—sat in the hot, sun-scorched verandah pulling the pankha-rope to and fro. The rope was attached to a pleated cotton cloth stretched on a rectangular frame hung from the ceiling inside the room. All doors and windows were covered with screens of *tatties* of fragrant *khus* grass. Water was sprinkled over them from time to time by a *chhokra*-boy.

Earlier, the bearer used to carry palanquins and sedan-chairs, now he had become the equivalent of a valet. *Bavarchi* was Turki for cook. The *khidmatgar* was the butler. *Khansaman* or comptroller of the royal household, now meant a chef. In north India most *khansamans* and bearers serving the Sahebs belonged to the Muslim community which, by and large, had become the Biblical drawers of water and hewers of wood.

The ayah was contributed by the Portuguese, and was usually a Hindu or a Christian. She worked as nanny, nurse, lady's maid and enjoyed a position of privilege in the bungalow. Often she had a smattering of English, and was always dressed in a superbly starched, snow-white Indian skirt, blouse and long scarf. In the evenings ordinary mortals saw her pushing a baby's perambulator through the Company Gardens. Often she sat down on the clock-tower steps and gossiped with other ayahs, while the town band played English and Scottish airs and the baba-log played on the grass.

The ayah was quite indispensable in an English household.

Saheb was Arabic for master, and was generally used in north India as a term of respect. It had also come to denote an Englishman. During the days of the Hon'ble John Company an Englishwoman was referred to as *bibi*, Turki-Persian for lady. Later, 'Ma'am' was Indianised into Mem—now all White women were called Mem Saheb.

Baba, Persian for a venerable old man, had also come to mean English children.

William Cantwell's residence in Ramna, Dacca, was a large, picturesque bungalow, set amidst an acre of beautifully maintained gardens. His servants were also of the classical mould. They were well-trained and spoke kitchen English. Right now, they were busy preparing for Christmas, the biggest social event of the year. It was called Burra Din—Big Day—by the populace.

The Cantwell baba-log were away in England. Mrs. Freda Cantwell spent her mornings playing mahjongg with other

Englishwomen. Since the last three months she had become busy with soldiers' welfare work.

Last night the Cantwells had attended the second show of a Norma Shearer film. They had a late breakfast and had still not come out to sit in the sun. It was a bracing December morning. The garden was full of the sharp, cool, scent of sweetpeas, the sun shone brightly, and large butterflies flitted from shrub to shrub in the flower-beds.

Rosie Bannerjee arrived at ten o'clock. Nervously, she got off her bicycle and was scared to see Ronald Jones, William Cantwell's Eurasian clerk, come out of the office-room. Mr. Jones was known to be a bloomin' tatler and a scandal monger. By evening, the news would spread in Dacca's Eurasian and native Christian circles, that Miss Bannerjee was frequenting the Cantwell residence.

Ronnie Jones gave her a faint smile, said "hello" and rushed out, looking terribly busy and important. He was carrying a file marked "Urgent". He rode on his motor-bike and shot out of the gate. Rosie entered the verandah. There was nobody around. She peeped through the window and noticed the old *khidmatgar*.

Abdul was dusting the cake-stand, which piece of furniture was also called "Abdul", because its top was carved like a Turkish-cap-wearing servant.

In colonial North Africa every housemaid was called Fatima, in the Civil Lines of north India, Abdul more or less meant a cook or bearer.

Timidly, Rosie knocked on the *gol-kamra* door.

The bearded *khidmatgar* looked up and saw the Black Padri's daughter. Must have come to invite Mem Saheb for the Big Day. He came out and salaamed her, but did not bow low. He was far more snobbish than Woodland's Karim Khan. His family had served the Sahebs for the last four generations.

"Is Mem Saheb in?" asked Rosie, gulping.

"Yes, Missy Baba."

"And Saheb?"

"He also."

Just then Rosie heard William Cantwell's booming voice as he called out, "Darling, what on earth has happened to Tipoo? He's barking himself silly."

"He's chasing the squirrels, Bill," came Freda Cantwell's cheerful reply. Both were somewhere inside the immense bungalow. The next instant it struck Rosie: she must go back, must not get involved in dangerous games.

Nationalism etc., were all right, but not these hit-and-run conspiracies.

God. How stupid could I get. She stepped back in order to beat a hasty retreat.

Right then Freda Cantwell came out, followed by a playful lap-dog. Tipoo was the big Afghan.

"Good morning, Mrs. Cantwell!"

"Oh, hello! How are you, Rosie?"

"Fine, thank you, Mrs. Cantwell. How are you? Hello, Dusky." Her mouth had gone dry. Dusky wagged his tail.

"Yes, Rosie? Have you come about the church fete?" She was talking to Rosie the way she spoke to the postman or the newspaper vendor. She didn't even ask her to sit down. Rosie was merely the daughter of their native protege, fit to be treated condescendingly.

Mrs. Cantwell wouldn't dream of being rude to Jehan Ara or Uma Roy. Nawab Qamrul Zaman Chowdhry and Barrister Pritish Roy met the Cantwells as their equals. In fact, the Nawab considered himself far superior to the English rulers. He referred to them as monkeys, red-faced barbarians and wily traders, who had used deceit to usurp his royal ancestors' throne.

A few minutes earlier Rosie had decided to tell Mrs. Cantwell that she had come to remind her about the charity bazaar, and go back. To hell with the Underground and the struggle for freedom. Now with a sudden, renewed self-confidence and courage she raised her head and said boldly, "No, Ma'am, I've come for something quite different." She took out the postcard from her cardigan pocket and said, "Leelabati's grandmother is probably dying. She has written to Mamma."

"Oh, no. Not that miserable grandmother again! Abdul, call the ayah, will you?" Freda Cantwell strolled down to the cluster of ferns. The ayah came out. Rosie told her in Bengali about her grandmother's illness. The woman began to cry.

Mrs. Cantwell returned. "Don't worry, Leela," she said gently. "Had your grandmother been seriously ill, she would have sent you a telegram."

"Mem Saheb, would you please let me go?"

"Certainly, but you must provide a replacement, I don't like to be understaffed during Christmas week. We're going to have house-guests."

"Miss Saheb, is Daisy still in the Compound, or Sushila?" Leelabati asked Rosie.

"We need a trained ayah at the bungalow, Miss Saheb," Abdul Gafoor put in gravely.

The venerable old *khidmatgar* was obviously Mem Saheb's trusted advisor. The head gardener had arrived to water the potted plants. She left the problem to Abdul and walked down to the end of the long verandah. Rosie followed her. "Mrs. Cantwell," she said urgently, "Mamma has brought Leela up as her own daughter. She is worried about the girl. When this postcard arrived, she did think about the replacement. Our tailor's niece has been working as an ayah. Shall I send her to you"?

Freda Cantwell turned towards Rosie. This was the crucial moment.

"Tailor's niece? Which tailor? Our Hasan Ali?"

It was apparent that Mrs. Cantwell was a typical English colonial housewife, deeply interested in matters pertaining to tailors and servants. Rosie was confused. Quickly she said, "No, Ma'am, an old man who used to work for the Compound, Wajid Khan. He has gone away to Calcutta. He has a widowed niece who came to see me a few days ago, looking for a job. She doesn't know pidgin English but is hard-working and honest. She is actually a genteel purdah-woman."

"Send her, if you know her. My things keep lying around, Bill doesn't lock his trunks. We trust our servants."

"I'll send her with John or Joseph." Rosie looked visibly relieved as she addressed the ayah, "Leelabati, you explain to Kulsum Bano her duties when she comes here in the evening."

"Yes, Rosie Baba," Leela nodded eagerly.

Freda Cantwell began inspecting her chrysanthemums. Rosie said goodbye and ran towards her bicycle. By the time she was out of the gate she had broken into a cold sweat. It was eleven o'clock in the morning.

She went straight to Chandrakunj and reported to Deepali, after which she rushed back to Lily Cottage. An hour later Uma Roy's Oldsmobile arrived at Chandrakunj.

Dr. Sarkar was sunning himself in the front verandah, reading the newspaper. He was surprised to see a stranger on the stairs. Such affluent patients hardly ever came his way. Blankly he said, "Nomashkar" while Uma gave him a sweet smile and introduced herself.

Dr. Sarkar led her into the sitting-room. Deepali had posted herself behind a door, waiting for her cue. Uma called out to her.

"Yes, Uma-di," she answered, coming in.

"The article I asked you to write for the college magazine.... Have you done it?"

"Yes, Uma-di."

"Good," Uma took a deep breath and turned to the host for small talk. After a while she said, "Benoy Babu, I have come to you with a request. I am going to Comilla, we have a little place there in our village."

"You mean, your country villa!" Dr. Sarkar said, smiling.

"Well...er, I mean... would you allow Deepali to come with me for a short holiday? She could spend her Christmas vacations in the country."

Dr. Sarkar had never let Deepali go out of town alone, but he could not say no to such a responsible, matronly lady.

It also occurred to him for the first time that due to his perennial shortage of funds, he had never taken his children anywhere for a holiday.

"It seems you have already made your programme," Dr. Sarkar addressed his daughter.

"Uma-di mentioned it the other day when I went to see her," she replied coolly. "May I go, Baba?"

"Yes, you can. When do you plan to leave?" he asked the eminent visitor.

"Tonight. I would like to reach Daudkundi by the night steamer. Thank you, Benoy Babu. Deepali, pack your bags, I'll send you the car in an hour or so."

After a long time Deepali saw her father laughing happily as he talked to Uma Roy. How easily he had allowed her to go! Surely Uma Debi knows some magic. She belongs to Comilla, that district is famous for its Tantrik sorceresses. She seemed to have charmed Dr. Sarkar in no time. Deepali looked up at the portrait of her late mother. Uma sat directly below. As was her habit, after every few minutes she took off her round, gold-rimmed glasses, cleaned them with the corner of her sari, fluttered her eyelashes and put on her glasses again. She is so plain, poor thing, but her eyes are not bad, come to think of it. You never know about these females who have missed the bus. They live in a cloudland of their own and can fall for the unlikeliest of men.

After Uma Roy left, Deepali went to her room and packed a small tin-trunk. She did not have a leather suitcase. Busy pondering the unpredictable lady's obvious interest in her father, she forgot about the dangerous mission she was about to undertake.

At half past three in the afternoon, Miss Roy's limousine rolled up at the gate to fetch her.

11
The Ayah

THE woman was cloaked in a white "shuttle-cock burqa". Only her hands were visible. She wore no glass bangles and a rosary dangled from her right wrist, which indicted that she was a pious widow.

The ayah was accompanied by a lanky youth. An armed sentry stopped them at the gate. The boy said his name was John, he was a new inmate of the Mission Compound. Rosie Missy Baba had told him to bring an ayah to the Bungalow.

The sentry nodded and let them in.

A narrow canal rippled underneath the bridge which connected the gate with the avenue. Lilac clouds floated in the sky. At a little distance the bungalow sparkled in the setting sun. The garden was full of English flowers. Through the white net of her veil, Kulsum Bano viewed the picture-postcard scenery and marvelled: English people create a piece of "this other Eden, demi-paradise", wherever they choose to live.

Mem Saheb was still having her siesta, and Saheb had not come back from his office. John took the girl to the trellised verandah at the back. Leelabati was all set to leave for Narayan Gunj and was waiting anxiously for them.

The new woman observed such strict purdah that ever since she had left the Mission Compound with the lad, she had not spoken a single word to him.

Muslim women were called *bibi*. John said to Leelabati, "Why didn't Rosie Baba tell you? This *bibi* is deaf and dumb. How will she work here?" He spoke in English.

"You are a nut, kid. She can't be anything of the sort. Just too darn shy to speak to a stranger. You sit right here, Johnny, I'll be right back. Come along, honey." (Earlier Leelabati had worked for an American missionary family.)

Kulsum obviously did not comprehend her "git-pit". John perched himself on a stool and yawned. He was to escort Leela all the way to the steamer-station. Rosie Baba was very considerate about these things.

Leelabati took the new girl inside and explained the work. She was not at all surprised by Kulsum's shyness. A person like her was bound to feel lost in a Saheb's bungalow. Leelabati also knew that the girl would soon get over her diffidence. She led Kulsum from room to room and also showed her the *botal-khana* where liquor was stored. "In the evenings," said Leelabati, taking her right thumb to her mouth, "Saheb-Mem Saheb get sozzled. After that there is no work. They are a nice couple, dull and good-hearted. You'll be quite happy. It's only a matter of seven-eight days...

"And this used to be the *karkary-khana*, crockery room. Now I live in it. You make yourself comfortable in here."

Kulsum pushed her yellow trunk under the cot and sat down. Dusky came in, wagging his fluffy tail. Kulsum lifted her feet and cried, "Allah, this is going to be a nuisance. We think dogs are unclean. Please tell him to go away." She looked terribly annoyed.

"You just ignore them, right? They are well-trained dogs, won't bother you. Look, I must leave now. Okay?"

"Would someone tell me which dishes are pork and ham so that I do not touch them?"

"Abdul will tell you everything, Kulsum-bibi. Now let me go." She picked up her attache-case.

"Do you have lizards?"

"Plenty. Tata, bye-bye, and Merry Christmas!"

Kulsum looked around. Leelabati had pasted colour pictures of Calcutta film stars on the walls. Kanan Bala, Leela Desai, Miss Patience Cooper, Mr. Najmul Hasan. The Cantwells' old journals and newspapers were stacked in a corner. *Good Housekeeping. Punch. Daily Sketch.* A bundle of *True Story* magazines. A few Vicky Baum novels. An old *Picture Post* with

Jean Harlow as the cover girl. The place reeked of coconut oil and stale bacon. Kulsum felt sick and sat down near the window in order to get some fresh air. What on earth am I doing here? she asked herself.

She picked up a few months' old copy of *The London Illustrated.* A handsome young man smiled at her, Albania's Ahmed Zog, the only Muslim king in Europe. The poor kingy-wingy and his queen had fled to Greece when the Italians bombed Tirana. Kulsum sat admiring his good looks, when somebody coughed outside.

Quickly she turned the magazine upside down and came out. "Mem Saheb would like to see you, daughter," Abdul Ghafoor informed her solemnly.

The Cantwells sat under a garden umbrella, sipping Darjeeling tea. Kulsum bowed low and salaamed.

Mrs. Cantwell regarded her from head to toe like a sergeant inspecting a recruit. The girl fidgeted nervously.

"*Thora-thora Angrezi jaanta?*"

"No, Mem Saheb."

"Where work before?" The lady tried her pidgin Urdu.

"Calcutta, Mem Saheb."

"For English family?"

"No, Mem Saheb. Mohammedan."

"Belong Calcutta?"

"No, Mem Saheb."

"Hmm. Bill, Reverend Bannerjee's daughter has sent this girl. Seems all right."

Bill nodded, without looking up from *The Statesman.* A peon came with the evening mail. At once Kulsum covered her face with the *anchal* of her sari. Cantwell noticed her quick reaction and said, "How is this wretched woman going to work if she keeps hiding her face?"

"Bill, Rosie told me she is not working-class, she's a purdah-observing genteel widow."

Tipoo arrived and tried to be chummy with the new ayah. She recoiled and stepped back.

"Are you afraid of doggies, Kulsum?" Freda Cantwell asked with concern.

"No, Mem Saheb. We no touch them but."

"Oh, yes, of course. Abdul doesn't either."

"Darling. A purdah-woman who avoids dogs and can't follow even kitchen-English...how on earth are you going to manage?"

"Oh, Bill, she'll be here only for a week. How could I not let Leelabati go?"

Mrs. Cantwell was used to her English-speaking ayah. In the same breath she spoke to Kulsum. "You may go now. Stay in your room and come out only when I call you. Keep your purdah."

Kulsum looked blank.

"Oh," Freda Cantwell groaned, and repeated in her broken Urdu, "You go room. I ring bell. You come."

"Yes, Mem Saheb."

Freda was a kind-hearted woman. Her stand-offish behaviour with Rosie was an in-built part of the system. She was considerate to good servants, and Kulsum was a good servant.

They were going to Dacca Club for Christmas Eve. At six-thirty Mrs. Cantwell went into her dressing room to get ready and rang the bell for Kulsum.

The new girl brushed the lady's shoulder-length golden hair and narrated her sob-story. No father, no mother. Husband dead. Cruel relatives. Previous employers gone to East Africa. All alone in the wicked world. By the time she had finished she was shedding tears.

"Kulsum," Mrs. Cantwell said with genuine sympathy, "Don't cry. When Leelabati comes back, I shall send you to a friend of mine with a good chit. Now, now. Take heart. Go and wash your face."

Kulsum wiped her eyes gratefully and resumed her duties.

On Christmas morning the front verandah was filled with bouquets and presents (called "dollies" in Anglo-India) sent or brought by the city's middle-class notables, mostly businessmen. Some of them had come for Burra Din's Salaam and were received briefly by the Saheb.

On Boxing Day Freda Cantwell went to inaugurate the native-church bazaar. She told Rosie that the new girl was all right.

While Mrs. Cantwell was away at the bazaar and Mr. Cantwell had gone to the Club, Kulsum asked Abdul Ghafoor if she could help in the morning chores. Unfortunately, the bearer had fallen ill and the *khidmatgar* was doing his work, too. "Besides," he said importantly, "Mem Saheb wants me to oversee everything."

Kulsum said she would certainly pitch in. "Uncle," she suggested, "you get your *chhokra*-boy to polish the cutlery, I can do the dusting."

"Would you, Daughter? Good girl. I do the master bedroom and Saheb's study myself. I'm sure you'll do the job properly." He gave her the duster. He had natural sympathy for a fellow Muslim. Her tale of woe had also given him an idea. He had a ne'er-do-well bachelor son. Why not marry this poor waif to him? Such a nice, dependable girl, she would reform him in no time.

Abdul gave the keys of Saheb's office-room to Kulsum and dawdled off to the kitchen.

From the charity bazaar Mem Saheb was to go to the Club to preside over a ladies' work-party. They were knitting pullovers for Indian troops. Bill Cantwell had gone for a Civil Defence Committee meeting. Both of them would have their luncheon at the Club and return in the afternoon.

Mr. Ronald Jones could have turned up, but he was away in Calcutta, enjoying that metropolitan city's famous Christmas season.

Kulsum surveyed the office. The steel cabinet was securely locked, but some papers were lying around. She closed half-open drawers, collected all used carbon papers, emptied the waste-paper baskets and tidied up the place. Just before the

Cantwells returned home she was in the ironing room, pressing her mistress's evening dress.

The Plumers arrived from Calcutta late at night. By that time Kulsum was fast asleep in her room.

In the morning she caught a glimpse of Gilbert Plumer and his enormous lady as they strolled in the garden. Mr. Plumer was one of the topmost police officers of the province. After breakfast Mrs. Cantwell told Kulsum to attend to Mrs. Plumer.

She went to the guest-room and kow-towed to the Mem Saheb. Mrs. Plumer looked the jovial sort. The Cantwells were young but colourless, the Plumers were middle-aged and flamboyant. Perhaps the active, glamorous, outdoor life of the Indian Police had made them so. He looked every inch the huntin', shootin', fishin' type, she was good-natured, happy-go-lucky, and disorganised. Kulsum liked her immensely. She had taken to the Cantwells, too. As human beings they were all right. Good people in their own way, only doing their duty, perhaps.

Phyllis Plumer spoke fluent kitchen Urdu as she took out her clothes from a crocodile leather suitcase. She told Kulsum that the suitcase used to be a man-eating croc in the Ram Ganga. "This river flows through a big jungle. Jim Corbett lives nearby. Have you heard of Corbett Saheb, Kulsum? Plumer Saheb shot this croc in the Ram Ganga, in the Himalayan foothills of U.P. Plumer Saheb is a famous big-game hunter. He has bagged many a tiger in the Sunderbans, too." She began to hum a merry tune and pulled out a grey skirt from her holdall. Next she rummaged through the entire luggage for a white blouse. While doing so, she upset her husband's official files she had earlier put on a chair. Kulsum started rearranging them neatly.

Mrs. Plumer noticed the girl fumbling with the papers. She had held them upside down and was trying to put them together. Before she could tie them with the red tape, Mrs. Plumer shouted, "What on earth do you think you're doing?"

The girl turned pale. She was badly frightened.

"Give the lot to me! You people are so stupid. Illiterate fools. Don't you know this reads from left to right? Now you have doubled the work for me. Look, you just sit there and keep giving each sheet to me. Oh, bother."

The job took nearly half an hour but was finished at last.

Mrs. Plumer briskly instructed the ayah. "Put this steel box over here. When Plumer Saheb wants its key, you come and tell me. The key...Good God, where is the key? I'm getting on, you know. Keep misplacing my things."

Both of them hunted high and low for the key and eventually discovered it in Mrs. Plumer's toilet box.

"This is what happens when I try to be too careful. I kept it in here so that I would remember where it was."

She dropped it in her handbag after the ayah had left the room.

At dinner table the ladies discussed the latest hats worn by the Duchess of Kent, after which they went to bed. Cantwell and Plumer returned to the drawing room. They drank and talked in sombre undertones. They had closed the doors. Kulsum was in the dining-room, standing in for Abdul Ghafoor. She had asked him not to delay his Isha prayers.

After a while Cantwell called out: "*Koi hai...*Abdul!"

Kulsum covered her face demurely and knocked on the connecting door. It was opened by Cantwell. He looked at her as though he was seeing her for the first time. Kulsum blushed. Coyly she said, "Huzoor. Abdul, he is praying."

"Why are you still awake, Kulsum?" he asked in broken Urdu.

"Ironing Ploomer Mem Saheb's frocks."

"Get some cigarettes, will you. Do you know where the carton is kept?"

"Yes, Saheb."

She returned in a few minutes and stopped at the door. "May I come in, Saheb?"

He nodded. She went in, opened the tin of Goldflake, and located the missing bottle-opener.

The Sahebs carried on their conversation. Mr. Plumer regarded her with interest and said, "I say, Bill, that's some wench!"

Placidly Kulsum continued to empty the ashtrays after which she returned to her room.

Gilbert Plumer had come up to Dacca for an urgent conference. One meeting was held at Cantwell's bungalow, and was also attended by Uma Roy's uncle. That morning the bungalow was crowded with police personnel. Kulsum had a severe headache and mostly stayed in her room.

Before going back to Calcutta, Mrs. Plumer gave her ten rupees as *bakshish.*

On the eighth day Leelabati returned from her village. She whispered to Kulsum: "Granny was hale and hearty. She didn't mention her letter but obviously she played this trick to call me over for Christmas, otherwise Mem Saheb wouldn't have let me go."

That same evening Uma Roy's motor car brought Deepali back to Chandrakunj. She looked radiant, for she had thoroughly enjoyed her stay in beautiful Comilla.

On January 9, 1940, the police sealed certain riverways and raided the hideout of Rehan Ahmed and his comrades. They were not there.

12
Lily Cottage

T HEY were going to have a tea-party at Lily Cottage. Esther Bannerjee was icing her plum cake, Daisy was making cucumber sandwiches. Exquisitely cross-stitched tablecloths and cushion covers had been laundered the previous evening. Coconut pastries had been covered with a white net frilled with bottle-green glass beads. The newly embroidered tea-cosy looked splendid, adorned as it was with an English lady in period costume, standing among the hollyhocks.

Rev. Bannerjee was in his Sunday best, pacing the front verandah. From time to time he looked worriedly at his pocket watch.

Rosie had locked herself up in her room.

At four o'clock a horse carriage pulled up at the Mission Compound gate. Rev. Henry Biswas, Mrs. Mary Biswas, Mr. Luther Biswas and Miss Edith Biswas scrambled out and made for the parson's house. Miss Edith Biswas was gingerly carrying an attache-case.

Esther Bannerjee rushed out to welcome the important guests. She led them into the sitting room, apologising profusely for the inconvenience of their long train journey from Punjab.

The Biswas family mumbled, "No trouble. No trouble at all, Esther sister, no trouble, Esther auntie," as they took their seats. They sat upright and grave, as though posing for a group photograph.

Young Edith fidgeted in her cane chair till she spotted the ancient gramophone and broke the awkward silence: "Esther auntie, may I have a look at your records?"

"Certainly, my dear," the hostess replied effusively.

Edith stood up, straightened her frock, and walked across to the corner. Mrs. Biswas eyed the room critically. These people are as poor as church mice...ha...ha, but Esther Bannerjee is a good housewife, puts up a brave front. Anyway. Clergymen are not so ill-paid, so where does the salary go? Martin's brother's wife says Rev. Bannerjee has widowed sisters in the village, a whole bunch of poor relatives, and he supports all of them. Saintly old man. Well, well.

The two clergymen began talking to each other.

"My Rosie has embroidered this tea-cosy," Mrs. Bannerjee said to Mrs. Biswas, trying to start a conversation.

Mrs. Biswas smiled politely. By this time she had observed that Mrs. Bannerjee did not wear any gold ornament except a thin gold chain with a tiny Cross. Even her cotton sari had been darned in one place. Mrs. Biswas smugly surveyed her own fineries. Over a white petticoat she had draped a sari of bright pink Japanese georgette, pinned on her left shoulder with a golden brooch. She had tucked her lace kerchief under the left half-sleeve of her black satin blouse. She had gold bangles on her wrists and gold earrings, and a rope of cultured pearls around her heavily powdered throat. Even the clips in her hair were studded with seed pearls.

Fifteen-year old Edith looked gawky in her loose frock of purple velvet, white socks and black shoes, and like all prim and proper native Christian unmarried girls, she had wrapped herself modestly with a georgette dopatta.

Mrs. Bannerjee began serving tea. Rev. Biswas seemed a nice man, but evidently he was dominated by his wife. Luther Biswas was tall and skinny and very insignificant-looking. He was a science master in the Mission School to Ludhiana. After a couple of years he might even go as lecturer to St. John's College, Agra.

Last December when Luther had come to Dacca with his choir and met Rosie, he fell madly in love with her. He returned to Ludhiana and told his parents about the Bengali parson's white-skinned daughter. "She is so fair, Mamma, she looks almost like a European girl, Spanish or Italian, you know," he had told Mary Biswas in awe. As he went on and on about Rosie Bannerjee, his father sent a formal proposal to Rev. Bannerjee.

The parson in Dacca showed the letter to his wife.

"Our Rosie deserves a better match," Esther Bannerjee said reflectively.

"Yes, indeed. But you know our community has a dearth of well-placed young men. The lads usually leave school to become clerks and stenographers. Our girls go in for higher education and acquire superior airs, then they marry upper-class Hindus or Muslims. This is happening all the time. Do you want our Rosie also to marry a non-Christian and be damned eternally? Raise her children as heathens? Poor Luther is not the most eligible bachelor in the world, but let's be realists. I am growing old, we have no money. Rosie is too attractive to gad about all alone. Remember what troubles you had to face before Bishop Brown introduced me to you? These are evil times. We must thank the Good Lord that He has sent us a nice boy like Luther. Your prayers have been answered, Esther," said Rev. Bannerjee.

Without asking Rosie, like a traditional Indian father he accepted the proposal. It would never occur to him that his dutiful daughter might not be a realist like him and might object to his choice. Rev. Bannerjee would have preferred a Bengali Brahmin Christian. Both he and his wife were top-grade Kulin Brahmins of north Bengal, but you can't have everything. The Biswases seemed all right. Still, Rev. Bannerjee was rather uncomfortable on one account: they might be of "untouchable" stock. Rev. Biswas's grandfather was an army clerk who had gone to Punjab and settled down in Ludhiana, one of the largest missionary centres of north India. Rev. Henry Biswas did not know any Bengali. His own mother was a Punjabi Christian. His wife Mary was also Punjabi, and unfortunately, Rev. Bannerjee had noticed with dismay, she did look slightly low-caste. Anyway, such a family was the best he could get in the circumstances. Rosie was already twenty-one, she must get married. The important thing was that during the missionary conference last year, Rev. Bannerjee had come to like the boy, Luther. He was mild of manner, and a devout, honest Christian, so different from the flippant young men of today. And he adored Rosie and would always be a devoted husband.

A week ago the Reverend had received a letter from Ludhiana. They were coming to Dacca to "perform the engagement ceremony". That was when Esther Giribala informed her daughter.

Rosie was dumbfounded. It was preposterous. How could her parents do this to her? Perhaps they were joking. Perhaps the Biswases were coming for something else and Mamma was merely pulling her leg. She went about her daily routine in a daze, not quite convinced that her father would be so unthinking and mindless. She felt too shy to ask him about the matter and she didn't take her Mamma seriously. She could not confide in Deepali for she was away in her arty Santiniketan, and she did not want to go with her problems to Jehan Ara. Her grim silence was interpreted by her parents as a well-bred maiden's natural shyness in "matters pertaining to her nuptials". Rosie looks so sad because she has to leave us and go away to distant Punjab, her father thought fondly. The bombshell fell at night when Rev. Biswas's telegram arrived at Lily Cottage. Rosie gaped at her parents, rushed into her room and locked herself in. She didn't come out in the morning. No tea. No breakfast. No lunch. Her mother was distracted with worry. She should look her best before her prospective in-laws. And here she was, behaving so strangely.

The Biswases were going to stay with distant relatives in the city. At four o'clock they turned up at Lily Cottage. Now, for the first time Rev. Bannerjee was worried about his petulant daughter.

Daisy brought in the tea. Mrs. Bannerjee served Bengali roshgullas to Luther, in order to "sweeten his mouth" as a good omen. She liked Luther, too. He may not look like

Robert Taylor, but he's such a nice fellow. Mrs. Biswas, however, was going to be a terrible mother-in-law. It was a distressing thought.

Mrs. Bannerjee offered the cake to Edith who raised her little finger and delicately picked up a slice saying, "Thank you, auntie. Where is Rosie sister?"

"Coming just now..." Mrs. Bannerjee faltered. "Not well..." Helplessly, she looked at her husband.

"What's the matter?" asked Mrs. Biswas, lifting an eyebrow.

"Nothing, nothing at all...she's been studying so hard for her exams...that's why...she's got a nasty headache..."

"Does she get these headaches often?"

"Yes...No...quite often..."

"I see. Well, unmarried girls don't get frequent headaches without reason," Mrs. Biswas said darkly.

Esther Giribala was shocked. She looked appealingly at her husband, who hastily turned towards Rev. Biswas, trying to discuss the latest war situation.

He was cut short by Edith's loud voice. "Auntie," she asked, "may I play these records?"

"Yes, my dear, certainly." Mrs. Bannerjee was about to add that her Rosie was very fond of Western music, but kept quiet. She was still fuming at Mrs. Biswas, the witch. How dare she!

Edith sat down on the cotton carpet and began inspecting the 78 r.p.m. records. An English official had sent the lot to Lily Cottage before returning home.

Mrs. Bannerjee got up. She went into the dining-room and closed the connecting door behind her. Then she swept across to Rosie's door and knocked on it. Tearfully, she said, "Rosie, please, listen to me..."

She waited in despair for some minutes, then returned to the parlour. Sitting down in her chair she cast a glance at her husband. He left the room, crossed over to his daughter's door and knocked softly. "Rosie, listen to me. I am your old Papa. Just give me a minute," he said humbly.

Rosie opened the door. He stepped in. Clad in a white sari, her long hair flowing down to her waist, she stood in the middle of the room motionless, like a statue of some heathen goddess. Suddenly her father remembered. This was exactly how Esther Giribala had looked, draped in a white sari, hair flowing down to her waist, when Bishop Walford Brown had called him to his Palace to meet her.

But there was a difference. How had Rosie become so different from her own mother? Esther had seemed a picture of submission when called forth to meet her future husband. Rosie's eyes glowed with fiery rebellion. She looked like a silent Fury. Nowadays this stubbornness is called self-confidence. But he only wished her well. He wanted a secure, respectable future for his beloved child. Why had she become so angry with her poor old Papa?

Suddenly she knelt down and flung her arms around his legs. "Papa...Papa," she whimpered. "Tie me to a stone and throw me in the Ganges. Poison me, but don't ask me to marry that moron. He is too ridiculous for words, Papa, how can I marry that giraffe...?" She started sobbing. "That mouse...that stupid cobbler."

"Mouse? Giraffe? Cobbler?" her father repeated in disbelief. "He is a good lad, Rosie... Do you want me to lose face? They have come all the way from Punjab."

"No. No! No!!" Rosie shrieked hysterically.

The parson tried to calm her down. Her sobs grew louder. He lost his temper and thundered: "What do you intend doing? Want to marry some oily Hindu, some rakish Mohammedan? Have you forgotten what the Hindus did to your mother, you luckless wretch?" Trembling in his wrath he forgot that he could be heard in the parlour.

He was facing a catastrophe at the hands of his own offspring. God, what have I done to deserve this? Never in his life had he roared like this. Stealthily, Mrs. Biswas came up behind him and posted herself near the door. She had overheard the entire dialogue. Esther Bannerjee followed her. She looked half dead.

Rosie saw Mrs. Biswas. She got up from the floor and shot into her bathroom. As she banged the door shut behind her, Rev. Bannerjee swung round and saw Mrs. Biswas. He was petrified.

Silence raged for a few moments. Then Mrs. Biswas hissed like a dragon: "So we are cobblers. Sweepers. God damn you all. Roast in hell. Bloody swine. Henry!" she screamed, marching back to the sitting room. "We did not come here to be insulted so outrageously. Get up! At once, I say, at once. This minute."

Esther Bannerjee came running. Tears were rolling down her puffy cheeks. "Please, Mrs. Biswas, for the sake of Lord Jesus, forgive us...Rosie is...is...delirious...because of her fever."

The two clergymen stood very still, avoiding each other's eyes. Mary Biswas sniffed into her tiny kerchief. Rev. Bannerjee hung his head and went into the verandah. Mrs. Biswas carried her kerchief to her eyes.

"Come along, my dear," her husband said gently, placing his hand on her shoulder, "let's go."

Mary Biswas shook his hand off and yelled, "We are not rich. We came all the way from Ludhiana to see the Princess. You invited us. We travelled Inter class, four people. It costs money, you know. Coming and going. Ludhiana is not next door."

"Hold your peace, my dear," her husband said, embarrassed. Luther had cast his head back and was staring at the ceiling.

"Inter class fare for four people. My Edith is only eleven, but they charged full fare." (Edith was fifteen.) We are not rich. We don't embezzle church funds."

"Keep quiet, Mamma," Luther said with acute discomfort.

"Shut up, bloody fool! Oaf. I am talking to this lady, what's her name, Mrs. Bannerjee. You wrote to us. You asked us, through Mrs. Barkat Masih, to come down to Dacca and meet your precious daughter."

"Mamma, please," Luther pleaded, sweating profusely.
"Pipe down, donkey!"

Meanwhile, Edith had very diplomatically started playing, *It was on the Isle of Capri that I found her.* Luther Biswas turned off the gramophone, glared at his sister and returned to his chair.

"We made inquiries," his mother went on. "I wrote to my sister-in-law, Henry's cousin-brother's wife... She is Matron at the government hospital out here. She knows big-big people. Shy knows everything that goes on in this god-forsaken town. She investigated and wrote back. I told Henry here, I told him: 'Marjorie sister has written that the girl does not have a good reputation. She has *Hindu* boyfriends. Meets them at night in nooks and corners. She has become a *Congressi, Communist.*" But this son of a mule...he has fallen in love with the fancy Missy Baba. As if we had a dearth of proposals. We are getting offers from Agra, Sialkot, Meerut, everywhere. Mr. Edward Khan is a Deputy Collector in Meerut, no less. His daughter, Catherine Shirin, is studying in Lucknow in Isabella Thoburn College. He wants her to marry our Luther. My son is such a gem. What does your girl have, may I know?"

Outside, in the verandah, Rev. Bannerjee stood near a pillar. In the last one hour he had suddenly begun to stoop.

Mrs. Biswas continued, "But this son of a toad has fallen in love. So we come scurrying all the way from Punjab. What do you have to show for yourself? You don't even have any jewellery. My son is going to be a lecturer at St. John's college, Agra..."

"My dear..." Rev. Biswas tried to put in.

"Mamma..." Edith squeaked.

"Does your hoity-toity daughter imagine by any chance that some ICS chap will marry her? With the kind of stinking reputation she has, she won't be able to hook even a peon."

"Mary, please..." her husband protested feebly.

"You keep out of it, Henry Biswas! I had heard a lot about Lily Cottage...Huh. I wouldn't have such rickety furniture in my servants' quarters. And you see, we also can't live on the pay of a native clergyman. We have our own lands and property. Father God has blessed us in every way. If the Missy Baba had the good sense to wed our Luther, she would have lived like a queen." Mrs. Biswas forgot that a few minutes earlier she had complained of her poverty.

Suddenly she remembered and groaned again, "Five hundred bucks, we spent full five hundred on this trip!" Ludhiana had many U.S. missionaries and she, like Leelabati, had picked up some American slang as well.

Meanwhile Luther had rushed out to hire a hansom cab. He came back, and for the first time he lost his temper. "Mamma," he bellowed, "you are disgracing yourself! Don't create a scene. Behave yourself, please." He caught her by the arm and dragged her out to the waiting carriage. Rev. Biswas followed her. Edith picked up the attache-case which contained the engagement ring and a pink sari of Banaras silk. She clambered onto the front seat. Rev. Henry Biswas went down to the gate, returned to the verandah. Rev. Bannerjee was still standing by a column, his eyes fastened to the floor. Henry Biswas extended his hand and said hoarsely, "Sorry, Reverend, I am very sorry. Not your fault. I'll pray for your daughter."

His Bengali host did not raise his head. Esther leaned against the entrance door, crying silently. Luther came to the verandah, walking with dignity. He bowed a little and said, "I'm sorry, uncle, please don't mind my mother. Goodbye."

"God bless you, my son," the old man replied quietly. Luther hurried back to the hansom and got into the front seat next to his sister. All the inmates of Mission Compound had gathered at the gate. Little, blind Ruth stood under a tree looking unhappy and bewildered. Daisy had informed everybody about the disaster. By tomorrow the entire native Christian community of Dacca would come to know.

The carriage circled round Lily Cottage in order to reach the main road. Luther was leaning out of the window. He caught a glimpse of Rosie who sat motionless on the bathroom steps, facing the backyard. He raised his hand to wish her a feeble goodbye. The carriage rattled on towards the city.

Rev. Bannerjee went into his room and sank into his armchair. After a few minutes he moved to his bed, feeling hollow inside. As he crouched in the dark he suddenly burst into tears. What had shocked him more than Rosie's refusal was the sudden realisation that the world had changed and he didn't even know.

13
Wandering Minstrel

Rabindranath Tagore's Santiniketan is situated in a place called Bolpur, a hundred miles from Calcutta. It used to be a desolate region, notorious for its highwaymen, but was turned into "the abode of peace" by Debendranath Tagore, father of the poet. He had everything except *shanti*, inner peace. He went to the Himalayas, didn't find it there and came back, dejected. Some years later, he happened to travel through the dangerous area of Bolpur. While he was crossing the awesome heath he saw a lone, shady tree and told his men to stop there. They set down the sedan chair and spread a rug under the tree's shadow. There he sat down cross-legged, and began to meditate.

Suddenly he attained peace. Therefore, he came to be called Maharishi, great sage.

Later, he bought the piece of land from a fellow Zamindar, built a marble shrine under that tree and inscribed upon it the words...

Amar praner araam,
Moner anand,
Atmar shani

Repose of my spirit. Joy of my heart. Peace of my soul. It came to be known as *shanti-vriksh*, the Tree of Peace.

Maharishi Debendranth Tagore also founded an ashram. In 1901, his son Rabindranath Tagore set up a school and modelled it after the forest universities of ancient India. It became a place where one could actually find boys and girls sitting at the feet of their gurus, reading Indian philosophy. They lived in small huts, led tranquil lives, respected their professors and did not know "student unrest". Jawaharlal Nehru's daughter, Indira Priyadarshini, who was destined to meet a violent end, spent the academic year 1935 at Santiniketan.

On a mellow autumnal evening in September, 1940, Deepali Sarkar, undergraduate at Santiniketan, sat down cross-legged under the Tree of Peace and read the inscription gloomily. Professor Murtaza Hussain, famous academic at this hallowed university, had told her last year at Dacca Radio Station that she must let her dreams come true. So here she was, trying to fulfil her dreams of becoming an accomplished musician.

Repose. Joy. Peace. How did the Maharishi attain all that in an instant? Come to think of it, Buddha had also achieved Nirvana under a tree.

Once the gods churned the cosmic ocean and brought forth a wish-fulfilling tree called Kalpataru. In its flowers one could smell the fragrance of one's choice. And it granted boons.

Let's pretend, she said to herself, that this dusty old tree under which the Maharishi found peace, is my Kalpataru. She picked up a leaf and made a secret wish. It had nothing to do with God or spiritual attainment.

It was uncanny. "Alakh Niranjan." Hail to the Power behind the universe! A zestful shout came floating with the evening wind. Some Shaivite yogis of Gorakhnath were passing by. They had smeared their bodies with the ashes of cremation grounds to conquer the fear of death. They could also be kapaliks who wore garlands of human skulls around their necks and performed terrible rites. Their fleeting presence scared Deepali Sarkar who was known for her fearlessness. She decided to rush back to the hostel before one of the yogis cast his spell on her.

Leaves crackled on the dog-path. There was a footfall. Nervously she stood up. A tall, good-looking sanyasi almost materialised in front of her. She felt relieved. He was a gentle monk of Krishna, not a frightful Tantrik ascetic.

Many such wandering minstrels passed through Bolpur, which lay in the region of Birbhum. Here, four centuries ago, Chaitanya had founded the cult of Krishna which continued to be popular in Bengal. The devotees of Lord Krishna sang and danced ecstatically like the 13th century

Sufi poet Maulana Jelaluddin Rumi's Whirling Dervishes of Turkey.

This *bairagi* had a long, glossy beard. Ringlets fell in cascades over his broad shoulders. Glowing in the twilight, he almost looked like a stage sadhu. "Om Namo Bhagavate Vasudeva..." he greeted her with the Vaishnavite mantra, and strummed his two-stringed lute. She joined her palms in obeisance.

He grinned and said, "May we sit here for a while, to rest our tired bones?"

She was taken aback.

"Child," he said smoothly, "we have a feeling that you have become a little confused. It often happens. The path to salvation is difficult and thorny. All you need is reassurance." He glanced around slyly and sat down on the edge of the platform. Next, he took out a cigarette from his ochre bag, regarded it lovingly and put it back.

She remained speechless.

"Child," he continued, "you have done us a great service and we are proud of your fantastic courage."

"You," she managed to utter at last.

"Yes, child, we."

She was hit by a wave of depression and unhappiness. "Please go away. I am not going anywhere now, as cook or ayah or anything. Do you realise what a narrow escape it was? Even now somebody may discover. That's one reason why I bolted to this place. To stay away from Dacca as long as I can. How did you know you'll find me here?"

"Our occult powers, child. We also know that every evening you sit here under the Tree of Peace to do your homework."

She could see his face clearly in the gathering dusk. A gust of wind scattered the puja flowers lying at the shrine.

Far away, Rabindranath Tagore was strolling in the sal avenue.

"Gurudev!" he exclaimed, and scrambled to his feet.

Suddenly, Deepali felt with a pang that the evening was unique, almost unreal. A time like this would never be repeated.

"Can you imagine what it must have been like for those Russians who used to see Tolstoy walking about among the birches of Yasna Polyana? Players' Navy Cut. That's the brand I would like to get, if I can."

She began to laugh. He was so funny.

"Any news of your Saheb?"

"Transferred to Chittagong, probably as a punishment for his failure to nab you all. But the new fellow is also quite friendly with Rev. Bannerjee. His sister is a missionary in Assam. Miss Alice Barlow."

"How is Rosie?"

"Should be all right. Haven't met her for some time."

"Nobody suspects her?"

"No."

"Could you find out from her the date of Charles Barlow's arrival in Khulna? Do you know his code name?"

"Uma Debi told me, before he arrived from Chittagong."

"Good girl! When did you last run into the Typhoon?"

"She's no typhoon. How can a fatso be called a typhoon? You have to be light and airy to be a typhoon. She may be destructive but she is no...."

"You seem to be in a lousy mood this evening."

"She is in Calcutta, staying with her brother. I had gone to Cal with my father to record some songs. Couldn't meet her. She doesn't write to me, I'm not important enough. I was asked to do a job and I did it That's all. Like a gangsters' moll, if you want my honest opinion. She is not a cardholder. It is also rumoured in Dacca that her police officer uncle has given a surety to the Government of Bengal that she will keep away from politics. You, of course, must know all that."

He frowned. "No, I didn't. All right, Moll Flanders," he said after a pause. "Look. There is a paanwallah down there, near the main gate. I'll meet you in the mango grove. Another thing, William Cantwell had a desk job in New Delhi, he had no experience in flushing out tough chaps like us. Charles Barlow is an old rogue. His father and grandfather were also

Bengal Civilians. He knows the province like the back of his hand. All of you keep that in mind. During the Terrorist days he sent many a revolutionary to the noose. Tell Rosie to be extremely cautious while sending us information. She must not in any way annoy or displease her father. It's very important. Now go." And he gave her some money.

She found him dancing, and singing a Chandi Das bhajan in the mango grove. She shoved the packet of cigarettes into his bag. He gave her a beatific smile. It was time for moonrise. Leaves rustled in the breeze. Lights came on in students' huts across the wood.

Deepali saw a broken red glass bangle lying near her feet.

Red bangles are worn by brides—a broken red bangle is not a good omen at all. Now I'm becoming superstitious, too. She touched the piece with her right toe. A chameleon sprang out of a flowering creeper. Far away in the girls' hostel they had started singing a Tagore song.

"Anil Kumar Das will be your contact out here," she heard the "yogi's" soft voice.

A group of sturdy Santhal women passed by.

"You look like one of Kalidas's heroines, roaming the moonlit woods. But I think you are more like Walt Disney's Snow White, looking after her seven dwarfs who keep hiding themselves in the forests."

"They are very tall dwarfs," she laughed, and added, "Am I also not Cinderella?" She glanced ruefully at her dusty, inexpensive sandals.

"I must run along. Blessings, child!"

He walked away rapidly and was soon lost in the forest.

She returned to the shrine to gather her books. The stray leaf she had picked up was still lying there, shining in the moonlight. A magic leaf! Well done, Kalpataru!! Thanks! Now I must return to my room and write the latest instructions to Comrade Rosa. Goodnight, Moon. Goodnight, Forest. Goodnight, Tree of Peace!

14
Miss Rosie Bannerjee and Solidarity

W_{HEN} the Biswas family's hired carriage rattled past, Rosie was sitting on the bathroom steps, still in a state of shock. She had overheard Mrs. Mary Biswas's ringing tirade. "Marjorie sister" had given her the story. The Bannerjee girl has a bad reputation. She has Hindu and Muslim boyfriends. She has become a Communist. How did it all leak out? Deepali and the comrades had promised strict secrecy. How would Papa react? He may put me under lock and key, may even disown me. Throw me out of the house.

At nightfall she emerged from her room, dreading the encounter with her parents. They were not in. Instinctively she knew that they would be in the chapel, praying for her. She was right. Just before dinner-time she saw them coming through the corridor which connected Lily Cottage with the church.

At dinner table her father did not say a word. His unexpected reaction puzzled her. He was given to delivering long sermons, now he seemed speechless…. She noticed his swollen eyelids. He had been crying. Both her parents had been crying. Dinner was eaten in complete silence. From that day on Rev. Bannerjee stopped talking to his daughter.

He had realised that he should not have invited the Biswases without her consent. He was sorry about his thoughtlessness, but the information about Rosie's politics had stunned him. He had also learnt about the Party office and the Nawabpura study circle. She had airily told him some cock-and-bull story about doing social work in the slums. She had been lying to him—she had become a liar and a cheat, joined a gang of ruffians who wanted to overthrow the Government of India.

Now he had acquired a Cross of his own which was too heavy to bear.

Rosie heard from Deepali, who wanted to know something about the new man, Charles Barlow. She tore up the letter from Santiniketan and burnt it. If they ever get to know about "Kulsum Ayah", I can be tried and imprisoned. Why am I punishing my meek and mild father? Was it his fault that Mamma had to begin her life as a child-widow? Is he responsible for being sneered at as a "rice Christian"? I have come to understand this unhappy situation. Can my Marxist analysis change the existing world order? Perhaps it can in the long run, but how can I go on hurting my poor Papa?

As soon as the summer vacations began, Rev. Bannerjee sent the girl to Lalmunir Haat, an upcountry town where his sister, Flora Bannerjee, taught school. She was an eminently sensible woman and would be a good influence on her confused and unhappy niece.

On her return she rejoined college for her B.A. (final). As a result of near-famine conditions she had seen in Lalmunir Haat, she became more rigid in her political views. The existing social and political order must be changed overnight through revolution, not through the woolly pacifism of Mr. Gandhi who was, in fact, an agent of the bourgeoisie.

Jehan Ara arranged for her to coach a girl called Yasmin Majid. The job gave her some diversion and also some badly needed pin-money. The girl Yasmin seemed a bit mad, too, she had dreams of changing the sorrowful human situation through dance and music. On a Sunday morning Rosie went to Arjumand Manzil to thank Jehan Ara for getting her the tuition.

Jehan Ara gasped when she saw her friend. "Rosie!" she exclaimed. "You've lost your glow! Get a hold of yourself, it's not the end of the world. You threw the Biswases out, jolly good. You had the guts to defy and refuse. When my marriage is arranged by my father, I'll merely bow my head and say, Yes."

"Your marriage, Bibi?"

Suddenly Jehan Ara hid her face among the cushions and began to cry.

"Gosh, what's the matter, Bibi?" It was Rosie's turn to be surprised.

"Nothing, Rosie, nothing at all,"said Jehan Ara, sniffing.

For the first time in her life Rosie looked at her friend with a certain sympathy. This lucky, high-born young lady—living in the tranquil safety of her little palace—she can be unhappy, too. Well. Like all good-for-nothing poor little rich girls, marriage is her only problem. Not that I blame her now, look at what my otherwise enlightened Papa did. Muslim girls are often betrothed to their cousins. Maybe Bibi has no eligible relatives in her family, and some stranger will be selected for her. Rosie recalled her Mamma saying some time back, that Begum Qamrul Zaman Chowdhry was worried about Jehan Ara. She was already twenty-four and may become and old maid. The sons of Muslim zamindars were usually indolent loafers. The middle classes were producing eligible young men, highly educated and successful in the professions, but Jehan Ara must have an aristocrat of equal status.

Bibi herself was an introvert and didn't talk of her personal life, even with Deepali who was her closest friend. It dawned on Rosie that she had been so self-centred she had never thought about Jehan Ara. Probably even Deepali had never bothered about her. It would never occur to them that a wealthy young woman could be unhappy. Unhappiness was for people like Rosie and Deepali, who had never had enough money even to indulge in simple pleasures like buying a nice sari. And we become so selfish in the pursuit of our own interests and ideals.

Remorsefully, Rosie regarded her melancholy friend who was now wiping her tears with enormous dignity.

"I say, Chimp—" Rosie tried to resume their usual school-girl banter.

"Yes, Toad," Jehan Ara replied feebly. There was silence again. Rosie was embarrassed. She felt she had grown up in the last few months, become an old woman. Mature and sad and wise. A few months ago, before the Luther Biswas Fiasco, her reaction would have been different—she would have contemptuously dismissed a tearful Jehan Ara as stupid and sentimental, a leech fattening on the blood of her estate's starving peasants.

But isn't that true, she told herself suddenly: isn't poor Bibi a parasite, shamelessly living off her jute plantations? My sympathy for her is misplaced. I was carried away by the feudal splendour of the scene—the unhappy princess, crying. I must correctly analyse the situation. We are fortunate, Deepali and I. We have Solidarity to fall back on. Solidarity shall help us in solving our personal and emotional problems. Poor Jehan Ara, imprisoned within the fortress of her religious-feudal-cultural pressures. She has nobody to help her.

Jehan Ara half sat up and wrapped the end of her superfine jamdani sari round her right arm. "Rosie Bannerjee," she said sternly, "have a *dekho* at yourself in the mirror. You look haggard. How do you intend holding out on your own in the future? Are you strong enough to be a rebel?"

"Solidarity—" muttered Rosie.

"What the hell is that?" Jehan Ara asked crossly. Then she blew her nose into her superfine hanky and shouted, "Mala—"

Mala, her personal maid, appeared in the doorway.

"Tea," she ordered and turned to her visitor. Rosie remembered—even the tea they drank in Arjumand Manzil came from their own gardens in Sylhet.

"I have given myself over to the Movement, it is going to be my moral, intellectual and emotional support. The Communist International—"

"Don't be daft, Rosie," Jehan Ara said curtly.

"Jehan Ara Begum, you have absolutely no idea. You do not know what all is going to happen in the world—"

"Do *you* know?" asked Jehan Ara, graciously.

15
The Cloud Messenger

AFTER that enchanted evening seven months ago, he had vanished once again. No clouds, no swan brought her any message from him, the way they did for Kalidas's heroines. Anil Kumar Das had asked her about Charles Barlow's movements—she could tell him nothing because there was no letter from Rosie. That was odd, and it worried her.

Third Year examinations were over. The campus was almost deserted. Deepali had stayed on to finish a special course in medieval folk music. Daily she collected her mail from the warden's office. No letter from him, none from Rosie. In May she completed her work and got ready to return home. On the evening she was to leave for Bolpur railway station, she went to the office to pay her bills and picked up her letters. The postcard from her father made her sick with remorse. He informed her that after a long time, Bhavtarni Debi had opened the store-room and found the Balucher saris missing. She was grief-stricken but he was happy because now, finally, there was nothing worthwhile left in Chandrakunj for their old friends, the thieves, to steal. "I advise you," the poor man added as a postscript, "not to feel sorry about the theft, and concentrate on your studies."

The stylish, light-blue envelope had the Zaman-Chowdhry crest embossed on it. She walked across to Kala Bhavan garden and sat down at the feet of the black-clay Buddha. She wanted to read Jehan Ara's letter at leisure.

She had not met Bibi for quite some time. When she had gone to Dacca for her Puja holidays, Bibi had left for her estate. Rosie was away in Lalmunir. Ever since Deepali joined Santiniketan, she was cut off from her old Dacca circle. She had also acquired that special halo which the Vishwabharati students carried about them. Jehan Ara had warned her not to become too arty, Rosie had envied her.

Eagerly she opened the blue envelope.

"...Rosie's improbable engagement party," wrote Bibi Jehan Ara, "would have seemed hilarious had it not been so sad. Mrs. Bannerjee had come to see my Ammi and was complaining about her daughter. Rosie is back from her aunt's place. She dropped in the other day.

"Last year in March my father went to Lahore for that famous Muslim League Session in which they passed the Pakistan Resolution. He was so excited about it, and full of all manner of plans for the future. On the way back he stopped over at Aligarh where my grandfather had also studied. Abba returned home and told me that he would send me there again, now for my M.A. Now that I have given my B.A. previous exams, he seems to have changed his mind. I don't know what his present plans are for me. I dare not ask him. Our elders maintain that they know what is good for their children, and do their best for them.

"But look at Rosie. Showed the green flag to Mr. Luther Biswas. I told her, 'Both you and I are the products of our particular milieus. How far can you rebel? The Brahmin Christians of Bengal can be very conservative. Your father happens to be one of them.' I do not know why Christianity is equated with Western modernity. Basically, it is an orthodox Asian religion.

"She said, Solidarity was going to help her—and the Communist International.

"Ah! I happen to know about all that. Perhaps I know more than both of you put together, I told her.

"You and Rosie sometimes talk utter nonsense. Absolute drivel. Hope you don't land yourselves in trouble.

"My brother Nayyar is getting married pretty soon.

"A maulvi saheb of Jalpaiguri has come to stay in our bitchy 'Aunt' Shama's neighbourhood. Maulvi Majidullah. A not very well-to-do theologian. Scholars are usually very poor in our country, aren't they? He teaches in some local seminary and has a brilliant daughter called Yasmin. She is in high school. Excellent in music but weak in maths. Her mother wanted her to be coached in that subject. I thought of our Rosie, and recommended her to Mrs. Majidullah.

"Yasmin came to our place. A sweet-tempered, jolly sort of girl, but a bit crazy. You know what I mean. After her mother left the room she whispered to me, 'Apa,' she said confidentially, 'my parents want me to study unnecessarily. I don't want to go to college, I want to be a professional dancer, like Simki and Sadhana Bose.'

"I was taken aback. I said, Yasmin Bibi, you belong to a family of Syeds and old-fashioned clerics. How on earth are you going to become a professional dancer?

"She shook her head and replied, 'Never mind, Apa. Some day I'll show you. I'll become as famous as Rukmini Devi.'

"Crazy.

"Now Rosie goes thrice a week to Sagun Bagicha to coach Yasmin Majid. I am worried about Rosie. She looks so unhappy. And desperate—"

That explained why Rosie had become 'incommunicado'.

Deepali put the letters in her bag and was about to get up from the Buddha's feet when she saw Anil Kumar Das approaching her. She was peeved.

He would pester her again about Charles Barlow. He came closer and grinned from ear to ear. Without uttering a word he handed her a book. It contained a brief note: "Sorry, couldn't get in touch with you all this while. This time you let us down badly. Obviously there must have been some hitch. Anyway, now follow Anil's instructions carefully."

She looked askance at him.

"Uptil December he was hiding in Noakhali, right now he is somewhere in the Sunderbans. I have just come back from there. Went to give him a new battery for his radio-set," Anil whispered, squatting down on the grass.

"What has he asked me to do?"

"Shall tell you presently, Didi. I thought you had gone back to Dacca, but on the way back from Noakhali I came to know that you are still here."

"Anil, what is it?" she asked irritably.

"What is what? Nothing." He smiled again. "He has merely called you to the Sunderbans."

"Did I hear right?"

"Yes, Didi?"

"He has called me where ...?"

"Where...? There... over to the Sunderbans."

"He must be out of his mind."

"Maybe. Maybe not...."

This Bengali ambivalence could be infuriating. Without raising her voice she said sharply, "Please don't waste my time."

"I am merely repeating the message. You have got to go to the Sunderbans," he beamed.

"Is it easy to get there? And why?"

"It's not at all easy to get there. The journey is long and tortuous and full of all manner of danger," Anil replied gleefully. "And why he wants you to go there, Didi, how do I know? I am not supposed to ask questions, nor are you. He merely said to me, Anil, you go right back to wherever she is and tell her she is needed here for an urgent meeting."

"Who else is going there for the meeting?"

"He said: tell her that Surendra-da, Mahfuzul Rehman and his wife, Ayesha will be coming over from Barisal. You from here. Mahmoodul Haque from Dacca. And he has asked you to bring the following things for him." Anil fished out a piece of paper from his kurta pocket. It was a list of some British newspapers, magazines and books.

"How do I go?"

"From here you go along by train to Ranaghat. There you will meet one of our boys at the railway station. He'll escort you to Khulna via Jessore. From Khulna another comrade will take you to Bagher Ghat." He picked up a straw and etched a complicated map on the moist ground, explaining to her the various train and steamer routes. Suddenly, like a ssconjurer, he produced a couple of hundred-rupee notes from his loose, long pocket, "Sent you the fare, too. Said, tell her I have become rich, so all of you come over to the forests and have some fun, for a change.... The money won't last long, and I too may not..." Anil faltered, repeating the message.

"May not what...?" she asked anxiously.

"...May not last long. His situation is pretty dangerous, you know."

"I think he likes to dramatise, like all of us Bengalis. Nothing is going to happen to him." Nothing happened to me even though I spent a week in the lion's den, she added to herself, remembering "Operation Cloudland". Yet she had indulged in some drama when she told him about it under the Tree of Peace.

"Let me know when you decide to go, I'll be around," Anil said and abruptly disappeared in the gathering dark.

Deepali stared at the black clay feet of the Buddha. The friezes on nearby huts looked like the decor of a huge open-air stage. The monsoons were advancing towards Birbhum. Clouds had risen in the Bay of Bengal and passed over the Sunderbans... She strained her eyes and spotted a white crane flying in the dark sky. She remembered Kalidasa's play, *The Cloud Messenger* and chuckled. Thank you, Cloud!

Back in her hostel room she went straight to the writing table. Now I am going to hoodwink my poor father once again.

"Dear Baba," she scribbled quickly, "I am writing this in a hurry to inform you that some final year (Musicology) students are going to tour the interior of Santhal Pargana in order to collect Santhal folk songs. They want me to come along, since I am specialising in folk music. (The trip is being financed by the Department of Music.) I'll come home as soon as I can. Don't worry. Your loving daughter, D."

16
The Sunderbans

THE Sunderbans, "beautiful woods", stretch from the district of 24 Parganas to Baqargunj and Khulna. They are the abode of the Royal Bengal Tiger, and their wildlife is world-famous. The rain forests are sparsely inhabited by fishermen and woodcutters, and remain one of the most accessible and awe-inspiring regions in the world.

At early dawn Deepali Sarkar's boat sailed downstream from Bagher Ghat, and by midday the river had turned into a broad green tunnel snaking through thick woods. At sunset the boat reached the lonely pier of a fishing village. An old man stood there, holding a lantern. With his white, windblown beard and glowing lantern, he looked like Father Time. The boatman greeted him. The two figures seemed almost symbolic.

The boatman spoke to Father Time, addressing him as Maulvi Saheb. In Bengal all venerable Muslims were addressed as Maulvi Saheb, anyway, even if they were not theologians. They were speaking in Khulna's coastal dialect. Deepali climbed across to the tiny bamboo-jetty. The maulvi said to her, "Come along, daughter."

The canoe sailed away, leaving Deepali behind, alone with Father Time in the Primeval Forest. Suddenly she felt scared. The maulvi carried her little trunk and bedroll. She followed him to the mud-track. He walked briskly, facing the strong river wind.He had probably spent his entire life here, toiling and praying, and would die here, unknown and unsung.

"What do you do for a living, Baba?" she asked.

"Catch fish," he replied, with simple dignity.

A fisherman! Again very symbolic!

What have we done for him and millions like him? she asked herself rhetorically, trying to shake off her fear, and increased her pace with renewed vigour.

"Have the others come?" she enquired, trying to sound casual. He made no reply. Perhaps he does not understand my upcountry, urban Bengali. She repeated her question. He shook his head in the negative. She was gripped by fear once again. Nothing could be done now. Here I am, all alone, surrounded by the savage Noakhali people. The area was known for its bandits. She found herself praying to Kali, the terrifying goddess of her ancestors.

"Here we are, daughter," the old man said. "That's my humble abode."

She looked ahead. A bamboo hut stood by the stream, its thatched verandah covered with flowering creepers.

"What a lovely house!" she exclaimed.

"Part of it was destroyed by the last cyclone, but with Allah's help we have repaired it. You know, daughter, He sends us a lot of cyclones, but also gives us the strength to survive them."

A lamp burned in a doorside niche. The old man hastened to the verandah and shouted, "Zainab!"

A thin old woman wrapped in a tattered cotton sari came out. In the half-darkness she squinted at the newcomer and smiled, as though approving of her. The maulvi disappeared into the shadows.

"Come in."

Deepali followed her into a large space. "I have put your cot here, in my room," the old woman said briskly. "My husband and my sons sleep in the front room. The boys have gone to Khulna."

But where on earth is *he?* Deepali wanted to ask.

Nobody had mentioned him all this time, not since she left Bolpur for Bagher Ghat. Tired, she sat down on the cot. She realised that she hadn't spoken to the old woman yet, which was very rude of her. What am I doing here, she asked herself suddenly, just as she had wondered when she had found herself inside Ayah Leelabati's room in Dacca. Too late, it was too damn late. She tried to smile.

"It's a long voyage," Zainab was saying. "You must be worn out. Eat." She bustled about and respectfully offered her guest some sweetened rice balls.

Deepali had seen a lot of poverty, but this was heart-rending. She picked up a rice ball and looked around the shadow-filled room. Outside, in the verandah, the maulvi had begun his night prayers.

Apparently, Zainab had sensed her discomfort and guessed her thoughts. These humble, illiterate people are so intelligent. Deepali made a mental note. Did I ever expect to meet a sensitive, intelligent fisherwoman in the backwaters of the Sunderbans?

Zainab offered her a glass of buttermilk and said, "He is sitting out there, by the water."

"When are the others coming?" she asked timidly.

"Others? You have come here to meet him, haven't you? He is a good boy, deeply religious. He does not say his ritual prayers regularly, but he told me that he meditates on Allah most of the time. Told me about you. You are a good girl, too, and have a trusting nature. It's so obvious."

Rogue! Meditates on Allah! Why must he fool these simple people? But aren't I fooling my own family? And what is all this about me having a trusting nature? She stood up nervously. What is the old hag driving at? She's not all that innocent. She is a witch of these black forests. O, Divine Mother, help me. "Excuse me, I'll just go out for a bit," she said and left the room, suddenly feeling very frightened.

What must this old woman be thinking? That I am a tramp. Why must I worry about what this insignificant fishwife of coastal Khulna thinks about me? But I still believe in Old Morality, and I was also told that the Party discarded the Glass of Water Theory long ago.

There is no bloody Underground conference out here. He called me just like that, and I came running. She walked along the stream, frowning and feeling thoroughly miserable.

"Dr. Livingstone, I presume!" a cheerful voice greeted her in the dark. He sat on an upturned canoe, smoking. "I always sit here and wait for the moonrise. It's a gorgeous sight." He spoke like a tourist guide, and sounded so casual, as though it was the most normal thing for them to meet on a mid-summer night in the heart of the trackless Sunderbans.

He was clean-shaven. It was the first time she had seen his entire face. He was really quite nice to look at.

He noticed her surprise and chuckled. "I got fed up. First it was the Muslim beard of Rehman Mian, then the Muslim beard of the Baul fakir, followed by the Hindu beard of the Vaishnav monk. Now I can tell you a thing or two about beards. Nobody can recognize me out here in the Sunderbans' dark interior. So in honour of your visit, I borrowed a blade from my host's son and swish..." he gestured with his right thumb.

Tigers roared from across the stream. She sat down on a mossy stone. For some moments they contemplated the riverscape. He lit another cigarette.

"Just before you came," he said slowly, slipping from his casual cheerfulness to thoughtfulness, "I was thinking of Alaul. Have you read him?"

"Alaul...?"

"Yes, Syed Alaul. The Muslim poet of 17th century Bengal?"

He was always subtly conscious of the Muslim aspect of Bengal. This surprised her.

"Why couldn't you just say the poet of 17th century Bengal?" she said argumentatively, glad to find an impersonal topic.

"Why not? If Tagore can proudly write of his Hindudom..."

"Goodness! You're talking like a...like a...Muslim fanatic..."

"Really? You take it for granted that all Indian and all Bengali culture is Hindu..."

She shuddered. Have I come all the way from Bolpur for this?

She recalled his visits to Chandrakunj, disguised as a Baul fakir. He had once lectured her saying, "Always remember, there are two aspects of India, Hindu and Muslim, just as you have two or more aspects of your deities. At several points these aspects merge into each other, but we must not ignore their identities and must analyse them scientifically. They can co-exist peacefully. Now, Lenin in his theory of nationalities..."

He could be such a bore...

He threw his empty matchbox in the river and returned to Alaul.

"Once his boat was attacked by Portuguese pirates. He fought them and braved the cyclones and managed to reach the Arakan coast of Burma... He says that on a dark night a bright green boat..."

The river and the sea and the forests had become one under a liquid moon. The Sunderbans had begun casting their spell. Rehan continued his recitation...

"A bright green boat, tossed by the tempest, sailed on towards Arakan. A high wind swept it off the coast and carried it to an island...far away... He came ashore, famished and wounded. He lay gasping on the sand, when a young woman arrived.

"She said, 'I'll take you home. A man should not be forlon, shelterless and without hope...

"'You are a human being, aren't you? Not the angry spirit of the dark and lonely and hungry ocean?' she asked. 'Because the sea, raging in its fury, keeps dashing against the shore but can never submerge the earth. For the earth is strong. It carries the load of man's injustices and iniquities. The sea can't give shelter to even a little canoe. You must have huge, peacock-shaped barges to face the sea.

" 'Houses are built on the earth. The moon is pretty, but there are no houses on the moon. Homes are built under the coconut palms. I shall be your home...' "

Rehan finished the recitation and grinned.

Suddenly the wind dropped. It seemed to Deepali that the river river also stopped flowing for a moment.

Soon the wind stirred the *sundari* leaves again. The stream began to flow. Deepali listened intently to the sounds of the moonlit jungle.

"Why have you called me here?" she asked.

"For an important meeting."

"This fisherman and his wife don't seem to know."

"They are not supposed to."

She took out the two hundred-rupee notes from her purse and asked, "How did you get this loot?"

"Royalty for my book. You didn't spend it? How did you manage to travel?"

"I, too, got the royalty for my gramophone records."

A happy smile broke over his face. "So, two capitalists are out on a safari in the Sunderbans."

"Where are the others going to stay?"

"Who?"

"The other comrades."

He roared with laughter.

She was stunned. "So you lied to Anil."

"As Allah is my witness."

"And you thought I would come running?"

"You did."

"I don't think it's very funny."

She stood up and turned towards the forest path.

"If you go on walking on this track you'll reach Dacca in a few months. You'll meet a number of tigers on the way, and the rivers are full of man-eating crocs," he called out.

A long black line appeared on the surface of the shining river, a crocodile was crossing over swiftly to the other bank. Deepali ran back, shrieking.

He said thoughtfully, "I'm sorry, perhaps I shouldn't have invited you here. I had no right to."

She said nothing.

"For the last three years I have been hiding here and there like a common criminal. Charles Barlow has sworn to himself that he'll get me, dead or alive. What do you think I am? 'Spirit of the dark and angry and lonely ocean?' I wanted to see you before I was caught. I'm sure you are aware of the fact that I am...sort of...fond of you..."

She stared at him, wide-eyed. The situation was dangerous and absurd.

Suddenly she broke into uncontrollable laughter. He seemed relived.

"Uma Debi says I giggle like a silly schoolgirl. Am I very foolish?"

"Yes. Otherwise you wouldn't have rushed down to the Sunderbans to meet a chap you hardly know! Let's go in and I'll introduce you properly to our hosts."

The memory of the old couple's humility saddened her.

"Who are they? How do you know them?"

"Their sons have become our Party workers."

"What have you told them about me?"

"That I'm going to convert this heathen lass to the True Faith, after which I'll marry her."

"Aren't you ashamed of yourself?"

"What is wrong with getting converted to the True Faith of Marxism and marrying me?"

They walked back to the hut. Zainab served them fish-and-rice after they sat down on a colourful reed mat. A fishing net was spread behind them on the bamboo wall. Their shadows loomed large against the light of the lantern. In a few minutes the stooping silhouette of a bearded man appeared on the wall.

"Baba," Rehan addressed the old maulvi, "this is our Kulsum Bano."

Little did I know, she thought, when I became "Kulsum Ayah" that the name might stick to me for life. She shuddered.

"Kulsum-Deepali," he continued, "some day, Baba, I'll explain to you how, through Communism, we can erase the senseless difference between Kulsum and Deepali."

The Party line again! Never for a moment does he forget the blasted Party line... For an instant she felt as though Dr. Benoy Chandra Sarkar's shadow appeared on the wall, too. Guiltily, she bent down over her plate as conversation in the coastal dialect continued around the dining-mat. He seemed utterly at home with these meek people. Once again she wondered about him. Who was he? What were his antecedents?

She didn't know. Perhaps it was the mystery that surrounded him that made him so attractive.

Early next morning she went down to the stream to see the fantastic sunrise. The world must have looked like this on the morning of Creation. A spotted deer darted across the swamp. Expectantly she heard a footfall, swung round and saw him.

"Good morning, Miss Sarkar!"

"Morning," she said primly.

"Had a good sleep?"

"Yes, thank you."

"Not too many mosquitoes, I hope?"

"No."

He lit a cigarette.

"Let me give you the magazines I have brought for you. Or would you like to see them after breakfast?"

"What's the menu?" he asked grandly.

"Chicken and pulao...or whatever you eat in the morning. You people are such gourmets."

"Silly girl, we don't eat pulao in the morning."

"Why, once I had kebabs at Jehan Ara's place and she told me that they had been prepared in the morning."

"Who is Jehan Ara?" he asked. They started strolling back to the hut.

"Friend of mine. Nawab Qamrul Zaman Chowdhry's daughter. Utterly feudal, but sweet."

"Ah, I see."

They returned to the shack. Zainab served them last night's leftovers. "I'll go down to the village today and bring some eggs and bread for you. Also other foodstuff," she said to him in English.

"Indeed. And make them feel small. I could also get better stuff but they are too proud to let me spend my own money on food. I am their guest. Kindly make do with what they offer."

Feeling thoroughly ashamed of herself, she began drinking the steaming hot tea sweetened with jaggery. They could not afford sugar. Rehan brought his portable radio-set from his room and tuned into Calcutta to hear the morning news relayed from AIR, Delhi.

It was a long and langorous, slow-moving day. "You can touch the dimension of time out here. It's torture, not doing anything, just hiding to save your life. One can't go on reading and writing. And when you do nothing, you brood. Let's go boating. We'll come back by lunch-time," he suggested after a while.

They went down to Abul Hashim's bamboo jetty. He had already left in his fishing boat, so they untied his canoe.

"The forests are more dangerous as we go south," he said as they drifted downstream. Rowing the canoe, he seemed a natural part of the scene. She wondered again: who is he? What is his background?

He had started humming a boatman's song. Kingfishers flew across the sparkling river. The sun had come up and the air was warm and hazy.

After a while he stopped singing and said reflectively, "Bengal is so beautiful, and how deeply it has suffered. I am also part of this suffering."

"Do you belong to a village?" she asked.

"Yes. You have seen Maulvi Abdul Hashim. My father is just like him, except that he is not a fisherman but a peasant. Humble and patient and innocent."

She didn't want to appear nosey, but how had the son of a humble peasant managed to go to the London School of Economics? After a pause she ventured to ask, "How did you go to England?"

"England?" he repeated crossly. "Who the hell is talking about England? Look at what England did to us."

The outburst baffled her. Perhaps she had become too personal. He stood up, punted for a while, sat down again. Holding on to the oar he said, "I went to London in 1933. You want my bio-data? Here it is. Did my F.A. from Aligarh. Returned to Dacca for my B.A. After that ...I...I got a ...scholarship and went away to London."

"On your return home you jumped into the fray."

"That's right."

"You write, too?"

He looked at her in astonishment. "You are so literate! How else do you think I got royalties on a book?"

"Do you write short stories?"

"I do not. I am a journalist by profession. Didn't I come to your house disguised as a Baul fakir to get material for my underground magazine? Have you really never heard of my book?"

"Is it a novel?"

He shrugged and looked at the sky. "Girls!" he exclaimed plaintively.

"Tell me, please. What is the title of your book?"

"*The Condition of Peasantry in 19th Century Bengal.* Uma Debi should have lent it to you."

Uma Debi again.

"You seem to have idealised a lot of people," she said.

"I have, indeed—you are one of them. Look, Deepali, would you like to work on our Cultural Front?"

"I'll do whatever you say."

The canoe was passing through a leafy tunnel.

"Do they have this kind of a strong movement in Europe, too?" she asked.

"Yes. They have fought a terrible war in Spain."

"Tell me more about yourself. About London, when you were a student there."

"When I was a student in London!" He put the oars aside and leaned back. He was completely relaxed and seemed to be enjoying himself. "We used to meet the Left-wing intellectuals of England. They didn't treat us like an inferior subject race, and we wallowed in contemporary English literature. Isherwood. Auden. Spender. Louis MacNiece. It was a very exciting time and was being called the Pink Decade."

"Are English people Left-wing too?"

"A few. All Englishmen are not arrogant imperialists of the kind you see out here in India. In fact, most them are very nice people. But they become a different breed the moment they cross the Suez."

He trailed his fingers in the cool, clean water and continued reminiscently, "And we had a number of remarkable Indian intellectuals living in Britain at that time. When I returned home in 1937 I found that the young men in our universities were ready to join the Leftist movement. We also admired Jawaharlal Nehru. And the Terrorists joined us and gave up their old bomb-throwing ways. Deepa, you and I are fortunate to be alive in such stirring times and be able to do something for our country…"

She gulped and looked mistily at him. They had reached the end of the tunnel.

Zainab had cooked the day's meal. After finishing their fish-and-rice they made for their respective rooms for a siesta. Zainab went down to the stream to wash clothes.

Deepali was fast asleep when he came to her door and knocked. She got up with a start and rubbed her eyes. He hesitated a little and came in. "Where are those magazines?" he asked rather foolishly.

"Just a minute," she said, getting up.

He lingered by the door and scratched his head awkwardly while she opened her little trunk. Then he saw Zainab trundling back with her washing and hurried out. Deepali followed him with a huge packet. He gave her a radiant smile, looking really pleased. They spread a mat on the verandah facing the river, and sat down.

Instantly he got absorbed in the journals. She picked up a book to keep him silent company, but found it tough reading, so she began scrutinising the jungle scene printed on the mat. An orange tiger peeping out of the bush. Khulna district was famous for these mats. What artistic people! Artistic and starving, she said to herself, admiringly, and stole a glance at him. He seemed to have become oblivious of her, his nose buried in *New Statesman* and *Nation*.

After a while he lifted his head and chuckled, "Time for high tea."

With Zainab's help she made rice cakes and fried some bananas and poured syrupy sweet tea into aluminium glasses.

"Ha..." he exclaimed, nibbling at the rice cake and reading, "Lovely."

"More tea?" she asked eagerly, after some time.

"Yes?" he said, frowning. He didn't like to be disturbed while reading. "Yes, please. Thank you."

She made fresh tea for him.

"The situation is becoming alarmingly domestic!" he said lightly, taking the glass from her.

The thoughtless remark hit her. What do you take me for, she wanted to say but it would have been a cheap retort. She reddened and fixed her gaze on the river. Why did I come here? I am merely his whim. All women are men's whims, not comrades. This business of camaraderie and intellectual companionship is all bosh. Hot tears welled up in her eyes. Blissfully ignorant of her reaction he continued reading till the sun went down.

A boat arrived at the jetty. Maulvi Abul Hashim came ashore, dragging the net behind him. Another Sunderbans day was done.

They spent the next day in the nearest village, talking to farmers and fishermen. They ate with them and explained the movement to them. Deepali was scared. "Suppose one of them is an informer?" she whispered.

"No," he replied. "They are our men. Living in such misery you don't except them to be on the side of the Government. Besides, they do not know my real identity, and this place is fifty miles of impossible terrain from the nearest police station."

On the third day they had walked a couple of miles along the river when they spotted a gleaming white motor launch. Quickly they hid themselves in the trees. It was a Government launch, probably some district officials passing by, touring the backwaters. Or perhaps a party of Englishmen or upper-class Indians who had come for a tiger-shoot. The launch disappeared round a bend in the river. Deepali had paled.

"Tch, tch—" he whispered disapprovingly. "Afraid of a civilian motor-boat?"

Gunshots echoed in the distance.

"Now we are done for," she said in despair.

"Obviously a hunting party, cruising the rivers. They won't come our way. Nobody can flush us out of here easily."

He listened a while to the green resounding silences of the woods, and continued, "The Muslim peasants we met yesterday...their ancestors fought in the Peasant War against the British a hundred years ago. The Faraizi Movement was led by the revivalist Wahabi maulvis. I have told you about them, haven't I?" He had solemnly resumed his 'extension lectures'.

"Rehan, you have absolutely no doubt about this path you have chosen for yourself?" she asked, as they came out onto the mud track.

"Absolutely none," he replied. "There can be no room for doubt once you have recognised your real enemies and their agents.

"Remember two very important points: If you read the history of India in careful detail, from the time of the coming of the Muslims, a thousand years ago, you will not find a single Hindu-Muslim riot mentioned by any historian. There were battles between rulers—no riots, till we come to the last century.

"Also, the sense of nationalism was born in the last century when people realised that for the first time in history, the wealth of the country was being taken out.

"Just take Khulna and Noakhali. Now they are full of robbers and destitute fishermen. In the Mughals', and the Nawab-Nazims', time these coastal districts used to be prosperous because of their maritime trade."

The picked their way through tropical flowers.

"Do you know that during the last two hundred years the emerging nations of Europe waged wars against one another, mostly in order to capture Indian trade?" he wagged his forefinger. She burst out laughing.

He wrinkled his brows. "What is it?"

"Somebody ought to witness this scene. In this perfectly romantic setting, Comrade Rehan Ahmed is talking about trade and commerce in 17th century India..."

On the fourth day, as they went out rowing, they came upon an ancient river-side temple.

"This is waiting to be explored," he said gaily and rowed across to the landing steps.

According to a folk belief of Bengal, Rama and Sita had spent part of their 14-year-long exile in the Sunderbans, too.

Rehan and Deepali ascended the worn-out stairs.

"Let's have a *dekho* at the sculpture. Obviously Sun period, tenth century," Rehan declared, gazing at the mossy structure. Deepali looked at him with awe. Golly, how much he knows about everything.

A half-blind, toothless priest came out of a cell. Rehan had forgotten to take off this shoes. He noticed the priest and said to Deepali in English, "If this bloke objects, tell him I am your lord and master, Rahul Das Gupta, M.A., England-returned."

Expecting good *bakshish* from the tourists, the priest called them in. They found themselves standing before the idol of the eight-handed goddess Durga. Rehan assumed an expression of pious devotion. The priest put red paste on their foreheads, picked up some flowers lying at the feet of the deity and showered them over their heads.

"Hurray! The chap was very sensible, got us married!" Rehan shouted playfully in English.

Deepali flushed a deep crimson. Rehan gave some coins to the old man and escorted her out. She was visibly shaken. He noticed her agitation and grinned. "Look, I was only joking. I have seen exactly the same scene in every Indian film. The hero and the heroine turn up at a secluded forest-temple and the lone priest garlands them and, lo and behold, they are married with God as their witness. Fantastic!"

"Shut up." She sat down on a broken pillar and began to cry. He was bewildered. My God, I didn't realise it would have such significance for her. O, my God. He said earnestly, "Look, Deepa, I was ragging you. For goodness' sake, of course we are not married. Who the hell says we are married? You must admit that you are exceptionally stupid. And anyway, how can you still believe in temples and mosques and churches? We have discarded all that as superstition. What a foolish girl!"

Suddenly the absurdity of the situation dawned on her. Here they were, a Bengali Hindu girl and a Bengali Muslim young man, both professing to be Marxists, he hiding from the British and telling her in English, which he spoke with a British accent, not to take the temple business seriously. Once again she broke into helpless giggles...

Next morning, as she sat in the kitchen helping Zainab with the chores, Rehan shouted from across the bamboo wall.

"Deepali, come here...at once!" He sounded highly agitated.

She rushed to his room.

"Hitler..." he uttered, ears glued to the radio.

"What's happened to Herr Hitler?" Old Abul Hashim asked placidly, taking down his fishing-net from the wall.

"He has attacked the Soviet Union! This...this radically alters the entire situation."

Three days later Deepali and Rehan were standing on the crowded river-front of the nearest village. Boats were leaving for Bagher Ghat. Villagers were carrying lovely Khulna mats they had woven, for nearby market-towns. The mats would be sold all over Bengal and beyond, and adorn arty sitting-rooms. Their weavers would get the barest of profit for their labour.

Fishermen were going out for the day's haul. It may be big, it may be small, all depended on Allah's will.

Deepali was leaving the Sunderbans and going back to "civilisation". At Bagher Ghat she would board a steamer for Narayan Gunj, sailing via Barisal and Faridpur. The last three days had been spent in great tension and worry. Rehan had started waiting for a Party directive. All the top Communist leaders were imprisoned in Deoli Jail, in faraway Rajasthan. It would take them some time to get in touch with somebody underground in the god-forsaken Sunderbans. The monsoons had set in. "I don't know how long I'll have to stay here," he had grumbled on the way to the pier. "The comrades in Calcutta seem to have forgotten about me. And even you are running away." He had been sulking and had stopped shaving. When they got to the pier he stood a little away from her and talked to Maulvi Abul Hashim. People had opened their umbrellas. Soon it started raining.

"Time to leave, Kulsum. Allah be with you." Standing on the windy pier, the wizened fisherman resumed the role of Father Time. She winced. Why did everything seem so ominous? She had deceived him, too. Like his wife he sincerely believed what Rehan had told him...that soon she, Deepali Sarkar, was going to embrace Islam and marry this remarkable young man.

The crook. She turned to say goodbye to her beloved crook when she caught sight of Zainab. The old woman came running towards the landing-stage, clutching her umbrella and a small bundle.

She scrambled up to Deepali and shoved the parcel in her hands. "Kulsum Bibi," she said shyly. "I forgot to give it to you when you left in the morning. I bought this for my future daughter-in-law, but Rehan Mian is like our son, too. So you take it now as our humble present. We'll buy another sari next year...when our Qasim brings his bride home."

Deepali trembled a little as she opened the newspaper wrap. It was a bright red, inexpensive sari of Japanese silk. They must have saved hard to be able to buy it. She felt miserable and turned round to thank her, but the old woman had disappeared into the crowd.

The river swarmed with all manner of country-craft. Maulvi Abul Hashim beckoned to her to get into her boat. Right then a majestic *shampan* came into view. It was in full sail and over-loaded with passengers. Maulvi Abul Hashim saw it with his sharp, river-eyes and gestured to her to wait. She stepped back, wondering. The *shampan* neared the jetty. The voyagers started pouring out. A young man jumped onto the pier with the agility of a monkey and ran towards Abul Hashim. He resembled the old man. Abul Hashim said something to him, he looked around and made a dash for the corner where Rehan stood under a banyan, smoking.

The young man had tied his sarong with a leather belt and looked very efficient and smart. Minutes later she saw the two men walking towards her. Rehan strode with unusually bold, carefree steps. He sidled up to her and whispered, "This is Abul Qasim, our hosts' son, and a diligent comrade. He has brought a message, Uma has called me to Calcutta at once—They have received the latest directive."

"Hail to thee, Uma, O omnipresent goddess," she muttered acidly.

"Beg your pardon?" he asked, puzzled.

"Nothing. All right, bye."

"Wait, I am coming with you part of the way. We'll leave tomorrow. Come back to the hut and help me pack. We'll leave first thing in the morning. God, what a relief."

"I am going right now, right back to Dacca."

"Of course, you'll go straight to Dacca, but tomorrow. Come along," he said masterfully and resumed talking to young Abul Qasim in an undertone. She ran down towards the boat. He paid no attention to her. Abul Hashim had watched the scene, he gestured to her to return to the shore. The old man knew about life.

He called her again.

After a little hesitation she returned to the embankment.

Part II

Part II

17
Arjumand Manzil

IN Persian it meant "the auspicious house". It was pure Lucknow rococo, and therefore its ornamentation also symbolised the decline of a magnificent civilisation. The noble, awe-inspiring grandeur and exquisite beauty and purity of Indo-Mughal architecture had given way to the often hybrid, though more utilitarian, styles popularised by the Europeans in India. Arjumand Manzil could have even been built in what came to be called Victorian Gothic. But its construction was finished in the year the young queen ascended the throne of England. That was the year the Zaman Chowdhrys arrived in Dacca to live in their 'auspicious house' as absentee landlords of Faridpur.

Like most noblemen of the era, they were connoisseurs of the fine arts, and possessed an excellent library. During the Time of Troubles many a private collection had been ravaged. Fortunately, the Zaman Chowdhrys' books had remained intact, and had been brought to Dacca from the country seat in Faridpur. The scriptorium contained Hindu epics translated into Persian six hundred years earlier, at the behest of the independent Sultans of Bengal. There were also some manuscripts of early Sufi literature written in Old Bengali. The Zaman Chowdhry documents included a number of imperial firmans issued from Agra and Delhi, Court diaries written by the Kayastha scribes of Murshidabad, and land records signed by Lord Cornwallis, Governor-General of India.

Of course, the most valuable family possession was a copy of the Holy Quran, calligraphed on gold leaf by an Emperor of Hindustan.

The Zaman Chowdhrys represented a civilisation which had been as all-pervasive as the latter-day Age of Victoria. As such, these Bengali aristocrats of Arjumand Manzil had much in common with the Khans of Crimea, the Aghas of the Balkans and the Pashas of Constantinople and Cairo. They were also different from the Khans and Aghas and Pashas of the West, because they were *Indian*. This inner duality had been no problem in earlier times; now modern concepts of Pan-Islamism and nationalism had turned it into a political dilemma.

At noon the sun shot through the rose-patterned stained glass windows and made multicoloured designs upon the library's walls. At night the bright tropical moon lit up the stylistic Tree of Life on the Isfahani carpet. In lamplight the room glimmered with its multitude of silver-framed photographs. Some of the portraits revealed the drastic changes the process of history had brought about in the fortunes and attitudes of the Mussalmans of India.

The large portrait of a nobleman of Delhi commanded respectful attention as it faced the main door. With his flowing white beard and gentle, benign face, the old man looked like a Hebrew prophet, and he had warned his people of the impending doom if they didn't modernise themselves. He was Sir Syed Ahmed Khan, Father of the Muslim Renaissance of post-1857 India. Sir Syed's co-religionists had been smarting under the crushing defeat of 1857. He tried to haul them out of their medieval cloisters and place them with a bang in the Age of Lytton Strachey. To a large extent he had succeeded. In 1875 he founded the Mohammedan Anglo-Oriental College at Aligarh, near Delhi; in 1920 it became a university.

Sir Nurul Zaman Chowdhry of Arjumand Manzil had been one of the early graduates of M.A.O. College, Aligarh.

A signed portrait of Mohammed Ali Jinnah, a former Indian National Congress leader, held pride of place over the carved rosewood writing table. Mr. Jinnah had revitalised the All India Muslim League in 1937, and had already acquired a large following in Bengal.

But the portrait of Rabindranath Tagore suddenly reminded the visitors that they were inside a fiercely Bengali household... Water-colours of Dacca's Mughal monuments decorated the library's light green walls.

The All India Muslim League had been established in Dacca in 1906, and Sir Nurul Zaman was one of its first members. Like many Muslim gentlemen of Dacca, Sir Nurul, too, had been fond of Urdu which was the language of culture in north India. His children had been taught that language along with their own mother-tongue, Bengali. Lady Chowdhry wrote articles in Urdu which were published in the Muslim women's powerful feminist Urdu press, which had flourished in north India from the turn of the century. In Bengal, as in the rest of India, language politics was to figure prominently in later years, but its faint rumblings had already become audible.

Both Sir Nurul Zaman and Lady Chowdhry had died in the 1920s. Their only son and heir, Nawab Qamrul Zaman, was unhappily married and spent most of his time in the library, devoting himself to the affairs of the Muslim community. Politics was the favourite pastime of most educated Indians, particularly of Bengalis.

On a cloudy morning in July 1941, Nawab Qamrul Zaman reclined in his long armchair, smoking his silver water-pipe. He was planning to write his speech. In the afternoon a meeting of the provincial Muslim League was to be held at Arjumand Manzil. The Nawab stroked his forehead with his golden fountain pen as he thought about the opening paragraph. After a few minutes he picked up some notepaper from a walnut teapoy and began writing in Bengali.

While Nawab Qamrul Zaman sat writing in his peaceful study, the rest of Arjumand Manzil hummed with brisk activity. Chairs were being arranged in the hall for the League meeting. The gardeners were busy cutting flowers for the vases. A houseboy was cleaning the ashtrays, another brushed the carpets. A placard in Bengali which read, *Pakistan Is Our Birthright* had been placed behind the chairs on the makeshift dais. Nawab Qamrul Zaman's only son and heir, Nayyarul Zaman, was overseeing the arrangements while humming a Tagore song...oblivious of the inherent contradiction in the situation!

Inside, the women's quarters wore an air of festivity for an entirely different reason. Nayyarul Zaman was to get married three days later. He had never seen the girl, who was the daughter of a wealthy landowner of Dinajpur. Relatives had arrived from Faridpur, jewellers brought their wares to Arjumand Manzil. Bird-like Begum Qamrul Zaman inspected the ornaments loftily, or ordered her own designs. "Girls these days do not like our old fashioned jewellery," she would complain to a hanger-on. Her daughters and servant-maids gathered around, excitedly discussing each piece. One of the housemaids, called Mala, always wondered that the family already had heaps of jewellery, but they continued to buy more. Still it's the will of Allah that they should have everything, and I nothing. So be it.

Wedding songs were being sung in the back-garden. Nawab Qamrul Zaman looked out of the window and got up to take out a file of *Al-Mashrique*, 'The East'. This monthly journal in Urdu had been started in 1906, when Lord Curzon had combined Assam and eastern Bengal and formed the Muslim majority province of East Bengal. The partition of Bengal had been vehemently opposed by the Hindus, but this shortlived partition was the forerunner of the demand for Pakistan.

Nawab Qamrul Zaman returned to his armchair and began quoting a paragraph from the editorial and the first issue of *Al-Mashrique*. Carefully, he translated into Bengali... "We, the Muslims of India, realised that we had no alternative but to have a separate organisation. The aggressive and rude tone and attitude of the Hindu Bengali press has taxed and worn out our patience..."

The Nawab put the old magazine aside and went on to write his own speech, in which he gave a brief account of Muslim affairs from 1906 to 1941. He mentioned the Pakistan

Resolution which the All-India Muslim League had passed earlier at Lahore. He looked around for the latest copy of a Muslim League weekly being published from Delhi, which had carried a map of the proposed state of Pakistan. The Nawab wished to mention some important points about Assam and Bengal while referring to the map. When he couldn't find the journal in the room he frowned and rang the bell.

A servant appeared at the door.

"The new *Dawn*," the Nawab said, "ask Nayyar Mian if he has taken it. I need the map of Pakistan."

"Huzoor, Nayyar Mian has cut it out and pinned it to the wall in the front verandah. Shall I take it off? But the wall will be spoiled."

"Oh, all right. You may go."

The servant disappeared. The Nawab returned to his papers.

Abdul Qadir, the coachman, drove his rickety carriage straight into the imposing portico of Arjumand Manzil. Deepali Sarkar stepped down. Almost mechanically the old man drove out, his head bent as usual, crouching on his coach-box, a compelling figure of doom.

Deepali ascended the marble stairs and was about to turn in the direction of the zenana when she caught sight of the map of Pakistan. Nayyarul zaman had pinned it on the wall directly above the cluster of potted palms. Deepali stopped by and read the caption: "Punjab, Assam, Bengal, Kashmir. Sarhad (North-West Frontier Province), Sind, Baluchistan, P-A-K-I-S-T-A-N."

There was nobody around. The servants had left. The place was full of a languid peace and the special stillness of a Sunday morning. Deepali remained engrossed in the map. The silence was broken by a gentle voice:

"Daughter Deepali, what are you studying so carefully?"

She turned round. Nawab Qamrul Zaman Chowdhry stood in the doorway of his study, smiling benignly.

She liked Jehan Ara's distinguished-looking, highly sophisticated father. He was so refined and urbane. She could talk to him as freely as she did to her own Baba. She joined palms in respectful greeting, and asked, "What is this, Uncle?"

"Ah, that! You ought to know. When, Inshallah, Pakistan comes into being, you too, shall be a Pakistani..."

"Me, Uncle?" she pouted, traversing the length of the verandah to reach the library.

The Nawab smiled fondly. Jehan Ara was his favourite child. Deepali was her friend and a nice, quiet girl. Deepali's father had been his schoolmate. Zamindar Romesh Babu had been a close friend of the late Nawabzada Fakhrul Zaman. Theirs had been a friendship of three generations.

"You are late, my dear," he said to the fresh-faced Sarkar girl. "You were supposed to help Bibi in some sewing and stitching for Nayyar's bride...something of that sort," he said vaguely.

"I'll go in presently. First, I would like to ask you something. May I?"

"Certainly, come in."

She entered the library and slumped down in a sofa-chair.

"Give me a few minutes, just let me finish the last page," he said courteously, noticing, at the same time, that the poor girl wore half-broken sandals, and the most inexpensive cotton sari one could buy in Dacca town. It upset him: because of his naive idealism her father had no business to treat his children so shabbily.

After qualifying from Calcutta Medical College, Benoy Chandra Sarkar had become the Chowdhrys' family physician, but for old friendship's sake he refused to take any fees. So the Nawab started sending costly presents to Chandrakunj. The doctor stopped coming to Arjumand Manzil. Later, he went off to jail. When he returned, his practice floundered. On the two Muslim festivals of Eid, Jehan Ara gave expensive saris to Deepali. Dr. Sarkar said to his daughter: 'You can't reciprocate. Why accept gifts from her?' Deepali had to tell Jehan Ara: 'My father has a lot of personal pride. He feels bad about the presents you all give. You'll understand, won't you?'

Dr. Sarkar even stopped paying them social visits. He was fast becoming a recluse. The Chandrakunj family's situation distressed Nawab Qamrul Zaman but nobody could do a thing about it. Still, a young girl deserves better clothes, he thought furiously.

"Now, my dear, tell me about youself. I happened to meet Benoy Babu in a bookshop the other day. He told me that you had gone off to the interior of Santhal Pargana to collect folk songs."

"Yes, Uncle," she said feebly.

"Your father was very worried about you. That the monsoons were about to set in, and you must be facing all kind of hardship in those primitive Santhal villages..."

Deepali avoided his eyes and hurriedly changed the topic. She addressed the Nawab with much bravado. "Uncle," she said blithely, "are you so sure that Pakistan will come into being?"

"God willing, yes. Very soon. That reminds me, I may as well finish writing my spcech before I explain to you what Pakistan is all about. Excuse me." He picked up his pen and papers and began writing with a flourish. She watched him, fascinated. He was such a majestic picture of self-assurance and well-being.

Deepali stood up and began examining the bookshelves. She stopped before a volume with an English title: *The Travels of Mirza Abu Talib Isphahani.*

"Oh! Haji Baba of Isphahan..." she exclaimed.

Qamrul Zaman Chowdhry looked up from his writing table. "No, this was a local fellow. A Bengali, more or less, although he was born in Lucknow." The Nawab's Bengali chauvinism had suddenly come to the fore. "He was probably the first notable Indian to visit England. He went there in 1799, after he had had his fill of adventures at home."

"Really? Well! Trust a Bengali to do a thing like that. Was he an ancestor of yours?"

"No. His father came from Iran. As a child he became an orphan and was brought up by Nawab Muzaffer Jung."

"...?"

"See," the Nawab replied patiently, "my father had a flamboyant kind of friend called Syed Ahmed Ali, Nawab of Chitpur, Calcutta."

"That rings a bell, Uncle, I have heard my aunt talk about his gold-plated album."

"Right. Your grandfather also met him in Calcutta. Muzaffer Jung was Nawab Ahmed Ali's ancestor. The district of Muzafferpur in Binar was named after him. Mirza Abu Talib also married into his family, and went off to England in 1799...the year Tipu fell."

The Nawab grew silent. They way he had said, "the year Tipu fell," had infinite pathos in it—1799 was the great, heartbreaking watershed.

He resumed after a pause: "Abu Talib's book is in Persian, otherwise you could have read it. Among other things he informs us that his ship's Bengali crew was bone-lazy and rascally!" He laughed.

He stopped and added after a few moments, "Mirza Abu Talib mentions in his book that in the house of a judge called Mr. Dosey, in London, he saw some rare Persian and Mughal miniatures. Many Englishmen, he writes, had acquired such treasures from the ruined aristocracy of India. On an illuminated volume of Nizami, Abu Talib saw the personal seal of Nawab Sher Jung."

"Pardon me, Uncle, so many Nawabs confuse me. Who was Sher Jung?"

"Never mind." He yawned and leaned back in his chair. "Abu Talib says that he had seen this book in the poor nobleman's library back home. He came across a lot of priceless Mughal books, paintings, cameos and seals in the houses of Hastings, Sir Fredrick Eden and others."

Why were these people so sad and backward-looking? Deepali wondered. Because they had lost an empire? Would the British be so unhappy and full of nostalgia, too, after they lose their dominions? Did the Imperial Guptas also brood for centuries after they had been vanquished by the Huns and Scythians?

"Uncle, why do you dwell so much on the past?" she ventured to ask.

"Past? No. Right now I am thinking of the future... Pakistan! Just give me a few more minutes, after which I'll answer your questions."

Deepali settled down in her chair once again.

Her gaze wandered to the water-colours. The Mughal monuments of Dacca...Lalbagh Fort. The Seven-domed Mosque. Bibi Peri's Tomb. Hussaini Dalan....

Nawab Qamrul Zaman Chowdhry is the heir to the Muslim past of Bengal. She recollected that her home district, Mymensingh, contained lovely monuments of Buddhist and Hindu Bengal. So, am I the heir to the Hindu past? Don't these two heritages have any relationship with each other?

In the Sunderbans Rehan had given another interpretation of history. She decided to ask the Nawab: how would Pakistan benefit poor Abdul Qadir, the coachman?

Rehan had said: Deepali, ninety per cent of the population of India is poor and illiterate. The talk of culture and spirituality and philosophy is meaningless for a people who have to struggle desperately to get their daily bread. Poverty also makes a nation characterless. We have become just that.

The sun burst through the windows and lit up the rose-pink painting of Lalbagh Fort. It had been built by Emperor Augranzeb's son, Prince Mohammed Azam, Governor of Bengal, in the seventeenth century. Rehan had said (she had begun to think in the way Rev. Bannerjee would prefix his speech with the phrase: 'Jesus had said'): All our monuments, our superlative handicrafts, our music and dance and literature...all this belongs to better times. Our communal tensions and our poverty are the direct result of British colonialism. The badly exploited agricultural land and a growing population are bound to cause group conflicts.

"There we are! Now, what did you want to ask, my dear?" the Nawab said, putting his papers aside.

"Uncle," she spoke quietly," why do you want India to be divided?"

The Nawab puffed at his silver hookah for a few seconds and answered, "Deepali, Indian Muslims are, on the whole, a poverty-stricken people. Incidentally, even the well-to-do among them are not so prosperous as they should be.

"Because they like to eat well and live well and do not save much, hoping that God will take care of tomorrow. Most Hindus neither eat well nor live well, and save furiously." He gave a little laugh. "Well, that's the Muslims' fault. Bad national habit. Anyway, there was a time before John Company's loot, when the Bengali Muslims, in general, were quite well-off. They had their handicrafts and their lands. This was true of the rest of India, too. In Bengal alone there were one hundred thousand Islamic schools. One hundred thousand! It is not an exaggeration—their records still exist. Look at the condition today. Even Rabindranath Tagore has admitted that the Muslims of Bengal are victims of social and economic injustice."

"But once we are free, Muslims will be all right in a united India," Deepali interrupted him.

"United India? Alas, no! And besides, when was India ever united? The British welded it into one country. You are a child, I cannot have a political argument with you. I do not even argue with your father. When we were both young, I tried to make him see reason, but with great derring-do he went off to court arrest. Now he is making his children suffer."

"He is an idealist," Deepali replied loyally. "Tell me about Pakistan."

He smiled sadly. "Perhaps you are a little crazy too, like your father and uncle. Look at the way Dinesh got himself hanged. Poor lad. Who remembers him now? Why did he have to lose his life? Even your Jawaharlal Nehru says that the terrorists were misguided and politically immature."

He stared reflectively at the end of the long, snake-like crimson pipe of the hubble-bubble. Merry notes of wedding music floated in from the garden.

He leaned over and wagged a finger at Deepali. "But you take my advice. Do not ever get involved in some crackpot, dangerous politics. Your uncle has already made the supreme sacrifice..."

"Sacrifice," Deepali said with vehemence, "renunciation and sacrifice are the ancient traditions of our land, from the Buddha down to Mahatma Gandhi and Jawaharlal Nehru and..."

"Hmm..." the Nawab smiled a trifle ironically.

"Uncle," she said with great urgency. "Please do not let the country be partitioned."

"Child," the Nawab replied calmly, "you and I belong to two entirely different schools of thought. Look, we welcomed the partition of Bengal in 1905. In order to undo the partition you started the Terrorist movement, and began throwing bombs at innocent people. Do you know that in Dacca alone there were five hundred secret groups who flung hand grenades at Englishmen?"

"Five hundred?" she repeated, wide-eyed, and thought: I belong to the tradition of the bomb-throwers. He represents the opposite camp. Why did this polarisation occur among the Bengalis...?

Rehan had said: 'The British snatched Bengal from the Muslims, so they crushed them and created a new, loyal, Hindu land-owning class who later became leaders of the Hindu Bengali renaissance. Muslims became the underdogs. Tagore belonged to this new Hindu zamindar class...'

Nawab Qamrul Zaman continued, "The Muslims are in the majority in Bengal. They would have gained from the partition of 1905, and now the establishment of Pakistan will benefit them. My dear, you have not seen the plight of the

Muslim peasantry, groaning in the clutches of the Hindu zamindar and moneylender."

"You are a landowner too, Uncle!" she said defiantly.

The Nawab rang the bell. An attendant appeared soundlessly, like a genie. The Master waved towards the water-pipe. The servant picked up the clay-cup topped with a silver cover, and carried it out. The Nawab turned to the girl and said mildly, "Doesn't the Indian National Congress have landowners and capitalists in its fold?"

"I am not member of the Congress, Uncle."

"Then what are you?" he asked, alarmed. "My dear child, I do hope you have not turned into a Communist! This is the latest malaise afflicting unhappy Bengal." He regarded her with deep concern.

"I am not a Communist, either," she laughed hollowly. He did not seem convinced. She said, a little boldly, "I...I merely want to serve my country, and work for freedom."

"Go ahead, my dear, but the freedom you talk about would not be for us Muslims."

She was dismayed. There was so much bitterness in him, such despair. Are Rehan and I and all the other Leftists living in an unreal intellectual world created by our theories...?

The genie returned with the chillum full of fresh, fragrant tobacco and red hot coal. He placed it atop the slender neck of the *pechwan*. He retreated to the door without turning his back towards the Master and vanished. Feudal etiquette.

She asked sweetly, "Uncle, why is it said that the All-India Muslim league is a body of Nawabs? Nawab Liaquat Ali Khan, Raja Amir Ahmed Khan of Mahmudabad, and...Nawab Qamrul Zaman Chowdhry..." she broke into mischievous giggles.

"Muslims are not the only loyalists in India as alleged by the Congress. What about the Hindu zamindars and rajas and title-holders who kow-tow to the Sahebs!"

"Uma Roy is very rich and yet she..."

"I have heard about Pritish Babu's strange daughter. Perhaps you have become her follower? In that case you had better be careful."

Deepali looked at him uneasily. He continued. "Sorry, I am a conservative. My ideas are bound to annoy you."

"Uncle..." she said now, a little uncertainly, "I merely wished to say that we could work together for unity instead of partition."

"Where the hell is unity? The anti-Muslim Arya Samaj of Punjab and the Hindu militancy of Maharashtra and Bengal...are they symbols of peace and goodwill? Don't forget that these movements were started before we thought of setting up a separate political platform."

"I don't know about other provinces, but in Bengal Hindus and Muslims share a common culture."

"Did your community ever admit the fact that the folk music and folk literature of Bengal are largely the contribution of the Muslims? By 'Bengali culture' you only mean Hindu culture. During the last century your press even started the language controversy. They said Bengali was not the language of the Muslims, they declared that Bengali literature and culture were exclusively the heritage of the Hindus. I can show you those newspapers in my files." He gestured towards a bookshelf. "By God, Deepali, we wanted unity. But now, such hatred for us! Such contempt. Like the Christians have for the Jews in Europe... Have you read *Anand Math...*?

"No."

"Your Hindu Bengali press called Nawab Sir Salimullah a toady. All these Hindu knights of Bengal...are they not toadies...? Till a hundred and fifty years ago there certainly was unity. The Hindu gentry wore Mughal dress and read Persian..."

"Because the Muslims were the dominant ruling class," Deepali put in, but the Nawab went on with increasing fervour. "Persian and Arabic words form twenty per cent of the Bengali language."

"But, Uncle," she cut in impatiently, "both communities started their revivalist movements and were encouraged by the..."

"British! I agree. Well. Why did we let ourselves be manipulated by them?" He collected his papers and carried them to the writing table.

Girls in the distant back-garden had now started a Sufi song. She listened carefully and, with a pang, recognised the words. It was a mystical Bengali lyric by Lalan Shah which Rehan had sung to her in the Sunderbans. *My neighbour lives in a house of glass/But I have never seen Him. A deep river separates Him from me/How I wish He could come to me.* Rehan had often talked of the Sufis, their social consciousness, their humanism, even their romances. He had told her, with a mischievous glint in his eye, about Syed Murtaza Anand, how a married Brahmin woman, Anand Maya Debi, had fallen in love with him and become his devotee and how, because of her, he had come to be called Murtaza Anand. "In every country, the Sufis usually belonged to the working classes and led the masses against the autocracies of their times. In Bengal the Hindu sanyasis and the Madari fakirs fought together against the Company's forces in 1770." He had proceeded to talk about Bengal's great singing Sufis: Sheikh Madan Baul, Shatolan Shah, Hasan Reza, Lalan Shah, whose lyrics had inspired Tagore's poetry and music...

Deepali smiled secretly as she sat there in the window seat, thinking of the great singing comrade, Rehan Ahmed. He had quietly slipped into the fortress-like library of this reactionary ogre and come to her rescue. With sudden reassurance she turned to the Nawab and said, "Pardon me, Uncle, you represent your class. All this is class politics. Both the Congress and the Muslim League represent the bourgeoisie." She stood up triumphantly and moved towards the door.

The Nawab regarded her for a moment, walked over with majestic steps, and placed his right hand upon her head. "My dear," he said gently, "I hadn't realised that you had become so learned. It worries me. Girls shouldn't become too clever, it complicates life for them. They become unhappy. I wouldn't like Jehan Ara to join the university. Too much knowledge would unsettle her... Now, run along and help her stitch the wedding dresses. That is our tradition—our fancy sewing is done at home so that girls become expert needlewomen. And that should be a young lady's real interest. Needlework!" he chuckled.

"Aye, aye, sir!" she gave him a naval salute (as a young man he had done a stint in the Royal Indian Navy) and darted out. She was feeling marvellously light and happy, her heart still singing of Rehan...

Jehan Ara was in the garden, singing Lalan Shah's song with her sisters and cronies as they sewed the wedding clothes. Deepali came out of the portico and walked briskly past Arjumand Manzil's private theatre hall. She noticed that the hall had been opened—perhaps they were also going to stage a play during the marriage celebrations.

The "magical throne of King Vikramaditya" had been lying in the godown for more than thirty years. It belonged to a more relaxed era when touring companies visited Arjumand Manzil and performed popular Bengali pays like *Shahjehan,* *Tipu Sultan, Siraj-ud-Daulah, Mir Qasim* and *Kirani Jeevan.* The plays reflected the intense patriotic fervour and Bengali nationalism of Hindus and Muslims alike. They never tired of seeing plays about the 18th-century Muslim rulers who had fought valiant but losing battles against the conquering English. While Tipu Sultan, "the Tiger of Mysore", and "Siraj-ud-Daulah" and "Mir Qasim", the tragic Nawabs of Bengal, strutted about on the Bengali stage brandishing their wooden swords, every schoolboy in England was being taught how villainous and cruel these "despotic native chieftains" had been, who were finally vanquished by such glorious empire-builders like Wellsley and Clive...

The fact was that Bengalis loved theatre, just as much as they loved to sing. The villagers had their folk troupes, the urban middle-classes their dramatic clubs, the landlords their private concert halls called *jalsa-ghar*. (*Jalsa* or musical soiree was also a relic of the Mughal regime.)

When, in 1885, Nawabzada Fakhrul Zaman Chowdhry built this playhouse, there had been thirty-four theatrical companies performing in the city. An Urdu stage had flourished in Dacca even before 1857, for which they used to invite actresses from faraway Lucknow. A Victorian Bengali or Victorian Urdu melodrama had to be seen to be believed.

Fakhrul Zaman had also written an opera in Bengali called *Raja Bhoj*, based on the mythological story of King Vikramaditya and his magical throne. For the opera the talented princeling had designed a throne complete with the figurines of thirty-two "sky maidens". The throne, along with the other props, had been locked up after the untimely death of the Nawabzada. Sir Nurul Zaman, and after him his son, Qamrul Zaman, had taken to politics and the playhouse had gradually fallen into disuse. Whenever Deepali needed any swords, beards, crowns or costumes for her college plays, she came straight to Arjumand Manzil. Jehan Ara ordered the servants to open the *jalsa-ghar*'s store-room and lend her friend whatever she needed. Deepali had never been inside the playhouse nor seen this magnificent throne before. It had been buried deep under the other props.

That Sunday morning the old major domo of Arjumand Manzil remembered the "throne" and had it dug out of the back room.

It had been scrubbed and placed under a flowering cotton-flower tree for the young ladies to sit on and do their fancy sewing.

Deepali went round the theatre hall which stood by itself, next to the summer house, and entered the zenana garden. She came upon an incredibly peaceful and idyllic scene. Jehan Ara sat in a corner of the spacious throne, cutting a blouse. Najma, her younger sister, was busy at a sewing machine. Akhtar, the youngest, and some other girls squatted on the grass, singing. One of them played the harmonium.

All these young women seemed the least concerned about the fate of the country or humanity. Birds chirped in the foliage. Dark clouds hung low over the trees.

"You are late!" Jehan Ara said reproachfully.

"Sorry!" Deepali grinned.

"Our cousins, Sarah and Hajira, from Faridpur," Jehan Ara introduced the guests.

"Rosie Apa hasn't turned up," said Najma.

"She'll come after her church service. Why were you held up?" Jehan Ara asked Deepali.

"I was having an argument with Uncle in the library."

"What kind of argument?"

"Hectic. About Pakistan."

"What did you say to him?"

"I told him that this is a scheme thought up by the British."

"You were arguing with Abba?" asked Jehan Ara, taken aback.

"Now, if our elders are wrong about something, they ought to be corrected," the girl who had been playing the harmonium said gravely. Deepali was surprised by her defiance.

Jehan Ara laughed. "Deepali, this is Yasmin Majid, our new friend. A bit crazy…like you."

The girl flung her long plait back and gracefully raised her right hand to her forehead in a polite *adaab*. She was about seventeen and had large, very expressive eyes.

"I'll give you something simple to do. Take this," Jehan Ara pushed the mound of *eau de nil* china silk towards Deepali. "Just start stitching this on it." She gave her friend a gold-and-silver roll of Surat border, and turned to the young girl. "Yasmin, this is our old friend, Deepali."

"Of course, Kumari Deepali Sarkar. I have all three records of yours, Deepali-di. On one of your songs I have composed a dance, the one about the mountain stream!"

"Ah! I always forget that our Deepali has already become quite a celebrity and needs no introduction!" said Jehan Ara affectionately.

Just then Rosie arrived.

"Here, hem this blouse," Jehan Ara threw an unfinished blouse at her after she got off her bike. "No time to waste."

"Sing, girls, why have you stopped singing?" Shamsa Khatoon popped her head out of a first-floor window and shouted down.

"Busybody," whispered Najma to Rosie. "And a crony of my mother's. How cleverly she has got her niece's marriage fixed with my brother."

Blackbirds chattered in the cotton-flower tree. The garden was in full bloom. The air was heavy with the fragrance of magnolias. Yasmin wandered off to a thicket and returned with some flowers. "Have you noticed," she said to Deepali, "that different fragrances have their own *tones*? Deepali-di, give us a Nazrul song."

"Hmm—Let me think," Deepali replied, absorbed in her pile of china silk. She hummed a little and began a romantic lyric composed by Bengal's revolutionary pet, Qazi Nazrul Islam.

Narcissus burns in the fire of Spring

Akhtar took up the refrain and started playing the harmonium. Yasmin began to dance in the flowing Manipuri style—she was an excellent dancer. Jehan Ara continued her needlework. Deepali crooned:

Where are you my love? My heart aches...

Abruptly Jehan Ara stood up and walked away towards the distant kitchen.

"Blue thread," Najma announced, "Akhtar, I need some blue thread."

"Didi," Akhtar said sweetly to Deepali. "Could you please go upstairs and get us some blue and purple reels from Jehan Ara Apa's room?"

"That's fine, ordering your elders about," said Najma. "Lazybones—why don't you go yourself?"

"Can't," Akhtar stretched out her right foot. "Hurt my toe. Can't climb all those stairs five hundred times a day. Akhtar bring this, Akhtar bring that. Please, Deepali-di." She gave her a bunch of keys. "Here, this one is the key to Bibi's wardrobe, the reels are in the Blue Boy's chocolate box on the middle shelf. And in case you find her work-box in the same almirah, bring us some D.M.C. silk coil, too. I don't know why she can't keep all her reels together, and not under lock and key."

"I need rose-pink and bottle-green silk coils," Najma added. "Thank you, Deepali-di."

The grand staircase led straight to Jehan Ara's room on the first floor. Deepali went up the broad, carpeted stairs whose railings of intricate Burmese carving always fascinated her. Still humming the Nazrul song she went into her friend's spacious bedroom, crossed over to the huge wardrobe, unlocked it and found the fancy work-box. She had to rummage in it for the rose-pink and bottle-green silk coils, for they were mixed up in a jumble of odds and ends. As she tried to untangle the coils she saw the photograph, lying on the satin-lined bottom. It was Rehan Ahmed of a few years ago. On the right hand corner he had inscribed:

To Jehan Ara Begum, the lady of my dreams,
From Rehan Ahmed, London, April 16, 1936.

Deepali experienced a brief blackout and tried to hold on to the wardrobe knob. Someone slammed a door in the adjoining room, which brought her back to a dizzy consciousness. She blinked and looked around. It was the same familiar room. The carved Burmese four-poster. The Turkish divan. The Georgian dresser. The Bokhara carpet. The curtains of Kashmir embroidery. The Chughtai paintings on the walls. Everything was in its place, nothing had changed. Happy laughter rose from the arbour.

With trembling hands she put the photograph back. Closing the almirah, she saw herself in its tall mirror. She looked horror-stricken, blighted. Her legs were shaking. She leaned against the wardrobe to compose herself before going down.

Sarah and Hajira were still singing in the garden. Akhtar played the harmonium. Yasmin was dancing away in rhythmic frenzy. Najma and Rosie were absorbed in their work. Deepali gave them the threads, hoping not to be noticed. She sat down in a corner of the throne, still in a state of shock.

"Be careful, Didi," Yasmin swung around, "you are sitting on the broken leg."

Deepali gaped at her foolishly.

"Have you observed this fantastic throne?" Yasmin asked conversationally, twirling around, "Twenty-eight celestial dancers turned wooden…and stuck to the three sides of the royal seat of Raja Indra." She etched out her words through her hand and neck movements. "Four of them support the heavenly throne on their block-heads…hee…hee…one of them is broken. So Bibi's servants have put bricks there." She pointed below.

Najma handed her the unfinished sari and border.

"Going to the loo," Akhtar announced and limped off towards the house.

The throne was rocking like a storm-tossed *shampan*. Jehan Ara returned from the kitchen. The hazy blue-green garden hissed like the sea at high tide. Sarah began cutting a piece of pink brocade. She had spread it on a Khulna mat and was sitting on her haunches. Mala sat opposite, pressing two corners of the brocade with her thumbs. The women seemed so stationary. Why didn't they sail away?

"Let us pray to Allah," Mala said aloud, "that very soon, before the next Eid Moon, we make Jehan Ara Bibi's wedding dresses, too."

Jehan Ara glared at her and slouched over her sewing. Her eyes filled with tears. She dried them discreetly. She was sitting at the other end of the throne. Deepali stared at her blankly. Sarah and Hajira broke into a merry song. Rosie climbed out of the throne, pretending to look for a pair of scissors. She came near Deepali and whispered, "Dunno why, but whenever someone mentions her marriage, she has the same reaction. Some time back she broke down before me, too. What can the matter be…?" She picked up a pair of scissors and primly returned to her place.

Slowly, the garden stopped heaving and became still. Fearfully, Deepali glanced around. The girls were engrossed in their work. Nobody had taken any notice of her.

Yasmin had ambled off to the tank and was looking at the lotuses. She came back and perched herself on a side railing of the throne.

"Amazing," she remarked.

"What?" asked Sarah, looking up from her sewing.

"Everything."

There was silence again. The wind rose and scattered some flowers on the grass.

"Amazing throne, too," Yasmin said aloud.

"*Singhasan Battisi*," Sarah put in.

"Pardon me?" Yasmin asked absently.

"Thirty-two Tales of the Throne."

"Ya, I know. What thirty-two and a half..." Yasmin said to nobody in particular.

"Lunch is ready," the ancient major domo cried hoarsely from the back verandah. "Pick up the things and come in, it's going to rain."

Rosie, Najma, Hajira and Sarah got up and strolled away towards the house. Mala collected the clothes and followed them.

Yasmin addressed Jehan Ara and Deepali. "Listen, Apa, Didi. See. We three are sitting here upon this fake throne right now. Let's pretend we are the three celestial nymphs supporting the throne. And never mind about the one which got broken. So, like these nymphs, we shall challenge any Raja Bhoj who wishes to ascend the royal chair and is not worthy of it. Like it happened in the fantasy."

"You are quite mad, Yasmin!" Jehan Ara said, smiling wanly.

Yasmin continued, "Your great-uncle turned the story into an opera. Someday I shall create its ballet."

"I'm sure you will," Jehan Ara said indulgently.

Deepali finished the last half-yard of the border and lifted her head. Jehan Ara noticed her ashen face.

"Deepali!" she exclaimed. "What's the matter? Are you all right?"

"Just a little dizziness and headache."

"Perhaps you need glasses. Have you had your eyesight tested? Perhaps you are not used to stitching for two hours at a stretch. I'm sorry. My mother insisted that I invite you and Rosie for these sewing sessions. 'They ought to know the difference between a needle and spade,' she said, 'before they get married!' But you look ill. Go upstairs and lie down in my room. I'll have your lunch sent up. Shall I call the doctor...?"

"Don't be silly," Deepali replied peevishly. "I think I would like to go home, Baba will give me some medicine. Don't worry. Yes, perhaps I should get my eyes tested," she added tiredly. "Let me go home."

"That's not fair, you know," Jehan Ara replied mildly. "You spent the vacations roaming the countryside on some crackpot arty mission. Santhal Pargana, wasn't it? Now you pay us a flying visit. Half the time you spend talking politics with my father. We haven't had a proper gossip session. We haven't even discussed Rosie's Improbable Engagement Party...! All right, you're looking pretty miserable. Have lunch with us and go..."

Yasmin looked on with concern. Mala and another maid came back to carry the remaining things inside.

"Mala," Jehan Ara ordered, "tell the chauffeur Deepali Bibi will go home at two-thirty sharp."

It had started drizzling. Rosie rushed out to carry her bicycle into the verandah. She came back and exclaimed, "Deeps! You look unwell!"

"I'm fine, Rosie," she replied curtly. I must not make a spectacle of myself. Go in, she told herself, straightening up. Have lunch. Smile. Talk. Return to the ever-gloomy Chandrakunj. Pack up. Go to Bolpur. Join your B.A. final class. Your time is up. It will be measurable on lonely roads.

Calmly she accompanied Jehan Ara, Rosie and Yasmin into the Auspicious House.

18
The Nightmare

THE hostel garden was lit up with the glitter of fireflies. She was sitting on a pile of ancient palm leaves. *I shall write to you with saffron by the light of the glow-worms, and send the letter to you through Ambassador Wind...*

Just as we give over our words to the air. Suppose we don't speak at all. The fireflies vanished. The weird tree of Gorakh tamarind groaned overhead. The Tree of Unrest. Durga's temple was blown away in the costal cyclone, it was a massive cyclone, brother. The library has no doors, only walls. No exit. He comes out of the bookshelves slyly, like a mouse. Shaven-headed. Bespectacled. Wooden sandals. Clod. Clod. Clod. He gives her a palm leaf.

This monk teaches at Santiniketan's China Bhavan. Prof. Hussain sailed past on a dinghy marked "Unsafe Boat." She tried to read what the Japanese bhikshu had given her.

Can't understand a word. The final exam would be held in this unknown language. She shivered. Rumble of thunder and lightning. The monk disappeared. Now she stands alone listening to an ancient poem. *My voice is your thunder. My tears your downpour. The fire in my heart is your lightning. You and I are alike, Brother Cloud, so why do you trouble me?*

Soft, silky light. Magnolia flowers glow like dim lamps. Walking by the stream he comes towards her.

That beloved of the moon-birds, long-haired, dark-eyed, lotus in hand, pouring nectar from his fingers, Avalokiteshwara Padmapani.

She stands in the Kala Bhavan garden, happy and secure. He sits in the art school verandah. He has a Turkish cap on, smokes a silver hookah. Water-colours everywhere. Trampling the young grass. Wearing a crown of flowers, he approaches her. Loknath Lokeshwara.

She laughs gaily. He lifts his face like Pan and plays his flute. Silver-bodied, a sun emerging from the black clouds.

Amitabh. Boundless light. Compassion. Love.

Came closer. Took off his glasses and stared at her. He had no eyes, no nose either, no ears, no nothing. Egg-face. You can paint me anyway you like.

She screamed.

"Take this," he said and stretched out his empty hand.

"What is it?"

"Glass of Water. No theory. Go and worship. What kind of Communist sympathiser are you? Don't go to the temple? My child, I hope you have not become a Communist." He spoke in the voice of Nawab Qamrul Zaman Chowdhry.

"Worship who?"

"Yourself. All of us worship ourselves."

"But today is the Festival of Snakes."

"That's why I gave you a glass of milk."

"Which century is this?"

"From beginning to end...an instant...ho...ho...ho..." He began to dance like a harlequin.

She lifts her hands as though carrying the brass tray for ritual temple worship. With heavy steps she returns to the ghostly tamarind. Snakes slide around its knotted roots. The forest is full of light. "The Festival of Serpents!" Rosie Bannerjee, the compere, announces off-stage. The chorus starts reciting Sarojini Debi's poem.

"Shining Ones, awake! We seek your chosen temples in caves and sheltering sandhills and sacred banyan roots ... O, lift your dreaming heads from the trance of ageless wisdom, and weave your mystic measures to the melody of flutes..."

Flutes in the background. "We have brought for you milk and maize and wild fig and golden honey. We have sanctified the air with joss sticks. Protect our helpless lives and our troubled dreams...! Swift as streams and soundless as the dewfall, subtle as lightning and splendid as the sun...seers are ye and symbols of the ancient silence, where life and death and sorrow and ecstasy are one..."

The stage collapses with a thud. The tamarind begins to shake and rattle, the ancient hermit tree haunted by old ghosts and sorrowing spirits. The half-blind temple priest shouts: Shri Rama and Queen Sita have lost their way in the Sunderbans. Hari-Har-Hari-Har. Help! Help! The tamarind groans. Kapalis are sitting under its shade. All-India Kapali Conference. They are burning their herbs to perform their fearful Tantric rites. Lots of Kapalis. Fearsome wandering yogis, they wear garlands of human skulls and make all manner of horrible magic.

One of them jumps in through the window. Here...he offers hashish. Smoke this. No thanks, I don't smoke. Excuse me, are you a juggler? Last time I saw you dressed as a wandering minstrel of Krishna! Alakh Niranjan. *Amar Praner Aram Moner Anand. Atmar Shanti.* Pardon me... Your beard is made of jute, you are a phoney yogi. Phoney king. Imitation throne of Vikramaditya. The whole world is phoney. My name, Miss Harimati, famous gramophone singer.

The Kapalis touched their skull-garlands. They waved their tricolour, red hammer-and-sickle and green crescent-and-star flags, rang their bells and descended into an underground monastery. Child, have you read the anti-Muslim novel, *Anand Math?* the man with the red Turkish cap asked. She left him in his doorless library and started running, running till she reached the Lotus River. A green canoe appeared on its crimson waves.

The boat sails on with no mast, no oar, no sound. The boatman has no eyes. No nose. No nothing. Egg-face. Silent movie. Soundless reel. She is sitting in the boat. Bang! Lalan Shah appears in the wings. Died long ago, still singing. Wears a long white cloak. Dim, vapoury. Even on a clear day you can't see him. I am Love, he sings, theatrically. I can't be comprehended. Can't be seen or gauged. Mr. Lalan Shah speaks his lines well. In his wraith-like hand he holds a *kadam* leaf.

He sings on the harmonium: There is a house of glass in which my neighbour lives. I have never seen Him. A deep river separates us. How can I cross it? I wish He could come over to me Himself, O Brother Boatman...

He gives her his visiting card. She reads it. Mirza Abu Talib Isfahani, member, Communist Party of Great Britain. He has a broad-brimmed Tipu hat on, and he wears a long robe of crimson velveteen. He is also an egg-face. In a second he becomes headless.

Huge lizards. They grew and grew till they became alligators. She broke into a cold sweat and trembled. One turned into a suitcase. Gilbert Plumer sprang out of it like a jack-in-the-box. Long, multicoloured tunnel. Dark ocean. The oarless barge sailed away without a river. The lamp burns with no flame. The flame glows without a lamp.

The woods are flowing. The river is stationary. Human beings stand rooted like trees.

Elephants. Row after row. An elephant of black terracotta stands near the redstone tank. Flaps his ears foolishly. Bang! Lalan Shah announces in English: Nawabzadi Jehan Ara Begum, affectionately known as Bibi, was murdered in cold blood. She is alive but has died. Point of mysticism that. Another bang. Crack of lightning.

She woke up, shivering. A thunderstorm raged outside. After a while it died down. The clouds dispersed. The moon was at its full. It peeped in as though it would slip out of the mist and drop into the room with a thud and burst into cold flames.

She wiped her face and tried to think coherently. Was she back in Santiniketan, the abode of peace, to have nightmares?

The bloody crook. Two-timer. Swindler.

She got up and drank a glass of water. The moon was swept away by the clouds. Washed off the sky.

Shan't even recognise the rogue.

A naked bulb shed its dim light in the verandah. Burnt-out moths lay in a heap on the floor directly underneath. Krishnachura leaves swished in the wind. The frogs had become silent. Once in a while a cricket sang out. She stretched her hand and picked up a tiny terracotta elephant from her dressing-table. He had bought it for her at a village potter's shop before they left the Sunderbans. He had said jovially, "Here. Keep it as your little Ganapati, your elephant-god. He'll bring you luck!" She had cherished this little gift, even treated it as a kind of totem. She had become superstitious.

Shortly afterwards they had sailed for Bagher Ghat. He had grown a beard again and disguised himself as a coastal fisherman. Somewhere along the waterway, he had stepped ashore and disappeared in the ocean of night. Why, then, had he said that now that Russia had become an ally in the war, there was no need for him to worry? She put the elephant under her pillow and fell asleep again.

Faceless men appeared on the river-bank. Steamers swarmed the Padma, loaded with wedding-parties. A red palanquin arrived, borne by lantern-carrying goblins. They set it down on the gangway.

Jehan Ara stood in front. The ship hooted its siren. Its name, *Passing Show*, shone brightly in liquid darkness. Sailed away. Bibi vanished. The palanquin was empty.

Somebody was weeping non-stop. Louder than the siren of the fast receding *S.S. Passing Show.*

The Bridegroom arrived. Faceless.

She opened her eyes, feeling disconsolate and ill. Outside, the Oriya gardener's little daughter was crying incessantly. Look here, Bibi. I snatched the thug from you quite unwittingly. Cross my heart and hope to die, I hadn't a clue. Not the foggiest. So forgive me and herewith I return him to you... She found herself weeping aloud.

Her next-door neighbour rushed in. "Gosh! It's you, Deepali! I thought it was the gardener's daughter making a racket so early in the morning! What's happened? You all right? Is everything all right at home?"

"Everything is fine, Abani. I just had nightmare after nightmare...like a horror film..." she sniffed, and got up.

Abani stared at her in astonishment. "Deepa," she said after a few moments, "you are going to play a *bhairabi* next month, aren't you?"

"Yes, I am. Why?"

"You look like one already."

Deepali crossed over to the dressing table and looked at herself. Dishevelled hair. Ashen face. Red eyes. Perhaps she had really become a *bhairabi*. An ascetic woman, a medium for Tantric practises, a yogini who dedicated herself to Lord Shiva and lived in dark forests as a figure of boundless mystery. They were going to produce a dance-drama in which she had the role of a lute-strumming *bhairabi*. She was to sit under a wood-apple tree and sing the classical melody called Bangla Bhairav...

"Oh, well," she replied trying to sound casual, "I'm going to be a stage *bhairabi*, so last night I saw a *bhairabi's* dream!" She laughed mirthlessly.

The girl lingered for a while then went back to her room. Deepali started making her bed. She lifted her pillow and saw the humble clay elephant. She took a deep breath, picked it up and threw it out of the window. The little toy fell soundlessly in the tall grass rippling in the fresh, early morning breeze.

19
Monsoon Melody

THE rainy season has a mystique of its own in India. The months of Sawan and Bhadon have been celebrated in art and literature as harbingers of music and romance. "In the fireflies' light," said an ancient poet of Bengal, "she goes out to meet her lover. Willows weep by the stream. Water-hens cry. Deer stand quietly under the trees on a rainy night when the glow-worms light her way..." In north India, young girls drape themselves in rainbow-coloured saris and wear glass bangles the colour of green paddy. Some of the haunting rain-songs they sing were composed by Amir Khusro, Delhi's 14th-century Sufi poet and musician. Monsoon songs are rendered in various modes of the "cloud-attracting" classical melody called Malhar.

Many Malhars were composed by Emperor Mohammed Shah. He had remained absorbed in his music while Nadir Shah arrived with his massive army, sacked Delhi in 1739 and whisked the Peacock Throne away to Iran. After which poor Mohammed Shah composed some doleful ragas.

In a white, trellised balcony, surrounded by *kadam* and plantain leaves and dancing peacocks, the forlon lady awaits her man. He has gone away to distant lands or has been lured away by the *sautan*, the co-wife. The lady pines for him on rainy nights and cloudy days when the papiha-bird's call sounds like *pi-kahan...pi-kahan...pikahan...*Where is he...? Where is he...? Pi, or Piya was the swain, the inamorato.

This mansion, lit up at midnight and resounding with laughter and music, did not look different from the white palaces depicted by long-ago miniaturists. Delicate, very large-eyed women sat around an indoor fountain, playing stringed instruments and little drums. Outside, peacocks slept on the branches of a rose-apple tree. This could have been a 17th century scene, except that it was Arjumand Manzil, Dacca, and the time was August, 1941.

Rom jhom, the clouds rain... Yasmin Majid was singing a Mohammed Shah Malhar. *Rom jhom, the clouds rain...Soom sananananana, the easterly blows. Crickets croon, jhoom jhananananana...the bells on my toes tinkle as I go upstairs. Lightning flashes; I tremble with fear and pine for the ever-merry Mohammed Shah Piya....*

In their compositions, north Indian musicians called themselves Piya...the woman's beloved. Traditionally, a woman always addressed her Piya in her songs and yearned for him. The lyrics depicted women's emotions.

In Sufi imagery the woman was the human soul, the Bride, dying to meet her Bridegroom. In Vaishnava poetry it was Radha, the perfect devotee, calling out to Krishna, the Divine Lover.

In some dark and rainy area of Time, the Merry King Mohammed Shah is still singing his songs, thought Yasmin philosophically, and put down her tamboura, the four-stringed lute. They were shortly to leave for Dinajpur where Jehan Ara's brother, Nayyar, was to wed a girl he had never seen.

My millionaire Babul, I am about to forsake your house. We are the jasmine blossoms of your garden, in great demand in every home. O my worthy Father, why are you sending me so far away? You have given double-storied mansions to my brothers. To me you give a foreign clime! O my wealthy Father, we are the cows of your field, birds of your garden, to be driven away at your will...

Yasmin stopped singing and shook her head. "For the last seven hundred years our women have been singing this song and have meekly accepted the situation."

"You try to change the situation, my dear, when the time comes for you to marry. Right now, can't you sing something cheerful?" asked Shamsa Khatoon.

"This is an Amir Khusro song, sung at every north Indian wedding."

"We are the boys' folk, silly. We are going to bring the girl here. Her people will be sad, we are happy. Give us a joyful ditty..."

Yasmin ignored Shamsa Khatoon's request and broke into another popular north Indian wedding song. "Now, this," she announced like a compere, "was composed by Bahadur Shah I, the last Mughal king..."

"Oh, Bahadur Shah Zafar," remarked Akhtar. She was painting her long nails. "He always wrote very mournful lyrics. Not that I blame the poor fellow."

"*O my Babul, I am about to forsake your home,*" Yasmin began the tragic king's song. "*Four kahars lift my doli. My relatives and friends are left behind. Take charge of your house, O Babul mine, I'm off to my Piya's land...*very mystical song this...," Yasmin added thoughtlessly. "The four *kahars* can be the four pall-bearers. The bride is the human soul on her way to meet her bridegroom."

There was a stunned silence in the hall. The fountain continued to ripple. Akhtar stopped varnishing her nails and stared at Yasmin. "Now I am convinced," she said furiously, "that you are nuts. Imagine talking such nonsense on an auspicious and happy occasion like this. Thoo...thoo..."

"Why?" Yasmin replied calmly. "My father says that true believers ought to remember their impending end seventy times in a day."

"Shut up!"

"And this song is a must at all north Indian weddings."

"North Indians must be potty, too."

"Come on everybody," the major domo cried from the gallery. "We're ready. Where is Bibi?"

"Sleeping!"

"Sleeping? For god's sake, wake her up or we'll miss the boat," exclaimed Shamsa Khatoon.

Akhtar hadn't finished her toe-nails. She said, "Never mind. The old tub has been chartered by Abba."

O, my millionaire Father. We are cows of your garden, birds of your fields. The words had got all mixed up. He was also singing. The glorious Piya. The Sultan of high romance. He was standing near the summer-house. She could not understand the words of his song. There was such a babel of noises floating up from the hall downstairs. Musical instruments. Laughter. Servants shouting. Songs.

"He has come," somebody announced.

She woke up and looked around. There she lay on her four-poster like the lady of the miniature paintings, waiting for her Piya while lightning flashed across the sky, the jasmine bloomed, and the bevy of maidens sang around a rippling fountain. Ugh...by the light of the fireflies she had also gone to meet him on a dark night.

Mala stood near the bed. The ceiling fan moved overhead like an officious old fool.

"Who has come?" she sat up.

"Bibi." Mala switched the bedside lamp." All the invitees. Everybody is ready to leave."

"For what? To go where?" she asked stupidly. Her mind was addled.

"To join Master Nayyar's wedding party and sail to Dinajpur. Get up, quick!"

"Oh." She gathered her long hair into a bun and closed her eyes again. Between my dreams and yours there now lies the path to the Day of Judgement.

"Bibi, hurry up. You are delaying everybody."

Mala rushed out of the room. She was dressed in a new sari given to her by the Begum. She wore silver ornaments. She looked so happy and excited. Blast this social system, he used to say. Blast, blast. Bibi got up, and padded barefoot to the window. This monsoon shall pass, too. "He has come," she had heard in her sleep. She smiled at her foolishness. She is the forsaken woman of Indian rainsongs, waiting for her runaway Piya. He had not returned. Along with his politics had he also been enticed by some ruddy *sautan?* Who knows.

She selected a sari of pink Banaras silk from her wardrobe, and pulled a rope of pink Burmese pearls out of her workbox which contained his snapshot She got ready and went downstairs, smiling.

Here comes Nawabzadi Jehan Ara Begum, the guests whispered to one another in awe.

In the portico she noticed that Najma and Akhtar were not talking to Yasmin. Like Mala, Yasmin was also dressed in her best clothes. A rainbow-coloured sari. Costume jewellery. Bata sandals. How bravely she was trying to face the affluent classes. Jehan Ara felt sick with anger. Yasmin was an extraordinary child, a budding creative artist, bursting with unusual ideas. At this moment she looked very much a part of this uneven, unjust, crazy scene. A typical lower middle class girl, one of the unimportant members of the baronial entourage. Her father, Maulvi Majidullah, the humble cleric, was smiling at everybody. He was to solemnize Nawabzada Nayyarul Zaman's nikah at Dinajpur, to the daughter of another wealthy Zamindar. At this moment he was probably silently praying that his beloved daughter Yasmin also marry a rich young man like Nayyar, and live happily ever after.

Blast. Blast. Blast. Jehan Ara was about to let out a hysterical shriek but she suppressed it with tremendous self-control and got into her motor car.

"Why are you scowling, Bibi? Still groggy with sleep?" Najma asked her placidly.

The peacocks are out, dancing on the green. The Unknown Bridegroom is about to arrive at an Unknown Door.

Listen to the sound of plants growing in the green silence... Yasmin said to herself as she was herded into a motor-lorry along with the less important women of the wedding party.

20
Song of the Seasons

RIVERWAYS are crowded with wedding-boats, for the rains also come as the "season of nuptials" in Bengal. There is water everywhere, which makes the landscape look larger. It is a the time for sowing seeds, of renewal and greenery.

Yellow jute flowers have wilted. Sickles shine in the fields. Cargo ships will carry the "golden fibre" to Chandpur, Madaripur and Narayan Gunj. The money will go to Calcutta and Scotland.

The clouds are passing, farmlands are full of paddy. Sufi songs are being sung in village chowpals. The sound of drums and castanets rises from the temples. Radha-Krishna. Radha-Krishna. Radha-Krishna.

Chandi Das's Radha. Ram Prasad's Kali. Dargahi Faqir's Allah. Allah, O Allah. O Allah...

"The clouds have grown old," the ancient poet had said. "The night has placed her moon-pitcher in the sky's courtyard... Ashwin's hot sun has saddend the water-fowl." The sugar cane crop is ready. The rivers have calmed down. Huts are being repaired. Pavilions and bazaars have been decorated for the annual visit of the goddess Durga.

In the autumn month of Karthik, a pale lotus-moon sails in the clear sky-pond. Ochre dust blows about. Parrots dangle on barley stalks. Fishermen have thrown out their nets in bright moonlight. The notes of their flutes haunt the travellers going away to distant lands. The sky-river flows in space. Passing clouds and white cranes are its sandy banks; stars its hyacinths. The cowherd sleeps on the cool and moist bank of the stream...

The paddy crop is ready. The markets are full of buyers and sellers. Singing competitions are being held in village chowpals.

Rice... Rice... Rice...

"Golden" Bengal grows rice thrice a year and remains hungry.

In early winter-time, betel nut trees are laden with pink nuts. On moonlit Paush nights, the fishermen's nets are filled with a silvery haul. Around the bonfires peasants sing the ballads of ancient warriors. Cottage floors are carpeted with hay. Jackals come out at night. The mustard blooms. Boat races are held.

Monkeys are shivering in the cold, long night of Magh. The dog sits by the oven. Witches have lighted their fires on moonless nights.

Lady Dawn can been seen through the mist. She wears red flowers and puts on a red veil, for she is on her way to her in-laws. The Sun peeps from behind the banyan tree. His face is betel-juice red. He wears the sacred thread and caste-mark on his forehead... Early in the morning, his rays fall on the bullock who lies happily on the crossways, covered with mustard flowers. There is frost on his eyelids. Wrapped in tattered quilts, pilgrims sit in the lanes, chanting Radha-Krishna.

Auburn leaves fall in the woods. Tigers roar under the cool moon of the month of Shishir. Orchids blooms on the hillside. Clay idols of goddess Saraswati have been dried in the sun, for her festival. Mustard is ready to be harvested.

Spring arrives in the month of Phalgun, accompanied by honey-makers, and passes through green bamboo groves where the southerly wind blows.

"Come to the flower-wood at midnight, O Bumblebee! I shall light the lamp of the moon and talk to the dew. Come softly, O Bumblebee, so that your song and my dream are not broken, and the flowers and twigs do not wake up," said the poet in his love song of spring.

Loafer-wind roves from forest to forest. The *palash* is in flower in the honey-month of Chait. Uncle Sun is growing angrier by the hour. He has become red like the parrot's beak. He has dried up the ponds and tanks. Storms have blown thatched roofs away. Masts and sails are broken. Strong gales have denuded the trees of their fruit. The bazaars are full of mangoes, the *jarul* flower is in bloom.

Famine stalks the land. Allah give us rain... Allah give us rain... Allah give us rain... Allah... Allah.

"And then the army of dark clouds began to advance from the Bay of Bengal. The Season covered his body with the pollen of *ketaki* flowers. Instead of skulls he wore a garland of flying cranes. He plaited his hair of dark clouds. He picked up his staff of rainbow and lightning. To scare forlorn women whose men are away, the Season arrived in the garb of a sorcerer. The sky turned into a dark banyan of rain, whose beard touch the earth... The aboriginals have sprinkled blood in the roots of the trees. They are drinking toddy and worshipping Durga of the Forests." So said the poet of ancient Bengal.

The rivers are in flood. Meghna and Brahmaputra. Padma and Madhu Malti. Bhairab and Sib Bansari, Karnaphuli, Surma, Dhaleshwari. On the fifth day of Srabon the snakes are worshipped. Elephants trumpet in deep woods. Serpents have come out. Witch-doctors are in business once again, curing snake-bite with their mantras. People have taken out their umbrellas as they cross delicate bamboo-bridges. The stormy rivers swallow butterfly-canoes. They sweep away entire villages. Trees are uprooted. Cattle and men are drowned in the deluge.

"O, Allah, my luck is bad, the flood took everything away. O, Allah. You made the world but you took back my jute, my paddy, everything from me. How much more am I destined to suffer, Allah? I told her I would sell the jute and bring for her a nose-ring made of gold. But my crop was washed away by rushing waters.

"O, Boatman, how many humans, how may cattle were taken away by the river? Allah...Allah. O, Allah..."

21
Quit India and People's War

Aᴜɢᴜsᴛ, 1942. They could have been a bunch of carefree young people going out on a picnic. Three men and a girl. One of the men carried a heavy cloth bag. They left the carriage outside the gate and came down the weedy garden path. One of them shone the torch around till its light fell on an old man sleeping precariously on the edge of the verandah.

They came closer and inspected him gravely. "Snoring away at 7.30 p.m. Lotus-eater! Sad relic of Zamindar Romesh Chandra's ambrosial times."

"There is a story in our religious lore," said one of the young men, "about the Seven Sleepers of Kahf. When they woke up they found that their coins had become several hundred years old; new currency was in use in the bazaar."

"The Zamindar's granddaughter has also taken to the latest currency. She thinks *we* are the Sleepers."

"Let's leave the bag here and go back," the girl suggested crossly.

"No. We must see the Zamindar's granddaughter. Come along, don't be difficult."

They waded through the tall, wet grass till they reached the courtyard wall and knocked on the door.

After some minutes the kitchen window was opened. Somebody peeped out.

"Good evening, Miss," one of the men said cheerily. The other two whistled a merry tune softly, and waited.

The creaky door was unchained. "At such a time and in such rough weather!" Deepali exclaimed.

"Seems late because of the clouds. May we come in?" asked Mahmoodul Haque.

They followed her to her back verandah and sat down on cane stools.

"We were passing by, so we thought we may as well say

hello to you," Jyoti beamed through his thick, horn-rimmed glasses.

"Nice of you to have come."

"Er... Look." Jyoti picked up the cloth bag. "These are some books I had borrowed from Rehan Ahmad. In case I don't come back, kindly return the lot when you meet him next. With my thanks."

"Where are you going?" Deepali asked.

"Oh, here and there, nowhere in particular. We came to know that your people were away in Faridpur and you would be alone, so we sort of dropped in."

"Speak for yourself, I didn't want to come. I don't like to meet traitors and toadies," Rosie said gruffly.

The men looked embarrassed. Mahmood clapped his hands to kill a mosquito. Jyoti weighed his empty matchbox like a discus-thrower and flung it out. Mushir lighted a cigarette.

"I'm glad you came," Deepali said hollowly. "Khokhu was not well, so Baba left with the younger boys. Some kind of celebration in my aunt's family. I'll go tomorrow morning. As for your remark, Miss Bannerjee, I choose to ignore it."

Rosie raised her voice. "Do you see that room in front, Jyoti-da? Exactly two-and-a-half years ago it was there that this grand lady made me take the oath of loyalty to my country. Little did I know then that she would turn into a British agent."

"I have not turned into a British agent, I am merely following the latest Party directive. We do not approve of the present outbreak of violence against the British. According to the correct analysis of the situation, we ought to help the Allies. It's no longer the imperialists' war, it is the people's struggle against Fascism."

"Oh, yeah?" Rosie scowled.

"At this very moment how valiantly the Russian comrades are fighting back the Nazis," Deepali continued. The wood-apple tree heaved in the strong wind. "Let's go inside. We'll make some tea," she suggested.

"Right. Let's have our final *adda*," Mahmood agreed happily.

"Why final?" Deepali asked. "Can't we remain friends?"

"No tea, I'm in a hurry to get back home. The carriage is waiting outside. My parents will be worried," said Rosie.

They went inside the stuffy drawing room.

Lightning flared as Deepali opened the window. The clouds hung so low she felt she could stretch out her hand and touch them.

"Do you happen to know that Kanaklata Barua was killed yesterday?" Mahmood asked her sombrely. She gasped.

Mushir walked up to the cracked marble-top centre table and began speaking like Melville de Mellow, All India Radio's chief English newscaster. "And here is the latest bulletin:

"CPI Comrade Rehan Ahmed, accompanied by Miss Uma Roy, is dining and wining with British officials at the Imperial Hotel, New Delhi.

"Leftist Urdu poets have joined the British Indian Army as majors and colonels.

"Miss Uma Roy is working on the Cultural Front against Fascism and may soon be awarded the Kaiser-i-Hind Gold Medal, like her esteemed mother.

"CPI intellectuals are writing an article a day for the new English weekly called *People's War*.

"And finally, Barrister Pritish Roy has received his knighthood."

Rosie cut him short. "Let's go. My parents..."

"Goodbye, Deepali," Jyoti said. "It was nice knowing you."

"The currency has changed in the bazaar," added Mushir.

"Which currency? Don't sound so bruised and sarcastic. One can differ in politics," responded Deepali severely.

They turned towards the portrait of Dinesh Chandra Sarkar and saluted it. Before she could finish her sentence they were out of the front door and had vanished in the dark.

Deepali picked up Rehan's books and began closing the doors and windows.

The shower drenched half of Abdul Qadir's tattered bedding and hit his face. He got up muttering angrily, dragged his mat near the wall and went off to sleep again.

22
The Rebel

Rosie dropped her three friends at three different places, then went home. She asked the coachman to wait under the banyan outside the Compound gate. His horses stamped their hooves in the mud and neighed unhappily as Rosie walked down towards Lily Cottage.

She had passed her B.A. in the first division and had joined the university to study for her Master's degree in Economics. Her avid interest in higher learning had assured her father that she had given up her idiotic politics. She would have no time for it—she was so busy. He was proud of her and had forgiven her for what she had done, last year, to the Biswases. He had started looking all over again for a high-caste young Bengali Christian man. This time he would definitely take Rosie into his confidence and get her opinion on the matter. Right now she was absorbed in her postgraduate studies, stayed late at the university library, attended seminars and tutorials, also went to a suburb to teach her student, Yasmin Majid.

Even when she came home late he did not admonish her. He trusted his daughter, despite the fact that the times were changing fast.

In his Sunday sermons he had sorrowfully pointed out the New Immorality. The War had brought it to Calcutta, which had always been a sinful city, anyway. Only now it had become worse. And, alas, it was affecting Dacca as well.

Army contractors and businessmen had appeared on the scene as a brash new class of go-getters. Money seemed to have assumed tremendous importance. Life had become feverish. The War was being fought next-door in Burma. Calcutta had been bombarded, albeit lightly. Japan had shaken the Empire's foundations in the East.

After the Fall of Singapore on February 5, Rev. Bannerjee held a special service in the church, and prayed for divine mercy. The choir sang *The Rock of Ages*. By March the yellow pygmies occupied all of Burma. Refugees poured in, walking all the way from Rangoon and Mandalay. Tents were pitched in the Mission Compound for Anglo-Burman and Burmese Christian evacuees. Rev. and Mrs. Bannerjee looked after the sick and the ailing with utmost tenderness and care.

After the British defeat in Malaya the military hospitals of Bengal overflowed with sick and wounded British and American soldiers. News started coming in about Subhas Chandra Bose and his Indian National Army.

The old warriors of Bengal, the terrorists, got busy once again. The outbreak of violence on August 9 horrified Rev. Bannerjee.

Rosie came home at half-past nine—she had never been so late before. Her parents were waiting patiently at the dinner table. She went to her room, changed her wet clothes and entered the dinning-room, smiling sweetly.

Her mother brought hot food from the kitchen. The Reverend said Grace. Rosie looked at her watch slyly, through half-closed eyes.

Rev. Bannerjee raised his head and began to eat. Rosie played restively with her spoon.

"Eat, child," he said.

"Yes, Papa," she ate a few morsels and rose from the chair.

"Rosie, what is the matter? The whole country is on fire, at the mercy of ruffians, and you come home at ten o'clock. At least take Joseph with you when you go out."

"Yes, Papa. But, see, on the first anniversary of Gurudev's death we are going to have a concert. We held a meeting about it and then, as usual, the *adda* started!"

"*Adda* in such dangerous times! Bullets are flying about, bombs are exploding."

"Yes, Papa," she got up and moved towards the door.

Suddenly it occurred to the old man that the university had closed down because of this so-called Revolution. She was trying to fool him.

"Rosie"

"Yes, Papa."

"Sit down."

She did so.

"Have you once again joined the traitors?"

"No, Papa"

"Rosie," he pleaded. "The government which made us human beings out of savages, which delivered us from fiendish idolatry and showed us the path of Jesus—"

"Oh, no, Papa, not again." Rosie banged the table with her fist and spilled a glassful of water. Her mother quickly scrubbed the table with her napkin, and glared at her.

"Sorry, Mamma. Listen, Papa. Why didn't you go and tell all this to C.F. Andrews, a White man and a much bigger clergyman than yourself?" She smiled triumphantly.

"Quit India, Quit India!" Rev. Bannerjee got up angrily and began pacing the room. "Stupid fools! Asses! If the English leave, we will return to the barbaric dark ages of tyranny and corruption! They saved us."

Rosie looked at her watch again. Her father was addressing her with great emotion. "The Golden Age of India—I'll tell you what it was like. The Hindus threw their infants to the 'sacred' crocodiles and killed their daughters when they were born, and the Muslim thugs strangled wayfarers. Indian culture! How many English missionaries saved widows from funeral pyres? And when they tried to pull them out of the flames there would be riots right there, on the cremation ground. Hindu culture, Hindu culture! In Chitpur's Kali temple they used to offer human sacrifice."

Rosie burst out laughing. "But, Papa, in your civilised Christian Europe thousands of women were burnt at the stake as witches. And when here, in India, Hindus and Muslims were living happily together, Europe mounted the Inquisition!"

"Keep quiet, Rosie," Esther Bannerjee reproved her timidly.

"And listen, dear Papa," Rosie was enjoying herself. "Look what the Christians did to the Jews in Europe and Russia. And when you talk of the untouchables, can a chimney-sweep or a charwoman dine with a lord in England?"

"Do not confuse the issue, Rosie," her father said sternly.

She remembered another point. "You always criticise the despotic rulers of India, especially Siraj-ud-Daulah, who is my hero. Weren't people beheaded right, left and centre in Elizabethan England? Look at the economic and cultural condition of England before they started looting India. Earlier, they didn't even have carpets in their castles."

The parson took off his glasses, wiped them with his handkerchief and looked proudly at his rude, cheeky and brilliant child.

"Many Kulin Brahmins of Bengal," he began, "continue to be polygamous."

"Yes, but, Papa..."

"Stop it, Rosie," Esther beckoned to her to leave the room. She took a deep breath and got up.

"All right, Rosie," her father said morosely. "Turn the British out, then see what happens to all you ultra nationalists. The moment they leave, your beloved Hindus and Muslims will be at one another's throats. There will be a horrible civil war. Bloodbath. You just wait and see. Then you will remember what this ignorant old parson told you." His voice choked.

Rosie was moved. She said gently, "Papa, I was arguing with you just for the fun of it. I mean, I am a star debater of my college, aren't I? Have won so many trophies. I'm a nationalist, but I am certainly against the violence which has broken out with this so-called Quit India Movement."

"You know, my child, that at this time of crisis when Britain is losing on every front—"

"We ought to help in the war effort...of course, of course," she said vehemently. "I agree with you, Papa."

"All right, let your Papa go to bed, Rosie," Esther Bannerjee sighed with relief.

"Yes, Mamma." Rosie went to the door and peeped out. The rain had stopped. "What a pitch dark night, Mamma...Look! Thousands of fireflies, thousands... glimmering in our kitchen garden. Papa..." She turned to her father. "Oh Papa, I was just teasing you." She stood behind his chair and put her arms around his neck. His glasses become misty.

Rosie decided that so much emotion was enough for one evening. She said casually, "The university is closed, of course, but our literary society is holding this concert of Tagore Music."

"Hmm." He sounded satisfied.

"Goodnight, Papa." She bent down and kissed his head. "Goodnight, Mamma."

"God bless you, child," the parents said almost in unison.

Rosie hesitated for a moment, looked at them, then went quickly to her room.

Rev. Bannerjee stood up and began pacing the room again. He touched the flower vase on the sideboard, looked at the framed "God Bless Our Home" and "The Last Supper". He stared at the picture for some moments. Then, as was his wont, he crossed his hands at his back, bent his head, feeling contented and grateful to God, and went towards his own room.

Having finished her chores, Mrs. Bannerjee made two cups of Ovaltine and went into Rosie's room. She wasn't there. Mrs. Bannerjee turned towards the bathroom door and said aloud, "Rosie, the washerman will come in the morning. Take out your..." But she could not complete her sentence. For some unknown reason her jaw fell. Her sixth sense told her that Rosie had run away. There was no light in the bathroom. A strong gust of wind came through the door. She took a few steps and peered in. The door which opened to the kitchen-garden was ajar.

Rosie might have gone out to catch fireflies, she often did that. Mrs. Bannerjee went out and shouted, "Rosie!" There was no response. She came in, took her umbrella and went out again.

Daisy, the servant-girl, would be fast asleep in her quarter. Wading through the slush, Esther Bannerjee went round the entire Mission Compound. Everybody was asleep. Moths were circling around the naked bulb in the portico of the church. All was calm. All was quiet... Rosie... Rosie. Where have you gone? Why have you done this to us? Where have you gone all by yourself, in this dark and dreadful night?

She came back, took off her muddy sandals and went slowly from room to room, putting out the lights.

Her husband dozed in his armchair, waiting for his nightcap. He had dropped his chin to his chest. Instinctively he sat up when he heard her footfall. Without looking up he extended his hand to take the cup of Ovaltine from her.

Esther Giribala went in and said, "Paul, our daughter has run away."

He shook his head, rubbed his eyes and gaped at his wife. He moved his lips but his voice had failed him.

Esther nodded in the affirmative and knelt down by his chair.

Rev. Bannerjee sat very still for a few moments. Then with trembling hands he tried to locate his glasses. She picked up the black steel case from the bedside table. He put his glasses on and took the Bible out from under his pillow. Esther sat down on the stool and covered her head.

"Let us pray," he said quietly.

23
Ganga and Brahmaputra

"I sent you so many letters after I surfaced from Underground, why didn't you write back? I was worried about you. I thought your father had found out about your Sunderbans trip and put you under lock and key, or married you off hastily. Anil informed me that you were all right, so I couldn't understand the reason for your silence."

They ducked to avoid a sudden crash of spray. A steward slept soundly on a wet bench. There was nobody else on the deck.

"It has been almost thirteen months since that July night when I got off the dug-out in Khulna. Kept hiding here and there. In December the Party leaders were released from Deoli jail. I was so busy afterwards... I wouldn't have come to Dacca even now if they hadn't sent me for some urgent work."

Silence.

"Have you joined Rosie's camp?"

The steamer forged ahead on tumultuous waters. He tried to light a cigarette. The matches had become moist. A cold wind blew over the Padma. She shivered.

He offered her his raw-silk *chader*.

"You'll catch cold."

"Never mind. Take it."

She got up to go to her cabin.

"Where are you off to?"

"Abdul Qadir Mian is escorting me back home. He is there, across the net, in the second class cabin."

"Last year you were roaming the Sunderbans, happy as a lark."

"That sort of thing will never happen again. One just cannot go on breaking the rules of middle-class society."

"Oh, I see."

After a long pause she asked, "How did you find me, of all places, on board this particular ship?"

"Easy. Went to your house. Abdul Qadir's wife told me you had gone to Faridpur and would be back on a certain date. I went to Faridpur. It was easy to find out the time of your departure for Narayan Gunj. So here I am!"

"You could have waited in Dacca."

"Couldn't. I'm not very rational about you."

The clouds and the river had become one. The captain stood in front of his cabin, a tall, gaunt man with a long, white beard. A powerful searchlight lit up the river as far as the eye could see.

"How is Rosie?" she asked.

"Don't you know?"

"No idea. Jyoti dropped in to return some books of yours. She had come with him, and Mahmood and Mushir, just before I left for Faridpur."

"Get me a box of matches from somewhere."

"I am no longer your courier for the Underground. Sorry, wrong number. Besides, an Indian male, even when he calls himself a comrade, will always consider himself a woman's lord and master..."

"So you have become a feminist but are upholding middle-class norms at the same time!" he laughed.

A troop-carrier sailed past.

"Very strange," she changed the subject. "When Comrade Randhive declared that this is a People's War, why did the nationalists turn against the Party? Specially Rosie. She is very immature politically. I explained to her what you had written in your letters, that the Communist International had taken on the Nazis and the Fascists with such valour..."

"You were educating your friends through my letters but couldn't drop me a few lines!"

"Very strange," she continued solemnly. "On the 8th of August the Congress parted ways with the CPI, although it was Jawaharlal Nehru himself who had first recognised the danger of Fascism," she finished, as though she had been reading out a newspaper editorial.

"You are quite right. I can see that your political understanding is on the increase!"

After every few minutes a wall of foaming white spray rose, dissolved and spread itself, wave after wave, on the deck. The night was coming to an end.

"Why are you in Dacca? Secret mission?"

"The days of secrecy are over. I have been sent to hold talks with leaders of the Provincial Muslim League."

The ship began to toss and roll. The noise of its engine became louder. "Rosie even called me a traitor. Jyoti, Mahmood, Mushir, all of them were unhappy that I didn't agree with their theory of revolution."

"Why didn't you? You are Dinesh Babu's niece."

"You told me not to."

"When?"

"In your last letter."

They got up and walked down to the searchlight. A river of light was flowing over the Padma.

"How long will you stay in Dacca?"

"A week perhaps. The political situation has become very complex. The All-India Muslim League has turned into a powerful populist movement. It would be foolish to ignore Mr. Jinnah's mass appeal or his demand for Pakistan."

The bearded skipper pricked up his ears and moved a bit closer to hear the conversation.

"Isn't he the ancient spirit of the river?" she whispered.

"Don't romanticise everything. He may be the Ancient Mariner and all that, what interests me right now is that he may be a staunch follower of the Muslim League, hoping that soon these Indian rivers will turn into Pakistani rivers. Geography is changed by human beings."

The shipmaster turned round and was greeted by an enthusiastic "Assalam Aleikum" by the young man. He was now telling his companion, "Bengal is a Muslim majority province and the Muslim masses are waiting for progressive leadership."

"The Nawabs of Bengal are Muslim League leaders, and they are so reactionary," she replied hotly. With his keen river-eye the captain noticed that the heathen woman was very much in love with this upright follower of the Lord Prophet. But it distressed the Ole Man of the River when the fellow declared, "We, the Communists, shall have to move closer to the Muslim League. We shall provide progressive leadership to our masses. I am predicting this tonight…in the month of August, 1942. Remember my words!"

The captain returned to the helm. The pair walked away.

She was thinking furiously: He will go to Dacca and hold talks with Nawab Qamrul Zaman, who else? The Nawab is the top League boss locally. He'll go to Arjumand Manzil and meet Jehan Ara. Who is he? What is the terrible mystery behind it all? She recalled the Gothic romances she used to read as a schoolgirl.

Arjumand Manzil was no Gothic castle, it was quite a normal household. But why didn't Jehan Ara ever mention him? Why didn't he ever talk about her? This man is a double-crosser, a two-timing crook. Sudden tears filled her eyes. She bent over the railing and stared hard at the dark waves. She remembered the nightmare she had had in Santiniketan. On waking up she had decided never to meet him again. She had not answered his letters. Still, he had chased her down the Ganges and here he was, smiling away so cheekily.

Would it be too cheap to ask him about that photograph in Jehan Ara's cupboard? It was dated 1936, this is 1942. A lot of Ganges water has flowed down to the Bay of Bengal. What happened between '36 and '42?

She shuddered and held fast to the cold steel of the railing. The steamer had gathered speed.

"Where are you staying in Dacca?" she asked distantly.

"At Woodland! Sounds incredible! There was a time, not so long ago, when that citadel of bourgeois eminence was out of bounds for the likes of us. We had to smuggle a budding Party sympathiser in, to take a message to Uma Roy. Remember?" He touched her hair playfully. She shook herself away. He laughed heartily. "Now that the CPI has become legal I am staying as Uma's guest in Sir Pritish's own guest-room. When did you last meet her?"

"Haven't had the honour for quite some time."

How timidly she had gone to Woodland that foggy December evening in 1939, carrying a secret message from the unseen demi-god, Rehan Ahmed. Only two-and-a-half years ago. So much had happened since then. I have grown up, she wanted to tell him, can't be fooled by you any longer.

It was no use. The declaration would amuse him no end. She could see the usual mischievous glint in his eye.

"Do come over and meet us someday at Woodland," he was saying with mock gravity.

"I thought Miss Roy was in Delhi."

"Was. Came back to Dacca with me. Her parents are in Calcutta at the moment, so we have the freedom of the house. The comrades assemble there in the evenings. Imagine holding Party meetings at Woodland!"

"You certainly have moved up socially!" Her voice was sharp with irony. "Here, Woodland. In Delhi, Imperial Hotel."

Reddening slightly he replied, "Uma checked in at the Imperial—her parents usually stay there. I was staying with a friend in Old Delhi. Who told you?"

"Divine inspiration."

He looked at her. "You have certainly changed." After a pause he said, "You have become bitter. Why? Give me the reason, please."

She continued to gaze at the misty horizon.

A military flotilla passed by. She walked down along the first-class cabins and spotted a figure in white. Lone White girl in a flowing, milky-white nightgown. Dejected and pensive. Flaxen hair streaming in the wind. Diana of the Uplands.

Perhaps the daughter of a top executive of the Scottish steamship company. Perhaps boyfriend Duncan was also aboard one of those troop ships, and she was worried about him—

"Ahoy there!" he shouted from behind and broke her chain of thought. They returned to their canvas chairs.

"I have to collect those books left by Jyoti. Can I come to Chandrakunj?"

"No, I'll send them to Woodland. I do not wish to meet you ever again."

"And you won't tell me tell me why."

"No."

"That's odd."

Diana of the Uplands went inside her cabin. The steward woke up. The steamship blew its foghorn and passed the bend in the Padma. The path of light became wider as the mist slowly lifted. They leaned over the railing and watched the ocean-like river. The waters of the Morning of Creation.

There was light as far as the eye could see. Light and water. In the beginning there was a void, and darkness was upon the face of the deep. And the Spirit of God moved upon the face of the waters. God said let there be light, and there was light. And God divided light from the darkness.

Allah said Be, and it Became.

Allah also created Adam and Havva, and left them at each other's mercy. He looked at the old skipper standing at the bridge. Noah is taking us to some unknown Ararat, ha...ha.

The searchlight spanned the waters. Light and darkness. Life and death. Happiness and sorrow. Sanity and madness. Thesis and antithesis. The confluence was left behind at Gowalandu Ghat. This river was composed of the almighty currents of the Ganges and the Brahmaputra. Which of its waves was the Ganga and which Brahmaputra?

A question for the mystically inclined! He chuckled.

She sneezed.

"Let's go inside," he suggested peaceably.

"No."

He offered her his mantle again. She took it. He placed his hand over hers on the railing. She didn't remove it.

Shore lights became visible, dimly twinkling in the distance.

Narayan Gunj approached them swiftly. The steamer entered the lights of the busy river-port. Jute stations hummed with activity. The searchlight fell on a 17th century Mughal bridge. It appeared like an enlarged sepia-brown print of a drawing by William Daniel, R.A.

The bridge, the paddy fields, the highway to Dacca, everything was the same as ever, seemed to be serenely waiting to welcome them back. The world had gone awry. Perhaps it was still intact. Happiness existed. It was possible perhaps to find some personal joy in life—after all, there are lots of people in the world who are happy and at peace. Is it a cardinal sin to become selfish in the pursuit of one's personal happiness? she wondered as she wrapped herself in his *chader* of home-spun silk, and inhaled the refreshingly cold, early morning river-wind.

24
Charles Barlow, Bengal Civilian

The Lays of Ind
by Aliph Cheem

For my dear son, Jim,
Camp Mymensingh,
Christmas Day, 1889

CHARLES Barlow placed his glass of whiskey on the tepoy and turned the yellowing pages carefully. A rare book, indeed. Its author, a Capt. Yeldham of the 18th Hussars, wrote under the *nom de plume* of Aliph Cheem. The collection of satirical verse was presented by Charles's grandfather, Sir Edward Barlow, then a divisional commissioner in Bengal, to his son James, who was shortly to become a Bengal Civilian himself. Nearly half a century later, James's son Charles held a similar post in the same province. Three generations of ICS men. It was almost like the caste system, except that to be a senior British administrator in 20th century Bengal was like wearing a crown of thorns.

Charles Barlow smiled sadly as he looked at the hilarious sketches. The characters—English and Indian—used to be part of the fascinating life of a Bengal Civilian fifty years ago.

It was a Sunday morning, and *The Lays of Ind* was a perfect book for relaxation in these troubled times. He glanced through the poems, some of which caught his attention. This one sounded very funny. He started reading:

... The Prince then was one of those natives
Who Britons would be if their faces were whitened,
He eschewed chewing chillies or betel or bhang,
He talked English well with a Telugu twang.
In some little matters he was black to the bone,

He was fond of display, in a barbaric way,
Tho' he played on the flute. As a signor may do't.
He adored the sharp tones of the Indian drums
And the horrible groans that from native pipes come...

Oh, God. Of course it's time we quit India. Charles turned some pages and stopped at *The Deserted Bungalow*:

There stands on the isle of Seringapatam,
By the Cauvery eddying fast,
A bungalow lonely, and tenanted
Only by memories of the past
It has stood as though under a curse or spell,
Untouched since the year Tipoo fell.

Stirring they were those times, forsooth,
And bold the hearts of our men,
Who lunged through water and rocks and slaughter,
And carried the tiger's den—
Heroic the onset and crushing the blow
That was struck near this lonely bungalow.
When siege was over a Colonel dwelt
With his wife and daughters here,
In command of the fort where the bloody sport
Had cost Mysore so dear—

Soon a time may come when this bungalow in Dacca will be tenanted by memories of the past, too.

Tipoo barked outside.

How much we hated our most valiant foe, Tipu. We patterned our peons' liveries after his dress. We named our dogs Tipoo. Even today the Afghan left behind by the Cantwells is called by that name.

Abdul tiptoed in with yesterday's Calcutta newspapers. He placed the bundle on a table and left. They were full of depressing news of War and the Indian insurrection. Newspapers can wait. Charles picked up the book again.

We—and the lesser breeds.

We—he cast a lazy glance at the crowded mantlepiece: Grandpa, Dad, Mamma, Uncle Sydney, Aunts Mabel, Maud and Matilda—and so amazingly true to type, smug, self-righteous, triumphant Victorians. All safely enshrined within their silver frames, while country-made bombs burst around the city of Dacca in August, 1942.

Sir Edward Barlow had been to Hailybury. He really belonged to the age of the Later Mughals, for in Murshidabad he had been trained by John Company's English civilians who had, in their own youth, worked under Nawab Mohammed Reza Khan, Muzzaffer Jung, Naib Nazim of Bengal, Bihar and Orissa.

Sir Edward Barlow, pince-nezed, writing solemnly at his escritoire, Calcutta, 1881. He had contributed to the Imperial Gazetteer of several districts in Bengal. How, after a hard day's work at the Kutchery, he must have sat down in his verandah and shouted, "*Chhokra,* lamp *lao,*" and started writing about the medieval temples and mosques of the region.

Masud always maintained that we distorted Indian history to suit our own designs. We maligned the Muslim kings of India and created the Hindu-Muslim rift. Perhaps we did—to some extent. Victors are at liberty to write the vanquished's annals any way they want—but why did the Hindus and Muslims allow themselves to be hoodwinked by us?

Sir Edward's daughters: Aunt Mabel. On a dark and rainy night she boarded a steamer at Gwalando Ghat and sailed away to the United Provinces in the west, to set up mission schools for girls. At thirty-five she was carried off by cholera and was buried in a lonely churchyard at Seetapur, Oudh.

Are the highly educated young ladies of modern India grateful to selfless women like Mabel Barlow?

He got up and crossed over to the fireplace.

Dad, and Mum. Calcutta, 1904.

Dad had read Botany and Zoology at Balliol College. When he returned to the Mofussil in Bengal, he spent his spare time writing authoritative books on the flora and fauna of his province. He was killed by a Royal Bengal of the

Sunderbans. The villagers of a tehsil in Khulna district had petitioned him to save them from the man-eater. James Barlow took up his gun and simply walked into the woods he knew so well. He never came back.

He gave his precious life so that those semi-primitive wood-cutters could live. That's how we have served these thankless Indians.

Sir Edward died in 1908. He had started his career as a civil servant of the Hon'ble John Company, survived the Mutiny and enjoyed the balmy days of Empire. He had his share of problems too; he solved them well, rounded up many a Muslim guerilla—we call them Wahabi fanatics who hadn't given up the fight even after the Mutiny. All of them were either hanged or sent off to the Andaman Islands.

Sir Edward Barlow had grieved when Lord Mayo was assassinated by Sher Ali, but he lived on to thankfully hear the news of the execution of Bengal's first terrorist, Khudi Ram Basu.

Sir Edward had seen it all. He had been invited to many a nautch party. He had also presided over academic meetings attended by India's first women graduates. He was a member of the senate of Calcutta University, and served on the governing body of the Royal Asiatic Society.

He met most Indians condescendingly, and did consider them an inferior people. The Orientals could never be the White man's equals. He was firmly of the view that ancient Greece's victory over Persia in the Battle of Salamis in 480 B.C. decided Europe's supremacy over Asia for all time.

The distance between the rulers and the ruled was necessary for the security of the Raj. Earlier, many an Englishman had adopted Mughal culture—there would have been no British Raj today had all Englishmen in India gone native. The Mughals did, and look what happened. They lost their empire.

Uncle Sydney. Killed during the March to Qandhar. Had been an adjutant to Field Marshal Earl Robert. Sir Edward

Barlow didn't mourn him much because the boy had died for his Queen and Country.

Aunt Maud. Drab and stern. Bible in hand. Went off to distant Canton to save the souls of heathen Chinamen. The Boxers attacked her Mission Compound and murdered her.

Aunt Matilda. Attractive and vivacious. Jilted by her fiancé, a dashing young officer of the Bengal Lancers, after which she also took to religion. Set up a mission in the Garo Hills. Still lingering in an Old People's Home in Maida Vale, London.

Dad and Mummy, with their three children.

Alice. It's odd. The moment we cross the Suez, we become terribly devout, even zealots. Alice was plain. Still, some drunken box-wallah would have been only too happy to marry into the distinguished Barlow family of Bengal. She preferred to run the mission set up by Aunt Matty in the jungles of Assam.

Saint Peter would certainly get confused welcoming so many evangelist Barlow women.

Wing Commander Richard Barlow, RAF. Bomber pilot. Unmarried. Shot down over the Rhine six months ago.

Charles Barlow, ICS. Married. One son. He started imagining his own obituary in *The Statesman* and *The Times of India*, in case a rebel's home-made bomb got him one of these days—

> Charles Barlow, ICS. Survived by Pamela Barlow, now serving with the WACS somewhere in Britain. One son, Thomas, aged nine, schooling somewhere in Wales.

Get back to the past, Charlie. The past is safe and full of peace.

First Anglo-French War, 1744–48. The Carnatic Wars. The Victory at Plassey The Victory at Masaulipatam The Victory at Buxar First Mysore War Rohilla War First Anglo-Maratha War Second Mysore War Third Mysore War Fourth Mysore War Second Anglo-Burmese War The Santhal Insurrection The Sepoy Mutiny The Battle of Ambala The Gorkha War Bhutan War Second Anglo-Afghan War Third

Anglo-Afghan War Third Anglo-Burmese War The Battles of the North-West Frontier—

Charles moved away from Grandfather Barlow's collection of books about the wars England had fought in India during the last two hundred years.

"Abdul," he shouted irritably.

"Yes, Saheb?"

"Get the bath ready." He stroked his face. At thirty-eight I have become world-weary. At eighty-seven Grandpa, I am told, was hale and hearty, and full of optimism.

Edward, James, Richard, Charles.

He looked around for something else to read, and stopped before Aunt Matty's books.

Kipling, Hunty, Marion Crawford, Col. Meadows Tylor, Flora Annie Steele, Maud Divers. *The Confessions of a Thug. Tara. Tippoo Sultan.* Ah, and here is the stuff Dick, Alice and I read in the nursery! *Little Arthur and His Bearer. Little Arthur and His History. Little Arthur—*

We read these books as sweet little imperialists. We were even allowed sometimes to play with the "nigger" children.

Quit India. Yes, we made some mistakes. A lot, perhaps. Who didn't? The Romans. The Sassanians. The Abbassids. The Ottomans. The Czars. The Mughals. Imperialism is not a lesson in ethics. But we were certainly the most enlightened of them all. Look at the French, and the Dutch and the Belgians.

It had started raining. Through the large window he watched the diamond-like drops of water falling over mango leaves.

We were bewitched by this exotic country.

Masud once said, "Your Beefeaters and Guards do not wear strange uniforms. The display of the Coronation is not barbaric, the headgear and robes of your bishops and popes are not funny at all—! The Orient is exotic, strange and barbaric!"

Both Masud and Ramanathan were great nationalists. They were also keen to join the Indian Civil Service. Masud

Ali is posted somewhere in the Punjab, Ramanathan in the Maratha Country. Both have turned into pucca Brown Sahebs.

We created the most splendid colonial society in history and we succeeded in giving the Indians a massive inferiority complex. No other imperial nation had done that to its subject races. I had Indian friends at Oxford. Came back to India and became a Saheb again. Couldn't be helped. Perhaps unconsciously I do resent Indian intellectuals, and I do like faithful domestic servants and starving peasants. They call me Mai-Baap, "father-mother", and grovel at my feet.

He lit his pipe and sighed.

After his first appointment as joint magistrate, Barisal, he had written to his mother. "The district is an old den of terrorists. Am I going to let these fools destroy Bengal? It is my Bengal, too. My family has lived here for a hundred years. I have wondered, Mummy, about the connection between the Bengali Hindu cult of Kali worship and their current phase of terrorism. The Divine Mother is appeased by blood. Now she desires the blood of Englishmen..."

Tagore is our product, too. He would not have written the way he did if he hadn't read Shelley and Keats.

Hypocrites. Harp on non-violence and wallow in riots and massacres.

However, the question is, the Irish also give us a lot of trouble—we do not have such contempt for them. Because they are white?

I was also secretly happy that I couldn't lay my hands on Comrade Rehan Ahmed or his moll, "Kulsum". I do not like to arrest these brilliant people.

Comrade Rehan Ahmed. Chap from the LSE. The place was crawling with Jews and Commies, they used to say.

Oxbridge-educated Indian nationalists were not enough, we also produced Indian Communists in England, and sent them back to this country to harrrass us.

Masud once said, "We would have acquired modern education even if you hadn't come. Both Raja Ram Mohun Roy and Tipu Sultan admired France!"

He picked up a group photograph. Alice, Richard, Charles, with their Eurasian nanny, Cynthia MacDonnel. A thick-nosed, prim and proper, bitter and disgruntled half-caste woman who hated Indians and called herself a 'Scotch lass'. Her natural father, Angus MacDonnel, had sold his house, Caledonia, to an upcountry Zamindar. "We are the rightful owners of Caledonia. It has gone to the natives and we have become homeless," she used to grumble.

Poor Miss MacDonnel. She was rather pathetic. Must have died by now.

And the Sarkars of Caledonia-Chandrakunj. Suddenly, he remembered with a pang.

He was married in 1931, the year he had Dinesh Chandra Sarkar arrested. He was sorry when young Sarkar's appeal was rejected by the High Court. Tom was born the day Sarkar was hanged in Alipur Jail. Thank God, he was born four hours *before* Dinesh Babu's execution; had he come into the world a few hours later, people in the bazaar would have said that Dinesh Babu has returned as your son to take his revenge.

What a horrible thought, poor Pamela had gasped.

As a matter of fact even I had unconsciously felt relieved that Tom was born four hours *earlier*. Christ! One can go round the bend living in this crazy country.

Pamela, sketching a fisherman in Khulna. As a young Sladie, she used to be starry-eyed about India. Perhaps she still was.

Pamela Barlow was story-book material: she was not exactly a Bright Young Thing of the Roaring Twenties; nor was she cut out to be a Burra Mem Saheb of India. Her parents were pure Bloomsbury. Her father had been a Fabian socialist. She had spent a year at Oxford, studying art history. She had

been Vishwam Ramanathan's girlfriend. Before returning to
Madras, the swarthy, intensely handsome South Indian had
passed her on to Charles.

He often wondered: I am bald and fat and dull, why on
earth did she accept me? Because I belonged to the world's
most prestigious civil service?

She sympathised with nationalist Indians. During their
honeymoon cruise in the Sunderbans, Charles beseeched
her to be careful and not cause him embarrassment on
account of her attitudes and opinions.

In the second year of her marriage Mrs. Barlow
disappeared from their bungalow in Barisal. She was
discovered living as a house-guest of a bachelor Scottish
planter on a green hill in Assam.

Calcutta's glossy society magazines reported that the
charming artist-wife of Charles Barlow recently spent a month
in the tea-gardens, sketching the coolies.

Bengal's European society continued to be agog with
scandals about "the beautiful bohemian from Chelsea". Every
second year she sailed back to Britain and travelled in Europe
with her artist friends. In the summer of 1939 she took her
son Tom with her. She was staying in the Barlow family home
in Baker Street when the war broke out. She joined the
WACS. Occasionally she sent him snapshots of herself in
army uniform, doing her bit for England. Her long silences
distracted him with worry for he was still madly in love with
her. He hated her too, for what she was—a highly intelligent
and talented woman with independent views, who didn't give
a damn for the traditions represented by her stolid husband.

Pamela Barlow was the exact opposite of the Bible-
thumping Barlow maidens. The surviving ones—aunt and
niece, Matilda and Alice—had stopped praying for her as
they knew she was a sure candidate for Gehenna.

According to the grapevine of Dacca Club, Pamela was
now living with an American colonel billeted in the Barlow
home in London.

Charles returned to his armchair and turned to *The Lays of Ind* once again. The past was safe and uncomplicated. It may have been full of heartbreak for those who were living it out as their present; for their successors it could be smoothly retold as a fascinating story. Must go back to old Aliph Cheem and his cheroot-smoking officers.

An affectionate smile played on his lips as he read the advertisements: *The Life of an Indigo Planter. English Etiquette for Indian Gentlemen, Social and Official.*

A Hilarious Account of Baboo English. Life of a Tea Planter in Assam. Behind the Bungalow. Some chapters: *Dog Boys. Mashalchi. Hari the Tailor. Abdul the Bearer.*

Abdul Ghafoor, my loyal bearer. As long as he is alive behind my bungalow, I am safe and secure. As long as my cake-stand continues to be carved like a fez-wearing Turk, the world is safe.

I am feeling groggy.

Rev. Paul Mathew Bannerjee entered the gate. It was one in the afternoon. Abdul Ghafoor stood in the portico talking to the head peon. Saheb has been sitting in the book-room, drinking, Perhaps he has had no news of Mem Saheb and Tom Baba from England, and is worried.

Bannerjee came up, water from his umbrella dripping onto the verandah's shining floor. "Can I see the Saheb?" he asked in a terror-stricken voice. "Where is he?"

"In the library, Padri Saab."

"Please tell him I want to see him urgently. It would be very kind of him if he sees me this instant."

Abdul Ghafoor went in.

Charles opened his eyes.

"Saheb, the Black Padri has come."

"Who?"

"Black Padri, Bannerjee Babu."

"What does he want?"

"He is very upset. Wants to see you."

"Send him in."

Bannerjee entered the room humbly, sola hat in hand.
"Good afternoon, Mr. Barlow."
"Hello, Padri Saab! Is it so late already? Do sit down.
Have a drink. Oh. You don't drink."

The visitor lowered himself into a chair, placed his hat in
his lap and looked around. Charles poured some more
whiskey in his glass, and said, "To Victory!" Rev. Bannerjee
nodded vaguely.

The room looked misty. I am drunk. Hurray! The Black
Padre sits in front. I have always wondered how one can
change one's ancestral religion. How does one peel off one's
skin and wear another? For instance, if I become a Buddhist
or a Mohammedan! Ha, ha. The Black Padre dressed in
black suit and white dog-collar looks so absurd. Comrade
Rehan is absurd. I am absurd. Sir Edward Barlow was absurd.
India, the whole world, all humanity is so ludicrous that one
ought to weep.

"Mr. Barlow."
"Hmm." Black Padre has come to me with some petition.
Must dispense justice, being the Mai-Baap, Father-Mother, of
the natives.

"Mr. Barlow—" the clergyman took out a newspaper-
cutting from his coat pocket and presented it to him. A
headline had been underlined in red pencil.

Charles Barlow read the news and frowned. "I'm sorry,
Reverend," he said after some moments. "I didn't know that
your daughter, too—"
"I had no idea myself. None at all."
"What do you expect me to do?"
"She has been misled. Please save her—somehow." He
spread his hands in a gesture of appeal.

Charles was rattled. He shook himself out of his private
world to resume his duty to the Crown. "Your daughter," he
said gruffly, "is not a child. She knew what she was doing. She
may soon get over this romanticism, or she may go on

making a mess of her life." He spread his own hands. "My sister Alice has wasted the precious years of her life preaching the gospel to Naga tribes. The human mind works in strange ways."

"Mr. Barlow—"

"Mr. Bannerjee. If it is proved that Miss Bannerjee's hand grenade killed somebody, she will be sentenced for life. I can do nothing about it."

Tears welled up in the parson's eyes. Charles looked away. It also indicated that the interview was over. The old man persisted.

"Mr. Barlow, I am told that Miss Barlow is in Pabna these days. Please trunk-call her and ask her to meet Rosie in the prison hospital. She may be badly wounded. Have penned this note to Miss Barlow. If you would kindly send it to her through your courier." He gave a letter to Barlow and regarded him hopefully.

Charles started reading: "Dear Sister-in-Christ, in this darkest hour I turn to you and beseech you to—"

A peon came in with an envelope placed on a silver platter.

Charles read the cablegram. His lips trembled and he was still for a few moments. Then he got up, waved to the peon to leave and in a hollow, but firm, voice addressed the clergyman: "Excuse me, I'll be back in a few minutes."

He took the envelope and left the room.

Bannerjee was bewildered. The letter to Miss Alice Barlow fell on the carpet. He picked it up and waited patiently.

Fifteen minutes. Half an hour. Forty minutes. An hour passed. The parson came out of the study and made for the outhouse. He found the servants gathered near the duck-pond, whispering to each other. Abdul Ghafoor approached him. "What is the matter, Abdul?" He asked.

"Mem Saheb gone. Saheb is in his bedroom. Just now he called me and said, Abdul, Mem Saheb is dead. The cable has come from England. The German-wallah was dropping bombs—what do they call them, Padri Saab—rockets—?"

"V-2 rockets."

"Must be. It hit Saheb's house in London. It was night-time—Mem Saheb was sleeping."

"But they have air-raid sirens. People go down to their basements."

"Saheb only said the bomb destroyed his grandfather's house and killed the Mem Saheb. I do wish, Padri Saab, that Mem Saheb had come back from Vilayat. She had gone to put Tom Baba in school. The war started and she could not return."

"Yes I know, Abdul."

"Tom Baba is safe in his school boarding-house. Matty Miss Saheb is also safe. Mem Saheb had put her in a place where the Sahebs leave their old relatives to die. But look at Allah's will. She is ninety and alive, and Mem Saheb is dead."

"Yes, Abdul."

"Saheb asked me to tell you that he will see you in a few minutes. He has gone to wash his face."

Bannerjee walked back to the side-verandah.

Charles came out.

They sat down in cane-chairs.

A bird cooed incessantly in the mango grove.

After some moments Charles remarked, "We call it the brain-fever bird, don't we?"

Bannerjee admired the Englishman's stiff upper-lip. Still it was his duty to say a few words of comfort.

"Do not grieve, Mr. Barlow. The good lady has gone to a better place."

Charles stared at him. The good lady was probably in bed with that American officer when the bomb fell.

The parson took Charles's long silence to be in the sacred memory of his beloved wife. He began, "God in his infinite mercy—"

The Englishman laughed bitterly. "God in His infinite mercy destroyed my beautiful house and killed my lovely wife."

The remark shocked Rev. Bannerjee. He said grimly, "God is merciful, my son."

"Quite. In His infinite mercy He asked a tiger to devour my kindly father. He got my innocent aunt raped and murdered by the marauding Chinese. He made the Germans shoot down my brother's aeroplane. Right now He is busy killing millions on war fronts all over the world. And that benevolent Lord sends down cyclones and floods and epidemics to your beloved Bengal. He also maims and blinds innocent children."

Bannerjee was accustomed to hearing such blasphemous outbursts by people overtaken by sudden affliction, for they knew not the mysteries of the Divine Plan. Quietly, he took out his pocket Bible in order to read the 23rd Psalm.

Charles Barlow viewed the kindly old man with admiration. How, like a conjurer, he had produced the scripture and was hellbent, as the Americans would say, on consoling the bereaved husband. Well, hellbent is not quite the right word. Charles smiled to himself while the parson put on his rimless glasses.

"Give it to me, Padre Saab. I would like to read the Book of Job," he said.

Rather reluctantly the clergyman handed over the Bible to Charles, who opened the book with woeful glee.

"Here, listen to this, Reverend... *My days are past. My purposes are broken off*—Oh, ho, hear this—*When the Almighty was with me, when my children were about me, when I went out of the gate through the city, when I prepared my seat in the street, the young men saw me and hid themselves and the aged arose and stood up, the princes refrained from talking and held their hands on their mouths*—It seems, Reverend, that old Job was a senior member of the ICS—"

"Mr. Barlow—"

"And listen to this... *I was father to the poor*—Yes, yes, Mai-Baap—*and I broke the jaws of the wicked and plucked the spoils out of his teeth.... Then I said I shall die in my nest and shall multiply my days like the sand*... but my nest has been burnt down by a V-2 rocket, and upon my right hand rise the socialist youth. Terrors are turned upon me, they pursue my soul as the wind, and my welfare passeth away as a cloud...

"Now, Padre Saab, I shall read out to you from the Revelations of St. John. Let me see, here it is. *Babylon is fallen, is fallen that great city because she made all nations drink of the wrath of her fornication...*"

"Please, Mr. Barlow, please."

"And I beheld and heard an angel through the midst of heaven saying with a loud voice, 'Woe, woe to the inhabiters of the earth...woe, woe, woe....' And there was a war in the heavens in which they fought a dragon, and in which my dear brother Dick was blown to pieces....

"Now, Padre Saab, which one is that about the punishment of the great whore sitting on the waters...?" Abruptly, he shouted, "*Koi hai*, Abdul...!"

"Yes, Huzoor—"

"*Tiffin mez par ekdum jaldee...*"

"Yes, Huzoor..."

They went into the dining room. Rev. Bannerjee said Grace. They ate in mournful silence.

The desolate bungalow by the Cauvery. The desolate bungalow by the Padma. Must get some sleep and get ready to face the avalanche of condolences.

He accompanied the parson to the door and said gently, "Reverend, I will trunk-call Alice today. I'll ask her to find out about Rosie and let you know. But I'm sorry, I cannot try to secure her release. The law will take its own course. But, of course, if she tenders a written apology—"

"I don't think she'll do that."

"In that case I can do nothing. Goodbye." He placed his hand on the old man's shoulder.

"God bless you, Mr. Barlow."

Rev. Bannerjee picked up his umbrella from the rack. His feet had become leaden. Now he knew that Rosie was perhaps destined to spend the next fourteen years in jail.

With his head bent, he almost crawled out of the gate, as though he were accompanying a hearse. He stopped by the roadside and looked up at the sky. It had not rained for some hours. Where shall I go now? He took a few steps, stopped and started trudging again...

25
Comrade Rehan Ahmed

THAT Sunday morning, when Charles Barlow went into his study to peruse *The Lays of Ind,* not far from his house Miss Uma Roy was having a late breakfast in Woodland. Karim Khan had brought in the newspapers which arrived by the latest train and steamer from Calcutta. Uma scanned the headlines. The Quit India Movement had snowballed. Both the British-owned and edited *Statesman,* and nationalist *Amrita Bazar Patrika* were full of gory news.

The guest-room door opened in the side-verandah where the breakfast table was laid for two. Rehan had just finished shaving. He sauntered out, wiping his face with a monogrammed towel. She pushed the *Patrika* towards him as he sat down.

One of the smaller headlines drew his attention. He began to read aloud: "Sensational arrest. Miss Rosie Bannerjee, daughter of an up-country parson, and Miss Sandhya Ghosh—"

Karim Khan appeared with the silver teapot.

"Have your tea first," Uma urged.

"Tea can wait," he said irritably. "Do you realize, Uma, that both Jyoti and Mahmood have got themselves killed?"

"How?" she gasped.

"At Isherdee. They were attacking the police station. Rosie was badly wounded, it says here. For all you know, she may be fatally wounded."

"Poor girl."

"Mahmood and Jyoti and Mushir, all of them."

Oh Jyoti, Jyoti. He came to Chandrakunj to return my books. He knew he was going to die. All of them knew. It was like a suicide squad.

For a few minutes he sat very still.

"Socialist Front, indeed," he muttered. "Only the other day Jyoti had argued with me. He said: 'Aruna-di, J.P., Lohia. All of them are so bravely directing the revolution from Underground, while you, an old revolutionary, have become a renegade.'"

"Don't grieve, Rehan. Only a year ago you could have gone like this. Your tea is getting cold."

"Uma, how can you be so cold-blooded?" he said in a shocked voice.

"Sorry! Look, you have been a gypsy for so long. For the first time in your life you've found a decent place to live in and good food to eat. So look after your health, at least while you are my guest."

Little does she know! he thought angrily. It would embarrass her if I told her about the kind of luxuries I gave up to become a gypsy. He dried his eyes and said, "Sorry, Uma, I am very upset."

"Now eat properly. You have to be out all day again to meet your Muslim League leaders. The very next day after your arrival you dashed off to Faridpur." She buttered the toast for him, sprinkled salt and pepper over the omelette and placed a fork in his hand like a nanny.

"That's a good boy," she coaxed.

He bent his head over the plate and began to eat.

"How was your father?"

"Who?"

"Your father. You went to your village in Faridpur to see your people, didn't you? That's what you told me when you left."

"My father? Yes, yes. He is fine, thank you." He swallowed a morsel and picked up the newspaper again. She grabbed it from his hand.

"No, finish your breakfast first. You got here very late last night. The Party office is working overtime?"

"Last night. Oh, last night I had gone to see Deepali home. Escorted her from Naryan Gunj."

"Deepali?"

"Yes. Have you forgotten her already? Deepali Sarkar."

"I didn't know that you had kept up with her."

"It wasn't such a world-shaking matter that I should have informed you. In fact, she, too, sailed back from Faridpur yesterday. I happened to meet her on board the steamer. Shall I tell you the name of the steamer? It is called *Lorna Doone*."

"Karim Khan," Uma yelled, "I tell you every day not to give me half-boiled eggs."

"Uma, the heavens won't fall. Get another egg."

"You don't know servants. These people shirk work in Mummy's absence."

"Come on, Uma," Rehan said, laughing. "If a Congress Socialist overheard you, he would say—This is how the Communists shout at their domestic staff!"

"Shut up."

"You are becoming a battle-axe. Watch out." He began to eat his omelette.

Caesar arrived, lumbering up the stairs, and lay down in a heap at his mistress's feet. She eyed him with disdain.

The bearer brought a hard-boiled egg. Rehan winked at him on the sly. The old man suppressed his smile and posted himself near the door.

Rehan waited for her to cool down and said, "By the way, Uma, I wanted to tell you something."

"Karim Khan. Ask the washerman if he has ironed my saris."

The bearer got the hint and left.

"What is it?" she asked.

"I am going to marry Deepali."

Uma was flabbergasted. She took off her glasses and blinked at him.

"Why, Uma? What's the matter?"

"We are old friends. Why did you keep this a secret?"

Women! He reddened and said gravely, "This is something terribly personal. Entirely my own business. I also believe that a woman can never be truly impartial about another woman."

"So this is what you think about me—"

"Come on, don't be such a martyr. I'm sorry if you feel hurt. But you'll appreciate that I have never, but never, discussed anything personal with you or with anyone else. I am a very private sort of person."

There was a short silence after which Uma said, "Well, I like her, too. You forget that you met her through me."

"Not true. I met her entirely on my own, when I jumped into the Chandrakunj jungle, disguised as a wandering minstrel. And, lo and behold, I fell for her like a—like a—"

"Grow up, Ronu, grow up!"

"Uma! Eat your hard-boiled eggs. You took the news of Mahmood and Jyoti's deaths so coolly and now look at yourself!"

Uma hardened her face and began to tap the egg with a tiny silver spoon.

"Sorry. Perhaps I should have told you much earlier about Deepali, but they were abnormal times. It's quite a job carrying on an underground love affair. And then, for some reason, that stupid girl had more or less given me up."

Uma remained silent.

"Look," he said earnestly. "I think the world of you. I can't go often to my village to meet my father and sister. I have lost my mother, I don't meet my relatives in Dacca. So you have become a kind of substitute family for me. I hate being sentimental, but you know what I mean."

Uma gulped. Her eyes became moist. Dreading an emotional outburst, he got up and fetched his packet of Players Navy Cut from the guest-room.

Fortified with a cigarette, he said cheerfully, "Now, let's have a cuppa, eh?"

She lifted the tea-cosy in slow motion.

"Good old Uma!"

Can't blame her really, if she has become slightly possessive, spinsters do latch on emotionally to a chap like me. I must get out of this unhappy situation. Tactfully, without hurting the lonely woman. He started thinking of possible strategies, when she shot a pertinent question at him.

"Dr. Sarkar is an orthodox man. Do you think he would let her marry you? And will both of you be able to live on the meagre allowance of a Party wholetimer?"

"I should think so, Mrs. Grundy. Don't wholetimers get married? Their wives work, too. Deepali is a qualified musician."

"So she will sing for your supper! And I am not Mrs. Grundy, I am merely being a realist."

"I have met Dr. Sarkar a number of times, and as far as I can gather, he is not anti-Muslim. Like the anti-Semitism of Europe, anti-Muslimism can be very subtle in Bengal. Still, I didn't discern it in the good doctor. Anyway, we will just go to the commune in Calcutta. Deepali is twenty-one."

"I hope you don't land yourself in trouble."

"It is not going to be the first Hindu-Muslim marriage in India, for goodness' sake! All right, you do this: Go to Chandrakunj and tell her old man what a good boy I am. Deepali told me that he was quite impressed by you when you went to Chandrakunj for the first time. Now you find out his real views."

"I know the real views of the bhadralok. And anyway, no Indian father, however broad-minded he may be, happily allows his daughter to marry outside his community."

"Even your Anglicised daddy?"

"Who's talking about my dad?"

"Why?" he chuckled. "Suppose you ever wish to marry a Hottentot, wouldn't Sir Pritish allow you to? He is what I would call a 19th century Liberal Englishman."

"Who is talking about my marriage?"

"Uma, don't blush! Tell me, have you any damn fool in view? Let me know. I'll plead his case before Sir Pritish, you recommend me to Dr. Sarkar. It's a deal." He shook her hand vigorously.

"Don't behave like a street urchin! I think you're crazy."

"Beg to report, Ma'am, I am a nut."

It had started drizzling. The garden looked fresh and intensely green. There was a brief silence as Rehan puffed at his cigarette.

"You seem to have completely forgotten that poor cousin of yours," Uma said archly. He was taken by surprise.

"Which cousin?" he asked, frowning.

"Your former fiancée. You once told me vaguely in London, remember? You said you had a lovely girl, a cousin, waiting for you back home."

"Oh, that was so long ago."

"Where is she now? Still waiting for you?"

"Uma, you can be shamelessly nosey."

"Since you have asked me to recommend you to Dr. Sarkar, I must know. Have you told Deepali about the aforesaid cousin?"

"No, there was no need. And there is nothing much to tell. An uncle of mine wanted me to marry his daughter, with certain conditions, which I refused to accept. That was all, and it happened before I met Deepali Sarkar."

"And the poor girl is vegetating in your village!"

"In my village?" he repeated, surprised. "No. She lives right here, in Ramna. And now that you have reminded me of her, it occurs to me that the situation can be pretty awkward, because she is a friend of Deepali's. Why didn't I ever think of it before? Good Lord!" He stood up and banged his fist on the breakfast table. "Now I know why Deepali was so cross with me! For full one year. She must have come to know."

"She didn't tell you yesterday?"

"No. That's very odd. Women's minds work rather strangely, don't they? Now I'm in a real soup. Uma, dear Uma, I am up to my ears in woman trouble."

Uma looked much relieved. "Who is the girl, anyway?" she asked sweetly.

"The girl—which girl—? Oh, the cousin. You must know her, too. You may even have taught her in college."

"What's her name?"

"Jehan Ara Chowdhry."

Uma took off her glasses, rubbed her eyes and gazed at him incredulously, as though he had acquired a totally different identity. "You!" she exclaimed, "You are Nawab Qamrul Zaman Chowdhry's nephew?"

Rehan studied her for a few seconds then said, "Yes, Ma'am! But this is the second time in one morning that your reaction has baffled me. This discovery puts riff-raff like me in your class!"

She chose to ignore his sarcastic remark, put on her glasses and shook her head. "It is a morning of revelations!"

"Like hell."

"Jehan Ara is your first cousin?"

"Second."

"How are you related to the Nawab?"

"Listen," he said in exasperation, "I don't consider my Arjumand Manzil connection to be that important. Forget it."

"No," she said flatly, "it's important. I must know in detail, for Deepali's sake.

"Don't bring Deepali into it. *You* are dying of curiosity!"

"Tell me from the beginning." She settled back to listen.

"From the beginning? From the 16th century, period of the Mughals—or earlier, the medieval Sultans of Bengal?"

"Don't tease me."

"All right." He wiped his brow. "I'll be brief. My maternal grandfather, Nawabzada Fakhrul Zaman, was the younger brother of the late Nawab Sir Nurul Zaman Chowdhry."

A vapoury haze floated across the rose garden. The air was full of rain-washed fragrances.

"Fakhrul Zaman Chowdhry! I have heard of him. Sounds almost fictitious."

"Oh, he was the stuff legends are made of."

"Now I know why you behave the way you do."

"I beg you pardon?"

"Got your streak of adventurous romance from him. Minus his decadence, I hope."

"Thank you!"

"How much money this man must have wasted! I have heard that the fish in his tank wore gold nose-rings."

"It was a fair division of labour, Uma. The Zamindars wasted money and men like your Papa made their pile fighting their court cases. When my grandfather went to England, he took his cook, his hookah-bearer, his butcher and his sitarist along. In London the Ustad played the morning melody, Bhairavi, in order to wake him up. The butcher cut kosher animals in the prescribed manner.

"Grandfather was larger-than-life. We do not have men like him anymore. He had a Hindu friend, a small Zamindar. This man's wife had become his 'rakhi sister'. The chap died and the widow didn't have enough money to bring off the marriage of her daughter with the son of a big rajah.

"The engagement could have been broken. Fakhrul Zaman heard about the crisis. He was the younger son, but had his own lands, gifted by a childless aunt. Promptly he sold off one of his villages called Hirapur and bought a Rolls."

"I am told the wags called it Hirapur-on-Wheels," Uma interrupted.

"Right. And he drove straight to the friend's place and asked his adopted sister to invite the baraat, and as 'maternal uncle' he presented the Rolls to the bride.

"He was a connoisseur of Hindustani classical music and renowned Ustads were on his payroll. He also patronised the top-notch Jewish and Eurasian courtesans of Calcutta, and the classy demi-mondaines of Lucknow.

"He wrote and staged plays in Bengali and Urdu and invested in a theatrical company in Calcutta. Its manager absconded with the funds. That more or less ruined him.

"He died in 1908 at the age of forty-seven and left behind colossal debts, a wife and a sixteen year-old daughter, Maliha. The widow was claimed by an epidemic. The debts were paid off by selling the Fakhrul estate. Sir Nurul helped himself to the remaining assets of his late brother. Now only Maliha remained to be disposed off. Thereby hangs a tale—

"In her infancy the girl had been betrothed to her cousin, Qamrul Zaman. Now an impoverished and orphaned Maliha made no sense. So Lady Nurul Zaman found the frail daughter of a very rich landlord of Kushtia district for her only son and heir. The bride, Anwari Begum, brought jute plantations in her dowry."

Rehan began playing with his matchsticks. After a while he resumed: "A poor student of theology had come from the interior to study at a Dacca seminary. Once he visited Arjumand Manzil to invite Sir Nurul Zaman to a religious function. The old Tartar liked the country lad and engaged him as a tutor in Arabic for his son, Qamrul Zaman.

"After a year or so he decided to give his niece Maliha in marriage to this humble maulvi."

"Oh—"

"I think there was a reason behind this sudden decision. You see, Qamrul Zaman had been unhappily married and very much in love with his cousin and former fiancée, Maliha. They were living under the same ornate roof. I have been told that Maliha avoided meeting her cousin, but the bride, Anwari Begum, started throwing tantrums. To avoid further trouble Sir Nurul thought it best to get rid of poor Maliha at the earliest."

"Why? Qamrul Zaman could also take Maliha as his second wife."

"He could, but didn't. Most Muslims do not have two wives, leave alone four, as is generally believed."

"The Nawabs and Rajahs have regular harems!"

"Qamrul Zaman was not one of them. Even Maliha's father was not a bigamist."

"You have a sneaking admiration for your feudal relatives!"

"Qamrul Zaman is a very fine man and so was his uncle. Don't you admire your capitalist father as a human being? Or aren't you fond of him?"

"Please get back to the story."

"This poor maulvi was a Syed, a descendant of the Prophet. To marry a Syed was considered an honour. In earlier times many sultans and kings gave their daughters in marriage to Syed dervishes and scholars. The Chowdhrys of Arjumand Manzil were no sultans. They declared that they were merely following an old tradition, and this particular Syed was also an upright, highly moral young man.

"Maulvi Burhan Ahmed belonged to a village called Shonapur in Faridpur, which happened to be the same district where the Zaman Chowdhrys had their vast estate.

"The bride's uncle had cheated her out of her inheritance. As compensation he gave her a considerable dowry from her own father's money. For the poor farmers of Shonapur it was more dazzling than a royal treasure. My mother used to tell me that when the coolies were loading heavy trunks onto motor lorries to go to Narayan Gunj, the bridegroom raised his hand and yelled: 'Stop! I do not wish to be called Nawab Nurul Zaman's poor relative who fattened himself on the riches brought by his wife.'

"He refused to accept her jewellery as well. Said to his wife: 'Are you going to wear all this and make the poor village women of Shonapur feel small?' So all her ornaments were also left behind.

"The south wing of Arjumand Manzil as well as the playhouse had been built by Nawabzada Fakhrul Zaman. According to Muslim Personal Law, Maliha Begum had inherited them. She had been born and brought up in utmost luxury. Without a word of protest she left all that behind and sailed away to lowly Shonapur.

"Her husband had been trained in the Dacca seminary as a preacher, so he began teaching in the village mosque-school and led the daily congregational prayers. The two jobs did not give him much. His students sometimes paid him in kind—a little jaggery, a packet or two of tea. Some fish or salt, or kerosene oil. And he grew paddy in the few acres of land which he owned."

"That sounds pretty grim."

"You have been close to the Party. Have you no idea how our peasants live?"

"How did your mother adjust to a poor farmer's household?"

"Being a modern girl, you can never understand India's Muslim and Hindu women of an earlier generation. They had learnt to take their hardships for granted. And for all of them religion was a great solace."

"Poor and middle-class women, yes. But aristocrats like your mother?"

"My dear Uma, wealth and status sometimes make no difference to the reality of misfortune. Suffering is a great leveller. Rich or poor, all of them had been taught to be patient and dutiful and obey their male relatives."

"Had our women become morons and puppets?"

"They were no morons. Many of them were virtual dictators within their joint families. But in the western Church too, the bride takes a vow to obey her husband. Englishwomen had no property rights till—"

"Oh, I know all that. Please get back to the story."

"Well, therefore my Ammi never criticised her late father whose way of living had indirectly been the cause of her distress. She didn't even complain about her unjust uncle. She thought it was all predestined, part of her fate."

Uma took a deep breath. "Strange! You never told me all this before!"

"There was no need. My personal life is entirely my own. Why should anybody be interested in it?"

"I am. Don't you consider me your well-wisher?"

He recalled how, in his digs at Earl's Court, he had received a cable from home informing him of the death of his beloved mother. He had been ill and the news had made him worse. Uma used to come all the way from her own digs and look after him till he got well. She had cooked for him, taken his clothes to the laundry, given him his medicine. Only his mother had cared for him with such selfless devotion. He was grateful to Uma. She had always been a friend in need.

"Was your Ammi happy?" she asked.

He smiled sadly. "I remember, I was a small boy. On a dark night I did my school work by lantern-light in the thatched verandah of our bamboo hut. All of a sudden I heard voices. Inside, in the kitchen, my mother was crying softly and Father was shouting at her. I adored my mother and was very upset.

"I peeped in through a little hole in the reed-wall. Mother had worked hard all day and broke down due to sheer fatigue, and also probably because of her general unhappiness. She crouched by the mud-oven and wept. My father stood in the door and spoke gravely as though he was delivering his Friday sermon from the pulpit.

"He declaimed: 'Maliha Bibi, the second day of our marriage I told you that now you ought to forget that you are the daughter of the late Nawabzada Fakhrul Zaman and the niece of Nawab Sir Nurul Zaman Chowdhry. And from now on you must always bear in mind that...' He raised his forefinger '... you are now the wife of a poor Syed, and a daughter-in-law of the House of the Lord Prophet. And you must remember, Maliha Bibi, that the Blessed Fatima, peace be upon her, used to grind corn on a humble grindstone as the wife of Ali, the Fountainhead of Mysticism and the Fourth Caliph of Islam. And the daughter of the Sassanian Emperor of Iran used to often starve after she was married to Hussain.

" 'You are not fit enough to be even the dust on their holy feet. Do penance for your lack of patience, and keep fearing God. He is forgiving, merciful.'

"Abba repeated the benediction whenever he uttered the words 'Lord Prophet', and stroked his face piously. His beard was waving in the strong wind which came in through the open door. Despite the gravity of the situation I couldn't help smiling, for Abba looked so funny. I returned to my reed mat. Mother wiped her tears and resumed her chores. Abba went out.

"Afterwards, I remember, Mother never complained to him. In dutiful silence she continued to serve her husband and her in-laws. She was really proud of the fact that she was the wife of a venerable Syed.

"She said her ritual *namaz* five times a day, fasted during the month of Ramzan, and for me she offered all manner of special prayers at the saints' shrines." Rehan's voice choked as he looked away.

"Who were those people?"

"Who—?"

"Whose life of toil and hardship your father cited as a shining example?"

"Oh—Fatima, daughter of Prophet Mohammed, and Princess Sheher Bano, wife of his grandson, Hussain. Forget it, Uma. How can you be concerned with them? Forget about my mother's story, too." He got up and began pacing the floor.

"Once I told my father about communism. He lectured me on Hazrat Abu-Zar Ghafari, an early Muslim of the Prophet's time, who according to Abba, was the world's first communist. Then he held forth on the socialism of the Prophet and of the first Four Caliphs of Islam..."

"Oh. Rev. Bannerjee would tell you that Jesus and his disciples were history's first communists. That's how people become woolly-headed."

"I am not woolly-headed."

"Who's talking about you? Come back to the main point of your epic."

"Good Lord!" He sank down in the chair again. "All right. I was about twelve when my Senior Grandpa Nurul Zaman passed away. I remember him well. A real old-world Pasha. In his formal robes he seemed to have come straight out of the time of the Nawab-Nazims of Bengal."

"I have seen his life-size portrait in Arjumand Manzil."

"His son and successor Qamrul Zaman was my mother's first cousin, so I called him Uncle Qamrul. When I stood first in my middle school exam in Faridpur district, he persuaded my parents to send me to Dacca. My father agreed when Uncle Qamrul assured him that my Ammi's money was still safe in the bank and would be spent on my education. Despite this, my father sent twenty rupees a month by money-order. Uncle received it with a smile and deposited it in the post office account he had opened for me. I stayed in Arjumand Manzil where, in fact, I was being brought up as a sort of adopted son of Qamrul Zaman Chowdhry. His own son and heir, Nayyar, was a bit of an ass and naturally his father was sorely disappointed in him.

"Uncle Qamrul began planning for my future. Barrister-at-Law. A member of the ICS. A director in his jute mill. And the husband of his favourite daughter, Jehan Ara.

"She was about five or six years younger than me. I was very fond of her. When I learned about her father's intentions about us, the idea pleased me no end. But I was dead against government service, and had decided that after my M.A., I would either teach in some university or work as a journalist. I would have my own little house in which Jehan Ara and I would live happily ever after.

"Uncle Qamrul did love me dearly," Rehan continued thoughtfully. "Apart from the fact that I was so promising and so on, there was another reason why he was fond of me. His parents, specially his mother, had been enormously unjust to helpless Maliha. Uncle Qamrul wished to compensate by making me his son-in-law. Also—"

Uma had been listening with rapt attention. "Yes, also, also what"? she asked eagerly.

Rehan raised his eyes. "Uncle Qamrul had been very much in love with Maliha Begum. But as I told you, his mother had foisted this hysterical heiress from Kushita on him."

"And your mother liked him, too?"

"She did. But to her last breath she remained utterly devoted to her husband and served him as her lord and master."

"Bengali woman!"

"Yes, Indian woman!"

"Did she ever come to Arjumand Manzil?"

"Once in a while, to attend some family celebration. When a married daughter visits her parental home, she is loaded with presents. Uncle Qamrul went to town giving her the royal treatment. She left all the costly gifts behind, because Abba had ordered her never to accept a single penny from her wealthy family. She obeyed him."

"She must have been a great woman."

"She was."

The rain had let up. Rehan looked at his watch and tried to finish the narration.

"Your mother had a lot of ornaments which she left behind?" asked Uma with the curiosity of a typical middle-class Indian woman.

He was surprised once again. "Probably, I never saw them. They were kept in a bank locker by Sir Nurul for my sister, Rabia. Ammi's share of the family jewels had been apportioned by her aunt, Lady Zaman.

"When Uncle Qamrul wanted to send me to London, my mother decided to sell her jewellery in order to finance my education abroad.

"Uncle Qamrul told her: 'You save your ornaments for Rabia, I am sending Ronu to England on my own. Tell Maulvi Saheb that Ronu has got a government scholarship.'

" 'I will never lie to my husband,' she replied fiercely. So he told my innocent father some cock-and-bull story which satisfied him, and I left for England in 1933.

"When I came back four years later, the entire Shonapur village turned up at the jetty to welcome me. We went straight to the mosque where Abba offered his prayers of thanksgiving. Mother had been waiting for me most eagerly, but she passed away a year earlier. From the mosque we went to the adjoining cemetery. The next day, a music party was held in the village chowpal. Local bards composed songs in my honour. I had become a celebrity, the first "England-returned" young man of the area. When I came back to Dacca (you were still in London), I was told that the wedding date had been fixed. My Uncle Qamrul called me to his study and said that after the marriage, I should start looking after his jute business. He sat behind a heap of files and ledgers pertaining to his estate, and jute and tea plantations. He added that since I was now over-age for the ICS he would get me nominated to the Provincial Civil Service. A suite of rooms on the upper floor had been re-decorated for me and Jehan Ara. Everything had already been decided.

"I told him simply that I had become a member of the Communist Party of India. He was thunderstruck."

"I don't blame him," said Uma wryly.

"I was sorry to give him such a massive shock. Explained to him as gently as I could, that I had no intention of becoming either a deputy magistrate or the manager of his jute mill.

"Nor will I stay in Arjumand Manzil as your resident son-in-law. Jehan Ara will live in Shonapur. After all, I reminded him, your cousin had also been sent from here to begin her new life in a reed hut in Shonapur.

"Uncle Qamrul looked stupefied. He didn't seem to grasp what I was saying. After a few minutes he began to tremble with rage, but remained speechless. I showed him my Party card and tried to explain again why I had chosen to become a Communist worker. For the first time in my life I saw him explode.

"He was transformed into his father, the late Sir Nurul. He screamed at the top of his voice: 'You ungrateful wretch! Scum. You blithering idiot! You son of a dumb peasant, you offspring of an arrogant, self-righteous mullah! I made you an economist. You would have been ploughing your little plot of land, you would have been carrying bundles of paddy on your bare back. You would have become a half-baked mullah teaching village brats in your mosque-school. You luckless rascal!'

" 'I'll plough my little piece of land even now, dear Uncle, and I'll carry bundles of paddy on my back. I'll also teach, though not in a mosque-school,' I answered gently.

"He continued to yell. And it occurred to me that forty years ago, his Uncle Fakhrul used to write similar melodramas depicting the traumatic social and political changes which were taking place in India those days. The blood-and thunder plays were staged in his own theatre. I am told one was an opera about a 'throne of justice' in which he re-interpreted a mythological tale in modern terms. I have this feeling that poor Grandfather was vastly misunderstood. He probably had some kind of social consciousness, but couldn't quite express it fully and remained bogged down in his luxuries.

"Now, in the Arjumand Manzil of December 1937, the melodrama continued for three days and three nights. My uncle coaxed and cajoled, cried, pleaded. He reminded me that his prestige, the family honour, even his daughter's life were at stake.

" 'You would let your daughter die of tuberculosis, but you won't let her marry a Communist,' I retorted.

" 'Atheist! Anarchist! You are going to waste the best years of your life in prison. You will be beaten up, tortured, languish underground. They may even put a price on your head. If you don't die you will run from place to place, hunted by the police. What do you think will happen to my daughter then?'

"When he was saying all this in an emotion-charged voice I did feel a surge of filial love for him. I was sorry. 'She has known nothing but comfort and security. Would she be able to share such a dangerous life with you?' he asked me, not unreasonably.

"The argument went on. I was supposed to be marrying Jehan Ara soon, therefore, according to convention, she was now living in her 'pre-wedding seclusion', and could not meet me. Her mother had an attack of neuralgia. The son

Nayyar began avoiding me. The wedding was cancelled. Arjumand Manzil was plunged into sorrow and silence.

"Uncle Qamrul managed the whole thing in great secrecy. Till that time he had mentioned the wedding plans only to his immediate family and to my parents, because in zamindari society marriage negotiations are almost like statecraft. Sometimes the relatives, hangers-on, go-betweens and sycophants can create complications.

"Jehan Ara was an introvert. She had also been told to keep the engagement a secret, so she never mentioned anything about me to her college friends. That's why Deepali didn't even know that I was Bibi's cousin.

"I was staying in my old room at Arjumand Manzil. When I thought of Jehan Ara my heart sank. On the fourth evening I told her father my final decision: I will not give up my political life and will marry his daughter on my own terms. He said: 'Fair enough. From tonight the doors of Arjumand Manzil are closed to you forever.' Then he broke down and wept. After a few minutes—my Uncle Qamrul is very clever—he tried emotional blackmail. No. It was not emotional blackmail, though at that time I thought he was play-acting. In the arrogance of youth we tend to overlook the genuine feelings of our elders. Uncle Qamrul said, 'Maliha is dead, you are her son. You have done this to me.' He got up from his armchair with a little difficulty and left the room.

"I had not yet got over my grief for Ammi. When I heard those words I had trouble suppressing my own tears. I went to my room and began packing. I called Najma and said to her: 'Tell your sister to meet me tonight, after everybody goes to bed. Be very careful. In the summer house. I must see her.'

"Najma's face lit up with hope. She ran upstairs.

"Late at night, the girl tiptoed in and said, 'Come along'."

"I liked Jehan Ara immensely. I had been writing to her occasionally from London, kept her informed about my activities. No, I was not madly in love with her, couldn't be.

We had been more or less brought up together. In our society such alliances are often taken for granted, and mostly prove quite successful. For me, Bibi had always spelt peace and emotional security. I had always thought that whenever I returned home, from wherever, I would find her waiting for me like a shady tree, or a well full of cool, sweet water. When I met her after those four exciting years in the West, I found her to be the same, serene and graceful as ever. Now she stood there in the dark and cold summer-house, a picture of love and devotion. I was shaken.

"I made my decision on the spot. There was no time to lose because we could be discovered any moment. Her younger sister Najma and her personal maid, Mala, stood at a little distance to warn us if someone happened to come by. I said hastily, 'Listen, Bibi, just come away with me'."

"Now you have told poor Deepali to do the same," Uma commented dryly.

"Yes. Never mind. So I said, 'Come along. It's a frosty night, put on a veil. Nobody will recognize us. We'll get out through the playhouse gate, take a tonga and go to the nearest mosque.'

"'Easier said than done,' she replied calmly. 'You must be out of your mind.'

"'It's not difficult at all', I replied. 'All you require is a little courage.' I was forgetting that a conservative girl like her would not even dream of elopement. I had just come back from Europe and was agog with ideas of women's independence. I was also being trained for work in the Underground. For a daredevil like me running away on a dark night seemed easy. Why the hell can't this girl break her shackles when I am offering her glorious freedom? I said again, 'Bibi, look at the Soviet women! Look at Miss Amy Johnson, the aviator!'

"Despite the perilous situation, I saw the faint glimmer of a smile on her face. Perhaps she, too, thought that I was being juvenile. I repeated, listen, let's go straight to a mosque.

"She replied: 'You find me a maulvi in all of Dacca, all of Bengal, who would be willing to solemnise the nikah of a runaway daughter of Nawab Qamrul Zaman!'

"'My socialist father would. Come, let's go straight to Narayan Gunj and take the early morning steamer to Shonapur. But after that you'll have to forget that you are Qamrul Zaman Chowdhry's daughter, and always bear in mind that you are married to a poor farmer's son.'

"Unconsciously, I was repeating what Abba had said to my mother.

"Suddenly she broke down and cried. I was furious. I said, if you do not have the guts to defy your autocratic father, how will you fight in the revolution alongside your comrade husband?

"I was about to blurt out that I needed a brave girl, a real fighter, as my wife, and not a silly weakling like her. Better sense prevailed and I kept quiet. I lingered there another few minutes, hoping that she would agree to come away with me. She didn't. I left her there, shedding copious tears, and returned to my room. At the break of dawn I went away from Arjumand Manzil for good.

"A few days later I had to go underground and that was that."

"And then you found the kind of girl you wanted, brave and a real fighter, etc.," Uma remarked acidly.

"Oh, yes, I did. I met Deepali Sarkar exactly after ten months, in October 1938."

"I think you are a swine."

"Thank you. Er—Uma may I take your leave now? I must go and console Mahmood's parents, they are old and poor. Jyoti had no family."

"Yes, you must. Where is your sister?"

"In Shonapur. I have to go home again. My father has found a match for her, a petty clerk."

"Your house must be very beautiful."

"Yes. Its thatched roof is covered with yellow gourd flowers. Our kitchen garden is surrounded by bamboos and our tank is full of pink lotuses. We have our own betel nut trees. Not many. There is a cow in the barnyard and the palanquin of our womenfolk in the shed. The family boat is moored on our own tiny pier. Abba rows it across the river to conduct the Friday service in the big mosque. He has spent his life going from village to village in his boat. He knows no other mode of transport. He sat in a motor car only when he came to Dacca to put me into school. Uncle Qamrul's limousines used to be ready for him all the time.

"That reminds me, I'm meeting Uncle Qamrul this afternoon. Have to make an appointment through his secretary. Political negotiations, he being the Muslim League leader. Meeting him after that melodramatic exit in the winter of 1937—feeling a bit nervous, you know!

"Yes—my self-contained village. The picturesque huts. The mosque. The Kali temple. The *nat mandir* where Radha-Krishna devotees get together to dance and sing. The popular shrine of a Muslim Sufi saint. The pier. The chowpal.

"And the graveyard in which my mother is buried under a fragrant magnolia tree. She died when she had just turned forty-two. She was eighteen years older than me, but many people thought I was her younger brother. Had she been alive today, she would not have looked much older than you. When you start revealing your deep concern for me, you remind me of my mother."

"I remind you of your mother!"

"Yes. Except that she was very slim and sweet-tempered. Must run along now, bye!"

This man has gone bonkers, Uma decided, as he disappeared behind the guest-room door.

26
The Muezzin's Call

THE Nawab was returning from Dacca Club when he saw Bannerjee coming out of Barlow's house. He was trudging aimlessly like a tortoise, face lifted to the sky, looked utterly distraught. The Nawab told his chauffeur to stop. He got out of the motor car and overtook his old friend. He had read about Rosie in the morning's newspapers. He led her sorrowing father to his Buick and helped him climb in.

In a few minutes they reached Arjumand Manzil. The Nawab took his guest to a glazed verandah and made him relax on a chaise-longue. He spoke over the house-telephone to Jehan Ara and asked her to send in some tea. Nayyar was playing the latest New Theatres records on the gramophone in an ante-room.

Bannerjee took out the newspaper clipping from his coat pocket and handed it to his host like a robot.

"I have read it."

"I went to see Mr. Barlow. He refused to help."

Qamrul Zaman grunted in sympathy.

"Mrs. Barlow was killed in the bombardment over London."

The Nawab nodded.

"V-2 rocket."

A servant came in with a dish of dry-fruit.

"Barlow's ancestral house was also burnt down in London."

The Nawab blinked. The parson looked like a blackrobed messenger of doom who had nothing to impart except disaster news.

"What shall I do now? My friends have let me down. Shall I go away to Rangpur? But my sister writes to say that there are rumblings of a most dreadful visitation, a terrible famine, which may soon stalk the unhappy land of Bengal..."

Bannerjee had turned into Job. Allah have mercy. The Nawab waited for his hookah.

All of a sudden Bannerjee sprang up. "Nawab Saheb, I want to meet Dr. Sarkar. At once! Forthwith!"

"Please sit down, Padre Saheb. Relax. I'll send for Benoy Babu right away. Will he be able to help?"

"I want to meet Dr. Sarkar," the parson repeated firmly. The host rang the bell. Mala came in. "Ask Habib to go to Chandrakunj and tell Doctor Saheb I send him my salaams. It is urgent."

Dr. Sarkar arrived with his medical bag. "What's the matter, Qamrul Mian? I have just come back from Faridpur. Didn't even have my bath or shave when your motor car came. Is everything all right?"

"Everything all right, he asks!" Bannerjee flared up. "*I* sent for you. I want to tell you that your foolish daughter is the architect of this disaster."

Dr. Sarkar looked askance at the Nawab.

He answered slowly, "Rosie was arrested yesterday at Isherdee. The insurgents had attacked the police station. Some of them and two policemen were killed. Rosie was wounded. This is last night's bulletin. Tomorrow we may hear which jail she will be lodged in. Right now she should be in the prison hospital."

Nayyar was still at the gramophone. He overheard the conversation about Rosie, and as a tribute to her bravery started playing Qazi Nazrul Islam's famous song, "The Rebel". The song had set the whole of Bengal on fire, inspired an entire generation.

Another servant came in pushing a gleaming trolley. He was accompanied by Mala, who poured tea.

The three men listened silently to "The Rebel".

"Proclaim, O young man: I hold my head high and the Himalayas bow down before me. I have rent the sky asunder and plucked the sun

and the moon and the stars. I have shaken Paradise and Hell, struck at high heaven and have become somebody to marvel at…"

"Poets can be dangerous, so dangerous." Bannerjee shook his head.

The song continued: *I shatter everything. I break principles. I trample laws and rules and restrictions. I am the God of Annihilation.*

Proclaim, O young man, that my son is a damn fool. Why did he have to play this record to add fuel to poor Bannerjee's smouldering fire, thought the Nawab sadly. But the song was so compelling that he continued to listen…

I hold a flute in one hand and a war-bugle in another. I am thunder and lightning and the echo of the Trumpet of Israfael. I am the banner of the Day of Judgement, and the staff of Gabriel. I am the mighty river at flood. My raging waters enrich or destroy the earth. I am a shooting star. I am Mercury. I am Mahadeva who has ensnared the Ganga in the wavy ringlets of his hair.

I am sick of being bloodthirsty. I'll be content when the cry of the oppressed reaches the sky, when I break the spells cast by belief in 'Destiny'. I am the eternal and immortal rebel. I will kick the world and rise once again…

So help me, God. The Nawab shouted, "Nayyar, kindly stop it now, will you?"

Bannerjee fidgeted in his chair.

"Poets! Writers!! What have they turned this country into!"

"Don't say that, please. We love Nazrul Islam," Dr. Sarkar said mildly.

There was silence again.

Bannerjee raised his head and regarded Sarkar balefully. By this time he had been able to compose himself. He began tonelessly: "Benoy Babu. My obedient child was led astray by your daughter. I merely wished to tell you this, nothing else. As a responsible father you ought to have restrained the young lady. How on earth did she take up with those thugs and bandits?"

"Both of you probably think I am a retrogressive, arch-conservative Muslim, an oppressor of women, a backward-looking landlord. But you can see now, this is what happens when you give unlimited freedom to immature girls. This is precisely why I do not allow my daughters to stir out of this house without a chaperone," said the Nawab.

"Deepali promised me that she would never join the terrorists. I trusted her. She did so secretly, I could do nothing about it. Each new generation finds its own trail. You and I, Monmohun Babu, went forth on the paths we chose for ourselves. I can understand your anguish. When my brother Dinesh…" he didn't complete his sentence.

Another servant brought a massive silver hubble-bubble and placed it on a silver tray.

The clergyman said, "You, Nawab Saheb—how would the English quitting India benefit you? Jawaharlal Nehru has declared a thousand times that the government of free India will abolish the princedoms as well as the zamindari estates."

The Nawab had a pull at his hookah. The political situation had become extremely complicated. He felt as though he was the caterpillar in *Alice in Wonderland,* placidly smoking his hookah while things around him were becoming curiouser and curiouser. He suppressed a smile.

Allah is Great. This seedy parson and the indigent physician would both probably benefit from India's independence. But how will I fare? He had never bothered much about the economics of the question. Ronu had studied that aspect and created havoc.

He said thoughtfully, "Monmohun Babu, I, too, understand your grief. My favourite nephew has also joined the rabble-rousing troublemakers. You talk of the new generation, Benoy. This is a thoroughly ungrateful, thankless, heartless bunch of spoilt brats. Last year your daughter began talking to me about the noble deeds of the Congress leaders, their self-sacrifice, spirit of renunciation, blah, blah. I didn't feel like arguing with her, and didn't tell her that politics had taken a toll of my own personal happiness. My brilliant nephew has been swallowed up by the vortex."

"Which nephew of yours, Qamrul Mian?" asked Dr. Sarkar.

"You hardly ever meet me now, you have become a stranger to my affairs. Forget about it."

"Sorry! I didn't mean to be inquisitive."

Nevertheless, the Nawab continued, "I made his life for him, and what did he wish to do to me? Just this: demolish, destroy, set ablaze—rend the sky asunder.

"Monmohun Babu, you and I and Benoy, all three of us are sailing in the same boat. Ronu, Rosie, Deepali, they are all trying to punish us for the crime of creating a safe and comfortable world for them. Their mission is to destroy the creators of the society they were born into."

"But why?" the parson asked. "What kind of world will they create after they have finished with us?"

"I wish I knew," said the Nawab ruefully.

"Please forgive me, Benoy Babu," Bannerjee said with great humility. "I was very rude. The shock has unhinged me."

The Nawab addressed him. "Monmohun Babu, Allah is the Architect of Causes. Rosie may find some way out. Keep praying. Inshallah, she will come home safe and sound."

The parson shook his head uncertainly.

The muezzin called the faithful to Asar prayers. Bannerjee and Sarkar rose from their seats and took their leave.

The host saw them off in the porch. He watched his car leave the gate, then turned towards his private mosque.

After he had offered his prayers, he strolled down to the summer house. Tonight they were going to have a big dinner to celebrate the "Tradition of Abraham", the circumcision ceremony of Nayyar's infant son. Guests would start arriving after the sunset prayers. He sat down wearily on a bench and pondered. We three Bengalis, Bannerjee, Sarkar and I, we are standing at the crossroads, facing three different directions. The shepherd's staff the Padre holds in his hands, has already been attacked by white ants. He doesn't understand the situation. Even if he does, he can do nothing about it.

He was saying that Barlow remained utterly composed this morning when he received the news of his wife's death. Well, if they were not so courageous they would not have been ruling half the world. I'll have to go to his house tomorrow to sign the condolence register.

Pamela Barlow was known to be a flirt in Bengal's European society. Drank like a fish and she was so pretty. A bomb fell on her. How dreadful it must be to die such a death. Charles Barlow used to be quite unhappy because of her waywardness. Now what should be done about Rosie? Nothing can be done, I suppose. Rosie's mother Giribala was fifteen when she came to this house. She used to sit by the tank there and polish the silver. I used to hide behind that tree and throw little pebbles at her and tease her. How time passes, and changes. God is great.

"Nawab Saheb," a young clerk approached him from the avenue. "Telephone message from the League office. Shall I make an appointment for this evening?"

He read the name scribbled on a piece of paper. His face paled. "Ask the gentleman to come right away and place the relevant files on my table."

"Yes, sir."

The Nawab got up and walked back to his library. His gait had become that of a very old man.

27
Jehan Ara Begum

JEHAN Ara sat on the terrace knitting booties of light blue rabbit wool for her newborn nephew. Through the balustrade she caught a glimpse of her patrician father as he hurried down to the mosque. He took off his shoes, tied a kerchief on his head and entered the courtyard. The prayers had already begun. He stood alongside his syce and joined the service.

The corner of the rooftop was a kind of vantage point from where one could survey the entire Arjumand Manzil complex. The tiny mosque. The concert hall. The summer house. The little zoo. The outlying servants' quarters. The stables. The motor garages. The long *dalan* inside which the palanquins and sedan chairs and shooting howdahs of a bygone era were kept in a row.

The fabulous urban estate of the Zaman-Chowdhrys! In earlier centuries some of them used to die on the battlefield. After Lord Clive's Famous Victory nearly two hundred years ago, they had been breathing their last peacefully on their four-posters. They left behind indolent heirs to continue their line.

Among Muslim families a new bride was called the 'foundation stone of the next thousand years'. But there was also an Urdu couplet which said that one did not know the time of one's death, made preparations to live for a century, and knew nought about tomorrow!

And all year round, in pouring rain and scorching sun, the muezzin went up the slender minaret and called out: God is Great. God is Great. There is no god but God. I testify that Mohammed is His Prophet. Come for prayer. Come for Grace. God is Great. God is Great...

And the noblemen of Arjuman Manzil and their humble servants all flocked together to the house of worship, stood side by side and prayed to an unseen Deity. How did the most illiterate of the congregation also have this strong abiding faith in a purely abstract, metaphysical concept? Did that show their inner spiritual strength and the grasp of their minds? How did they concentrate without the use of the simplest of symbols? How did they so intensely love a Prophet whose image they were strictly forbidden to make? How were they so passionately devoted to a person who had never claimed any divinity and who had always insisted, in all humility, that he was merely a human being, a servant of God? Was it His followers' inborn understanding of His work and message or was it mere blind faith?

After visiting the Woking mosque on an Eid day, Rehan had written to her in one of his long letters that according to Engels, history was not entirely the result of economic conditions. Its course was also influenced by extraordinary personalities. And, Rehan had added, Mohammed was one of them.

The congregational prayer continued in the mosque. High and low stood side by side five times a day. But the moment they stepped out they became master and servant once again. Rehan had also said once that Islam had given mankind a practical lesson in democracy. It was repeated day after day, and yet the Muslims had divided their society into haves and have-nots in the name of predestination. Shouldn't they return to Islam's original teachings?

And Abba had said only the other day, that once Pakistan came into being, all would be equal in the new country, and there follow the principles of Classical Islam.

But then would Abba give up his life of state and bounty for the sake of Islamic egalitarianism?

Rosie and Deepali were endeavouring, in their own way, to achieve ideal conditions for humanity. While I, Jehan Ara, Decoration of the World, sit and brood and knit booties. Should I have got out of here that fateful night with Rehan?

Was it predestination that I didn't go, or merely the result of my own sheltered upbringing?

It was the bewitching hour between Asar and Maghrib prayers. In Bengal it was called 'the cow-dust hour', for this was the time the cows came home, raising pink dust with their hooves. They remained placid and continued to make lovely music with their bells even if they were unhappy. A harmless woman was called "cow-like". It was supposed to be a compliment.

The atmosphere became quieter as twilight spread over the sky. A hush fell over Arjumand Manzil as though a sorcerer, hidden in the ancient *sagwan* trees, had cast his spell and the flowers, animals, birds and humans had all fallen into a trance.

The domestic staff had come out of the mosque after Asar prayers and returned to their multifarious duties. Abba had sauntered down to the summer house. Now he also looked like a granite statue as he sat on a bench near the shrubbery.

In their private zoo a deer barked. Parakeets twittered in the aviary. Leaves stirred again. Father moved his right hand and etched something in the air with his forefinger. Was he writing Aunt Maliha's name or drawing the imaginary map of Pakistan?

His secretary approached him and said something. He rose to his feet and strode back to the library.

Tonight they were going to have a grand dinner to celebrate his newborn grandson's circumcision. She must go to the kitchen and supervise the cooks. The other day Mother had said harshly, and that too, in the presence of the super-cat, Shamsa Khatoon, "Your stars being what they are, you may never have a home of your own. May as well look after this house properly."

Sister-in-law was lazing around in her suite of rooms. Now that she had produced a son, she had also become subtly arrogant. Mother was as usual sulking in her bedroom. Why did she have these frequent bouts of melancholia? She had everything. A considerate husband, children. Now a grandson. Yet she was unhappy. Was it because she thought that her husband had still not forgotten his late cousin, Maliha...?

The booties were finished. May God give him a long life, my little Munnawer is so cute. I had even bought pink wool for him. Why can't boys wear pink?

"Bibi...Bibi..."

She looked up. Mala stood in front, panting. She had come hotfoot from the ground floor. "Bibi...he...he has come."

She missed a heartbeat. "Who—?"

"Ronu Mian."

"Ronu...? Don't stand there jabbering like a half-wit."

"As Allah is my Witness, I saw him with my own eyes. He is sitting in the book-room with the master."

"Rosie and Deepali's fathers had come..."

"They left long ago. He has come just now. Bashir told me. I peeped in through the garden window. The Master and Ronu Mian, both of them in the library. Behind closed doors. Secret meeting going on, Bibi."

Jehan Ara felt weak. "Don't you tell stupid lies, Mala."

"I swear by Allah and His Prophet. Come along and see for yourself."

"Secret meeting?"

"I swear."

Have her prayers been heard?

She put her knitting on the wicker-table and got up.

"Mala, wait. Where is my brother?"

"Gone out."

She went downstairs, followed by Mala, and tiptoed to the dining-room which adjoined her father's study. The connecting door usually remained closed. Her heart was beating fast. She peeped through a narrow chink.

He was there, right in front, across Father's writing table. He hadn't changed one bit. Handsome as ever, same attractive mannerisms. He was talking to the Nawab who sat stonily in his swivel chair. A lot of papers and a tea-tray were placed between the two men. Why hadn't Abba telephoned them for proper tea? She pressed her ears to the chink. He was saying: "Yes, sir, I'll give the details to Comrade Joshi."

Abba pushed his glasses over his forehead and began reading: "The points elucidated by Mr. Jinnah..."

She felt blighted. They were not talking about her, they were discussing Pakistan.

Her father cast a glance at the closed door. She grew nervous and moved away. Mala stood guard in the passage. She beckoned to her to stay on.

Now her father was collecting the papers. Ronu had got up.

"You can go inside and meet your aunt. She is not well," Father said tonelessly.

I know. I know Abba's coldness is a put-on, because he has so much self-respect. He is still very fond of his nephew.

"Yes, sir, I will."

Allah, please make Abba speak to him about me, Allah.

"Where is Nayyar Mian?" Ronu was asking.

"No idea. May have gone to play tennis."

Abba, please ask him to stay for dinner. Do not let him go away like a stranger.

"Will my aunt be in her room?"

"Yes."

"All right, Uncle, goodbye." They shook hands.

He bowed respectfully, "I'll contact Nawabzada Liaquat Ali Khan as soon as I reach Delhi."

"Good."

"Bye, Uncle."

"God be with you. May you live long."

He picked up a file and moved towards the archway. Mala beckoned to Jehan Ara. Hastily she went out of the dining-room door which overlooked the ladies' badminton court. I should have gone through the corridor, then I would have run into him, she thought with regret.

But suppose Abba had come up from behind? He had given strict orders that if Ronu ever came to Arjumand Manzil again, Jehan Ara was not to meet him. She ran out to the back-garden and sat down on the soggy "royal throne". She was breathless.

After a few minutes Mala arrived. "I peeked into the Begum's room," she reported, "Ronu Mian had gone in. She was fast asleep. He left. Now I don't know where he is." Instantly, she held her breath.

He was coming out of the passage.

On the roundabout way to the front gate he passed by the lotus pond. It started raining. He took shelter under the cotton-flower tree. Then he saw his cousin. The next moment he was standing near the painted throne, just like he had in the dream that night.

"Oh, hello, Bibi," he said nonchalantly.

"Adaab, Ronu Bhai."

There was no earthquake. The Trumpet of Israfael did not blow the world away. He stood in front of her, exactly like he had that terrible night of December, '37, when he said his final goodbye.

Mala hid behind the tree.

"When did you come, Ronu Bhai?" Jehan Ara assumed a matter-of-fact tone, too. She could keep up a brave front. All well-bred Indian girls were taught to bear their anguish in silence, cry on the quiet, and face the world with a smile.

Besides, a lady never created a scene.

"Came to Dacca a week ago."

"Where do you stay nowadays?"

"Redflag House, Bombay. What are you doing now? M.A.?"

"No. How is your father? Did you go to Shonapur?"

"Yes. He is fine."

"And Rabia?"

"She is fine, too."

There was a shower of wet flowers around them. A leaf fell dancing over her head. He was about to remove it from her hair when he checked himself. He looked at the sky and said, "Must leave before it turns into a downpour. Look, you must do your M.A. In political science, as I advised you once. Bye-bye, Bibi," he added quickly and ran towards the driveway. In her temporary mood of inner strength and firmness she decided against sending a servant after him with an umbrella.

He left as unceremoniously as he had come. He had materialised after so many years and after such intense prayers. But when he left the world remained the same. The *sagwan* trees. The birds. The sky. The clouds. The earth. Everything.

Mala came out of the shrubbery.

Jehan Ara returned to her private world of pain. Now she looked at the maid blankly.

"Bibi, wait, I'll get you an umbrella."

All of a sudden Jehan Ara let herself go. She banged the throne with her fist. "Why did he come, Mala? When I was sitting here, why did he? Why couldn't he go out through the portico? Do you know why he came here Mala? What was he saying?"

"Get up, Bibi."

"Why did he come?" She pounded the throne's carved railing. It had already become wobbly.

"Bibi, do not behave like a ... like a mad woman. What will people say? Do not become hysterical like your mother, Bibi."

Mala's words stunned her. Quickly she wiped her face.

A tiny brook had begun rippling by the throne. Mala helped her jump across. They covered their heads against the driving rain and ran towards the house.

28
Cow-dust Hour

"THANK you for the lovely song, though you hummed it too softly."

"How could I sing properly here on the road?"

"This desolate forest area is a road according to you! Last time I had seen a damaged marble statue somewhere here. Where it is?"

"Have you ever seen anything in this dump which is intact or new? We are so antiquated we even have a resident ghost. Oh, yes. Poor Diana the Huntress is still there, hidden by wild creepers. My soulful grandfather acquired her because he called this house Chandrakunj and translated the name into English as Luna's Grove. He also versified, after a fashion, in English. The other day I found his notebook in an attic. His poetry was sweet—O winged songstresses of the Garden of Moon/Trill they and lilt in emerald June…"

"Fifty years from now, if our grandchildren ever cared to read what we wrote, they would be amused too!"

"What do you think is going to happen in the near future?"

"The English will leave. We will have a socialist government, and sooner than you think we may have real communism. Pakistan will come into being. It will also be a socialist democracy, for the simple reason that the people of the entire subcontinent have the same economic problems. Meanwhile, first things first. I am leaving for Lahore tonight. Should be in Calcutta by the end of October. I'll send you a telegram from there to your hostel address. Take the train from Bolpur, come straight to our commune. I have given you its address, and right away we'll have our Party wedding."

"Only a tea-party for our wedding, not a dinner?"

"Party wedding, stupid. The comrade-in-charge will marry us."

"*The Owl and the Pussy Cat...*"

"Beg your pardon?"

"*... went out to sea in a beautiful pea-green boat. They took some honey and plenty of money...*"

"Your father will be livid."

"*... wrapped up in a five-pound note. The Owl looked up at the stars above and sang to his light guitar...*"

"Has he gone to see a patient?"

"*Pussy said to the Owl, you elegant fowl, how charmingly sweet you sing. Let us be married, too long have we tarried... They sailed away for a year and a day, to the land where the Bong tree grows...*"

"Bongs can be very orthodox. Tell me: Your father..."

"He is orthodox, but when it's a question of my happiness, he can overlook the social norms. My aunt, of course, will hit the ceiling."

"Wish I could meet your Baba this evening. He hasn't come back and I must catch the train tonight. It's a long journey: Delhi—Lahore—Rawalpindi—Peshawar."

"The royal road to Pakistan!"

"West Pakistan. Our region of Bengal and Assam will be called East Pakistan ... Don't took so glum!"

"I have suddenly remembered, it's Tuesday evening. My aunt will be back any minute from the temple. Run! Get lost. See you in Calcutta last week of October, *and hand in hand at the edge of the sand, we'll dance by the light of the moon...*"

"Who was that man hurrying out of the gate, Deepa?"

"Somebody who came to see Baba, Pishi Ma."

"And why should you be loitering on the rain-soaked grass? Tree-spirits can possess unmarried girls at moments like this, when Day meets Night. You were standing right under the peepal tree. Don't you know MacDonnel Saheb's low-caste woman has started living in it?"

"Oh, Pishi Ma! You always maintained that she lived in her dingy puja room."

"She did! Now she has shifted to this peepal tree. Abdul Qadir's wife saw her with her own eyes. It was a moonless night, the woman sat on a high branch, dangling her feet. Her legs had become so long that they touched the ground. Poor Sakina got such a fright that she was down with high fever for three days. Come in. Take this special prashad I have brought for you from the temple. In no time you will get married to a very nice man."

"Thank you, Pishi Ma!"

"And never again stand under the trees at cow-dust hour."

"Never again, Pishi Ma, never again!"

29
Shrimati Radhika Sanyal

My dear Deepali,

I must apologise. That fearsome night of August I was so rude to you before setting out on our perilous mission. I'm sure you'll understand. All of us have been through a dreadful crisis. Mahmoodul Haque was shot dead right in front of me. Mushir and Jyoti succumbed to their bullet wounds a little later. They were such fast friends and they died together. They were also my "teachers" during the study circle days, and they gave me a practical demonstration of their militant philosophy.

They had thrown hand-grenades at the police station. The police baton-charged and tear-gassed the mob; later they opened fire. I don't remember what happened afterwards, because when I regained consciousness I felt a terrible pain in my left leg. I was handcuffed and lying on the stone floor of the women's lock-up. After a while two warders came in carrying a stretcher. They took me out and put me in a van. I was driven to the district jail and locked up in a cell in the female section. They placed a lantern outside the barred door and left. The cell buzzed with mosquitoes.

After half an hour an old hag shuffled in, jingling huge keys. She looked at me and went out, grumbling. The jailer arrived. I was taken out again on a dirty stretcher, and put in a Black Maria. Two armed policemen sat inside. The van rumbled through the darkened town and reached the civil hospital. I was carried to the female general ward and dumped on a filthy bed. There was great commotion when the patients saw me handcuffed. An old woman began to lament loudly— her son had been killed in the uprising.

The doctor came late at night. He was followed by a surly nurse. My wounds were cleaned and dressed. I was given watery rice-and-lentil and a lukewarm cup of tea. The policemen continued to guard the entrance. I don't know why they didn't take me to the prison hospital.

I remained in the general ward for three days. Since I was surrounded by sympathetic patients I was transferred to a single room.

Fortunately, none of my injuries was serious. The doctor treated me with great care. They were government servants, but secretly most of them were sympathetic to the Quit India Movement. At nightfall some of the women patients of the general ward sneaked in. They brought me fruit and sweets and tried to look after me as best they could.

A week passed. One fine morning an English lady arrived. She came straight to my bed, bent over me and gently said, "Good morning, Rosie."

I was taken aback. A drab, middle-aged woman. Grey hair tied into a neat bun. Grey frock. Heavy boots. A typical soul-saver. She was Miss Alice Barlow, Charles Barlow's famous missionary sister in the Garo Hills. She spoke mildly and said my Papa was in a state. He had gone to see her brother and sought his help. He had come to know that she was here. Mr. Barlow trunk-called the English clergyman in this district. It's all part of the Merciful God's plan, my dear, she added, and took out paper and a fountain-pen. She said if I signed on the dotted line of the typed letter of apology, I would be released forthwith. The district magistrate would send me home with an armed escort.

I refused to sign. Miss Barlow didn't insist. The following morning she came again. A uniformed orderly carried a flask of coffee and a hamper full of fruit, cakes and sandwiches. The policemen and some of the hospital staff were impressed by my new importance. The nationalist doctors resented the attention. Miss Barlow resumed her preaching. She had begun talking at me as though I were one of the Naga tribals she wanted to convert.

The same evening a young patient from the general ward came in. The policemen on duty turned a blind eye to these nocturnal visitors from the female ward for they, too, secretly sympathised with me.

There was a very poor Muslim girl called Razia. Her father, she told me, was a petty clerk in the civil court. She said: Apa, all of us in the general ward have been praying for your speedy recovery, but if you sign the letter of apology we will never forgive you.

I said, Razia, I shan't disappoint you all, don't worry. Just then the sentry at the door coughed as a caution and Razia made herself scarce.

A couple of days later Miss Barlow arrived again. She was not alone. A Bengali gentleman accompanied her. She introduced him as Robi Kumar Sanyal, a senior district official. Mr. Sanyal would like to talk to you, my dear, quoth she. Mr. Sanyal repeated Miss Barlow's words: I wish you well. Don't you realise so much bloodshed, destruction of national property and lawlessness will lead us nowhere?

I remained silent. Miss Barlow still hoped I might relent. "Look, Rosie, the Booda was called the Prince of Peace. I do not have to tell you about Jesus. Mr. Gandhi also preaches non-violence. Why must you follow the path of Terrorism and—"

The visitors noticed that I was dozing, so they left with a sigh.

On the fourth day, Mr. Sanyal came again. Instead of Miss Barlow he was accompanied by a young man who resembled him. Mr. Robi Sanyal introduced him as his cousin, Mr. Basant Kumar Sanyal, advocate and journalist from Calcutta. Said he wanted to interview me for a Bengali magazine.

I was confused. How was Mr. Sanyal, a senior government official, permitting me to give such an interview? But these were abnormal times. Anything was possible. It was difficult to distinguish between friend and foe.

Mr. Basant Sanyal blinked rather foolishly. I am supposed to be very pretty and all, and used to such attention from men, but at that moment I must have looked awful. Bandaged head. Unkempt hair. Unwashed face. I was peeved. He asked me routine questions: family background, education, hobbies. And whatever I distinctly recalled of the skirmish of which I was an eyewitness.

Since I had refused to tender an apology and my injuries had been completely cured, after exactly two weeks I was told that I would be taken back to jail.

That last evening in the female ward the girls sang, in undertones, the revolutionary songs of Qazi Nazrul Islam. In the morning when I was handcuffed again and taken out of my room many women followed me to the verandah. Some wept. They knew that if it was somehow established in the court of law that I was one of those who threw the hand grenades (which killed two policemen) I would be imprisoned for life.

I was taken back to the district jail. When I was locked up in a cell I realised for the first time that I had become a political prisoner.

Mr. Basant Kumar Sanyal turned up during the visiting hour. He was carrying a bundle of brand new cotton saris. A bit shyly he said, "My sister-in-law, Ranjana Sanyal, has sent you these. You said the other day that the sari you had on in Isherdee had been torn."

I felt awkward. He said that his elder brother was a leading barrister of Calcutta and that he would defend me.

"Tell me, why are the Sanyals so concerned about me?" I asked.

He laughed, and said nothing. He continued visiting me daily and kept me informed about the legal position.

Then it dawned on me that Basant Sanyal had fallen in love. That was why he had not gone back to Cal. As a nationalist he was keen to help me—but there were a whole lot of girls imprisoned during the uprising. Why didn't he worry about them? I asked him, and he said those girls had their families to help them out or arrange for their legal defence. I had nobody. I had told him earlier about Papa and his loyalist views, but obviously that was not the only reason.

I think two things floored him: my looks, and the courage of my convictions.

One evening he came looking aglow. Said that I could be bailed out after furnishing a bond of ten thousand rupees.

Who would bail me out? The information was useless. As a matter of fact I had resigned myself to the idea of spending the next fourteen years in prison, maybe in the penal settlement of Andaman Island. I had also accepted the possibility that Papa would lose his eyesight crying silently for me or would simply die of shock and grief.

Miss Barlow had also come to the jail, but after realising the futility of her mission, had returned to her mountains.

Early next morning the door was unlocked. The jailer came in and said, "You can leave, Miss Bannerjee."

Basant Kumar Sanyal had furnished the bail.

He was waiting for me at the gate; Mr. and Mrs. Robi Sanyal were in the motor car. They took me to their bungalow in the Civil Lines. When I got there I was hit by the incredible difference in atmosphere. The human misery and squalor of the female general ward and the female prison belonged to a different world.

After a long time I bathed in a clean bathroom, wore a starched cotton sari and had proper food.

In the evening Basant said to me, "Pack up. We are leaving tomorrow."

"I don't have much to pack," I replied.

"I said this out of sheer habit," he was grinning.

"I'll take Rosie to the bazaar tomorrow," said his cousin's wife, Ranjana.

"She can do her shopping in Calcutta," said Basant.

"Why Calcutta...?" I cut him short.

"Because I am going to take you home as my wife."

Does this read like one of those bourgeois women's magazine romances we used to be so snobbish about?

Was I bailing myself out of the situation I had landed in because of my politics? Was it not as bad as signing the letter of apology? Would I have helped the cause of India's freedom by serving a long term in jail? Had I wondered that if I said, No, eventually I may have had to settle for somebody only slightly better than Luther Biswas?

I must be brief. A civil marriage in the present circumstances could create problems. So the very next evening a Brahmin priest was called. He ignited tiny pieces of sandalwood in a brazier and performed the Vedic rites (whatever they are). Basant and I went round this "sacred fire" seven times. I was renamed Radhika. Had the Sanyals been worshippers of Kali, they told me, they would have re-named me the militant Durga. They explained to me that they were Vaishnavs, worshippers of Krishna, so they renamed me Radhika, symbol of sublime devotion. Basant told me that in Bengal's Vaishnava sect every man is an image of Krishna and every woman, Radha. Lovely idea, that.

Look. Religion has no meaning for me. In church the parson would have repeated a few words. That Brahmin also intoned some mumbo-jumbo. Love, my dear, is the real thing.

Yes, I am also very fond of Basant. He may not be the world's most glamorous male, but he is quite presentable and a real gentleman.

After a few days we came down to Calcutta. Basant has this large bungalow in Ballygunj. They are a distinguished family. They welcomed me warmly. Mother-in-law and some aunts didn't seem terribly enthusiastic, because after all I am the daughter of an insignificant upcountry native clergyman. But they are a cultured lot and do not for a moment make me feel unwanted or odd, for they know that Basant adores me.

They are probably richer than the Woodland Roys.

Nirmalendu Roy is our next-door neighbour in Ballygunj, and a friend of my husband.

I grew up in want, now I'll have the good things of life. You have seen how we lived in Lily Cotttage...Papa's ideals of Christian poverty and all that.

Papa also used to talk of Divine Mysteries. So look how Basant met me through our enemy, Charles Barlow... If Barlow had not asked his sister to see me in the hospital, and if she had not come with Robi Sanyal and Robi had not brought his cousin Basant along...

Papa, of course, has not forgiven me for having married an infidel. As soon as we came here, Basant and I wrote a joint letter asking him for his blessings.

The other day I received his brief reply. He thanks the Lord that I am alive and well. But since I have left the fold and gone away with a polytheist and an idolator, he will never see me again. He will continue to pray, however, that the Lord deliver me from sin and evil.

Basant sends you his greetings. Why don't you come and stay with us during the vacs? I'll keep a guest room ready for you.

Yours,

Radhika Rosie Sanyal

Ballygunj,
Calcutta,
22nd October, 1942

30
Luna's Grove

Bhavtarni Debi peeped through the broken window. Uma Roy's sleek black car purred at the gate. The lady had come yesterday, too. Benoy was not at home. Today she had turned up again. Bhavtarni Debi had seen a lot of goings-on at Chandrakunj in her father's time, but those days unmarried women did not chase unattached men so unabashedly. Did Uma Debi wish to consult Benoy as a physician? She could send her servant to make an appointment, or send her car to fetch him like Nawab Qamrul Zaman used to do once. Why did she have to come herself? She did not even have the courtesy to step in and meet the doctor's elder sister.

Bhavtarni Debi distrusted modern women. There was more to Uma Debi's visits than met the eye. She had come only once before, to take Deepali with her for a holiday. Bhavtarni Debi was not too sure if Deepali had gone to Comilla. But who was she to stop her when Benoy had allowed her to go? And if Miss Roy had become so friendly as to take the girl with her to her own country-place, why didn't she ever come again? Why didn't her mother, Mrs. Archana Roy, ever visit Chandrakunj? Why had Uma Roy started coming again?

Bhavtarni Debi was upset. She kept standing in the window till she saw Tonu going towards the clinic. "Ask Miss Roy to wait," she heard her brother tell the boy. She returned to the kitchen.

The patient rose from the examination table. Dr Sarkar washed his hands in the basin and picked up a towel. He entered the drawing room, wiping his elbows.

"Good morning, Uma Debi."

"Oh, good morning to you, Benoy Babu."

"I'm afraid Deepali has left for Bolpur."

"I'm aware of that." She was smiling amiably. "Can't I come to see *you?*"

Dr. Sarkar lowered himself into a sofa-chair. He seemed uncomfortable as he tapped the side-table with his fingers. He had got out of the habit of making useless social conversation with females.

Uma viewed him amusedly. She had seen him nearly two and a half years ago when she had come here in connection with the "Ayah Conspiracy". He had greyed some more at the temples. Good-looking man that he was, he did resemble his late brother. She began talking feelingly about Dinesh Sarkar.

Tonu came in with the tea. Bhavtarni Debi had taken out some unchipped crockery but had forgotten to change the soiled tea-cosy.

After having discussed Dinesh Chandra, Uma paused a little. The next item on her agenda seemed to be the late Shibani Sarkar.

The doctor didn't like to talk to inquisitive strangers about his beloved Shibani. It was a kind of desecration of her memory. Uma Debi, however, asked him about her with such disarming sincerity that he unwound slowly. His sister had never been very fond of poor Shibani. The children were too young. He had just never talked about his wife to anybody.

All of a sudden this lady turns up and makes him feel that she is a friend, and that she also understands loneliness.

Uma Roy had come at four in the afternoon. She left before dinner.

Benoy Chandra Sarkar cut down the time of his evening walks and began to wait for her. The lads went out to play football or else they would have been surprised to see their father pacing the front verandah, looking restively at his wrist-watch.

Bhavtarni Debi's suspicions were confirmed. She had thought over the problem and had come to certain positive conclusions. One day she cornered her brother. "When is she going to pop the question?" she asked him rather crudely.

"Didi, don't be crass," he replied gruffly.

"One of the sure signs of Kalyug would be that women start proposing to men. So that is quite in order and anyway, she is ageing fast. Be a realist for once in your life, Benoy, and think of the enormous dowry she would bring."

"Didi!" The doctor was horrified. "Please do not talk such rubbish."

Bhavtarni Debi pursed her lips and smiled.

Late that night when everybody had gone to bed, she sat down cross-legged on her wooden footstool and began writing to her niece. "My dearest child," she wrote carefully.

Good news. Most probably your father will have a woman in his empty life. I'm afraid the lady is a bit odd, but Benoy seems to like her, and I am sure the match will be good for everybody: (1) We'll regain our lost social prestige. To become a son-in-law of Sir Pritish Roy is no joke. (2) You will move in high society and may marry a big shot through the Roy connection. (3) I am on my last legs. Who will look after poor Benoy if he doesn't marry again? So why not Uma Debi? (4) Don't tell your father about this letter.

Your loving aunt,
Bhavtarni Debi

One of Dr. Sarkar's patients called Mitra Babu was also a client of Sir Pritish Roy. He used to come often to Chandrakunj, mostly to chat with Dr. Sarkar. Lately he had noticed one of Sir Pritish's cars parked in front of the doctor's gate. He saw Uma going in and out of the house. He also knew that Deepali was away in Bolpur. He asked Dr. Sarkar if Miss Roy was getting her migraine treated. Benoy Babu was a truthful man. He answered simply, "No, she just turns up, like you do, for a chat."

Mitra Babu went home and told his wife. The very next morning Mrs. Mitra went to Woodland. Lady Roy was having her coffee and reading *The Patrika*. Mrs. Mitra sat down noiselessly in a chair.

"Oh, hello, Orundhati, good morning," Lady Roy said, smiling and put down the newspaper. "Coffee?"

"Yes, please, thank you."

Mrs. Mitra broached the subject deftly. "How is dear Uma?" she asked.

"Well, you know... her migraine trouble has made her slightly irritable...and..."

"That's why I asked."

"Luckily, for the last few days she's been quite cheerful."

"My husband always tells me that Dr. Sarkar's treatment works wonders..."

"Dr. Sarkar?"

"My husband also goes to him for his asthma. He saw Uma a number of times at Dr. Sarkar's place, so he came home and said to me that it was a good thing that..."

"Uma never told me..."

Mrs. Mitra was now gloating. She continued: "You must have heard of him, Dr. Benoy Chandra Sarkar. His daughter is quite well-known as a radio-singer... Deepali Sarkar, you know..."

"Oh..."

"Splendid fellow. Wife died long ago. Four children, one daughter and three sons. His father was a Zamindar, bought Caledonia and lived in it like a Nawab."

Lady Roy got the hint. She didn't like it and looked away, frowning. Mrs. Mitra went on, undaunted. "My husband says Dr. Sarkar is a good soul, almost saintly. First-class family. As for money, well...it is a transitory thing, anyway." At this point Mrs. Mitra got onto an entirely different topic. After fifteen minutes she returned to Dr. Sarkar. "Marriage has become such a problem for good-family girls. Do you remember my sister-in-law's niece, Anjali Dasgupta? Hair turned gray, acquired a middle-age spread. Got fed up with everything. Went off to Burma or perhaps Ceylon, and became a school-teacher. Imagine wasting one's life teaching a bunch of Burmese or Ceylonese brats."

Mrs. Mitra decided that this much was enough for one day, after which she began talking of other things.

Lady Roy was perturbed. She spoke to her husband that night. The news of Uma's frequent visits to Chandrakunj had reached Sir Pritish, too. He knew Dr. Sarkar. He said to his wife, "Thank God, at least she's got interested in somebody."

"She's thirty-two and no beauty, but not a down-and-out widower with four children, for goodness' sake. That nasty woman, Mrs. Mitra, made it a point to tell me that he is penniless," Lady Roy said unhappily. She was still hoping to find a good match for Uma who was growing fatter and more ill-tempered by the day. Ordinary people have lovely daughters. Our girl looks and behaves like a schoolmarm. Except for her useless "comrades", all eligible young men are driven away by her drab, high-falutin conversation.

A wealthy Sanyal family lived next-door to the Roys' son Nirmalendu's house in Ballygunj, Calcutta. The Sanyals' younger son, Basant, was just right for Uma, but the very first time he met her he began calling her Didi, and she had a long discussion with him on Modern Sensibility in Indian Literature.

And now he had gone and married a native Christian girl called Rosie.

"And, anyway," Sir Pritish said again, "Benoy Babu has class. His father, Romesh Chandra Sarkar, squandered his inheritance trying to compete with the Nawabs of Dacca."

"That's one point in his favour," Lady Roy sighed. Marriage to Sarkar was better than living the life of an unpleasant and unwanted old maid. Come to think of it, Dr. Sarkar must be an angel to have overlooked dear Uma's obvious shortcomings.

The following morning she asked her daughter indirectly about the doctor. Uma gave her mother a cryptic smile and started talking to her Alsatian.

She had still not invited the doctor to Woodland, and continued to visit him at Chandrakunj. One evening she asked him, "What are your plans for Deepali?"

"Deepali...? She is studying for her degree in music."

"After that...?"

"I've no idea, really. Never gave it a thought."

"Do you have a boy in view?"

"A boy...? Oh, you mean for her to marry? No, none. You suggest somebody. As you know, I can't give her a dowry."

"I'm very fond of her. I would like her to marry well, and soon."

"Soon? Why?"

"I think she should get married at the earliest. These are evil times."

"Evil times!" Dr. Sarkar burst out laughing. "You've begun to talk like my sister, Bhavtarni Debi. I thought you were a modern woman."

"You seem to be more progressive than me!"

"I'm quite old-fashioned, but I would never force Deepali to marry against her will."

"If she marries without your approval?"

"She wouldn't do that, she is an innocent child."

Uma smiled archly. "Every father thinks that about his daughter."

"Your father, too!"

Uma Roy was cornered. After a few seconds she said, "Supposing Deepali wishes to marry someone who belongs to a different community and religion?"

"Different community? Why do you say that?"

"Benoy Babu, there is this Muslim lad...Comrade Rehan...He has been to Chandrakunj, you have met him. I just heard a vague sort of rumour..."

"What rumour?"

"Benoy Babu, Dacca is a small town..."

"What is it?"

"Nothing…" Uma removed her glasses, put them back on, relaxed in the sofa, and began impassively. "Last year, as you know, she went off to the Sunderbans from Bolpur."

"Not the Sunderbans, Santhal Pargana," Dr. Sarkar tried to correct her, but she went on: "The Sunderbans. Last year, in the month of June, to meet Rehan. You, of course, must be aware of it. One of my dad's clients happened to see both of them at some god-forsaken river-port in Khulna district. This client came back and told me…" Suddenly she stopped short, horrified. Benoy Babu had blanched. Uma feared that he was in the grip of a heart attack. He was staring at her blankly.

"Oh, I'm sorry, Benoy Babu." He raised his right hand, indicating that she keep quiet, and closed his eyes.

After a few minutes he recovered from the obvious shock and sighed resignedly.

"I am sorry," Uma began again, "I thought you knew. Deepali is a truthful child. She would not be telling you lies."

"You have taught her to tell lies, Uma Debi," he answered wearily.

"I…how…?"

"You had supposedly taken her along with you to spend a week at your country house in Comilla. Till today I don't know where she actually went. All this is the result of your training, Miss Roy."

"It's unfortunate that you think so," she said agitatedly. "Shall I get you a glass of water?" She ran out, looking for the refrigerator and found a row of clay pitchers in the verandah. Outside, Abdul Qadir's thin horses grazed in the blue light of the evening. A stray goat was noisily munching the creepers which had partly covered Diana the Huntress. It was a dreary evening. Most evenings she had spent in Chandrakunj had been depressing. She, too, had been trapped by situations, like everybody else. Who was free? She lingered awhile near the pitchers and filled a glass of water. When she returned to the drawing room Dr Sarkar had already gone into his room and closed the door. She wondered if she should knock. Bhavtarni Debi came in. "What's the matter?" she asked sternly. "I heard voices."

"Nothing at all. Your brother is not feeling too well. Here, take this to him." She gave the glass of water to Bhavtarni Debi and hastened out.

She had reached Ramna when it occurred to her—suppose the doctor did have a heart attack and die? They did not even have a telephone. The possibility terrified her. She decided to return to Chandrakunj. He was such a nice man. He ought to live but if he died, Deepali would be totally free to do what she liked. She told the driver to go back.

Dr. Sarkar was walking on the lawn, looking quite normal. His sister walked along with him. The boys had come home. Uma heard them all laugh as they tried to chase the goat away from the statue of Diana.

Loonies. Living in Luna's Grove they had all become *loonies,* she thought morosely and returned home.

The very next morning she came again. The clinic was locked. Bhavtarni Debi had gone out to buy her groceries. Uma knocked on Dr. Sarkar's bedroom door. He opened it, still reading the newspaper.

"Oh, thank goodness." Uma heaved a sigh of relief.

"Why?"

"I could not sleep all night, I was so worried about you. I can't forgive myself for having given you such a rude shock."

"I've got used to bearing all manner of shocks, Uma Debi. In fact, I am glad you told me." He tried to lead her to the drawing room but she pushed him aside and barged in.

"You have become quite a hermit," she remarked, rather pointlessly.

He remained silent.

She took off her glasses and rubbed her eyes with her palms.

"Benoy Babu," she said after a pause. "I have only one request to make..."

"Well?"

"Please do not tell Deepali that I told you about the Sunderbans."

"You do not have to ask me. I am not going to say anything to her, anyway."

"Nothing at all?"

"Nothing at all." He proceeded slowly towards the door. "Deepali is an adult and a sensible girl. Do you think I am going to embarrass her by mentioning the episode?" He led her to the sitting room and continued: "As a self-respecting, orthodox father I ought perhaps to recall her forthwith from Santiniketan, shut her up in a room, get hold of a Hindu lad and marry her off. I wouldn't do any of these things."

She sat down expectantly. He began pacing the room as he spoke. "Because of youthful idealism or her romantic notions of love or whatever, she lied to me and went off on that foolish trip. But I am also quite sure that she didn't do anything she shouldn't have."

"How are you so sure?"

"You lived in England for how many, three-four years? How is your father so sure you didn't do anything that you shouldn't have?"

Uma was cornered again. She asked weakly, "So, would you allow her to marry Rehan Ahmed? I have known him for a fairly long time. He is a thoroughly irresponsible sort of fellow. Let down his own cousin. He has a hand-to-mouth existence. Do you know what a pittance a wholetimer gets from the Party as monthly allowance? How will Deepali manage? And how will she adjust in Muslim society? Wouldn't her marriage to a Muslim also affect your own medical practice? Most of your patients are *bhadralok*. Pardon me, Benoy Babu, I am trying to warn you as a sincere friend. I want you to be a realist. I would hate to see Deepali suffer after her reckless marriage. Of course, it is none of my business."

Benoy Babu was looking at the high, vaulted ceiling. He smiled and said briefly, "I have lost my wife and my brother. Both were young, they would have liked to live. I want people to be alive and happy. I do not believe in this nonsense of rebirth, one is born only once. One must not make others miserable in their short lives. If I were convinced that Deepali and Rehan are genuinely in love, I would certainly allow them to marry. Hindu society, my own medical practice, etc. are not more important than the personal happiness of my daughter. You ought to applaud my progressive views!"

Uma rose from the chair.

Dr. Sarkar escorted her to the limousine and folded his hands in a pleasant goodbye.

When she reached Woodland she was told by Karim Khan that Nawab Qamrul Zaman had telephoned several times. She rang him up. He sounded frantic, wanted to know Rehan's whereabouts. She told him she didn't know, and rang off. The next instant she rushed to her father's office-room and asked his secretary to reserve a first-class cabin and a coupé for her on the earliest steamer and train to faraway Bolpur. She had decided to rush to Santiniketan and meet Deepali Sarkar.

31
The Bridal Palanquin

Dᴇᴇᴘᴀʟɪ-ᴅɪ, Adaab!

Two days ago, on Friday, Jehan Ara Apa was married off to a rotund landlord from the interior. You will be surprised. So was I. But for some mysterious reason, the marriage was arranged in utmost secrecy. Even Bibi was only informed a week ago. The match had been fixed by a family friend, Shamsa Khatoon. Nawab Ajmal Hussain Murshidzada's first wife was an aunt of Mrs. Nayyarul Zaman. She died some years ago. No children. According to Shamsa Khatoon, Jehan Ara was already twenty-six. An eligible bachelor could not be found, so she obtained a widower.

Nawab Ajmal Hussain Murshidzada is almost twice her age and not highly educated. That hardly matters, according to Shamsa Khatoon. What matters is that he is as formidable an aristocrat as his father-in-law, Nawab Qamrul Zaman Chowdhry. He owns a Rolls Royce, and many race horses and elephants. Shamsa Khatoon said to my mother, the "boy" is only a matriculate. So what? Our Jehan Ara doesn't have to discuss Shakespeare with him.

My mother said the Nawab is a known philanderer. To which the lady replied primly, "Well, keep quiet. Jehan Ara's folk made all inquiries about the 'boy', and were satisfied. If they approved of him who are we, the outsiders, to worry? Doubtless, the 'boy' was once a bit of a loafer, was fond of the bottle, and so forth. But what else could the poor fellow do? His wife had died and he had tons of money. Jehan Ara is such a good girl. She will reform him…"

I tell you, Deepali-di, I am so angry with Shamsa Khatoon and Mrs. Nayyarul Zaman. Both of them ganged up to fix this misalliance. Bibi's father is not at all happy, but his wife got after him. "Do you want her to become an old maid? As long as she remains unmarried her younger sisters won't get any proposals." The Nawab remained adamant. So the Begum played her trump card: she had one of her famous "heart attacks".

Now that I am growing up I can understand a lot of things. The lady is just plain hysterical. The Nawab is a peaceable man and dreads his wife's tantrums. That's why he has spent his entire life sitting inside that depressing library of his. So, the Begum gave him an ultimatum: If Jehan Ara wasn't married to Nawab Ajmal Hussain, she, that is, Mrs. Qamrul Zaman, would conk out.

The Nawab still said No.

Then his delicate lady played her final trump card. I overheard the entire conversation and was greatly surprised. I had gone to Arjumand Manzil. Jehan Ara Apa was in the baronial kitchen, as usual, supervising the cooks. I sat down in the back verandah twiddling my toes, when I overheard the following dialogue. The Nawab was inside his wife's boudoir, talking ever so quietly, "I will not destroy Bibi's life." Whereupon the Begum retorted: "So you want her to run away with that no-good son of your darling Maliha..."

"Keep quiet, Anwari Begum, keep quiet," the Nawab said patiently. She went on screaming, "Don't you know? The devil is stalking Dacca once again. The other day he came here. I was fast asleep. As he slipped through my room, I woke up and rushed to the window. Saw him and your dearly beloved Jehan Ara by the lotus tank, talking in whispers. The next moment he was gone. I didn't say a word to your daughter but decided on the spot about Ajmal Hussain. Do you have any idea, Nawab Saheb, of what is happening right under your nose? You keep sitting in your gloomy study writing speeches about your marvellous would-be Pakistan. Do you want your daughter to blacken your face and cut your stupid nose and run away with that vagabond? Now I know why he is hanging around town.

"Even if they fail to elope, the very rumour that Rehan Ahmed is back in Dacca and has visited Arjumand Manzil, is enough to seal her fate. People would come to know how he refused to marry her five years ago and has turned up again and is seeing her secretly. With great difficulty Nayyar's wife and Shamsa have managed to find a match for the wretched girl. If Ajmal Hussain hears of the scandal…"

"What scandal?" the Nawab said. "Rehan merely declined to become our resident son-in-law, as he had become a Communist. And because of that I said No to him. Now I realise I made a dreadful mistake. Besides, he had come to Arjumand Manzil to see me about some political matter. I told him to go in and meet you. Seeing you asleep he must have gone out through that door and met poor Bibi by chance. I know my daughter better than you do. You have a sick imagination, Anwari Begum. And I tell you, if he asks me now, I'll let him take her away as his wife and keep her in his commune, make her live on his Party allowance of fifty rupees a month. She will be supremely happy living in penury with the man she loves, than as the begum of that undesirable landlord you have selected for her." He sounded determined and coldly furious.

Anwari Begum hissed back, "Your nephew will never marry her now. After that day when I spotted them by the pool, I asked my loyal friend Shamsa to investigate. Apparently, many people already know about it…" She paused for effect.

"Know about what? That busybody Shamsa is a bloody bitch."

"Don't you use foul language for my dearest friend— Shamsa operates the best grapevine in Dacca town. Her information is always correct. She told me that Rehan is being kept by barrister Pritish Roy's bovine daughter. He is a pauper, so he has become Uma Roy's gigolo."

The Nawab lost his temper and shouted, "Stop talking absolute drivel. You have no business to malign either Uma Roy or Rehan! Both you and Shamsa are sick women, sick beyond belief."

"Says you! Of course you must defend your nephew. Listen, according to Shamsa's information he may even marry some Hindu female, not Uma, some other gadabout..."

By this time the Nawab had left the room, obviously in disgust, because after that there was complete silence.

While husband and wife were having this bizarre dialogue, Najma had also joined me in eavesdropping. After a few minutes of shocked silence she said, "I hope it happens, I hope Ronu Bhai comes back. But don't tell Bibi about what Abba said just now, because she may start hoping again and Ronu Bhai may never turn up."

The whole thing sounded pretty mysterious to me and very, very sad.

Now poor Najma tried to discover her father's next move. Both she and Mala, the maid, turned into expert sleuths. It transpired that the same evening the Nawab summoned Shamsa from Sagun Bagicha and asked her about what she had said regarding Uma Roy and Rehan. The Nawab was livid. Shamsa got a fright. She almost trembled and quaked, "Sire, I do not know anything. I had just heard a vague sort of rumour and repeated it casually to your lady wife. Of course, it can't be true. Sir Pritish has a lot of rival lawyers, one of them must have started it."

The Nawab began frantic efforts to contact Rehan. He apparently wanted his nephew to rush to Dacca and solemnise the nikah before the tentative date fixed for Mr. Ajmal Hussain. The Nawab telephoned Uma Roy to ask his whereabouts. She was most unhelpful, said she hadn't a clue.

The Nawab firmly told his wife that he would not give his consent until he contacted Rehan and asked him if he was still interested in Jehan Ara. Anwari Begum hit the ceiling. She had a massive attack of hysteria. The Nawab couldn't care less. I really admired him. I used to go to Arjumand Manzil every day. He was desperately trying to reach Rehan, sending him telegrams to all possible addresses, making phone calls to Delhi, Calcutta, Bombay, etc. A wild goose chase.

When he could not be traced and Anwari Begum's condition took a turn for the worse, the poor nobleman accepted defeat. Didi, during those days I felt so sorry for him. He looked shattered. Jehan Ara was dumbfounded.

The marriage was a grand affair. All of us missed you and Rosie Apa. There is a still no factual news about her and a lot of wild rumours. For instance: she has tendered a written apology and come out of prison; she has been transported for life to the Andaman Islands; she has married an Englishman; she has run away from jail, handcuffs and all, and swum across the river. The latest is that she has married a wealthy Hindu advocate in Calcutta!

Despite the political unrest in the region, the Chowdhry-Murshidzada wedding was one of the greatest social events of the decade!

The bridegroom's gold-caparisoned elephant entered Arjumand Manzil's porch. The main hall of Arjumand Manzil was jam-packed with guests, mostly men. The entire upper floor had been turned into a zenana, overflowing with women and their noisy brats. Jehan Ara was in her room, also surrounded by women and children. She sat motionless on a divan, head bent, eyes closed, face hidden behind the bridal veil of red chiffon.

My father, Maulvi Majidullah, is a renowned theologian. He knows his Muslim Law. He had asked Nawab Qamrul Zaman to insert a clause in the marriage contract which gives the wife the prior right to divorce. The suggestion was vetoed by Jehan Ara's impossible mother, on the ground that no lady in that august family had ever done such a disgraceful thing as to seek a divorce. It was only the hoi-polloi, the servant-class women, who ran from qazi to qazi trying to obtain legal separation from their wayward husbands.

Abba is also the town qazi, the registrar of Muslim marriages. Dressed in his formal robes, looking very grave and thoughtful (and sweet), he came upstairs accompanied by the bride's father, brother and some male relatives, including three witnesses. In accordance with Islamic Law he asked, loud and clear, if Jehan Ara Begum, adult, daughter of Qamrul Zaman Chowdhry, of her own free will and in a state of total sanity, accepted as her lawful husband, Murshidzada Ajmal Hussain, adult, son of Murshidzada Arshad Hussain (who now dwelt in Heaven), against the dower of five hundred thousand rupees, embossed with the image of the King Emperor, and the currency of the present times. Half of which amount could be paid to her by her husband right away.

He asked the question thrice.

According to Mohammedan Law the girl must explicitly say, Yes or No. In India, customarily, she does not even utter a word. To speak would be the height of immodesty on her part. Therefore she merely nods or remains silent which is supposed to be a sign of her consent.

The same thing happened here. However, my father insisted that she speak so that he and the witnesses could hear her.

Just then Begum Qamrul Zaman, her mother, came forward and said, "Maulvi Saheb, she is too shy to raise her voice. She has said yes. Do you want her to shout from the rooftop?"

But my dear Abba wouldn't give up. He turned to the witnesses. "Did you hear the young lady say yes?"

There was some confusion. Because of the overcrowded room I couldn't see what was going on. I thought the Nawab was a bit hopeful that the nikah may not come off, thanks to the puritanism and strictness of Maulana Majidullah.

The suspense did not last more than a few minutes because I saw my father leave with a frown. Evidently the bride had either nodded in affirmation or mumbled an audible 'yes'.

Over the centuries we have acquired so many social customs from you all, Didi, which your community is discarding. For instance, your old women still say that once a girl is carried into her husband's home in a palanquin, she must leave that house only on a bier.

Awful. Jehan Ara Apa did not say No. She will not seek a divorce. And if she dies in his lifetime, her cortege will be covered with a red shawl signifying her good fortune that she is being buried by her husband. In case that fat lump of corruption kicks the bucket first, she will break her glass bangles and wear the widow's white sari for the rest of her life. (Why don't men go around wearing widowers' weeds?)

All these taboos are un-Islamic, my father once told me, taken over from the Hindus because they suited our men.

While I was on my way downstairs to see the remaining part of the nikah, I was buttonholed by Miss Gladys Jenkins, who taught English Literature to you all too, at Garden College.

"Jehan Ara looks like Thomas Moore's Lala Rukh!" she gushed.

I don't know who that lady is, but nodded vigorously so as not to show my ignorance.

"I dare say half a million rupees is a fabulous amount even for a Nawab to pay as bride-price."

I said, "Miss Jenkins, it is not bride-price, it is the wife's financial security guaranteed by the husband. The amount is fixed according to the earning capacity of the man. The wife is entitled to take it any time she so desires and realise it from his heirs after he expires."

"Yasmin, try not to speak baboo English."

"I mean, for instance, if this bloke goes phut," I gestured towards the hall.

"I beg your pardon?"

"And also a chap must pay up the entire *mehr* if he gives wifey a walking ticket."

Miss Jenkins was not amused by my command over the English language. She said, "Ah, but if the wife seeks a divorce she must forego that amount." Miss Jenkins also knew her Muslim Personal Law. "And that makes a woman's position inferior in Islam."

Deepali-di, as you know, we Bengalis love an argument. Here I was in a hurry to go downstairs but I must also defend Islam. So I said, "Miss Jenkins, Muslim women were granted the right to divorce nearly fourteen hundred years ago. You all in the West got it only in the last century."

Miss Jenkins said patiently, "I have always asked you girls not to speak chi-chi English—'you all', 'and all'."

"Okey-doke, Miss Jenkins."

That was the last straw. With an anguished expression on her wrinkled face, she turned to go.

Gladys Jenkins is sweet. She looked so cute in her formal dress, gloves, evening gown and all. Sorry, pl. delete 'and all'.

To return to the scene of action. All the other important English ladies were there, except Mrs. Barlow (on account of her giving up the ghost recently in England). For them the celebrations must have been pure Arabian Nights.

Down below in the ornate hall, my father was already in the process of asking the question thrice. Every time the groom said an emphatic, Yes! The register was duly signed by the couple. Abba delivered the wedding sermon and repeated the words of the Lord Prophet (Peace Be Upon Him) which he had uttered on the occasion of his beloved daughter, the Blessed Fatima's marriage to his cousin Ali (PBUH).

I found the sermon very moving and felt like crying.

Led by my Abba, the Muslim guests raised their hands and repeated the benediction in Arabic. Like confetti, dry dates were thrown over the assembly. This led to a mirthful scramble among the youngsters.

"Here, take one, Ronu, you'll also acquire a wife before the year is out," somebody shouted gleefully.

I had perched myself on a window-sill in order to have a sort of bird's-eye view of everything. It was then that I spotted this attractive stranger. He caught the dry date deftly, like a fast bowler, and threw some more towards others. The fun-belief is that if the unmarried eat these dry dates and pray earnestly, they will find a spouse in no time.

Ah, but dear reader, who was this dark-eyed stranger?

Hold your breath! It was Rehan Ahmed, none else! He had turned up at the time of the nikah, accompanied by Miss Uma Roy, and mingled with the guests. The Nawab saw him now and was petrified.

I wanted to go out, look at the moon and howl.

Rehan and Uma looked rather incongruous as a pair. Sir Pritish and Lady Roy were also present amidst the throng of distinguished guests.

Now, Didi, I must tell you who this mysterious Ronu Mian is. He is the famous Comrade you might be knowing, too. His mother was the Nawab's first cousin. In fact the Nawab was in love with her, but she was married off to some poor farmer-priest. The Nawab never forgot her, and that's why he always had a soft corner for her son, Rehan. He wanted him to marry Jehan Ara and stay in Arjumand Manzil for good. But Rehan had turned Red and refused to be a partner in the Nawab's jute business, etc. So the Nawab told him to get lost, which he did. Mala told me all this. As you know, now the Nawab wanted to make amends but it was too late.

Whew! What melodrama. What tragedy. Really. Now that also explains why Mrs. Qamrul Zaman is hysterical and why she hates Rehan's guts. Because she knows that her husband is still in love with Rehan's dead mother. My God. The emotional problems of the super-rich!

Nayyar greeted Rehan under the arch, "You have become like the Eid Moon! I'm seeing you after four-and-a-half years!"

"You can see the Eid Moon every year," he answered cheerily. "I came to Arjumand Manzil in Septembery—you weren't in!"

Right then Najma accosted him. "Where have you been, Ronu Bhai? Where did you go from Dacca? Delhi? Calcutta?"

"Oh," he said rather casually, "I went straight to Lahore. Then Peshawar. Spent the entire month touring the Frontier villages."

So that's why he didn't get the Nawab's telegrams and phone calls. Jehan Ara's bad luck. Now, that is predestination.

He continued: "In Kohat I got a telegram from Party headquarters to rush to Dacca for some work. Arrived this morning. Uma told me about the wedding, so we—I—came here just in time to attend the nikah and eat the dry dates!" Jovially he showed her the dates which he still held in his palm. He seemed so carefree and happy. I felt like murdering him.

Uma stood nearby, glaring at Najma. She asked him to join her parents on the lawn outside. As both of them strolled past, I said Boo to them on the quiet, and trudged upstairs with a heavy heart.

There was much commotion in the zenana. Women were leaning out of the windows, many had gone up to the terrace, all trying to catch a glimpse of the bridegroom who looked a clown in rich brocade. His pearl-studded velvet cap was the kind you see in the photographs of the Nawab Bahadur of Murshidabad. Suddenly there was another uproar. The bridegroom is coming, the bridegroom is coming! So he came, accompanied by his youthful best men and female relatives. He had flung back the floral veil which had covered his mug till the nikah, and was grinning from ear to ear. His mouth was full of betel-leaf. He was wiping off its red juice with his expensive hanky. He wore Mughal-style gold-work shoes, also studded with pearls. My God, that man is some Nawab.

Jehan Ara was escorted out of her room and brought to a gorgeous ottoman for The Mirror and the Holy Book ceremony. (It has no religious significance.) The couple were made to sit facing each other. A mirror and the Holy Quran were placed in between. The newly-weds were covered with a gold-work mantle of red chiffon. He was asked to recite a particular verse of the Scripture and see her reflection in the mirror.

The bride keeps her eyes closed and her friends urge the groom to say, "Wife, open your eyes. I am your slave." He resists but is eventually made to repeat the sentence.

Meanwhile one of his shoes is "stolen" by his sisters-in-law. Akhtar, Najma and I hated every minute of it. Most reluctantly we "stole" his shoes and teased him.

Downstairs on the lawns the police band played. *For He's a Jolly Good Fellow, The Blue Bells of Scotland* and *It's a Long, Long Way to Tipperary.*

The traditional shehnai-pipers were playing lovely ragas in the gatehouse.

Soon the time came for the bride to leave. Bibi had come downstairs. Chirpy females surrounded her again. Heard Nayyar yelling away: "Ladies, ladies, please make way. Make way, the bride's Elders are coming. The Elders are coming."

So a lot of "Elders" came in to bless the bride. They generally include aged relatives and old family friends. Your father came in along with other Elders, to place his hand on the bride's head. He did so and remained silent for a few seconds.

The Nawab had been crying silently. Most fathers of the bride cry, but I knew the reason for his bitter tears.

Rev. Bannerjee blessed the bride and placed a beribboned book entitled, *The Ideal Wife* near her. He turned to the baron. "Thanks be to the Lord," he intoned, "that you are sending your daughter away honourably and in accordance with the Law of your own Faith. Thanks be to the Good Lord." After which he crossed his hands behind his back, as is his wont, lowered his head and shuffled away.

Nayyar escorted her to the palanquin. Rehan was present among the throng of relatives. Shamsa Khatoon eyed him and shouted: "I say, Ronu Mian, now that you are here, you may as well bless your cousin..."

I was holding the velvet curtain of the palanquin. Rehan came forward, placed his right hand over Bibi's head and said, "All the best, Bibi." Then he added in a whisper—Didi, can you imagine what he said?—he said, "I still maintain that you ought to do your M.A. even as a private student."

Shamsa had cocked her ears. She asked me urgently, "What did he say to her? Did you hear?"

"Yes, I did," I whispered back. "He said, never mind that our plan failed. Don't worry, I'll carry you off from your castle in Dinajpur. Drop dead, Shamsa Khatoon."

She was aghast. Now I'm dreading the consequences.

An old crone bitched: "Ah, I remember, in the year 1910 dear Qamrul Zaman bade goodbye to his cousin Maliha from this very porch."

In the early hours of the morning the beautifully painted palanquin was carried out of the imposing gate of Arjumand Manzil.

I saw Rehan chatting happily with some friends on the front lawn. Didi, are all men so callous? I hope not.

Okay, Didi, 'bye.

Yours,
Yasmin Majid

Dacca,
22nd October, 1942

32
Kamal and Akmal

THE two infants were fast asleep in their frilled baskets. Jehan Ara, Rosie, Yasmin, Najma and Akhtar were all talking at once as they sipped their tea. Another golden afternoon in November. Only the calendar was different, and even 1943 was on the way out.

Rosie smiled at Jehan Ara's baby and turned to her friends. "I said to Basant my husband, I said, look Bibi has named her son Akmal to rhyme with his father's name, Ajmal Hussain. I'll call my son Kamal to rhyme with Akmal."

"That is sweet of you," Jehan Ara answered pleasantly.

"I told my husband, I said, Bibi has explained in her letter that Akmal in Arabic means most perfect. Basant laughed and said, in Sanskrit if you want the opposite of any noun you add 'A' to it. Let's hope Akmal does not become the opposite of Kamal. Basant is like that, you know. He is such an intellectual."

"Rosie, you were surrounded by your Party intellectuals before you got married, so you must be used to all this," Jehan Ara reminded her.

"Yes, but Basant is so different," she said proudly.

Nayyar's little boy. Munnawer, was pushing his pram down the verandah. The ayahs were sitting by the lotus tank. Rosie's ayah had come from Calcutta, therefore had superior airs. Unfortunately, even Rosie was giving herself airs. The not too subtle change in her distressed her old friends. They hoped it was short-lived and that soon she would start taking things in her stride.

"Rosie Apa, tell us what happened when you went to Lily Cottage yesterday," asked Akhtar Ara.

"Oh, nothing sensational, no fireworks. I had informed Mamma from Calcutta that I was so scared of Papa, I wouldn't come straight to Lily Cottage. Woodland people are Basant's family friends. Nirmalendu Roy is our neighbour in Ballygunj. He insisted that when we go to Dacca we stay with his parents. He trunk-called them from Calcutta. So we were met at Narayan Gunj and drove straight to Woodland. The same evening I went to Lily Cottage. Mamma had been waiting since the morning."

"The Return of the Prodigal!" Yasmin remarked.

"Yes. The Compound people had gathered at the gate. I got down from Lady Roy's motor car. The ayah with Kamal followed me."

"Did Basant Babu go with you?" asked Yasmin Majid.

"No. So Mamma came running and embraced me and burst into tears. She had decorated Lily Cottage with flowers and cooked a special dinner. When I went in she said, your Papa is in his study. Go in, he won't eat you up. I went in timidly. He was facing the window, reading. Mamma said, 'Paul!'

"He remained silent. He knew that I stood on the threshold. Mamma said again, 'Paul. do not be ungrateful to Father God. Thirteen months ago on a stormy night your daughter left this house and went out to court death. But the Good Shepherd looked after her and saved her. Give her your blessings, and behold! A little angel has come with her to this homestead!'

"Good old Mamma! She has started speaking the language of the pulpit. Anyway, perhaps Papa was waiting for his cue. His face hardened slightly, he slipped his glasses over his forehead and turned to me. Then he placed his hand on my head. Kamal began gurgling. Papa said, 'May God grant him a long life.' "

"He didn't ask about Basant Babu?" Jehan Ara wanted to know.

"No."

"Jolly good. The ice has been broken," commented Akhtar with satisfaction.

"Absolutely. After a few minutes Papa took Kamal in his arms and began to cuddle him. This rascal even spoilt his suit, but Papa didn't mind. When I was about to leave he asked, where are you going? I told him. He said, 'Why, isn't this your home?' I said I'll come tomorrow. So when I went there day before yesterday, I found him pacing the verandah. He was obviously waiting eagerly for his grandson. The moment he saw Baby his face lit up. Mamma asked me on the quiet, 'Why didn't you bring Basant along?' I said, I'll bring him tomorrow, but you see to it that Papa doesn't snub him."

"So, did you take him there yesterday?" asked Jehan Ara.

"No, I couldn't. Shall do so one of these days."

"Why are you taking so long, Rosie Apa?" Yasmin asked her former tutor.

Rosie said nothing. Master Akmal Hussain Murshidzada let out a big howl. All five girls started fussing over him. Jehan Ara said to Rosie, "Listen, you must take your husband to Lily Cottage this evening. Don't dilly-dally."

"Bibi, Basant is planning to shift to Delhi to practise at the High Court there. You see, we have a big house in New Delhi too, on Curzon Road. As soon as its tenant leaves, we'll go there. Last evening Basant began talking shop with Sir Pritish. You know, matters pertaining to legal practice, etc. And tonight the Roys are having a big dinner for us."

"Have they invited your parents?"

"Er ... No. They sort of won't fit in, and Bibi," Rosie said in a bored undertone, "I am not frightfully keen to show Basant that pokey little Lily Cottage..."

Just then Begum Qamrul Zaman came out of her room. The girls scrambled to their feet. Dressed in a red-bordered snow-white sari of exquisite Dacca muslin, the Begum looked as delicate and finicky as ever. She was followed by Mala who carried the silver paandan.

The Begum nodded. The girls sat down.

"How are you, Ma'am?" Rosie asked her deferentially.

"Fine, thank you." She beckoned to Mala. Trained to understand the slightest gesture of her masters and mistresses,

Mala went in and brought back a little velvet purse. It contained two hundred rupee notes and one silver rupee, which was always added for good measure. She slipped it under Master Kamal's little blanket.

"So, tell us, Rosie. Have you made up with your parents?" the Begum asked and opened her paandan to make betel-leaf *giloris.*

"Yes, Ma'am."

"Good. Allah is Great. All is well that ends well. And how is your mother-in-law treating you?"

"She is all right!"

The girls laughed.

The Begum spent another few minutes talking to the young women and offered them paan, which they took and salaamed her respectfully. After which she went back to her room.

Mala carried the huge paandan inside, came back and sat down on a cane stool near Rosie. She was a kind of lady-in-waiting rather than a servant, and talked freely with the begums, bibis, and their friends. She touched Rosie's jewel-studded bangles with pleasurable curiosity. Poor old Padre Saab's daughter marrying into a wealthy Calcutta family had been an exciting bit of news for the domestic staff of Arjumand Manzil. They knew that Rosie Missy Baba's mother, Giribala, had once worked here as an ayah. This was a real-life Cinderella story. It was all kismat.

Nawab Qamrul Zaman Chowdhry returned from the mosque after the Asar prayers. He spoke to Rosie and stroked her baby's head.

"What do you call him?"

"Kamal Kumar Sanyal!"

"Kamal to rhyme with our Akmal," Akhtar added cheerfully, and repeated what Basant Sanyal had told his wife about the prefix A.

"So, when you grow up you are going to take on my Akmal, eh? I'll pull your ears for that," the Nawab said pleasantly.

"No, sir," Rosie replied laughing, "Akmal becomes the opposite of Kamal, so your grandson is going to fight my Kamal."

"I'll give them both a good spanking, the rascals!" the Nawab said jovially. He went down the flight of stairs and began pacing to and fro on the lawn.

Jehan Ara had given Kamal baby-things of solid silver. The infant held a silver rattle in his tiny fist. "Master Kamal is born with a silver spoon in his mouth," Rosie remarked, happily sipping her tea.

Her friends were visibly embarrassed.

Yasmin was disillusioned. Was this the same Rosie Apa who had gone out into freedom's battle last year? She had refused to apologise to get out of her horrible prison. Do wealth and luxury and social position transform a person overnight?

Rosie addressed her loftily, "I say, Yasmin, you should settle down soon and Deepali ought to marry, too, and get away from that depressing Chandrakunj of hers."

"Chandrakunj is Deepali-di's home, Rosie Apa. Perhaps it is not at all depressing for her," Yasmin said gently.

"Nonsense. The parents' home is like a prison for an unmarried girl. One gets real freedom after one's marriage. Don't you agree, Bibi?"

Rosie had become a show-off and also a little stupid, Jehan Ara reflected sadly. She has to behave like an upstart; after all, her mother was once our kitchen-maid... The very next moment Bibi felt ashamed of herself for her unkind thought. Quickly she said aloud, "Yes, Deepali ought to find someone. When she does, I'll make all the arrangements. Her father is such a hermit, he won't do a thing. I'll come from Dinajpur and see to all the details. Only, I hope she lets us know beforehand."

"You must also bring your Rolls and all your elephants from Dinajpur for her wedding. Where is she, anyway?" Rosie asked primly. "You are in Dacca. Shouldn't she have come to see you?"

"Before Apa arrived from Dinajpur, Deepali-di went off to Delhi for her radio programme. The latest rumour in town these days is that Uma Roy is going to marry Dr. Sarkar. Deepali-di probably does not relish the idea and wants to be away from home as much as she can," Akhtar Ara told her.

"Uma Roy to marry Dr. Sarkar?" Rosie arched her eyebrows. "Nobody told me about it at Woodland. It's most surprising."

"Why? Uma being what she is, it would be her great good fortune if Benoy Babu accepts her. Though, unfortunately, people will think that he is marrying her for money," said Jehan Ara.

"Oh, I forgot, Rosie Apa, I've also got something for Kamal," Najma exclaimed and went in. After a few minutes she emerged, carrying an enormous, expensive English toy.

"Omigosh, you all have given such fabulous presents to my son!" Rosie said to the Nawab's three daughters.

"Don't be silly," said Jehan Ara.

Yasmin was sitting in a corner having, as usual, a detached view of the scene. She eyed her tiny packet sadly. Rosie had opened it, peeped inside to see the baby frock Yasmin had lovingly stitched and embroidered for Kamal, expressed her polite thanks and resumed her conversation.

A sleek silver-grey Jaguar drew up alongside the verandah. Nawab Ajmal Hussain Murshidzada got out and ascended the stairs. He was dressed in a black sherwani and tight white pyjamas. A Turkish cap sat jauntily on his head. He was munching a paan and looked very pleased with himself.

"Oh-ho-ho! Regular hen-party going on, eh...?"

Jehan Ara introduced him to Rosie.

"How do you do, Mrs. Sanyal," he said hurriedly and turned towards the passage which led to the grand staircase.

"He is a very shy person," Jehan Ara said sheepishly.

This black mountain of a man, munching paans like a he-goat—he has become the exquisite Jehan Ara's lord and

master, Rosie mused, and I get the marvellous Basant! Divine
Mysteries, as Papa used to say.

Nawab Qamrul Zaman was coming back from the garden.

"Bibi, could you come upstairs for a minute? Give me my
clothes, I have to go to a stag dinner," Murshidzada shouted
from the staircase landing.

"Coming—"

"And fresh paan."

"In a minute."

There are countless servants in Arjumand Manzil and a
dozen must have come with her from Dinajpur, but she
attends to him herself, Rosie marvelled again as Jehan Ara
hurried away.

Her father had reached the steps. He saw her running off
to obey her husband's command. He winced. Semi-educated
Maliha had done this, but this modern girl, a college graduate,
was also making the best of a bad marriage. He wished he
didn't have to be so ashamed of himself for Maliha, and now
for his own daughter. He had been mercilessly trapped by
life. Slowly he passed through the gallery and returned to his
last refuge, the library.

Basant Kumar telephoned from Woodland to say that the car
was being sent to fetch Mrs. Sanyal.

Rosie's ayah began packing the baby's paraphernalia.
Both Kamal and Akmal had been fed their bottles and had
gone off to sleep again. There they lay on the settee, side by
side, tiny, helpless beings, newly arrived in a strange world.

Outside, "the magical throne" began to glow in the sunset.
The hour when day encounters night can be very dispiriting.
According to Muslim belief there is a special reason for this:
daily the evening light reminds the human soul of the
impending final twilight which one will see in the hour of
one's death.

Evenings can also be trying inside vast and lonely rooms.
Nawab Qamrul Zaman felt claustrophobic in his study and

stirred out once again. He returned to his favourite bench near the summer-house.

The two infants gurgled in their sleep. "Babies smile when they see a lovely dream," commented Yasmin. "They must be seeing cherubs and rainbows and all manner of beautiful things." At that moment she forgave Rosie her new cheapness and arrogance. She said, "Rosie Apa, there is a lovely poem by Sarojini Debi—shall I recite it to you?"

"Yes, but quickly. My car is on the way."

Yasmin blinked and started her recitation.

Sleep, my little ones, sleep,
Safe till the daylight be breaking...
We have long vigils to keep...
Harvests to sow while you sleep...

She got up and began to dance, etching the words with her graceful movements.

Jehan Ara had come back. She whispered to Rosie, "You know, this girl is fay. She worries me."

"Oh, she will come to no harm," Rosie said indifferently, and closed the suitcase full of Arjumand Manzil presents. Yasmin increased her tempo as she recited.

Children, my children, who wake to inherit
Say, when your young hearts shall take to their keeping
The manifold dreams we have sown for your reaping,
Is it praise, is it pain, will you grant us for guerdon?
Anoint with your love or arraign with your pardon?

Nawab Qamrul Zaman had come up to the verandah. He stood behind a pillar and listened intently. Yasmin remained oblivious of his presence till she had finished. She noticed him and became nervous. He smiled reassuringly, stroked her head and strode down to the mosque.

The garden and the lotus-tank melted into the dusk. The muezzin called the Faithful to Maghrib prayers.

Kamal and Akmal continued to sleep.

Part III

Part III

33
Birds of Paradise

"If I had received your letter about Jehan Ara's wedding just a day earlier, we wouldn't have been here today!" Deepali said conversationally to Yasmin.

Mistress Saraswati arrived with coffee. She placed the tray on a wicker table and left. A bird of paradise flew down from a raintree and began strutting on the grass. Yasmin looked up. Dark Caribbean clouds had spread over the sky. A stream rippled through the greenery. An East Indian woman with a red bandana sat on the grassy bank, washing clothes. A tree-top dispensary displayed the signboard: **Dr. B.C. Sarkar, Plantation Medical Officer**. Patients waited under the shade. It was a motley group: Chinese, East Indian, Black. Man has this knack of creating a heaven for himself when he is exiled from his own, Yasmin said to herself.

"Didi, whatever happened?" she asked weakly.

"Master's phone," Mistress Saraswati called out from somewhere.

"Excuse me," Deepali said, getting up. As she walked up to the Spanish-colonial mansion across the lawn, Mistress Saraswati came back. "Madam says," she began, grinning, "that you are a dancer. You have come all the way from Pakistan."

"Yes, Mistress Saraswati. I have known your Madam for quite a long time. We belong to the same country...I mean, it was the same country till three or four years ago."

"Do you dance in the movies also? Like Miss Cuckoo of Bombay?" Mistress Saraswati got up and swirled around. "Like this...?"

Yasmin smiled. The woman with the red polka-dot bandana came over, carrying her wash. She put the basket down and joined Mistress Saraswati in her jig. Yasmin watched them, fascinated. It looked like a pre-war Hollywood movie with the tropical setting of a Somerest Maugham novel. Yasmin rubbed her eyes. She was finding herself in the midst of a strange hotch-potch of cultures. The woman with the red bandana looked like a swarthy Spanish gypsy, except that she wore a Muslim amulet around her neck. She was an excellent dancer.

Deepali returned from the house. The women stopped dancing. Deepali smiled at them benevolently. Quite the Lady of the Manor, thought Yasmin. "Such a carefree life, almost idyllic. This girl can be a fine dancer. Who is she?"

"The younger one? Mistress Khairunissa. Her husband, Sharafat Ali, is Father's compounder."

The girl asked Yasmin with awe, "You have come from Pakistan?" She uttered the word "Pakistan" as though it were a sacred name.

"Yes," Yasmin replied.

"Have you seen Noorjehan?"

"Noorjehan?"

"The great singing star. She sang, *The world hath no peace nor rest for me...*" Khairun crooned in reply. "Noorjehan sang this song in *The Family.* I have seen a lot of Indian movies. Miss Leela Chitnis B.A. and Ashok Kumar in *The Bracelet,* Prithvi Raj in *Alexander the Great.* When Alexander was invading India on horseback he led this chorus song: *Life is for loving. Love on...Love on...*"

"But these are antedeluvian movies! I saw them in my childhood," Yasmin remarked, amused.

"We only get to see ancient India movies out here. We have seen some of the latest ones too, like *The Rainfall*—Raj Kapoor-Nargis," Mistress Saraswati answered airily.

"These films make us happy. We long to see our Old Country. We can't go there—it would cost a lot of money which we don't have. We see the movies and imagine what our Old Country must be like," Mistress Khairunissa said wistfully.

Deepali's eyes brimmed over. She looked away.

"Forget it, Didi," Yasmin said to her softly.

"You are not an exile. Right now you are on top of the world. Famous dancer in your brand new country, and Dacca is still your hometown," Deepali said a little sourly.

"Sorry," Yasmin was crestfallen. She began to play with the coffee spoon. Doubtless, I am very pleased with myself, she thought. My happiness is too obvious. The world is lying at my feet, as they say. Promising career. Admirers. Fame. Limelight. Glamour. What does she have to show as her achievement? Or Jehan Ara? Bitterness and disappointments. All the same, I must not become conceited like Rosie Sanyal. "Although," she said aloud, "I have had to pay a fairly heavy price for my success and fame. Defied my conservative father, gave up my family. But the urge to serve art and culture was too strong…"

"Art and Culture, my left toe. You were only running after personal happiness. All of us are," Deepali retorted.

Perhaps she has begun to resent me, Yasmin reflected woefully. She was a noted singer in undivided Bengal, nobody knows her out here. I have become almost world-famous, with my pictures in the Western press. Gerald says if I try, I can even set up my "studio of oriental dance" in New York. Start a "modern oriental ballet" and so on. I won't tell her about the project just yet. And for all I know she may even be prejudiced. After all, I am a Pakistani and a Muslim, and she had to flee East Pakistan. Lived in Calcutta as a refugee…No, she is an old Marxist, can't be anti-Muslim. That's one thing about Leftists, they have no religious hangovers, and poor Deepali is such an old pal. Still, if I tell her about Gerald, she may become envious, cast an evil eye. Touch wood, I am so lucky. My famous, handsome, English fashion designer, Gerald Belmont. Look at her ugly fatso husband, Lalit Sen. Funny, how in looks, Barrister Sen is the Bengali Hindu version of Jehan Ara's rotund Nawab Ajmal Hussain. The only difference is that Mr. Sen is highly educated and does not chew betel-leaves.

Khairunissa and Saraswati were jabbering away in a strange language. Shonu called out from an upper-floor window, "Didi! Your phone call again."

Deepali got up and went in.

The East Indian women watched her leave. One of them turned to Yasmin and asked, "Why was Madam crying? I've often noticed, sometimes she just sits by herself and sheds tears."

"Dunno, Mistress Saraswati," Yasmin answered uncomfortably. "Perhaps she also remembers her Old Country and...and..."

"And what...?"

Yasmin quickly made up, "Well, you see, she had this childhood friend in Dacca, called Jehan Ara Begum..."

"Jehan Ara Begum?" Khairunissa repeated brightly. "That was a Mughal Emperor's daughter."

"This Jehan Ara's father was a minor Nawab of Bengal.

"Then...what happened?" Khairunissa asked eagerly.

"Jehan Ara Begum's love story was quite tragic. Your Madam must be saddened whenever she thinks of it, so she cries."

"Tragic? Something went wrong between lover and beloved? Who was the villain?" asked Mistress Saraswati.

"What kind of love—spiritual or romantic? Was her *piya* a prince or a commoner?" Khairunissa demanded to know.

These women had been brought up on a rich diet of Indian cinema.

"Spiritual and romantic both, perhaps," said Yasmin thoughtfully. "The hero was the heroine's cousin."

"Oh, just like Noorjehan's movie, *Khandaan*!" Khairunissa exclaimed joyfully. "Was he a prince?"

"Part prince, part commoner."

"That must have made the plot complicated."

"Very, and the heroine was deeply in love with him."

"I understand," Mistress Saraswati nodded gravely.

"But the cousin sort of ditched her and ran away."

"How dreadful! Oh, no…" the women cried in unison. "What a shame. Why…why…?"

"Er…because of his ideology."

"Ideology…what is that?" asked Mistress Khairunissa.

"It means…it means that…er…well, the hero believed that all human beings should be equal. There should be no rich man, poor man. See? The heroine's affluent father wanted the hero to become wealthy. He refused. You see, Mistress Khairunissa, in those day boys and girls used to sacrifice their true love for each other at the Altar of Ideology."

"They must have been nuts."

"They were, indeed. Me, too. I gave up prospects of a safe and mundane marriage for the sake of my…my ideology."

"And pray, Ma'am, what is your ideology?" Saraswati asked politely.

"Well—it's difficult to explain."

"Tell us. We'll try to understand."

"Okay, you can call it Idealism instead of Ideology."

"Another big word!" Khairunissa chuckled.

"Well," Yasmin continued. She was enjoying this conversation. "I learned classical dance so that High Culture could flourish in my country."

"And what is low culture…like ours…?" Khairunissa asked sweetly.

"Good heavens, no! What I mean is, things like classical dance and music and great literature, etc. I worked hard for their promotion in my new land."

"Lands are billions of years old, no land is new," Mistress Saraswati corrected her.

Zany women, these. Yasmin tried to go on bravely, "Ours is a young country."

"Is Pakistan a part of India?" Saraswati asked again.

"I beg you pardon, most certainly not!" Yasmin rejoined angrily. I shouldn't waste my time talking to these foolish creatures. "Look, I must explain again," she said patiently. "In 1947 the British colony of India became two independent nations. Now Pakistan is divided into two parts—West and East. I am from East Pakistan. We are all Bengalis over there and we Bengalis are rather strong on Art and Culture. I mean, what used to be East Bengal is now East Pakistan, divided by a thousand miles of hostile India."

"In short, you used to be an Indian, now you are a Pakistani," said Mistress Saraswati.

"That's right. And my government has sent me on a world tour," she emphasised.

"Your government?"

"Yes, the Government of Pakistan. You are still a British colony," she added a bit contemptuously. "You still have a colonial mentality."

Descendants of bonded labour, they'll always retain their slavish outlook. Bush coolies.

"Madam, what is your mentality like, in free Pakistan and India?" Saraswati asked amiably.

Cheeky. In the New World even the children of Indian coolies have become bold and independent. Why should I bother to argue with them? Yasmin kept quiet.

Deepali came back.

"My husband telephoned, he has arranged for you to give a performance at Government House—for the Governor-General. Saturday evening."

"For the Governor-General?" Yasmin repeated excitedly. Mistress Saraswati smiled. Yasmin noticed her sardonic grin and reddened.

"Excuse me, Ma'am," Saraswati picked up the coffee tray. Khairun curtsied and lifted her wash basket. They walked away towards the outhouses.

Yasmin watched them go. "Peculiar."

"They must be thinking the same about us! They are a very intelligent people, don't underestimate them. A hundred years ago their ancestors were brought here from eastern U.P. to work as indentured..."

"Yes, yes, I know. Listen, just tell me what happened... I'm meeting you after all these years, and here of all places, in the back of beyond."

"When the British freed their Negro slaves..."

"Didi, answer my question."

"You have always been a nosey-parker, Yasmin."

"Okay, but I do think you owe us an explanation."

"Owe you an explanation? Whatever for? And pray, who is 'us'?"

"Myself and your friend, Jehan Ara. Why did you suddenly drop her? It was most odd. Everybody noticed. What on earth was the matter?"

"*Oh dear, what can the matter be, Oh dear...*" Deepali hummed merrily.

"Stop being flippant. Bibi got married in October, '42. You never met her after that. Whenever she came to Dacca from Dinajpur, you were supposed to be either in Santiniketan or in Calcutta, for your radio programmes. You even avoided meeting me."

"That's not entirely true," Deepali answered slowly. "I did meet her once or twice afterwards, but didn't have the courage to face her. For the simple reason that I had a bad conscience."

"But why?"

Suddenly Deepali began to laugh. "Don't you know?"

"I don't. I heard some vague sort of rumours, nobody knew the facts. And Bibi never said a word."

"I did start telling you earlier this evening, but somehow lost track."

"Yes?"

"You asked me how we landed up in Trinidad, and I said if I had received your letter about Bibi's wedding just a day earlier, we wouldn't have been here today!"

"Didi, don't make it a whodunit!"

"It *is* a kind of whodunit." Deepali sighed. "You see, in the summer of '41 I quite unexpectedly found Rehan's photograph in Jehan Ara's work-box. Since then I had been feeling guilty as hell. I didn't know anything about his personal life and the discovery of that snapshot shocked me out of my wits. I didn't say a word about it to Bibi or anybody else, but stopped meeting him. Didn't answer his letters. He chased me up and down the Ganges and persisted. So I told him. Whereupon he narrated the story of his life, and also that the Nawab had broken off his engagement with Jehan Ara because he had turned into a dangerous Commie.

"Stands to reason. Any sensible father would have done that. And Rehan made me understand that all this happened before he met me, so I was in no way responsible for Bibi's unhappiness.

"In the first week of September, '42, just before Rehan left on his Punjab tour, we decided that the following month he would send me a telegram from Calcutta. I would go there and the comrade-in-charge of the Commune would declare us man and wife. By that time 'Party marriages' had come into vogue.

"In October I was in Santineketan, waiting to hear from Rehan, when Uma Roy turned up. She had come all the way from Dacca to see me. In the over-dramatic fashion of early Calcutta theatre, she proceeded to drop the bombshell: she had received a frantic telephone call from Qamrul Zaman Chowdhry. Apparently he had changed his mind. 'He asked me if I knew the whereabouts of his elusive nephew. I didn't. Even if I did, I wouldn't have told him. For the simple reason that now he would say, No, and for an entirely different reason: He is in love with you.

" 'Now, Deepali, do as your conscience tells you. If he returns to Jehan Ara, he would do so as a matter of moral duty, but he would make both his wife and you unhappy…' "

"In other words, Uma Debi was playing God…" Yasmin interrupted.

"Yes. 'Or,' she said, 'you go to Calcutta according to plan and deeply hurt your noble father, as well as poor Jehan Ara. Or you say No to Rehan. He is not very reliable, anyway. He ditched his cousin, he could do the same to you. Besides, how would you adjust in Muslim society? If the marriage does not succeed, will Chandrakunj take you back? You will have lost face, lost caste and burnt you boats. Jehan Ara is a highly-strung girl—she may even commit suicide if she comes to know of the perfidy of her best friend, Deepali Sarkar.'

"Uma Roy painted a picture of total disaster. Being young and inexperienced, I was horrified. Uma came and went like a devastating hurricane. I had nightmares of my Baba, my aunt and Jehan Ara, all jumping in together in the Padma river. I saw myself being persecuted by sword-wielding Muslim in-laws. I know! I am very susceptible. Anyway, after a few days I wrote to Rehan at his Calcutta address, informing him that this time it was really quits.

"Posted the letter on the morning of October 5th. On the 26th your fat envelope arrived, carrying the news of poor Jehan Ara's wedding to some silly Nawab.

"So, as I told you, if I had heard from you only twenty-four hours earlier, I would have gone to Calcutta and married Rehan."

"You could still have done that, explained to Rehan that you wrote to him more or less under duress."

"No, somehow it didn't work out that way. Rehan never met me afterwards. Perhaps he had got tired of giving me explanations about himself. And I had hurt him much too deeply. Perhaps a devil got into me—I accused him of double-dealing, because Uma told me that in August when he met me, he had also gone to Arjumand Manzil, ostensibly for a political discussion with the Nawab, but had actually met Jehan Ara..."

"She also told you he didn't care for his cousin and was in love with you. Couldn't he meet Bibi as a relative? Didn't you realise that Uma was only trying to confuse and scare you?"

"That's why, dear Yasmin, I have come to believe in Destiny." She laughed hollowly. "As a good Muslim, Bibi probably accepts everything as the Will of Allah. I don't really know about God, but I have certainly become a fatalist..."

"Now, shall I tell you the rest about Rehan Ahmed?" asked Yasmin after a long pause.

"Do!"

"In 1945 we held this All India Folk-song Festival... remember?"

"Yes, we Leftists organised things in a big way those days. What has happened now?"

"Forget about what has happened now. Listen to this. Comrade Rehan was very much there, supervising this and that. During the sessions he also began running after me."

"Rascal!" Deepali gave a short laugh.

"You, of course, were conspicuous by your absence."

"Didn't want to run into those two, Uma and Rehan. Preferred to sulk at home."

"Rehan Ahmed was in charge of the East Bengal Folk Singers' Camp.

"Another group had arrived from Manipur. They had driven Miss Alice Barlow away from the Garo Hills. The Communist Movement had become strong in the tribal areas of Assam. Those were the days, Didi! The Raja of Manipur's own brother had become a Communist leader. It was only five years ago, but already that era seems so remote and strange. How we used to take part in the Peoples' Theatre plays! Leading actors and actresses, dancers and writers, all had become 'sympathisers'. Remember Uday Shankar distributing our Cultural Front leaflets in the bazaars? All of us were full of joyous, patriotic fervour. We seemed to have forgotten that Golden Bengal was about to be cut up between two mutually hostile countries."

"Palestine and Germany have also been cut into two."

"That doesn't diminish our own miseries. We had such rosy visions of the post-war world, of free India which would turn into the land of milk and honey.

"In the Festival we had 'squads' from all over: Chittagong, Surma Valley, Manipur, Peoples' Theatre. Didi," Yasmin continued dolefully, "the Orissa Squad presented a folk song—
For the sake of my belly I went to Bengal/Knocked around, husked

paddy, slogged as a labourer/Received lashes on my bare back, danced with pain, met the god of Death/All for the sake of this belly."

"And we," Deepali interrupted, "came all the way from Dacca to Port of Spain... All for the sake of this belly."

"There was this song of a Gond tribe: *I sold my cow to pay the forest tax...I sold my ox to pay the forest tax. In the Englishman's Raj we remain hungry...*

"We were so sure that in our own Raj nobody would go hungry and all wound be well.

"The Hyderabad Squad sang that famous Urdu chorus... 'The Red Dawn of Freedom'—*We Red solidiers are the glory of our land, singing the crimson song...*"

"Yasmin, we were talking about Rehan..."

"Ah, yes. So he began to patronise me. I told him I was your friend. The information made no impact on him. Suddenly I got very bored. Disillusioned, fed up with everything. You know what I mean. In 1946 I obtained a scholarship in order to learn Bharatanatyam in the South.

"After Partition I went straight to Karachi from Kanchipuram, and stayed with a distant relative. He was very influential. A Central Minister from East Pakistan was his close friend. This hon'ble Minister has sent me abroad.

"Just before I left for London, I heard from Jehan Ara. She was in Dacca. She informed me that you all had sold Chandrakunj and emigrated first to Calcutta and then to Trinidad.

"She was sorry that you didn't see her before going away, nor ever wrote to her. What hurt her most was that perhaps the Indo-Pak bitterness had affected you as well."

"I wish I could explain to her the real reason. Perhaps she had guessed, and she also knew that I was not responsible for her unhappiness. Besides, she was mostly in Dinajpur. How could I meet her?

"We lived on in Dacca till 1948. Baba's patient, Mitra Babu, was an old fox. His wife was a bitch. Together they tried to foist Uma Roy on my unsuspecting father. Mitra Babu proceeded to exchange his modest house in Dacca for some rich Muslim's mansion in Calcutta's Park Circus. He left for India. So did Sir Pritish Roy. The government of East Pakistan rented Woodland from the Roys and turned it into the official guest house for VIPs. Partition didn't create any problems for the super-rich. The Roys still owned Woodland— Lady Roy would come over to Dacca, spend her evenings with old friends at Dacca Club, collect the house rent and fly back. In Calcutta they were staying in Ballygunj with sonny boy, Nirmalendu. He had become a business magnate on Clive Row.

"Now Mitra Babu wrote to Father asking him to come over to Calcutta at the earliest. My brother Khokhu had already left. He was now a member of the Hindu Mahasabha and a follower of Dr. Shyama Prasad Mukherjee.

"Eventually, one day, my father hired a cycle-rickshaw and went to Arjumand Manzil to consult Nawab Qamrul Zaman. The Nawab said, you must not go. We have a shortage of doctors. Hindu doctors are migrating to India. Now at last you can have a roaring practice. Baba said maybe, but what about the future of my children? So he sold Chandrakunj for a song. It was bought by a Muslim refugee from Bihar. We left for Calcutta. Nawab Qamrul Zaman Chowdhry cried when he said goodbye. Jehan Ara was away in Dinajpur.

"Abdul Qadir had come to our house as a child, when my grandfather first arrived in Dacca. He had loyally stood by us through all the ups and downs of Chandrakunj. We deserted him in his old age.

"We saw Charles Barlow at Gawalendu river-port. He was sitting alone on the first-class deck of the steamer, drinking. The sun was setting behind his back in the river. It was a strangely symbolic scene. Somebody on board the steamer told us that instead of returning to England, he was going off to Australia to become a sheep farmer.

"On reaching Calcutta we went straight to Mitra Babu's house in Park Circus. Baba had always treated him and his family free of charge. The least he could do was to take us in as paying-guests.

"Mitra Babu had decided that my father had fallen in love with Uma Roy. Lady Roy wanted her to find a husband and liberate herself from her idiotic fixation on Rehan. He was also in town but I never met him.

"Nirmalendu was a big capitalist and was embarrassed by his sister's politics. He also pressured her to settle down. She agreed. Perhaps she thought that once she acquired the status of a married woman, her friendship with Rehan would not be considered objectionable.

"My father, as you know, is a good-hearted man, and does not have a suspicious nature. He was no admirer of Uma Debi, but he had been uprooted and probably needed some kind of emotional support. Uma was flattering him no end. Everybody except Baba had a vested interest in the alliance. Mitra Babu was a wheeler-dealer. He thought that as a son-in-law of the Roys, Baba would help him in his business— Nirmalendu was a pucca Brown Saheb, and people like Mitra Babu could never hope to reach him directly.

"I was watching the drama in silence.

"Uma Debi had been a fellow-traveller and all that, but she couldn't overcome the inborn snobbery of her class. She had started patronising us, for we were poor refugees.

"I was looking for a job, Baba wanted to start his clinic. We had been living off our capital, the amount we received as the price for Chandrakunj. It was about to finish. Shonu and Tonu had become loafers. One year had passed and we were still living with Mitra Babu. Mrs Mitra began quarrelling with my aunt. Bhavtarni Debi was quite a battle-axe herself. The two women wrangled most of the time. I earned a little through my radio programmes and spent the rest of the time in museums and libraries. What made me feel worse was that Rehan was also in Calcutta and he knew that I was there, living as a struggling, unemployed refugee. Sometimes I sat in the Asiatic Society Library for hours, hoping that he would turn up to read a book. I rehearsed the sentences I would speak... It never happened.

"One morning I was loitering in the halls of Victoria Memorial. As I stopped under the portrait of Prince Abdul Khalique, son of Tipu Sultan, I heard Uma Debi's voice. When I turned round I saw her with an Englishman. She introduced him to me: an old classfellow of hers from London. She said to him, 'And this is Deepali, my brother Nirmalendu's personal assistant.'

"I was flabbergasted. I said, I'm sorry, you have made a mistake. I am not a personal assistant to any Nirmalendu Roy.

"Uma Debi stood there like a duchess, under the dome of Victoria Memorial. She stared at me and said, 'We shall talk about it later. Come along, Ben.'

"The Englishman looked embarrassed by the unpleasant encounter. I strolled away.

"The same evening she came to the house in Park Circus. I was standing outside. She got out of the car and began shouting. 'How dare you talk back to me in front of my English friend?'

"'You have become quite impossible, Uma Debi.' I tried to be civil.

"'Calcutta is teeming with refugee girls like you. Every fourth Bengali female has a singing voice like yours, you are not unique. Nobody is going to appoint you Governor of West Bengal! Thank me, that I have fixed up a job for you in my brother's Clive Row office.'

"'If you are under the impression that I will agree to work for your conceited, eccentric brother, you are sadly mistaken, Miss Roy.'

"'I am going to talk to your father,' she screamed, stamping her foot.

"'Go ahead,' I replied evenly.

"Baba and Mr. Mitra were not at home. My aunt had gone to Kalighat. Mrs. Mitra posted herself behind the door and eavesdropped. Uma Debi went back fuming. When my father returned home, Mrs. Mitra reported to him.

"After a while he came to my room. I had been crying. He said briefly, 'Don't lose your courage.'

"'Baba, are you really going to marry that terrible woman?' I asked him between sobs.

"He kept quiet. I said: 'Do you want me to become Nirmalendu Roy's secretary? Don't you know the kind of man he is? Besides, Sir Pritish has bought a house on Alipur Road for Uma Debi. She will stay in it with you. Obviously, I'll have to live there, too. Rehan will be a frequent visitor. It's a dreadful situation.' That was the first time I had mentioned Rehan to my father.

"After a short silence he said, 'Let's say goodbye to this country.'

"Go back to Dacca?" I asked.

"'No, to the West Indies. Mukul has written to me, he can get me a job as a medical officer on a sugar plantation.'

"Uncle Mukul was Father's first cousin. Years ago he had migrated to Trinidad. He was also a physician and had made a lot of money over here. Once he came home and visited Chandrakunj. He looked so prosperous in our genteel, poor surroundings. I remember he was smoking a very huge kind of cigarette I had never seen before. He told me it was called a Havana cigar. My mother had tried to keep up appearances, and gave him an excellent dinner.

"I asked Father, 'How will you shake *her* off?'

"He laughed and said, 'I'll tell her to accompany me to Trinidad. She will refuse—that's how.'

"That was precisely what happened.

"Father went to a steamship office and bought five tickets with the remaining Chandrakunj money. We said goodbye to India, and after a long voyage made it to the West Indies. Baba, my aunt, Shonu, Tonu and myself. Khokhu refused to come. He was in the process of becoming a minor leader in the Hindu Mahasabha.

"My aunt was angry: Laxmi, the goddess of wealth, had come to our threshold in the form of Uma Debi, but Benoy foolishly sent her back."

"Laxmi! My goodness! She would have made mincemeat of you all," Yasmin remarked. "Tell me, how did you meet Mr. Sen?"

"Uncle Mukul knew Lalit. His first wife was of Spanish descent. They were divorced long ago, no children. Lalit is a gentleman. I am quite happy. He bought this house for me. I have named it The Serenade. Odd sort of name for a house, people said. I was going to call it Saraband, but it reminded me of 'Saraband for Dead Lovers!!'" She fell silent.

After a few moments she added, "Father and Aunt stay with us as paying-guests. See, what a beautiful tree-top clinic Lalit has constructed for my Baba!"

Yasmin regarded her with amazement. After a while she said, "Which means that Bibi must be quite content with her Lord of Dinajpur?"

"Probably!"

"Is this a compromise or a kind of happiness?"

"Can't say."

A sleek chauffeur-driven car entered the gate. Barrister Sen stepped out, carrying his briefcase.

Dr. Benoy Chandra Sarkar climbed down from his tree-top clinic. The young women got up. All four walked together towards The Serenade...

Yasmin wandered into the drawingroom and looked out of a window. Bhavtarni Debi sat under a leafy tree, reciting her *shlokas*. A number of pedigreed pups played about on the grass. Servants could be seen carrying dishes through a glazed corridor which connected the kitchen with the dining-room.

Yasmin turned back and inspected the expensive furniture. She wondered if Deepali ever remembered Chandrakunj. But why should one keep remembering an unhappy past? Does Deepali ever hear her own old songs, Yasmin wondered again, as she opened the cardboard box of HMV records. Gingerly she took out one Deepali Sarkar bhajan and wound up the old-fashioned gramophone. The disc began moving. She fumbled with the sound-box. The needle dropped somewhere in the middle. All of a sudden a long-ago Deepali Sarkar sang out: *I wear what he makes me wear, I eat what he gives me to eat... Meera's Lord Giridhar Nagar...*

"Miss, lunch is ready," the Negro butler, Elias, announced from the doorway.

The Pakistani guest drew a long breath and closed the gramophone. On her way to the dining-room she passed by a side-table and saw Rosie's smiling silver-framed photograph. It was signed, 'Radhika Sanyal, New Delhi, 7.3.1950.'

34
Esther Giribala Bannerjee

IN a two-room quarter on the Mission Compound, directly beneath the framed GOD BLESS OUR HOME, Mrs. Bannerjee had hung the group photograph of Rosie's children—Kamal, Neera and Ella. She had decorated the rooms with paper bunting and Chinese lanterns. She had even tried to liven up the sitting-room with her own device. She had dabbed the walls with a sponge soaked in coloured water. It was a pity poor Paul could see neither the photograph of his grandchildren nor the colourful walls. Secretly Esther Bannerjee was happy that he couldn't see the huge, triumphant-looking Christmas card sent by the Biswases from Montreal. The entire Biswas family of Ludhiana had emigrated to Canada. Henry Biswas had informed them that they were going to have their first White Christmas.

Indeed. Now they could afford to cock a snook at the Bannerjees. They were no longer mere "rice Christians", they were *Canadians*. Luther had married a White girl. Edith wore New Look dresses and was dating a boy who was not only Canadian but *French*-Canadian. Sister Marjorie Das of the Government Hospital had come to the Mission Compound's X'mas Bazaar and shown Esther Bannerjee the snapshots her relatives had proudly sent her from the New World. Mrs. Mary Biswas had cut her hair and wore baggy trousers. "Now perhaps she thinks she is Yvonne de Carlo," Sister Majorie had bitched.

"Who is Yvonne de Carlo?" Mrs. Bannerjee asked innocently. But how right Mary Biswas had been about Rosie— she did eventually marry a heathen, didn't she?

This nasty Christmas card had come from across the seven seas, but none from Rosie who lived in neighbouring India. A few days before Christmas, Esther got busy with her annual chores. It hurt her to see her husband sitting by the window waiting patiently for the postman. This had become his sole occupation over the years—waiting for Rosie's letters which came once in a blue moon.

The postman passed by. The old clergyman recognised his footfall.

There was silence again.

"Esther, any letter from India?"

Esther was boiling rice on her kerosene stove.

It would certainly break his heart if she said no again. "It was not the postman, dear," she shouted from the kitchenette.

"Rosie hasn't come for so many years. Esther, have you decorated the Christmas tree?"

"Yes, dear."

"Where are the toys? Show me…"

"Toys?"

"For Rosie's children. I have a feeling they may arrive this evening. There is an aeroplane service now, between Calcutta and Dacca."

"Yes, Paul."

"We wait for her every Christmas. She doesn't come."

"Paul, it is not very easy for her to travel from India. Visa problems, you know."

"She hardly ever visited us even before Partition. Let's face it, she is ashamed to own us as her parents. She is a big shot's wife. Who are we? Mere rice Christians… Do you think she will remember us, Esther, after we are gone, or tell her children about us?"

He tapped his white cane on the brick floor. Esther remained silent. She had got used to her husband's monologues. He had retired from the Parsonage and shifted to the two-room quarter the Mission had given them. He had lost his eyesight as a result of an unsuccessful cataract operation, and acquired the habit of thinking aloud. He sermonised before an unseen flock, or lapsed into long silences. Now he was excited because Christmas was approaching and Rosie may turn up after all, and bring her kids along. How he had adored the infant Kamal.

"She wouldn't be celebrating Christmas now, would she, Esther?" he said again. "She has become Shrimati Radhika Sanyal. Perhaps even hides her former identity. She has totally merged herself with her husband's community."

"Didn't I, Paul, after I married you?"

The Reverend kept quiet and tapped his white cane again. Esther sat down near him and began cleaning the dry-fruit for her Christmas pudding. The ingredients had become expensive, nevertheless, she had managed. His pension was meagre. He still supported his widowed sisters in the village. Esther sold her jams and pickles and knitted sweaters, and embroidered table linen on a commission. The couple lived in penury.

In the evenings Esther Giribala took her husband's hand and gently led him out for his constitutional. White beard, sightless, holy-looking, the parson walked slowly by the lake. On misty evenings he looked like a Disciple of Christ, walking by the Sea of Galilee.

On a silent, peaceful winter night, Rev. Paul Mathew Bannerjee passed blindly on, to meet his Saviour. He could not meet his daughter for the last time. Mrs. Bannerjee sent a telegram to New Delhi. Rosie wired back: Mamma, come over to India at once, and stay with us.

Brahmin-born, proud Giribala Bannerjee would not deign to live with her married daughter and be supported by her son-in-law. Nor would she spend the rest of her days working as a glorified nanny to her uppity grandchildren. The Mission gave her a job as a warden in their girls' school. Unfortunately, she could not get along with the Principal.

One day she hired a cycle-rickshaw and went to Arjumand Manzil. Way back, in 1905, a fifteen-year-old Brahmin widow had run away from her in-laws' home, boarded a *shampan* at the river-jetty of her Faridpur village, and voyaged down to Narayan Gunj. Trembling with fear she had reached

Arjumand Manzil in Dacca and sought the help of her Zamindar, Sir Nurul Zaman. A decrepit Christian widow turned up at Arjumand Manzil and knocked at the mahogany door of the library. She had become a little confused, as somehow she expected to find the patriarchal Sir Nurul Zaman sitting inside, smoking his silver water-pipe.

Forty-five years ago, when she entered Arjumand Manzil, an adolescent Qamrul Zaman was deeply in love with his cousin Maliha, but had also fallen flat for this attractive village lass.

A patriarchal Qamrul Zaman opened the heavy door. A toothless, distracted-looking woman stood before him.

After she complained to him about the school's headmistress, he said, "Giribala Debi, Arjumand Manzil is still your home, your *maika*. Stay with us, we won't let you work in your old age. You need rest."

"Nawab Saheb, Paul was a very self-respecting man. He wouldn't like me to live anywhere as a parasite. I have no infirmity, my health is good. Please get me a job somewhere."

When she insisted, the Nawab secured for her the post of dining-hall supervisor in the women's hostel of Dacca University. She shifted to the campus and worked there diligently till she died of pneumonia a couple of years later. She was buried by her husband's side in the churchyard adjoining the Mission Compound. Her death was not reported by the press. Nobody knew that New Delhi's famous socialite, Shrimati Radhika Sanyal, whose photographs often appeared in glossy society magazines, was her daughter.

The Sanyals had thrown a house-warming party in their newly built American-style residence in India's capital. A telegram arrived from East Pakistan, sent by Nawab Qamrul Zaman. It was received by Basant Kumar Sanyal. He went over to his wife who was busy talking to a Fulbright scholar who had come to India to write a book on the Terrorists of Bengal. He said to his host, "I am told that Mrs. Sanyal is one of the heroines of the Quit India Movement. I am so glad to meet her." Basant smiled sadly and gave the telegram to his wife. He added quietly, "I'm afraid you are no heroine, Rosie. Your mother was."

Back in Dacca, the news of Mrs. Bannerjee's death cast a shadow of gloom upon Arjumand Manzil. She had been the last link with a now seemingly remote era, that of the feudal-British regime, the carefree days of everybody's youth. Besides, the Arjumand Manzil family had always sympathised with Esther and admired her courage and patience. They had also heartily disapproved of Rosie for the way she behaved with her parents.

Jehan Ara had come from Dinajpur. It was a golden winter afternoon. They were all sitting on the spacious ottoman in the back verandah. Jehan Ara's son, Akmal played on the lawn.

It seemed to be an afternoon full of distressing news. They had been talking about the late Mrs. Esther Bannerjee, when Nawabzada Nayyarul Zaman came in. He carried the voluminous overseas edition of London's *Daily Mirror*.

"Bibi, look at what your dear Yasmin Majid has gone and done, married a Tommy!"

"A Tommy?" Jehan Ara took out her glasses and looked at a bold headline.

Black Beauty Weds

Dark Dancer Yasmin Majid with her White Man, the caption read under the photograph. *The Barefoot Dancer says,* "I am in the seventh heaven of joy, like a hourie of paradise!"

The picture showed a barefoot Yasmin in a white sari, being carried in the arms of a grinning Gerald Belmont.

"Black Beauty. Dark Dancer. Is Yasmin a race horse? Sad. A girl from a family of venerable maulanas of Jalpaiguri—she has come to be called a Barefoot Dancer," Nayyarul Zaman commented ruefully.

"What does the English fellow do?" asked Begum Qamrul Zaman.

"Must be some Cockney shoeshine," Nayyar replied lightly.

"Fashion-designer...," Jehan Ara read out.

"In other words, a tailor," Nayyar remarked.

"Deepali had written to me about Yasmin's visit to Trinidad. She didn't mention any Gerald Belmont.... Yasmin may not have met him at the time," said Jehan Ara.

The Nawab's footsteps were heard. He was coming out of the gallery for his evening walk. The setting sun had lengthened the shadows of the verandah's pillars.

"Shh...keep quiet. Hide this newspaper," Begum Qamrul Zaman said urgently. "Do not let your father see it, he will be very unhappy. This is precisely why he has always been against women's unbridled freedom. Rosie liberated herself totally and hurt her parents till they died. Now Yasmin..."

Do I qualify as an Ideal Indian Woman, like Aunt Maliha and Esther Bannerjee? Jehan Ara thought bitterly, as she got up for her evening prayers.

35
Yasmin Belmont, Dark Dancer

"DEEPALI Didi, many thanks for your letter which I received some years ago. I'll tell you why I couldn't get round to writing to you all this while. I have been through an awful lot of troubles.

"I had told Gerald that I would like to marry him under Islamic law. He said, go ahead. We had a Pakistani friend who was a Left-wing intellectual, but had been trained earlier as a theologian. He had no religion now but remembered his Islamic jurisprudence.

"On a Friday evening Gerald and I, along with a bunch of close friends, left our Chelsea pub at closing time and went to this former cleric's house. There we had another round of drinks. There was some discussion about the amount to be fixed as dower. Somebody suggested five hundred thousand pounds. Eventually, five pounds was agreed upon by the 'congregation', after which the ex-maulvi asked me if I, in the presence of so-and-so, as witnesses, accepted so-and-so as my legally-wedded husband against five pounds of dowry-money, half of which could be paid to me right way. The maulvi asked Gerald the same question. He nodded agreement. Everybody, the bride, the groom, the witnesses and the "priest" were fairly groggy. The nikah over, we had another round of vodka, brought a day earlier from Moscow by a Leftist Urdu writer friend of ours. I did remember with a pang how my dignified father had solemnised the proper nikah of Jehan Ara Apa.

"After the marriage, we rented a mews in Chelsea. Surprisingly, I turned into an excellent housewife. Gerald was earning enough money as a fashion designer. I gave up dancing and eagerly awaited the birth of our child. We had a daughter. I called her Scheherezade. When she was a toddler I reorganised my troupe and began giving performances again. We could afford a baby-sitter.

"Suddenly, and quite unexpectedly, one day Gerald ran away with the Bengali lad who was my dance partner. I was horrified. Came to know that they had gone to Paris. A friend gave me their address. I went to Paris and took the train straight to the suburb where they lived. It was about ten in the morning on a bright Sunday when I landed up at their apartment. The door was half open. I barged in. The dancer was standing near the gas stove preparing breakfast. He wore a pink frilled apron. Gerald sat by the window reading the newspaper. The scene of "domestic bliss" revolted me and I felt like throwing up. Believe you me, I didn't utter a word and rushed out of the flat. Back in London, I consulted the ex-maulvi and wrote to Gerald to divorce me and pay the dower money of £500, as stipulated, to our theologian friend when he was sober.

"Gerald wrote back to say that we were never married. He never converted to Islam. The nikah ceremony was a lark. Everybody was roaring drunk. As for the dower money, he said, he vaguely remembered that it had been "fixed" either at five hundred thousand or five pounds. The marriage was not legal, therefore, the question of paying alimony didn't arise. He added that since I was too conventional to shack up with him, he had gone through the farce just to please me. Besides, since we had not been married under British law, the responsibility of supporting the child did not devolve on him. 'I was never really interested in women', he wrote. 'Your career as a dancer was on the decline. You were trying to make a go of your dance and yoga classes. You didn't even have the money to buy a return ticket to Pakistan. I liked you as a friend. You are warm-hearted and genuine, therefore vulnerable. Out of sheer sympathy and as your well-wisher, I 'married' you so that you could have a home and the financial support of your 'husband'. I had also thought that maybe I would be able to become 'straight'. I realised after some time that it was not possible. Didn't want to hurt you, so thought it best to come away quietly and begin a new life with the person I really love. It doesn't mean that we should part in bitterness. I hope we will always remain friends.'

"I had to leave the mews and shift to inexpensive digs. I could not earn enough as a dancer to give my child the kind of comforts and education she deserved. One day I rang up Gerald's mother. She called me over to her village in Surrey.

"Laura Belmont is a retired stage actress, wealthy and mean. We had a long discussion. She never got along with her only son and does not approve of his lifestyle. She took to her grandchild and offered to bring her up on the condition that she would first be baptised in the Roman Catholic Church. I was so desperate I said, Roman Catholic? You can bring her up as a Seventh Day Adventist, Buddhist, Shinto, Hottentot, whatever, as long as she doesn't have to starve and knock around like me.

"Now I am clerking in a City office. It was impossible to continue with the troupe, especially after the elopement of my star partner. He had become quite well-known in Europe as an "oriental" dancer. He is an East Pakistani, like me. We could not call ourselves Indian dancers, although the Manipuri, Kathak and folk dances of both India and Pakistan are the same.

"However, at the time, this was not my problem. The thing was that it was becoming increasingly difficult to face the stiff competition offered by classical dancers who had started coming in droves from South India to perform in the West.

"Last month, I glimpsed a ray of false hope. I came to know that Mr. Rehan Ahmed was in town. You know he is currently a minister in the provincial cabinet of Indian Bengal. I told you in Port of Spain how he had begun chasing me, way back in 1945. Times had changed. As an honourable minister he was staying at the Dorchester. I telephoned him, and was told that he was in the bathroom; please ring again. I did. He was lunching downstairs. Phoned again and was given the message that he was very busy with official work; next time he visited London he would certainly look me up.

"Do you correspond with Jehan Ara Apa? I wrote to her several times. No response. I think the Arjumand Manzil family also dislikes me because of what I have done with my life. What can I do? Heaven and earth ran away. I found no shelter anywhere."

Yours,
Yasmin Majid Belmont

36

Pilot Officer Akmal Murshidzada

THE announcer repeated over the amplifier: Mrs. Deepali
Sen, your friends are waiting for you in the VIP lounge. TWA
passenger Deepali Spain, sorry, Deepali Sen of the Port of
Spain..."

Some people laughed.

Lady of Spain I am waiting for you, Lady of Spain... A young
American impishly hummed the old tune and walked past.

A tall, slim boy in Pakistani Air Force uniform approached
her. "Aunt Deepali?" he asked shyly. "I am Akmal. Mummy is
in the lounge. Your flight was very late."

Pilot Officer Akmal Hussain Murshidzada accompanied
her to the VIP lounge. A sad-eyed, grey-haired woman rose
from the sofa. She was clad in a plain white sari signifying
widowhood. The sight distressed Deepali.

"This is my mother," young Akmal said nervously.

"I could not be present at your wedding, Jehan Ara. In
order to make up for it, I have come all the way to attend
your son's marriage." She made a sort of introductory speech
with forced gaiety.

Jehan Ara smiled wanly and muttered suitable words of
thanks and welcome. She had lost her husband a couple of
years earlier. Akmal was her only son. Somehow she seemed
a different person.

Deepali had never seen such splendour before, not in
Arjumand Manzil, nor in Woodland. Obviously, the upper
classes of Pakistan had become exceedingly prosperous. The
bride was the daughter of an East Pakistani business magnate,
although Deepali gathered that Bengali tycoons were fewer
in number than their West Pakistani counterparts. In fact,
the Punjabis of the West were ruling the roost, she was told
darkly. Good old Bengalis, preoccupied as ever with politics.

The floral veil was being tied to the bridegroom's forehead. Jehan Ara moved away to a corner and cried, remembering her late husband. Deepali looked at her, aghast. Indian... okay, Pakistani woman who had been married against her wishes to a horrid man who made her miserable all his life. She always defended him in front of others and served him hand and foot, and now she was crying her eyes out remembering him.

A few years earlier Jehan Ara's younger unmarried sisters had died in a plane crash. They were flying to England to visit their young nephew, Munnawerul Zaman, who was schooling in London. The plane broke up somewhere over the Alps. All perished. Their corpses were blown away by a snowstorm. The news killed their mother, Begum Qamrul Zaman, in Dacca. This time she had a genuine heart attack which she did not survive. Nawab Qamrul Zaman became very silent and spent his time in prayer. At the wedding reception of his orphaned grandson, Akmal, he sat still on a sofa under the canopy. As usual he had his Turkish cap on. Muslim gentlemen of an earlier generation considered it bad manners to remain bareheaded in company. He said a few words to the provincial Governor, members of the Cabinet and other VIPs, and returned to his shell. People knew the heart-breaking reason for his silence and didn't bother him.

He kept sitting like a statue, till his glance fell on Deepali. She stood to one side, talking to Jehan Ara's old servant-maid, Mala. The Nawab beckoned Deepali. She crossed over and sat down near him. Both remained silent, contemplating the glittering scene.

Deepali's eyes brimmed over. The Nawab said gently, "One must not cry, my child. One must bear everything... Forbearance is the thing."

After a while Deepali tried to start a conversation. She said, "In Calcutta the other day, I met your nephew, Rehan Ahmed."

Nawab Saheb tapped the carpet with his silver-topped cane. He replied after a pause: "Rehan is a big gun over there. He left his old revolutionary ways and joined the Indian National Congress. He has also been a provincial minister for some months. What is he up to now?"

"Uma Roy has lost her parents. Rehan has become General Manager of Nirmalendu Roy's firm. My younger brother Khokhu telephoned Rehan. He didn't come, sent his car instead, to fetch me. Khokhu, his wife and I went to the Roy bungalow at Alipur Road. Uma stays on the upper floor. She has let out part of the house to the Ahmeds. They live downstairs. Rehan's son is a problem child, he has run away. Uma's brother, Nirmalendu, never married. He is drunk all the time. Keeps sitting in the Bengal Club. All his affairs are being looked after by Rehan. I was told that when Rehan became a minister for a short while, he greatly benefited Nirmalendu and Uma's family business. That's why they are deeply indebted to him.

"Rehan was very upset about his precocious child. Told me he was just thirteen but had become a rebel and left home. He is also writing poetry, and sympathises with the young poets of Calcutta who call themselves the Hungry Generation."

Nawab Qamrul Zaman had bent forward and was listening carefully. Suddenly he gave a loud, bitter laugh. The wedding guests turned around in amazement. He had laughed for the first time since the death of Najma and Akhtar.

An ancient poet of Bengal called Abhinanda had said, "The tanks are full of lotuses. Bees are swarming over the mango blossoms. Even when the journey is short, the wind dances on the cart-track and the exile's heart is filled with sadness."

The journey from Dacca to Port of Spain was very long. Before going back to Calcutta Deepali spent an evening with Jehan Ara on the stage-throne under the cotton-flower tree. That was the spot she used to sit at with her friends years ago. Suddenly Jehan Ara asked her, "What is Cousin Rehan's wife like? Which Calcutta family?"

"No family. She is an ordinary sort of housewife. Uma Roy told me about her. Once it happened that Nirmalendu was dead drunk and driving through Garden Reach. He ran over an old man who died on the spot. The deceased was a gold-thread worker from Lucknow. Nirmalendu could have been hauled up for manslaughter but managed to get away. The victim was survived by a daughter who had nowhere to go. Uma Debi brought her home and made her in-charge of her wardrobe. A sort of glorified ayah. The girl was an excellent needlewoman and a good cook. She was also very plain and suffered from a massive inferiority complex. Rehan was a frequent visitor at Uma's place, he took pity on her. This happened about two years after Partition. He married the girl.

"Uma treats her like a bad mother-in-law. She continues to suffer in silence. Rehan does not take much notice of his wife.

"Zohra told me about Uma Debi's latest pastime. She has all manner of ailments and has long retired from politics. Early in the morning she limps down to Belvedere. A servant follows her, carrying a bucketful of dog-food. She calls all the stray cats and dogs of the neighbourhood and feeds them. Then she throws birdseed to the crows. After the good deed she returns home and starts persecuting Rehan's wife, Zohra. Rehan is mostly out, comes home late at night. Avoids meeting Uma. What a life."

Jehan Ara took a deep breath and got up to go inside. It was time for evening prayers. She left for the house. Rehan's younger sister, Rabia Qadiri, arrived from the kitchen. She had come to Arjumand Manzil from her house in Azimpura to help out with the elaborate arrangements for Akmal's marriage. She came near the "royal throne", looked at the evening sky and said," I must go for my prayers, too. I'll send my daughter Nasira to keep you company."

"Nasira does not say her prayers?"

"Prayers! She doesn't even believe in God. She has taken after her Uncle Rehan. Isn't it ironic that the son of Maulana Burhan Ahmed, as well as his granddaughter, both became atheists!" Rabia answered and walked briskly away. After some minutes a young girl came out of Arjumand Manzil. She was

Nasira Najmus Sahar Qadiri, a twenty-year-old firebrand student leader. That's what I used to be: twenty-year-old firebrand student leader, thought Deepali with a certain envy. During the last one week she had become friendly with Nasira, who had told her about the terribly complicated politics of East Pakistan. The Awami League of Maulana Bhashani. The famines in Khulna and Barisal districts. The peasant movement of Jessore. The police firings. The Language Agitation. Demonstrations. The riots at Adamjee Jute Mills. The Popular Front. The same old highly charged political atmosphere. Across the border, West Bengal presented the same kind of scenario.

"I was telling Jehan Ara about your Uncle Rehan Ahmed," Deepali said to her, as she perched on the throne.

"I know all about him," she replied with a frown. "My mother has always idealised her brother. Aunt Jehan Ara adored him and perhaps you, too, thought the world of him... we have better judgement. My uncle is quite a character. The Complete Idealist, as it were. International Goodwill personified. Today in Prague, tomorrow in Cairo, day after in New York. Today in this political alliance, tomorrow in that. Wherever there are greater chances of becoming a minister, and behold! he is there. A friend of Moscow as well as Washington. The Perfect Non-Aligned Man."

"Nasira," Deepali said amusedly, "yesterday's rebels have joined today's Establishment. You are a present-day rebel— you may become part of tomorrow's Establishment."

Nasira laughed derisively.

"Aunt Deepali, excuse me, but you have reached the stage when a person uses cynicism as a coat-of-mail. His angle of vision changes."

Deepali burst out laughing. "Nasira, dear, do you remember that Alice poem...

You are old, Father William,
The young man said
And you incessantly stand on your head,
Do you think at your age it is right?

Nasira began to laugh, too. "You ought to say this to your Pandit Nehru. He stands on his head in his yoga exercise!"

Mala brought coffee. After she went back Deepali said to Nasira, "You should keep meeting Jehan Ara, she seems so lonely. She can't get along with her sister-in-law, Nayyar's wife, and she does not want to live in Dinajpur. Her mother and sisters are dead. Her father...he is on his last legs, and she has always been slightly scared of him. Her husband is gone too—however bad he was, she had someone to turn to. Now the son has got married. He will go back with his wife to faraway Peshawar. Jehan Ara will be left alone."

"She may be lonely and all that, but I have no sympathy for her," Nasira said harshly. "Do you know Akmal wanted to marry me? I was very fond of him, too. But my father is small fry, a minor official in the provincial secretariat. We live in a tiny PWD flat in Azimpura. We are not in the social register. Aunt Jehan Ara didn't care one bit about her only son's personal happiness and selected an industrialist's daughter as her daughter-in-law. This class is unforgivable. I'm told Aunt Jehan Ara had a lot of social awareness once!

"Earlier she used to make a great deal of fuss over me, too. When I was born she named me Nasira Najmus Sahar, Victorious Morning Star. She used to make clothes for my mother, even gave us her cast-offs. How she patronised us! We were her poor relations." She picked up a little stone and threw it furiously into the tank. "And this old fogey, Nawab Qamrul Zaman—my great-uncle—he has spent years trying to get into the Central Cabinet in Karachi. Didn't succeed. Wasted his entire life in political manoeuvres. Old-guard Muslim Leaguer. When the people here mounted the agitation for Bengali, he raised his voice in favour of Urdu. The procession came to the gate of Arjumand Manzil, hollering: *Urdu bhasha cholbe na...* We shall not have Urdu imposed on us. He put on his Turkish cap and came out on the verandah, brandishing his silver-topped cane. Then he shouted back—*Urdu bhasha zoroor cholbe.* Long live Urdu! The crowd was so inflamed they could have lynched him. Luckily, he was saved. Now he is a political back-number and frustrated. But Deepali Mashi..." she stood up and declaimed, "Please do not get the impression that since we are against Urdu imperialism, or because West Pakistan is exploiting us, we will join India. Most certainly not. When it comes to a confrontation with India, we will die fighting for Pakistan. We will fight with the last drop of our blood! We are staunch Pakistanis. Okay, dear Aunt, I must leave. Shall come to the airport tomorrow to see you off."

"Where are you going now?"

"Home, Azimpura."

"Not staying in Arjumand Manzil for the wedding?"

"No, my mother is. She loves these fancy relatives of hers. I came here daily only to meet you. Goodbye."

She crossed the lawn quickly and walked away towards the gate. Deepali was taken aback by the girl's abrupt departure. Arjumand Manzil shone brightly in the gathering dark. The house was full of guests, musicians and servants. It reminded her of the festive time twenty-five years ago when Jehan Ara's brother, Nayyar, had got married.

After a couple of days Akmal was going away to the far-off Frontier Province of West Pakistan, across the vast stretch of India, where he was posted at a Pakistan Air Force station. Like his cousin Nasira, he was also a staunch Pakistani, a patriotic, zestful pilot serving in the defence forces of his country.

37
The Pacifist

"**D**EAREST Deepali, received your letter some time back; couldn't write earlier due to terrible worries. Thank God my son has come back from the frontlines. Right now he has gone to a concert with his girl-friend. You see, Kamal is a gifted musician. He could be a lawyer like his father and continue with his music. He said, Mummy, do you want me to don an embroidered silken kurta and turn into a sitar-playing sissy? I said musicians are not sissies, for God's sake. Whereupon he informed us that he was going to be a soldier; when the Motherland needed him he would die in the field of honour. I said, Kamal, think of us, your parents, you are our only son. He answered, did you think of your parents when you went off to fight in August, '42? You were their only child. I said, that was different. He asked, how? Then it was Britain, now it is China and Pakistan. Don't be tiresome, Mummy.

"So he went away to the Military Academy.

"In one of her rare letters, Jehan Ara had once written to me that she wanted her son Akmal to study medicine, but he was very keen to defend Pakistan against India. He joined the air force and became a fighter-pilot. You attended his wedding last year, so you would know all about it.

"Kamal was a second-lieutenant when this war broke out. He was sent to the Front. I went to all the churches and temples and Muslim saints' shrines and prayed as only a mother can pray. Also prayed fervently for India's victory (I ceased to be an atheist long ago. That was a necessary phase everyone went through in their youth). Anyway, so the multipurpose One God, or the multifarious department gods, heard me, and Kamal has come back safe and sound. Touch wood.

"And believe you me, I also prayed for Akmal's safety, as I always remembered those fateful words. It was you or my husband who had said that when you add A to a Sanskrit word it acquires the opposite meaning. One afternoon in Arjumand Manzil I told Nawab Qamrul Zaman about it and he said, would Kamal fight my Akmal? I said, No sir, Akmal will take on my Kamal. He said: Both are rascals. I'll pull their ears!

"A few weeks ago a European diplomat friend of ours was going to Dacca. I asked him to ring up Arjumand Manzil and get me some news of Jehan Ara. It was a risky thing to do as the war was on and Jehan Ara was our enemy, but I was concerned about her. We hardly ever write to each other. She never comes to India. I have not been to East Pakistan after my parents' death, probably because of the guilty conscience I have about them. I don't ever want to go to Dacca and visit the cemetery where they are buried. They must be so lonely in their graves. Well, the dead can't be gregarious but you know what I mean.

"So this European returned from Dacca and brought me the sad news: Pilot Officer Akmal Murshidzada was shot down while bombing a town in Jammu. His body was blown to pieces. He died in the field of honour—the sky of honour, to be more precise.

"The situation is so wonky that I can't write a letter of condolence to my enemy, Jehan Ara. And she is a singularly luckless girl if you review her entire life.

"My son is looking forward to the next round of fun and games, 'to teach them a lesson again', he says and grits his teeth. His counterparts across the border must be saying the same thing, and with the same intensity. I think from the time of the ancient Chinese warriors and the Mahabharata and the Assyrians, the world has never *liked* peace. Men do want to fight. In fact they love a war. Most women dislike it because their husbands and sons and brothers get killed. Otherwise they are also carried away by jingoism and the emotional clap-trap. Even I am stirred by the music played by our military bands. Nobody wants peace, its cranky to talk of peace. There is so much bellicosity in this muddled subcontinent of India and Pakistan and everywhere in the world, it is surprising that so many of us are still alive. The world's leaders would like all of us to perish. The world's leaders are like the all-consuming Kali.

"I'm glad you are away from it all, living on your beautiful island.

"Give my regards to Barrister Sen."

Yours,
Rosie

New Delhi,
October, 1965.

38
Good Luck Diary

January 1, 1967. Poosh 16, 1333. Ramazan 19, 1386 A.H.
Puh 18, 2023.
Name: Yasmin Majid Belmont
Address:

If this diary is found please return to the above address.

New Year's Day. I begin this brand new notebook, with the name of Allah, the Merciful, the Beneficent. Somebody has brought it for me from Dacca. It is called Good Luck Diary, but I am writing in it so it will turn into Bad Luck Diary. Tut, tut. Mustn't be ungrateful to God. I am better off than many. Forgive me, God, Thou knowest everything about me. I have been disobedient to Thee. I hurt my pious father, became a professional dancer. Married a non-M. Allowed my daughter to become a non-M. Lord, I tremble before Thee in fear of Thy wrath. O God, save me from punishment in the grave. I beseech Thee in the name of Thy Beloved Prophet.

I telephoned the senior Mrs. Belmont to wish her and my daughter a Happy New Year. They had left for Mass.

Dear Diary. Even old women in this country have no family feeling. Scheherezade is ill. Old Mrs. Belmont has dumped her in a hospital. I go there by train on Sundays. Come back dead tired at night. Monday morning I must be in the factory on time. Doc says I have a weak heart. Must not dance.

Dear Good Luck Diary. It happened three days ago. I came out of the hospital and walked down to the bus stop feeling miserable. My daughter had been exceptionally cold towards me. Perhaps her grandmother does not want her to have anything to do with me. S. is a little girl, but calculating like her father, and callous like her grandma. Perhaps she also doesn't want people to know that her mother is a coloured woman. She is a hazel-eyed brunette and has inherited the stunning good looks of her father. Obviously she does not wish to be known as a mulatto. Today she said bluntly, "Mummy, why do you take the trouble of travelling all the way from London every week to see me? I am all right." This broke my heart.

While I stood waiting for the coach, my tears mingled with the rain which lashed my face. Suddenly I felt that someone was watching me.

The stranger had heard me muttering "Allah, Allah". Also, I was clad in shalwar-kameez. So he gently asked me in Urdu if I had a relative in the hospital.

I looked up at him hesitantly. A fair, tall, broad-shouldered hulk of a man, perhaps a Pathan or a Punjabi. Not at all bad to look at. He was also waiting for the same coach. A moment ago I had been feeling totally lost and abandoned. His words seemed to me like a lighted safe boat appearing on the dark and stormy Brahmaputra. With deep gratitude I told him that I had come to see my daughter. Now she was all right and should be discharged soon.

Why then was I crying so bitterly? He didn't ask, but looked concerned. The brightly-lit coach emerged in the gray rain. We got in. He sat down next to me. Told me he was coming from Bedford. His car developed some trouble near this village, so he had left it in a garage and was going to London where he had his own business.

He belonged to Rampur, U.P., India. Migrated to Lahore, Pakistan, in 1949. Second migration to England six years ago. The usual pattern of immigrants. He seemed highly educated. Said: You are a Bengali but speak Urdu so well, and that too with a Punjabi accent! Told him that for the last so many years I had been working in a garment factory where most of my co-workers were Sikh women.

You work in a factory? he asked, surprised.

Yes, I said briefly. Didn't tell him that I started out as a celebrated dancer, ended up stitching shirts. That's how the mighty fall.

Dear Good Luck Diary. Maqbool and I spent the evening in Hampton Court gardens. He is going to buy a big house in Barnes. Didn't say anything else. But as a Persian proverb says: a wordless hint is enough for the wise.

Maqbool says I could join his firm at a much higher salary, but I don't like the idea. Don't want to be beholden to him.

He respects me. Meets me with great decorum. We are equals as friends. Then, he'll be the boss and I his employee. No, that won't do. Aren't I right, Allah? You go on leading me on the right path.

Old Mrs. Belmont has never invited me to her place in the country. Bitch. It is a regular manor house. Belonged to some rakish lord who left it in his will to the bloody woman. She used to be a high-class whore, as far as I can gather. Who else would dance in the Redmill Theatre? She is rolling. That's why S. flatters her. She has disowned Gerald for some reason. I never bothered to find out. Why should I?

My daughter is so rich but she has never given me a present, except a small handbag she brought for me last Christmas. Sees me once or twice a year. Anyway, may God keep her in good health and happiness.

My father has disowned me. I've been forgotten by my relatives. A woman from their strait-laced family went stray. My case rests with God. When my countrymen meet me here, especially the fellows from Dacca, they say with great enthusiasm, come to Karachi. The government will set up a dance academy for you. When I write to the Ministry at Karachi dealing with cultural affairs, there is no response. I am a person of no consequence. Who will pay any attention to me? That was in the very beginning—they wanted to please a Central Minister from East Pakistan, so they sent me on a foreign tour. It was part of East-West Pakistan politics. I didn't realise it then. *Dear Diary,* the world makes me sick. Did you notice the Indian Minister Rehan Ahmed's turnabout? Avoided meeting me here, in London.

One of the Sikh girls in the factory has taught me a song of the Punjabi Sufi, Baba Farid:

> *I am not scared of dying, O mullah,*
> *Let me have my fill of death.*
> *I don't demean myself if I turn into a dancing girl.*
> *Let me dance to please the Friend, for He is cross with me.*

Sunday, July 30, 1967. Rabi-ul-sani 1387. Sawan 15, 2024. Sarabon 14, 1474.

Seven months have gone of this year as well. One is alone and surrounded by so many calendars—Christian Islamic Bikrami Bengali. I don't know why the printers of this diary didn't include the Persian calendar as well. It would have added to the confusion of Time.

O boatman, O Rower of the Painted Boat. Turn your canoe around, tie it to the quay. How long will this stream flow? How long will you row this canoe? In what mood do you row, morning and evening? What mysteries do you carry in your heart? O brother boatman, does this river have no end?

I remember these *bhatiali* songs of the boatmen of my unhappy land, East Pakistan.

Wrote to Deepali today.

Rosie is visiting London with her husband and daughters. They have come on a pleasure trip. Happy and affluent. Staying with relatives in Hampstead. She got my address from Deepali and contacted me. Asked me to dine with them in a Piccadilly restaurant. I went. Didn't invite her to my dingy bed-sitter, nor told her what I did for a living.

Eventually we fell to talking of old days when both Rosie and Deepali were active revolutionaries. Rosie's children were accompanied by their hosts' teenaged London-born daughters. When I mentioned that as young girls our greatest ambition used to be to become heroines like Pritilata, Kalpana Dutt and Kanaklata Barua, the girls asked me sweetly if they were famous film stars of our time!

Kafka says that you can discern the meaning of certain words only through your own wounds. And Tagore also said something like that.

Keep quiet, Yasmin, you are crazy, I am looking at important business papers.

Tinkle tinkle tinkle...

Dancing again? The doctor has fobidden it...

Let me dance to please my Friend... Listen, Tagore has said that Memory is a worshipper who kills the present and offers its heart to the dead past.

What else does your Tagore say? He is boring me to tears.

Tinkle tinkle tinkle...Say you love me...I pleaded.

I love you, he replied.

Suddenly he got up, looked at his watch and said he had to rush for an important appointment. Went out and drove away. Maqbool is a self-made, successful businessman. Such men are usually v. selfish. He is also an egoist and arrogant and much pleased with himself. Though honest and truthful.

He had forgotten one of his files in my room. When I picked it up an open letter slipped out. It was a childish, feminine scrawl. Somehow I could not help glancing through the note. It said in florid Urdu:

My dear honourable crown-of-my-head, Khan Maqbool Ahmed Khan Saheb. The slave-girl pays her respects to you with folded hands, and begs to state that she has received the remittance. Further: the undersigned is fine, the children are also fine and remember you. Further: you have been away in England for so long. Come back and show us your auspicious face, or call all of us over there as soon as

*you can. And look after your health. My honourable parents-in-law
send you their fondest love.*
  Remembering you all the time,
  I am your humble wife,

Maimoona Khatoon,
by her own pen.

October 3. Deep night. The eye of the owl. The eye of the
cat. The eye of the forsaken woman. Silence sleeps. Yellow
autumn is a weak, helpless woman whose man has run away.
Maimoona Khatoon Autumn.

  In Arjumand Manzil they had a gramophone record of
Harimati or Dulari which Jehan Ara Apa often played: *Let this
world burn down where love is rejected and hearts are trampled
upon, where nobody is a friend of anybody.* Don't grieve, Maimoona
Khatoon.

Dear Diary. You belong to 1967. I have discovered you after so
many years, in the bottom drawer of the dresser. All the
pages are blank after October 3... What happened? Heart
attack. Prolonged illness. Hospitalisation. Living on dole.
Scheherezade has become a photographer's model. Doesn't
meet me.

  Maqbool suddenly stopped seeing me. Why should he
waste his time on a sick woman? I am told a pretty English
girl lives with him.

  Nadir dam...tana dire na...na dir dam ta na di re na...

  Gerald Belmont has become the editor of a Gay Lib
magazine. I am told that now a German boy lives with him.

Dear Good Luck Diary. Today after many years Maqbool rang
up. Sounded worried about me. Said in case I needed a job
he had a vacancy in his Hamburg office. Light job as a
receptionist. I refused politely.

Dear Bad Luck Diary. Today I went to Maqbool's office myself.
Time turns proud people into beggars. Asked him to give me

the receptionist's job in Hamburg. He was v. courteous and helpful. From next month, God willing, I shall be working in Hamburg. Sherry has vanished. Gone off to America, I am told. Snow is falling like silent music. Christmas is two days away.

Once during Krishna Chaturdashi, on a moonless night, I accompanied Deepali to the banks of the Padma. There, Deepali made banyan leaves into tiny boats and lighted earthen lamps—one each for all of us friends. She placed the lamps in the leaf-boats and floated them in the water. An old Hindu custom to decipher the future. Some of those lighted boats sank, some sailed away and disappeared in the dark.

Rehan Ahmed, I gather, has gone back to Dacca from Calcutta. In E. Pak. as well, I am sure, he'll become a Cabinet Minister.

A Punjabi devotional song: *Whoever once comes to Thy door, he crosses the ocean of sorrow...*

Now I am not too sure if He exists.

Dear Good Luck Diary. Maqbool turned up yesterday. Stayed for quite a while. Said Maimoona Khatoon was an imbecile. It was an arranged marriage. Didn't stay much with her. Up till now he was too busy expanding his business. Would I...?

Couldn't believe my ears. "Yes," I replied.

He has disappeared once again.

The manager of Maqbool's Hamburg branch is an aggressive Punjabi. Ever since the outbreak of war in East Pakistan he has been calling me a traitor. I keep quiet. Can't afford to retort as I have nowhere to go. Time makes one a coward, too. Maqbool's sister and two brothers were all killed in Chittagong. He has had a nervous breakdown. I don't know about my own people—they are in Dacca. How can I find out? They may have been killed, too. This morning a delegation of former East Pakistanis (present Bangladeshis) came to see me and demanded that I stop working for

Maqbool, who is a Pakistani. What do I do if I leave this job? I won't get another, my health being what it is. I have no academic qualifications. Maqbool is giving me a sort of pension because he has a bad conscience. My compatriots quarrelled with me and left.

This morning the Punjabi manager gave me notice. My services are to be terminated because I am a Bangladeshi. Horrified, I trunk-called London. Maqbool had left for Karachi.

Once again Bengal has sunk deep in the ocean of fire and blood. It is a big Dance of Kali...Oh, these are such cliches...I am so tired.

Four years have passed. Four years I have waited patiently. He may turn up again. It seems impossible now. He has shifted to that house in Barnes. I am here in West Germany, drifting from town to town doing odd jobs, lost in the crowd of Turkish and Asian workers. Better-off Bangladeshis avoid me, fearing that I'll ask them for help. The new generation of Bangladeshis does not know me, they have not even heard of me. For the older generation I am an embarrassment. Some of them have floated the rumour that I have gone round the bend. Am I really heading for a crack-up? After washing dishes in this cafe, I sit outside and watch the passing scene. A greying, coloured woman in Western dress, smoking in a corner, staring at the street—that's me. Waiting for nothing. Can Maqbool still appear out of the fog? Not possible.

One late evening I sat drinking my black coffee. A terrible, hawk-nosed Gulf Arab spotted me. He took out a wad of currency notes and showed it to me.

I have stopped sitting on the sidewalk.

Last night I didn't see my reflection in the mirror.

Frankfurt, January 4. Today I have written a black-robed ballet in Bengali. Sad, melancholy Indian mode, Purvi. *The corpses are coming back home the corpses are coming back coming back...*

Gosh, I can be morbid. Okay, I'll choreograph the ballet of spring in the happy mode Basant... One must try to survive.

All these people walking along the strasse are in fact heading for a cemetery or a crematorium. All living people are potential corpses. All people staying in my boarding house are going to die.

Jan. 24. Nothing happened in Frankfurt, going back to Hamburg. Now the river and the sea meet the ice. I tremble like a lowdown bitch.

My heart is like the over-crowded temple at Calcutta's Kalighat. Sacrificial goats are being cut round-the-clock, before the terrible idol of Kali. Her three red eyes stare into Gehenna. Pie dogs loiter on the temple floor. Women worshippers slice the goats' red flesh.

My heart is the Harlots' Alley of Sonagachi. My wishes and regrets, all garishly made up, stand against dirty walls, hoping that the next man will bring salvation. All doors are locked. *All lanes are closed. How do I go to meet Hari?* asked Mirabai. When the telephone rings, I tremble. It may be Maqbool, or my daughter Sherry. From this moment on, my punishment will increase.

My unseen persecutor will go on lashing me till my last breath. God Who is Merciful and Compassionate, Thou created me so that I live thus? And how will I die? In my life, O Magnificent Lord, many a time I have said to myself: this is the most horrible moment of my existence, not knowing that worse moments were yet to come. My God lowers my head in front of mine enemies.

Dear Bad Luck Diary. I am cracking up. A seventeenth-century Urdu poet said:

A perverse wind has blighted the entire garden, but the bough of the Tree of Sorrow called 'heart' has remained evergreen...

O boatman, put your oars away. Your canoe has broken apart. It's time to go.

Second heart attack. I have written to Rehan Ahmed's sister, Rabia (at her old Dacca address) that in case I die here and she hears the news, she may please have my funeral prayers arranged in a Dacca mosque.

I read somewhere about the second principle of thermodynamics. The world shall soon come to an end and the sun grow cold. Religion says it will be the Day of Judgement. The optimist says No, everything remains. Humanity shall live on.

Allah knows best. Who am I to understand His mysteries?

I want to die with dignity.

The Unknown Bridegroom is about to arrive.

Pain and happiness. Sanity and insanity. Hatred and love. War and peace. Poverty and affluence. Defeat and victory. Sin and virtue. Life and death. They are all separated from each other by a hair's breadth. In a fraction of a moment one can cross over from one state into another.

Dear Good Luck Diary. Last night my daughter Scheherezade called from Chicago. I wasn't at home. She left a message that today she will ring up again. After a long time I'll hear her voice. I am v. happy.

(unfinished)

39
Scheherezade Christina Belmont

Hamburg, June 16

"DEAR Mrs. Sen,

You do not know me, but I have heard a lot about you from Mummy. This is to inform you that my mother, Madame Yasmin Belmont, died in an accident. She was walking along the Elbe, slipped and fell into the water. I personally think that she *chose* to go into the river. I do not know you, but I knew my Mummy. I personally think that all of you, admirers of Tagore, Gandhi, Nehru, etc. were quite naive and innocent. You cannot cope today. I cannot cope either, but I have no pretensions and make no claims. All of you, including my mother, had a lot of pretensions. I know that I am like a straw floating on water, a broken feather adrift in the air, I am worthless as an insect or a worm; a cipher in the cosmos.

"I am sure you'll say that my negative and sick thinking is the result of Western European Decadence. Okay. But what was the outcome of your positive, healthy, noble, spiritual thinking? The point is, Mrs. Sen, that at twenty-four I am much more mature than my poor romantic unhappy woolly-headed mother. And far more experienced and worldly-wise than both of you. Name the thing, physical, mental, spiritual—I have experienced it. Name the swami-guru circuit—I have been in it. Drugs? Sure. I have tasted all and found them wanting. The recipe for morality prescribed by you folks was, of course, absurd.

"The tragedy with Mummy was that she came from a two-faced civilisation. As Bengali-Pakistani-Muslim she also tried to adopt Western attitudes. The inner collision shattered her. I'll tell you the reason why she died. For the last twenty years she had been living in poverty. She had failed to make the international scene as a dancer. Time was against her. A dancer's career does not last longer than ten years. Her personal tragedies and hardships aged her prematurely. She had also acquired a heart condition. But the real reason was something else. A few days ago I rang her up from Chicago to give her the good news: my photograph was about to appear on the centrespread of *Playboy* magazine. I was thrilled. It is the peak of success and glory for a model. Instead of congratulating me she called me a slut. I was surprised by her violent reaction. She became hysterical, yelled her head off and banged the receiver. After a few days I got the news of her fatal accident.

I do not understand why you people attach so much importance to the simple act of wearing or taking off one's clothes. Why such a hoo-ha about the human anatomy? I am a successful nude model, but I am not a whore. I am just a liberated, healthy, normal young woman. Period. My mother spent her life with the guilt that she stayed with a man for three years without being really married to him. I am sure after separating from my English father she would have lived like a nun.

"The other guilt which racked my poor Mummy was that she had to allow me to be brought up in the Catholic faith.

"I am writing all this to you because I came here two days ago from Chicago and found this diary on her bedside table. It's an old diary in which she had written, off and on, down the years. There are entries in Bengali, Urdu and English. It also contains your address. I know neither Bengali nor Urdu. You were her girlhood pal. Therefore, I am sending this pathetic notebook to you. I am sure you would like to keep it as a memento of your departed friend.

With regards,
Scheherezade Christina Belmont

"P.S. I don't know the whereabouts of my father. I believe he has become an organiser of the Gay Lib movement in London. After the age of four I have never met him. My grandmother is dead.

"Who is this guy, Maqbool Ahmed Khan? He ought to be lynched.

"P.P.S. I always marvel at the hypocrisy of your generation. Perhaps you envy us for our candour. Pardon me. I am writing all this to you because when I was small, my mother always used to lecture me about you and cite you as a shining example: what an upright, moral, courageous person you were; how you risked your life in the struggle for India's freedom, etc.

"The independence you achieved so bravely was such that it drove you out of your own country. I have also seen your great revolutionary hero, Mr. Rehan Ahmed. Saw him at London's Playboy Club, dining with his opponents from India and Pakistan. On the conference table, in international forums, they issue venomous statements against one other which lead to greater misery and tension for their common peoples. After conference hours they laugh and get together and chat, visit the same night clubs and chase the same White women.

"Mummy wanted to meet him, he avoided her. Had Mummy been an important person or still in circulation as a dancer, he would most gladly have met her. Sick sick sick. Your generation has disillusioned me no end, Mrs. Sen. The world you have made for us is pretty horrible. All this is old hat now, but I had to explain my position. Do forgive my frankness. Om shantih...shantih."

Scheherezade

40
Swami Atmananda Shanker Premi

A<small>T</small> Rome airport a young white swami stood ahead of Mrs. Sen in the departure queue. He carried a shining trident and a cloth bag. He walked along with the lady and sat down next to her in the aircraft. Shiva, Shiva, he sighed deeply after having tied the safety belt. Instantly he began telling his brown beads. They were made of the dried berries of an exotic Himalayan shrub called the "Eye of God Rudra". Mrs. Sen gave him a motherly smile. He remained grave and unmoved. She was dismayed. A young lad who has forgotten how to smile.

After a few minutes Deepali Sen could not help stealing a sidelong glance at him again. The face seemed familiar and set her thinking.

The swami noticed his travel companion's interest in him and took out some glossy magazines in French, German and Spanish. They were entitled, *New Dawn of Ancient Gods*. Solemnly he fished out a magazine in English and gave it to her.

"Thank you, son. May I know your name?"

"Swami Atom Ananda Shanker Premi."

"Oh, Atmananda... Bliss of the Soul. And your previous name?"

"I do not remember my previous name. I have forgotten my earlier life."

"Oh, I see." She looked at him a little intently. This was certainly not a stranger's face. Who was it, she had met him only recently... Yes, Charles Barlow, ICS. This may be his son.

Mrs. Sen remained silent. After some time she tried to start a conversation. "We'll soon be reaching Athens, and this is not even a supersonic jet. The rapid progress of modern science is mind-boggling."

"Modern Science! In ancient India we had flying chariots. Television had been invented in the time of the Mahabharata War, and that was *millions* of years ago. But the Englishmen stole all the hoary treatises of the Hindus and based their inventions on ancient Indian science. Now the Americans and the Russians say they have reached the moon. Nonsense! Nobody can reach the abode of the Moon God, Chandra Devata." The swami was talking like a robot.

"Where are you going?" Mrs. Sen asked, amused.

"Athens. I'll set up an ashram over there. After that India, Hardwar, abode of Lord Shiva."

"If you are going to India you should work in the drought-stricken villages of Bihar."

"The famished ought to worship the God of Rain so that they have a bountiful harvest. *Har Har Mahadeva.*"

"Son, you should do social work like the Ramakrishna Mission people. India needs social workers."

"The poor can come to the temples our Shanker Prem Foundation has set up. They can have the *prasadam* from there. You know, consecrated free food."

"Perhaps it was Lord Shiva's will that I meet you today, so listen carefully. Perhaps I knew your father, Charles Barlow of the Indian Civil Service."

The White sanyasi was taken aback. He composed himself and replied stonily, "Okay, Charles Barlow. But that's a stranger's name for me. I have not met him for the last ten years. He is my grandfather. His son, Tom Barlow, was my father."

Time flew past so quickly? "Son, if you..."

"Shiva, Shiva...Ma'm, what do you wish to find out? Why are you so interested in me?" the swami said curtly. "My grandfather, Charles Barlow, lives in Australia. Grandmother died in the London blitz ages ago. For all I know she may have been born again and died again, too. My father, Tom Barlow, is also dead. My sister and I were kids when our parents separated. My mother leads an immoral life. She has never bothered about us. Grandpa also married again...an

American girl...when he went to Australia from India in 1947. They were divorced, too. He had a son by that marriage, my half-uncle, Richard Barlow. Grandpa named him after his own brother, Wing Commander Richard Barlow who was shot down over Germany. This post-war Richard lives in Sydney and is gay. So is my sister. I don't know where this streak came from into our family, or else they were closet cases earlier. Anyway, my sister runs a lesbian club in Soho, London. My mother is a rich heiress. She lives with her French gigolo in Nice."

Thank God, at least she is normal, Mrs. Sen said to herself.

"I found peace at the lotus feet of my guru. Where did you meet my mother?" he asked.

"I have never met her. I live in Port of Spain. My husband is a barrister. Last year we went to Perth, where I was interviewed on television as an Indian-born singer. Your grandfather happened to see the programme and got my address from the TV people. He came to our hotel and took us for the weekend to his sheep farm. He was so happy to see me, as though he had met a long-lost relative. He had got my uncle arrested for the gallows, and during the Indian struggle for freedom I was on his blacklist. But somehow we had no bitterness when we met. Now he is so lonely. Old and forsaken. It is sad. He did tell me about his second marriage and divorce, also that his son Richard lived in Sydney but never met him.

"Mr. Charles Barlow misses you all very much. Is it not possible that at least once all of you go Down Under and meet him? He is a very old man and may not live long."

The boy continued to tell his rudraksha beads. "Mr. Barlow has to work out his karma," he replied coldly. "All blood ties are meaningless for a sanyasi."

Mrs. Sen looked away and didn't speak to him again. The plane began to descend over Athens.

Swami Atmananda Shanker Premi addressed her abruptly. "My Uncle Dick in an interior decorator in Sydney...I met him the other day in Paris. He told me he was going to Bangladesh to decorate a new five-star hotel. In case you meet him in Dacca, tell him that I shall be in Hardwar after the fifteenth of next month. This is the address of my ashram in that sacred Abode of the Gods." He gave Mrs. Sen his visiting card. "Please tell him to come and see me there, in the shadow of the lofty Himalayas. I'll try to show him the Right Path. He is too involved in Delusion. You, too, come to Rishikesh. Om Namo Shivayah."

The plane landed. The young swami got up and joined the passengers' queue. As he stepped down at the airport his tall trident and flag remained visible in the crowd for some minutes.

41
The Playhouse

At Dacca airport she was greeted by members of the Yasmin Majid Memorial Committee. They gave her a bouquet and a glossy brochure. The booklet mentioned her as 'An illustrious daughter of Bangladesh who has come from Trinidad to attend the cultural festival being held in the memory of another celebrated daughter of Bangladesh, the splendrous dancer and poetess, the late Madame Yasmin Majid Belmont.'

After her ignoble death, poor Yasmin had been declared a poetess as well. As an expatriate she spent half her life working as a factory-hand and a waitress, was insulted by her countrymen and shunned by her old acquaintances. She put an end to her troubles by jumping into a cold, alien river. If she had drowned herself in the Padma, she would have had the satisfaction that at least it was her own river she was jumping into. An irreverent thought. Deepali scolded herself and began shaking hands with the people who had come to receive her. Yasmin died, forsaken and an exile. Now her compatriots were spending a few hundred thousand takkas in order to pay "homage" to her.

The Festival Committee had offered Mrs. Sen return air fare, which she had declined. This was a ghoulish sort of journey she had undertaken on behalf of her late father, Dr. Benoy Chandra Sarkar and her aunt, Bhavtarni Debi. According to their wills she was taking their ashes to Hardwar for immersion in the Holy Ganges. They were also exiles like Yasmin, but they would find their own river for their last journey to oblivion. How can one think of immersing one's ashes in the Caribbean?

Hail to thee, O Ganga, O Padma, O Eternal India. Hail, hail. She smiled irreverently to herself again. This might be her final visit to the motherland. She might soon leave on her own Last Journey—after all, she had been around for quite some time.

"Shall we go to the Intercontinental, Mrs. Sen? The Indian delegates are also staying there. Or would you like to put up with friends?" the secretary asked her.

They were crossing the hall. A liveried chauffeur approached her. "Mrs. Sen, Madam?" he said effusively. "Nawab Saheb has sent me from Arjumand Manzil. Couldn't come himself to receive you. He read in the morning papers about the time of your arrival, so he ordered me to rush to Tejgaon and bring you home."

Deepali apologised to her hosts and began walking briskly towards the exit. The young chauffeur led her to a gleaming white Mercedes.

The Nawab must be very old now, in his mid-eighties. Does he still smoke his silver hookah and wear his Turkish fez? She smiled fondly. She hadn't informed Jehan Ara because she wanted to give them all a pleasant surprise. For long she hadn't kept up her correspondence with her friend. The distance between Dacca and Port of Spain could not be spanned by mere aerogrammes, or even by such lengthy letters as were once sent to her by Yasmin and Rosie. She had come here last in 1964, for Akmal's wedding. The following year Rosie conveyed to her the news of his death. She had not written a letter of condolence to his mother, it just could not be penned. Now she was going to meet them after such a long time. She felt excited and nervous by turn.

The Mercedes was cruising along the highway to Dacca.

"How is everybody at Arjumand Manzil?" she asked.

"They are fine, just fine, Madam," the lad answered and continued to drive with great concentration. Perhaps he had been recently employed at Arjumand Manzil and was very conscious of his importance as the Nawab Saheb's chauffeur. Arjumand Manzil servants had always been quite snobbish.

She closed her eyes and tried to think up the words she should use by way of condolence for poor Akmal. He had been killed in the 1965 Indo-Pakistan War and had been dead nearly twelve years. His posthumous son must be eleven, and Jehan Ara must be living only for that child. Her daughter-in-law may have married again. The times had changed. A bride no longer went into her husband's homestead in a red palanquin only to be carried out on a bier.

She opened her eyes and looked ahead, noticed the mark of a deep gash on the chauffeur's neck.

"Madam, would you like to hear Bangladesh Radio?" he asked proudly.

Somebody was singing a *bhatiali*, made famous by her guru, Abbasuddin Ahmed. The Song of the Padma Boatmen. After a few minutes they broadcast Nazrul's "Rebel"...

Proclaim, O young man. I hold my head high and the Himalayas bow down before me. I hold a flute in one hand and a war bugle in the other...

She could not help joining in the chorus and in an instant was transported to the time when she used to sing this fiery song with Rosie, Mahmoodul Haque, Mushir, Jyoti, Surindra and the rest. She didn't realise that the car had reached Arjumand Manzil.

A demented woman with grey, frizzled hair stood like a statue on the stairs. She saw Deepali coming out of the Mercedes and scurried away.

A servant took out the luggage. Deepali followed him into the gallery. The house seemed to be eerily silent.

"Bibi...Bibi!" shouted Deepali and turned towards the zenana. She had reached the grand staircase of carved rosewood when the crazy woman appeared again. She blocked Deepali's way and held her feet in a strong grip. Then she began jabbering, "Ah...Aa...Aa..."

Deepali was scared. The servant had gone towards the guest room with her luggage. She saw another man coming in. She asked him, "Where is the Begum? Upstairs?"

"The Begum, Madam? Nawab Saheb told her that you lived abroad and were coming home after a long time, so she must give you the best Bengali food. She has gone herself to do the shopping." He reproved the mad woman. "Hey, you! Don't bother the lady." He explained to the guest: "Madam, when everybody got killed, from that time this woman has gone off her head. She also lost her power of speech."

"Who...who...got killed?"

"Everybody, Madam... The senior Nawab Saheb. His son, Nayyar Mian, his wife and children. Jehan Ara Bibi, her daughter-in-law and grandson. Everybody. At midnight. All gunned down right here inside the house. This hag saw them all being shot, one by one, and she was struck dumb and lost her reason."

Lightning flashed across Deepali's vision. She trembled and felt she was rapidly turning to stone. Her legs gave way. A cold current passed through her body. There was a momentary blackout. She sat down on the floor and broke into a terrifying howl. Her hair fell over her shoulders. She felt she was not human. She was a carnivorous animal. The denizens of her own cave had been devoured by other, more dangerous beasts. Their carcasses had been picked clean by the vultures and covered by desert sands. She was a jackal scratching the earth with her claws, a she-wolf bemoaning her dear ones. She began crying like a wild cat. Her wails brought other servants rushing into the room.

They were all strange faces. The crazed woman blabbered vehemently. As a child cries in sympathy with another, she too began shedding copious tears.

Suddenly Deepali fell silent. She dried her eyes and said in a flat, dreary monotone, "Take me to Nawab Saheb. Senior Nawab Saheb. He must be in the library waiting for me. Tell him that I have come."

"He was murdered too, Madam," a servant replied, rather embarrassedly.

Deepali pounded the floor with her fists. "That smart aleck chauffeur told me that Nawab Saheb had sent the car to the airport.

"Bloody liars! Just now you said Jehan Ara Bibi had gone to the bazaar, though I don't know since when she has become such a plebian as to go to the market to buy her groceries," she added, growling in an undertone.

"The new Begum Saheba, Madam."

Now she crouched like a spaniel, whimpering. Her eyes turned into the overflowing Old Ganga. The insane woman sat down near her. Through a veil of tears Deepali recognised her: Jehan Ara's faithful servant, Mala. She was laughing like a hyena. Deepali snarled, too. The two women had seen the end of the world.

After a few minutes Deepali raised her head. With a tin of 555 in his hand, dressed in an expensive suit, Rehan Ahmed stood in the archway.

The only surviving member of the family and the lawful heir to the Zaman-Chowdhry estate. The present Nawab of Arjumand Manzil.

Deepali shook her head like a cocker spaniel and rubbed her bloodshot eyes. She felt she was Kali with her tongue hanging out, thirsting for more blood. As Kali's devotee-poet, Ram Prasad Sen, had said, she sat on the cross-roads of the universe, making kites. She was flying them merrily, and when one string broke and a kite floated away into space, she clapped her hands.

After lunch Rehan went back to the jute factory he had inherited in Narayan Gunj. It had belonged to Qamrul Zaman. Now he was its sole owner. His wife, Zohra, brought Deepali upstairs for siesta.

This used to be Jehan Ara's bedroom. A tallboy still displayed the wedding photograph of Pilot Officer Akmal Murshidzada in his Pakistan Air Force uniform, and his wife in full bridal regalia. In September 1965 this pilot officer had died fighting for Pakistan...

Deepali felt dizzy. She went across and sat down in the window overlooking the cotton flower tree, the "magic throne" and the lotus pond.

Zohra reclined on the divan and began complaining about Uma Roy.

"She made my life miserable," she said, dressing a betel-leaf with its lime and *katha* pastes. "She had grown senile. She used to feed stray dogs and cats in Belvedere. She also thought that Rehan and I were her pet canaries."

"She always had this attitude about Rehan," Deepali replied impassively. At that moment she was merely a spectator.

"She turned our son Furqan against us. He began taking drugs, became a hippy, ran away from home. We heard that he had reached Dacca. Rehan dotes on him. He said to me, let's say goodbye to Calcutta and return to Dacca. There we'll start our life anew. Uma had driven him up the wall. At long last he had seen her in her true colours. In 1968 we came over to East Pakistan. Rehan started some business in Khulna, he knew that district well. But basically, he is a political animal, so he jumped into the fray once again. Awami League. Sheikh Mujibur Rehman, and all that. We came to Dacca and managed to get hold of our sonny boy. Rehan reformed him and sent him to London for higher education. We had brought all our capital from India through the back door."

"Rehan had already become a capitalist?"

"Who hasn't become a capitalist? Haven't you?"

Zohra was not as stupid as Deepali had thought her to be.

"Afterwards what happened, everybody knows. Rehan told you at lunch-time. There was this terrible war. Some call it the War of Liberation, for others it was the dismemberment of Pakistan which took place with the active connivance of Indira Gandhi's India. Who killed whom is a big question.

"The Pakistanis say the Punjabis and Biharis were massacred by Bengalis. We say the Punjabis committed genocide in East Pakistan. The controversy would have raged till doomsday, but soon all the bloodshed was forgotten and almost everybody who was anybody got busy making money.

"During the war Furqan was away in England, so he was saved. Now he looks after his father's factory. We were hiding in a village deep in the Sunderbans, in Khulna district."

Deepali winced. Zohra didn't notice and continued, "Even after his return to East Pakistan, Rehan had scrupulously avoided meeting the ladies of his Arjumand Manzil family, but he used to see the old Nawab at political gatherings. The Nawab had also become a Mujibur Rehman man. How and why this entire family was wiped out, Rehan has told you."

"Yes, I have no desire to hear the details," Deepali said firmly. At lunch Rehan had narrated to her in a matter-of-fact manner, how his relatives were shot down at midnight. He had said, "A massacre dulls the senses. One does not grieve for it as one does for an individual killing. A massacre almost becomes a festival of death."

His younger sister, Rabia, and her husband and children had gone away to Calcutta as refugees. They came back, Rehan employed his brother-in-law in the factory. His niece, Nasira Najmus Sahar had not gone to India, she had been fighting here and there along with the Mukti Bahini. Later, she joined the extremists and refused to lay down arms after the war was over.

"What didn't I do for this foolish girl!" Rehan complained to Deepali. "She had got involved with the extremists. That would have got her into real trouble. I managed to extricate her from that bunch. Got her a Soviet scholarship. She was sent to Moscow's Friendship University, but she returned from there a Maoist! Now she teaches at a girls' college and has turned against me. I don't understand what these young people really want. This is an ungrateful, thankless generation," he told Deepali in the voice of Nawab Qamrul Zaman.

She remembered the bitter things Nasira had had to say about him when she met her in 1964.

Rehan had left for Narayan Gunj. His mod son, Furqan, had gone to the TV centre to produce his weekly youth programme. The servants were asleep in their quarters. A hush fell over Arjumand Manzil.

Deepali came back from the window-seat and lay down on the Turkish divan. Her glance fell on a framed piece of Persian calligraphy. Suddenly she remembered. "What happened to the library?" she asked her hostess.

"Looted," she replied briefly. "We are using it now as a godown for our Sylhet tea. You see, the books can't be replaced so we may as well utilise that big room."

Zohra Rehan was a chatterbox. She talked incessantly and chewed betel-leaf like a goat. After a while Deepali said to her sternly, "Okay, keep quiet, Zohra, and let me have a nap."

"All right, you snooze, I'll read this film magazine," she answered equably.

Not a bad woman at all, Deepali thought, closing her eyes. This plain and commonplace woman is Rehan's wife, therefore I am jealous of her, although even jealousy is meaningless now. Too late, much too late. All life is gone.

She opened her eyes again and found Mala standing in the doorway like a restless ghost.

"Why don't you get lost, you horrid witch?" Zohra yelled at her with uncontrollable anger.

"Please Zohra, don't," Deepali pleaded.

"Didi, this lunatic woman is always hovering around. She gives me the jitters."

"Sit down, Mala," Deepali told her gently.

She sat down on the threshold and began her Aa...Aa...Aa... Perhaps she wanted to tell Deepali something very important but could not.

Zohra closed her betel-leaf case and said, "You are Rehan's old flame, aren't you? Uma Didi told me all about you. She said Rehan didn't marry Jehan Ara because of you."

"You can say what you like now, Zohra, it makes no difference to me," Deepali answered calmly, "though Rehan didn't leave Jehan Ara because of me."

"Please don't mind what I said, I am a guileless person. See, I can't believe my own good luck. For the last twenty-eight years I have been Rehan's wife. Incredible! Didi, have you heard of Nawab Ahmed Ali of Bamboo Villa, Calcutta?"

"Vaguely."

"He was a descendant of Nawab Muzzaffer Jung and he married Lord Robert's sister and his son was married to King Wajid Ali Shah's daughter, and his daughter married an Egyptian pasha..."

"My aunt once told me that when her father bought Caledonia he found Ahmed Ali's gold-plated album lying there in the junk. He took it to Arjumand Manzil, or rather brought it here to this house, and asked Sir Nurul to forward it to Calcutta. That was how Zamindar Romesh Chandra met Fakhrul Zaman Chowdhry and began his life of fun and frolic."

"Well, the Nawabs of Chitpur were among the topmost families of Calcutta. You name it, they owned it. A place in history. Lineage. Good looks. Wealth and social status.

"Today, a direct descendant of Nawab Ahmed Ali sells tickets in a cinema hall... See what I mean, Didi? I am the daughter of a poor craftsman, real working-class. I have become the Begum of Arjumand Manzil. I am semi-literate and have an ordinary mind, and I have been sharing the life of a most unusual person like Rehan Ahmed."

"At least by marrying you, he proved at that time that he was a practising socialist."

"I don't know what a practising socialist is, nor am I sure you do. All I know is that as my husband, Rehan Saheb has had no complaints. When he joined the Cabinet I became a dignified minister's lady! *Allah gives honour or disgrace to whomsoever He wishes...*"

"Aa...Aa...Aa..." Mala produced her usual noise.

Arjumand Manzil has become a haunted house. Its ghosts chase me from room to room, follow me into the garden, do not leave me alone for a moment. One evening Deepali walked listlessly on the back lawn and saw Jehan Ara's lighted window. A shadow fell on its plate-glass. She closed her eyes and shook her head. Am I heading for a crack-up? It is not Jehan Ara... It is Zohra, sitting on her prayer rug, reading the Quran.

Jehan Ara has crossed the ocean of life but continues to make me feel ashamed of myself. Rehan rejected her because of the very riches he now owns. She had to marry the wrong man, lost her son, and herself died a violent death...so that Mr. and Mrs. Rehan Ahmed could stay in this house happily ever after.

Earlier, Deepali would have soundless conversations with herself, now she often muttered half-aloud. Sure sign of old age. She strolled across to the playhouse. It was a miniature theatre hall built in neo-classical style, and set upon the lawn like a huge, white doll's house. Once it was called Nawabzada Fakhrul Zaman's Folly, because he had sunk all his money into its lavish non-commercial productions. Very symbolic. Deepali again tried to find meaning and symbols in her surroundings. We take up a hobby or have a passion, she told herself, and submerge our lives in it. Mostly it does us no good, ruins us forever. She reached the entrance with its neat marble pillars. The main door was lying ajar. She had never been inside. A bit diffidently she stepped in. The setting sun had lighted up the hall through its numerous half-broken windows. The wooden floor was covered with layers of dust. Jehan Ara had once told her that the hall used to be fully carpeted, and the invited audience would recline against satin bolsters and enjoy the evening's entertainment.

Faded photographs hanging askew on the walls became visible. The Parsi Theatre, Dharamtalla Street, Calcutta. Master Mustafa, hero of "Siraj ud Daulah". Miss Tinkori Das the Younger. Miss Tara Das, heroine of "Sarla". Miss Gohar Jan, chief actress of Victoria Alfred Theatrical Company, Calcutta.

A portrait in oil glowed dimly above the stage. Deepali was taken aback. Rehan Ahmed in period costume! She went closer and read the name engraved on a small brass plate: "Nawabzada Fakhrul Zaman Chowdhry as Shahjehan."

She had a strange sensation—something was crawling over her feet. She screamed and jumped back. A mouse! She was about to rush out when a group photograph caught her eye. This was probably the cast of "Raja Bhoj", the opera Rehan's maternal grandfather had written and produced. The actor and actresses looked funny. Her own grandfather, Romesh Chandra Sarkar, sat in the front row with much aplomb, dressed as Raja Indra. She stared at the photograph for some minutes and ventured into the back room, hoping to find some more pictures of her Thakur-da. The place was full of mouldy props, moth-eaten costumes, East India Company's military "red coats", top hats and chimney hats, tarnished crowns, half-broken musical instruments, including a lyre. Canvas rolls of painted scenery stood in a corner. A lizard eyed her menacingly from behind a Grecian couch. Deepali was scared stiff. She ran out of the theatre hall as fast as she could and returned to the back garden.

The throne was still there under the sprawling tree. Its paint had been washed away by thirty-six monsoons. Many of the wooden figurines had been eaten up by white ants.

Deepali sat down on the edge of the throne and inhaled some fresh air.

On a pleasant summer evening Jehan Ara had once told her, "May Allah give him a place in paradise, my great-uncle was a truly gifted man. He composed beautiful music for his opera. He played Raja Bhoj. Your grandfather was King Indra, Calcutta actresses sang the parts of Urvashi and Rambha."

Mala was sitting on the grass. Rosie and Yasmin were also present. Jehan Ara had asked her maid, "Mala, tell us the story of Raja Bhoj."

"Bibi, Hindu folk, they say in the heaven of their gods there dwelt two-and thirty dancers. It came to pass that one day they tried to seduce the chief god, Shiva…"

"Good Heavens!" the girls laughed.

"So Shiva's wife, the chief goddess, Parvati, she was furious, naturally. Being a goddess she cursed the playful dancers to turn into wood. They did, and were fixed as decoration pieces on King Indra's magic throne."

"No, first tell us that story of the magic apple. What was it about"?

"The faithlessness of men and women, Bibi," Mala replied, contentedly chewing her betel-leaf. "Ujjain's Raja Bhartrihari, he was madly in love with his queen, Anang Sena. A yogi gave him this magic apple, you eat it and become immortal. The Raja gave it to Anang Sena. She presented it to her lover who was a stable groom. He was deceiving the queen. He passed it on to his other mistress who worked as a maid in the palace.

"Now, Bibi, the wench was carrying on with the milkman as well. She gave the apple to him. He had another woman tucked away in the village, she sold dung-cakes. She received the golden apple as a gift from the milkman. She placed it on top of her basket and went out hawking her dung-cakes. As she passed through a forest she was seen by Raja Bhartrihari who was out hunting deer. He noticed the magic apple he had given to his beloved queen, Anang Sena. His wife's infidelity broke his heart. He gave his kingdom to his brother Bikramjeet and renounced the world."

The audience was spellbound. Mala went on: "It is a cycle of tales, we'll leave them out. Eventually Bikramjeet was asked to judge a dance competition between two heavenly dancers called Rambha and Urvashi. The god Indra was so pleased with Bikramjeet's judgement that he presented the mortal king his own magic throne.

"Now, it was the same throne which had those accursed thirty-two sky maidens fitted to its golden railing and legs. When, in later times, no monarch turned out to be as good as Bikramjeet, the throne was buried in the earth. After a long, long time, Raja Bhoj had it dug out."

Now Jehan Ara had taken up the thread of the story. "Yes," she said, "I know. When Raja Bhoj proceeded to ascend the throne, one of the figurines came to life and challenged him. She declared that only that king deserved to sit upon it who was as generous as Bikramjeet. So every time Raja Bhoj tried to get to the throne, one of the statuettes stopped him and narrated to him a story about Bikramjeet's justice, loyalty, truthfulness, et cetera."

Yasmin had exclaimed, "Idea, Jehan Ara Apa! Your great-uncle composed an opera about Raja Bhoj, I shall choreograph a ballet. Actually, Bibi, to my mind this throne is a woman's heart. Let's pretend that we four—you, Deepali-di, Rosie Apa and Yours Truly, we are the four sky-maidens, turned wooden, who support this throne. Whichever Raja Bhoj worth his crown approaches it, we shall challenge him—Hey! just a minute. Do you have such and such qualities in you?"

Deepali rubbed her eyes. The ghosts of Jehan Ara and Yasmin vanished. A dumbstruck Mala sat on the tank-steps staring at her vacantly.

A car screeched to a halt on the drive across the trees. She heard Rehan's voice.

He came trampling across the grass and appeared before her like a useless thought. Krishna, Krishna. From where do you come in the cow-dust hour?

"Sit down, Rehan."

He sat down on the stage throne built by his mother, Maliha Begum's remarkable dad. Suddenly Deepali felt like challenging him. Stop! You can't sit on it...

"Sorry, got held up at the factory," he said, lighting a Dunhill.

"Busy re-building Bangladesh?"

He frowned and looked away.

Deepali had the uncanny feeling again that Jehan Ara was looking out of her window. It was Zohra Rehan Ahmed who had finished reading her scripture.

Hallucinations. Must run away from this shadow-land, back to my safe haven. Here, on every step, a spectre confronts me and tells me a story. The genii are incessantly repeating in my ears...shall I tell you more, shall I tell you more, shall I tell you more...?

Rehan also raised his eyes and glanced at Jehan Ara's window.

"Mala keeps muttering in her monosyllables. She wishes to tell me something, something about the massacre, perhaps. I am so sorry that I'll go away without understanding her."

"Yes, I, too, wish I could understand what she wants to communicate. Wish all of us could understand one another. We are all turned into crazed beings, muttering gibberish..."

Deepali didn't hear him. She was counting: Myself, Jehan Ara, Yasmin Majid—two of the three figurines broke down pretty horribly.

She began to hum an old song.

"Thirty-six years ago I heard you sing for the last time. There at the gate of your house, Chandrakunj. At the same cow-dust hour when you also recited "The Owl and the Pussycast!"

"Did I? I don't remember," she answered dryly.

A peacock glided by, lone and majestic in his indifference.

"There used to be a lot of Sunderban deer, too, in the Nawab's private zoo," she remarked after some moments.

"Yes. He was the last word in gracious living. We do not have men like him anymore," Rehan answered and added, "I still don't know who were the hoods who killed my uncle."

"*Who killed Cock Robin? I, said the sparrow, with my bow and arrow—*"

"I beg your pardon?"

"Sorry. I have acquired this unfortunate habit of turning everything upside down, inside out, and then I reduce it to the level of the ludicrous."

"Why?"

"What else can one do?"

He grunted.

"Early that morning when I arrived here from the airport, the shock of the information reduced me to the level of poor Mala. Did it help?"

"That was hysteria. Women often react like that."

"I know. There was nothing mystical or metaphysical about it, I had merely gone off, momentarily. Ages ago, I had a nightmare in Santineketan. I heard someone say: Nawabzadi Jehan Ara Begum has been murdered in cold blood. What would you call that? I am not one bit psychic."

"It's amazing you didn't know about this ghastly business. It happened several years ago, and Bangladesh got good coverage in the world press."

"Not where I live. At least not the details. I stay mostly in Florida, or I travel. We have no children, and my husband is too busy with his work, so I spend my time roaming the world. And I have not been in touch with old friends in India. Not that I have many friends left."

He smoked in silence.

"Do you know, after I lost my dad the father-figure of the Nawab remained in my mind as a kind of substitute. I had this comfortable feeling that at least he was still there, living in faraway Bangladesh. And what surprises me is that I haven't heard many people talk about him out here. He seems to have been completely forgotten."

"When a calamity wipes out thousands in one stroke, the details get blurred. Who remembers the countless families which perished during the London Blitz and in the bombings all over Europe? Would anybody have heard of Pamela Barlow a couple of years later even in England? There is an Urdu saying that nobody dies with the dead. This was, of course, a distinguished family, but a large number of eminent writers and artists were also killed. Too much death and destruction make the survivors secretly rejoice that they are still alive."

He took out his lighter. It didn't work. "Damn!" he uttered in exasperation. "Go and get me a box of matches and a packet of—" the next instant he faltered and checked himself. Her eyes became moist.

He asked hastily, "What is your programme after Calcutta?"

"Oh," she cleared her throat. "I have nobody in Calcutta. Khokhu also emigrated to Venezuela. I'll go to Calcutta en route to Bolpur. Being a sentimental old woman, I want to have a look at my alma mater. From Trinidad I came straight to Delhi because I had to go to Hardwar. I telephoned Rosie from the airport. She insisted that..."

"Which Rosie is this? Rosie Hasan?"

"No. Have you forgotten her?"

"Oh, that one. She got hold of the Sanyal boy in rather dramatic circumstances."

"What do you mean, got hold of?"

"You have become churlish! All sense of humour gone with the High Wind in Jamaica."

"I'm afraid it's you who have become a crashing bore."

"Have I, now? Well, my good woman..."

"And a pompous ass."

"Thank you. So, what is old Basant Sanyal doing?"

"Retired recently as a high court judge. Rosie is involved in cultural activities. I may hop back to Delhi for her youngest daughter Ella's marriage."

"That reminds me—our son Furqan is getting married in January. You are most cordially invited."

"Thanks. I have become a regular attender of my earlier times' friends' children's weddings."

"Watch your English."

"Never mind my English. Now I must go home."

"Sounds odd when you call West Indies home."

She eyed him hatefully, like the lizard which had darted out of long-forgotten props in the private theatre.

"Are you still play-acting Rehan?" she asked, trying to sound normal and casual.

"Pardon?"

"You used to be called the second Virendranath Chattopadhyaya because of the way you quickly changed your disguise. Now I know you inherited your talent for histrionics from your fabled grandpa. I have just seen his portrait in the playhouse. You also have an uncanny resemblance to him. And I have come to the sad conclusion that you have at last reverted to type, to your partially feudal origins."

"Haven't you?"

"Since I have seen you in your new role as the lord of the manor, being an optimist of sorts, I have been hoping earnestly that this is also part of your lifelong play-acting. Tell me, please, that you are still in disguise, that you really haven't turned into all that you once rebelled against."

"Is Kulsum Ayah also playing the wealthy expatriate?"

"How could you make such shameful compromises, first in Calcutta and now here?"

"Didn't you, in the Port of Spain?"

"I didn't sell my conscience."

"Says you," he shot back. "You went and married Uncle Scrooge."

"Lalit is *not* Uncle Scrooge! He is a generous large-hearted man."

"Ha! You and Rosie! Did you turn out to be any different from Rosie Bannerjee? Don't be so bloody self-righteous, seething with moral indignation."

"Don't yell, Rehan. People might think we are two cranky old people, two pensioners sitting on a park bench, quarrelling..."

"Over spilt milk, eh? We *are* old, Deepali. And you must bravely face a drastically changed world in which, as you told me, imperialist English evangelist families' offspring have turned into equally rabid *Hindu* missionaries! It's later than you think, my dear!"

"I had gone to see Chandrakunj yesterday. Found no trace of it. A new block of flats stands in its place, all concrete and glass."

"So? This is happening all over the world. How else do you think cities expand and new townships come up?"

"Found no trace of Abdul Qadir's family, either."

"There are a hundred million people in this country, another hundred million in Pakistan and nearly a billion in India. How would you find Abdul Qadir's family?"

He crushed his cigarette under his boots.

"There was so much bloodshed here and what was the net result? The local bourgeoisie turned the West Pakistani-Punjabi bourgeoisie out and took it place."

"You have become a silly woman. You do not know the situation out here and land up from the West to pontificate."

"Ronu. Shall I tell you a little anecdote?"

"Let's not slip into anecdotage, Mrs. Sen!"

"When we first arrived in Port of Spain, we rented a cottage facing a Moorish-style mansion. Two old ladies with snow-white hair used to sit on their balcony reading the Bible. A lot of priests and nuns came to visit them. They were regular church-goers and were known in the neighbourhood for their good deeds.

"Every morning at ten o'clock they got into a taxi and went downtown. They were accompanied by their Negro cook who carried a large canvas bag. I decided to introduce myself to these good ladies and go along with them one day to buy my groceries. They would tell me about the best shops and so on. Somehow I could not do so for a few days. One morning, when they got into a cab and left, I also hired one and told the driver to follow them. Thought I would stop at the same shops as them.

"But the other taxi went right down to the waterfront and pulled up before a shady-looking hotel. Sailors were coming out of the building and my cabbie looked askance at me. Meanwhile, the old ladies had got out of their taxi and entered the joint. About a dozen mulatto girls lounged in the gallery. They had artificially bleached hair and sat in a row, smoking. I was greatly perplexed and wanted to solve the mystery.

"After a few minutes the old women came out, followed by their cook. The bag he carried now looked quite heavy. All three got into the cab and drove away. My cabbie said, 'Miss, perhaps you are a newcomer here. These old ladies were famous whores forty years ago. They came here from New Orleans—now they own this flophouse. Every morning they come here to check the accounts with the manager and take the previous night's income home. They spend most of it on charity.

'Even monsignors of the Church visit them, they are so famous for their piety.'

"When I returned home and looked across the street, I found them sitting in their rocking-chairs, reading their Bibles.

"So, Ronu, most of us lead double lives. You are not Mlle Marie or Mlle Yvonne, you are the Negro cook who carries their canvas bag. You are also *involved*."

"Aren't you involved as well?" he retorted. "After you migrated to the West Indies, shouldn't you have organised a trade union movement and worked for the red revolution among the plantation labourers? But you chose to marry a wealthy fool with whom you attend Government House banquets, and vacation in Florida. Because you got tired or disillusioned or because you, too, had faced many hardships and now wished to enjoy the good things of life...

"You see, Deepali, to keep the lamp burning requires a great quantity of oil. And the trouble is that sometimes the oil runs out pretty soon. Now you have become a ringside spectator. You have your sympathy for the downtrodden. You hate injustices and wars, but you are no longer in the actual arena. To remain consistently inside the sphere of misery and struggle requires a hell of a lot of courage. Those who do so are considered eccentrics or plain fools.

"Of late I have been seeing your husband's name in the press. He is taking part in the island's politics. It is entirely possible that some day he may become the Prime Minister. You will be the Prime Minister's lady. Then, Deepali Sen, I'll come to meet you and ask you how free *you* are... You and I were two guinea pigs on which life made its experiments."

"But quite a few have turned out not to be cowardly like us..." Deepali answered slowly, suddenly feeling weak and defeated. "There are many who have kept the lamp burning."

"Yes, indeed. There are many who have kept the lamp burning. There are Hindu-Muslim riots in many states of India except Bengal. Why? Because of Bengal's strong Leftist tradition which was created by people like you and me. Some of us did fall by the wayside, but many more are still there... All luck to them." He threw away the cigarette stub and looked up...

42
Victorious Morning Star

A sad-faced girl came across the garden path and sat down at the edge of the red-stone tank.

"Adaab, Mamoo Jaan..."

"May you live long."

"Adaab, Deepali Mashi..."

"May you live long. Come and sit here."

Rather dryly Rehan addressed Deepali, "This is my sister Rabia's daughter, Miss Nasira Qadiri. I have told you about her, haven't I?"

"Mamoo Jaan, tell Mashi my full name. My mother's late-lamented cousin, Jehan Ara Begum, named me Nasira Najmus Sahar—Victorious Morning Star. And I met Deepali Mashi when she came here last—1964, for Akmal's—Akmal's—" her voice trailed off.

"I do remember. How are you, Nasira?" Deepali asked gloomily.

"Today I got to know that you had arrived from the West Indies. Otherwise, only cricketers come from there—ha, ha, ha! So I said, may as well come over and meet you."

The girl was too young to have become so cynical. "I'm glad that you could come," Deepali replied, "So glad. What are you doing these days?"

"Earlier I fought in the War of Liberation. Now I teach political science in the same college where you and Aunt Jehan Ara once studied."

"You fought in the War of Liberation," Deepali repeated in a monotone.

"Yes, ma'am. When you came here in 1964 to celebrate the wedding of Pilot Officer Akmal Murshidzada of Pakistan Air Force—on this very throne under this tree, I told you one evening that although we were against the injustices inflicted on us by the West Pakistanis, we were staunch Pakistanis and would defend Pakistan against India to the last drop of our blood—" She laughed with a bitterness which unnerved Deepali Sen.

"Nasira, how is your mother, Rabia?" she asked.

"My parents are fine, thank you. My uncle, as you can see for yourself, is flourishing." She glanced at Rehan with utmost contempt. Deepali grew more nervous. How this chit of a girl hated the almighty Rehan! He remained quiet. Perhaps he had accepted his defeat and laid down arms at the feet of this rude, cheeky, angry new breed. He was afraid of them. Or he had a bad conscience and could not face them. Deepali felt enormously depressed. I must run away from here as soon as I can. She changed the topic and asked Nasira about her old college.

A scooter arrived. Furqan brought it straight to the throne. "Having an *adda*?" he asked jovially.

"Yes, join us," Nasira replied.

Furqan, Deepali noticed, looked and behaved quite differently from his father.

"Cousin Furqan used to be a sympathiser of the Hungry Generation. Now he is going to be a leader of the affluent criminal classes."

Furqan kept sitting on his scooter and raised his hands. With mock gravity he declaimed: "Shantih...Shantih...!"

"Shut up, you bogus phoney pacifist!" Nasira retorted and turned to Deepali. "Excuse us, Deepali Mashi. We have been through an inferno, compared to which your struggle against the British and the Partition carnage were mere picnics."

"Perhaps we were mistaken about ourselves," Deepali answered humbly. "We thought we were 'the rebels' of Nazrul Islam."

"We have seen total destruction and the kind of bloodshed you cannot even begin to imagine. Now some people are calling themselves pacifists. Isn't it another kind of compromise? What should be the choice? Peace or the PLO? Peace or the Naxalites?"

"This is the basic question, Nasira Apa. Perhaps you do not want to lay down your arms because you continue to idealise that bloke, Tiger Siddique. You talk of perpetual revolution. Nasira Apa, you are a bit mixed-up, aren't you?" said Furqan amiably.

"To call somebody mixed-up is not cricket, you know. Deepali Mashi, this entire Arjumand Manzil family and millions—millions—were killed. I faced the Bengali-Punjabi and Bengali-Bihari hatred. I saw the role of the political leaders. Furqan Ahmed! When we confronted the machine-guns out here, as the son of a wealthy father you were enjoying yourself in London." She was ignoring the presence of Rehan who got up and began pacing the lawn.

Deepali felt actuely uncomfortable. Crazy Mala had gone away. She strutted back, nodding her head like a wooden puppet, and sat down on the grass. She was staring vacantly at the assembly.

Nasira said to Furqan: "Humanism and quietism and peace are indeed lovely words. Gandhiji advised the German Jews to employ non-violence against Hitler. Ha, ha! When Dacca was surrounded by tanks, should I have invoked William Penn and Bertrand Russell? Or George Fox and Tolstoy?"

"Perhaps you should have invoked Subhas Chandra Bose," said Furqan, smiling.

"Yes, indeed. Who remembers him now even in India?" Nasira replied. "Do you know he declared Nawab Siraj ud Daulah a national hero? He got a descendant of King Wajid Ali Shah of Oudh elected as the mayor of Calcutta. In Rangoon the neglected grave of King Bahadur Shah Zafar was rebuilt by him. The warriors of 1857 made the last Mughal emperor the symbol of India's independence. At his grave in Rangoon Subhas Bose and the officers of the Indian National Army took the oath to drive out the British. India became free not only because of Gandhian non-violence; the terrorists, and later the Indian National Army also convinced the British that they must leave."

"You know, Nasira Apa, Emerson has said that an interest in war reveals an immature mind. We Bengalis are supposed to be a weak, romantic, poetic sort of people. But from the time of the Sanyasis and Titu Mir and the Terrorists, down to Mukti Bahini and the Naxalites, we have indulged in violence like nobody's business," Furqan said peaceably.

"Okay, I put it to you," Nasira spoke vehemently, "Einstein was a pacifist. But wouldn't he have approved of Israel's expansionism? He would have. In the West even humanist Jewish intellectuals are against the Palestinians."

"In the West some Jewish intellectuals are moderates, too," Deepali put in mildly. After a very long time she was finding herself in a typical Bengali *adda*. She was also aware of the tremendous generation gap which separated her from Nasira and Furqan, and was reluctant to argue with them. Perhaps she had become out-of-date. Her old friend who used to take part in the *addas* of the past, was strolling on the grass, lost in thought. He was no longer her *adda*-holder comrade-in-arms.

"Every attitude is the product of a certain class. Pacifism will also benefit some people. First you become the owner of a jute factory, and then start preaching peace and goodwill," Nasira attacked her uncle and cousin once again.

Furqan laughed.

"And now perhaps you have also taken to religion," she added furiously.

"Religion contains the real spirit of peace. Do you know what Islam means? Peace! Shalom!"

"Don't we know how the CIA has spread its net all over the world through bogus swamis!"

"Nasira Apa, don't be daft," Furqan answered in his pucca British manner. " The fact is that now Jesus Christ is my hero, too, and Imam Hussain and his descendants—the

Apostolic Imams, and the Sufis of Islam—they were the real original quietists."

"The opium has affected you completely, alas." Nasira remarked sorrowfully. "Peace spread by religion, indeed! In the West army chaplains accompany their forces on either side of the battlelines and pray to the same god for victory. In the Indo-Pak wars, Hindu and Sikh soldiers carry pictures of goddess Durga and Guru Gobind Singh, and Pakistani forces raise the battlecry of God is Great, and invoke the help of Ali. Out here, in 1971, Islam raged on both sides of the war-front."

Squirrels played about under the flowering trees. Red lotuses bloomed in the pond. Deepali remembered what Albert Camus had said about man's constant questioning and Nature's perennial silence.

Nasira shouted again, "Did the bishops of England and the American clergy ever denounce the aggressive wars fought by their nations? Did the Ulema of Pakistan speak out against the war fought here in 1971?

"Shall I tell you about my Aunt Jehan Ara's friend, Yasmin Majid?"

"Ah! The celebrated daughter of Bangladesh! What about her?" Furqan asked, now with a certain seriousness.

"Aunt Yasmin went away to England before you were born. She made dance her career and married an English fashion designer. Her father, Maulana Majidullah, promptly disowned her. Aunt Yasmin, too, was unconsciously extremely pious like the rest of her family. She also knew that she had gone through a bogus nikah ceremony with Mr. Gerald Belmont. Later, Yasmin began to suffer from pangs of conscience. The 'marriage' broke up. Her daughter grew into a beauty and began to work as a nude model. The massive guilt destroyed poor Yasmin Majid. She committed suicide.

"I came to know all about it because, after her second heart attack in West Germany, she wrote to my mother. The maulvis did not forgive Yasmin for her waywardness, but thousands of Muslim girls were raped here during the War of Liberation, countless were forced to become street-walkers. Not a single maulvi in the Islamic world protested against the horrible situation." Nasira's face had become crimson.

This girl is the real Rebel of Nazrul Islam—Perhaps we were not, Deepali reminded herself again.

> *Men must fight*
> *And women must weep*
> *And women must weep*

Deepali repeated to herself and wiped her own tears.

"So, shouldn't I have killed, too? I shot a Punjabi soldier of the Pakistan Army with my Mukti Bahini service revolver. I was fighting in Comilla. I can't forget his last moments…How he groaned and writhed in agony. I see his tormented, dying face in my dreams, again and again." She continued to cry. "What shall one do? Where shall one go?"

"Nasira Apa," Furqan said gently, "once I saw a film in Cambridge, an anti-war film. There was a song called "Lily Marlene" which was very popular with German as well as British soliders. Aunt Deepali, the Allies get hold of this German girl and bring her to their camp and make her sing "Lily Marlene". Then there is this very English soldier, he is afraid of war and runs away from the battle-front. He is caught and brought back. A deserter must be shot. But the lad is ill, they can't shoot him right away. So they take him to the field hospital and treat him. When he gets slightly better they tie him to a stretcher and bring him out. The stretcher is tied in an upright position to a pole and then, in accordance with martial law, they shoot him…"

Rehan had come back and had been listening intently. He looked up and said slowly: "Perhaps I am a deserter, too. Nasira and Deepali, both of you can give me any punishment you like."

There was a terrifying silence. The delicate boughs of *jhao* trees continued rustling in the evening wind.

Nasira lifted her face, and for the first time she looked at her tired, unhappy uncle with a measure of kindness. She was about to say something when the upper-floor window of Jehan Ara's bedroom was opened and a shaft of light fell across the back garden. Zohra Rehan Ahmed shouted from above. "You all have had enough of your *adda*. The Yasmin Memorial secretary rang up. They are waiting for us at the club for dinner."

"Aa-a-a." Sitting on the tank steps the demented, speechless Mala made a feeble noise...

43
Richard Barlow

A flower-bedecked portrait of the late Mrs. Yasmin Belmont stood on a sideboard in the Banquet Hall of Dacca Club. Dinner was being served to the intellectual elite, ministers and new tycoons of Bangladesh, and their ladies.

"History is another name for humanity's inability to learn its lessons." Sea hawks continue to swoop down on the fish.

Dinner over, the guests adjourned to the drawing-rooms. Clad in a white sharkskin sherwani and tight pyjamas, Rehan Ahmed looked a picture of elegance. His hair had turned silver grey and he was the most distinguished-looking person in the gathering. Important, successful and affluent. At sixty-five he looked much younger than his age. Yesterday at the breakfast table in Arjumand Manzil he had said, "My late mother's soul must be so happy. Her uncle deprived her of her property and married her off to a poor cultivator. How Providence has made up for that injustice!"

The statement had astonished Deepali. Rehan had further said: "Look, for long years I went from pillar to post in united Bengal. Served terms in jail. Remained underground. Had the same kind of life in West Bengal immediately after independence. I grew tired. Then I got a chance to have some rest and comfort, first there and then here. It's as simple as that."

Earlier in the evening Nasira had said at Arjumand Manzil: "Furqan was going to be a poet of the Hungry Generation; now he will be the leader of the new-rich criminal classes of Bangladesh."

Dacca Club's chef had prepared excellent French dishes. Deepali wondered again, how much they must have spent on the Yasmin Belmont Festival. And she lived for decades as a penniless exile in the West.

A black moon dashed against the mountains and broke into splinters. Yasmin, you were a *ketaki* flower which attracted serpents. They killed you.

Conversation raged around her. They were talking of Pakistan and Bangladesh: we did this, they did that.

Suddenly she heard herself say aloud, "If Mr. Jinnah had not created Pakistan, there would have been no Bangladesh today. Actually, he is the founder of this new country as well."

People looked at her in surprise and said nothing. She continued to hold forth: "The concept of Mother India was given to the rest of the country by the terrorists of Bengal. They worshipped Divine Power in the image of Kali, the destroyer. They believed in the prehistoric Dravidian concept of the Mother Goddess. The British branded them as terrorists. Indians called them revolutionaries. Many among them were anti-Muslim as well. Bankim Chandra's novel, *Anand Math* was their Bible. The cross-currents of the politics of Bengal's Hindu *bhadralok* and Muslim gentry gave birth to East Pakistan, and the internal politics of West and East Pakistan created Bangladesh. Individual personality clashes, and the temperaments and actions of political leaders build or destroy entire nations."

The audience remained politely silent. She kept quiet and looked in front. Rehan's Cambridge-educated son, Furqan, was dancing with an English girl from the British Embassy. Furqan Ahmed's outlook had been formed by the attitudes of the West's contemporary young generation. He was post-Tariq Ali, and for him the New Left of France had also become *passe*. Does this lad know that once in British India, if you wrote revolutionary poems you could be sent to the Andamans? Are the doors of history going to be closed on us? Who remembers my uncle Dinesh Chandra Sarkar or Ashfaque Ullah Khan of Shahjehanpur?

What would happen to the newest rebel, Nasira Najmus Sahar, Victorious Morning Star? Wouldn't there be another backlash? How long would she be able to remain a rebel in a situation where Marxists are busy condemning one another as "revisionists"? According to extremists the moderates have joined the Establishment. Personal weaknesses, prejudices and neuroses affect the leaders' style of functioning. Commercial pilots' health and nerves are constantly checked so that they do not endanger the lives of their passengers. Political leaders' states of mind and nerves are never examined.

What did we do? What did our generation achieve? Now it seems to me that we were hitch-hikers who stood by the highway, raising our thumbs for a ride. A car stopped by and took some of us to Moscow. Others to Washington. Some of our friends got on to a camel's back and returned to Mecca. Others climbed onto a bullock-cart and went back to Banaras.

The car which stopped for me broke down in the middle of the road.

In the Vaishnava faith of Bengal every man is an image of Krishna, every woman a Radha, although they are not aware of this. So, was Rehan Krishna and I, Radha? That's what I used to believe in my youth.

Summer is about to come. In this lovely homeland of mine, *kadam* flowers will bloom. And lac flowers, and fragrant *sultana champa*.

"Mr. Rehan Ahmed told me that you had worked in the Underground against the British Raj." A young Bangladeshi journalist interrupted her chain of thought. He sat down respectfully near her. "Can I come to your place with my photographer tomorrow morning and interview you, Madam?"

"You cannot. The answer is an emphatic, No. Please go away. Leave me alone," she cried vehemently. People around her had been amazed by her little speech; this outburst convinced them that she was one of those cranky, disgruntled freedom-fighters, leftovers of the Raj, who find fault with everything in the present independent regimes of India, Pakistan and Bangladesh.

"I am sorry, Mrs. Sen," the newspaperman said gently and moved off. "What a bad-tempered old woman," he remarked to his colleagues at the bar.

Now speeches were being delivered on the floral dais about Madame Yasmin Belmont's services to the Art and Culture of East Bengal. Her rare qualities as a human being were highlighted. Deepali, too, would be asked to say something. After all, they had invited her all the way from the West Indies for this purpose. But it was strange, nobody had asked her to sing. Perhaps it had long been forgotten that she used to be the star pupil of Abbasuddin Ahmed, or that her gramophone records were a must for every Bengali household. Or that she had frequently broadcast over All India Radio, Dacca, which became Radio Pakistan, Dacca, and was now Radio Bangladesh, Dacca. The changing waves of sound—!

Even Rehan had not told the Yasmin Belmont Memorial Committee to include a concert by Shrimati Deepali Sen during the cultural programmes scheduled for the Festival. There seemed to be a strange kind of confusion everywhere. Rehan himself was lost in the world of high finance. Incredible.

Another young man came towards her. He bowed courteously and said, "We have just come to know that Madame Yasmin Belmont's diary is in your possession. Could you kindly lend it to us? We would like to publish it in a befitting manner. It is bound to be a literary masterpiece."

Deepali reddened with pent-up anger. She glared at the stranger, got up and went out.

As she stood under the last arch of the colonial building, a full moon emerged from behind the rose-apple trees. Like her, the moon also looked contrite. Secretly Rehan was ashamed, too; and Yasmin had been so sorry that she had simply removed herself from this earth.

A youthful White man sat at a small table under another arch, eating his solitary dinner. As he saw an elderly lady hovering nearby, he rose to his feet.

"Hello! It's so crowded inside that I came out," Deepali said hollowly. "At my age one can't stand too many people, you know. May I sit down?"

"Sure, ma'am. I am Christopher Taggart. Tourist, waiting for a friend. Oh, here he comes!"

Another blond young man strode down the verandah and joined them.

"Richard Barlow."

"Mrs. Sen."

"How do you do!

"Hello!" She pricked up her ears. "Small world, indeed! I happen to know your father. As a matter of fact, my family has known three generations of Barlows! I met your nephew on the way to Athens. Your half-nephew, Swami Atmanand Shanker Premi."

"Oh, Atom Ananda. Crazy guy." Dick Barlow smiled indulgently.

"Next month he will wait for you. In Rishikesh."

Dick Barlow sat down. Polite conversation followed. He was twenty-eight, a successful interior decorator in Sydney, and dissatisfied with life. His friend Chris asked a passing bearer to bring dinner. Richard said, "Arthur Koestler has written somewhere that some coincidences are quite baffling. Now, Mrs. Sen, look at your chance meetings with the Barlows. First you meet my nephew and then myself!"

"Also your father, in Perth!"

"Entire life is a series of coincidences," Christopher opined philosophically. He did not seem very bright.

The bearer brought fish and placed it before Richard Barlow.

He shook his head. "I have become a vegetarian. Please bring me some salad. This fish..." he addressed Deepali Sen, "for all I know, it may have been my late aunt, Miss Alice Barlow. She was a missionary in the Garo Hills, Assam. My great-aunt, Mabel Barlow, died of cholera in Seetapur Mission Compound. Miss Maud Barlow, her sister, ran a mission in China. She was done in by Chinamen during the Boxer Rebellion. Alice Barlow was murdered by tribal Communists in the Garo Hills. All three, according to their lights, achieved martyrdom. Right now, they must be singing in Heaven's Methodist Choir:

> *There is a happy land far, far away,*
> *Where the saints in glory stand,*
> *Bright, bright as the day.*

He began humming. He had been drinking and his face was flushed. "Mrs. Sen, as a schoolboy in the Australian Outback I, too, used to sing this hymn. Now I know better. First of all, there is no Heaven, and on earth there is no happy land anywhere. Europe-America-England-Bangladesh-India-Pakistan. Nowhere. And my nephew, Swami Atom Ananda Shanker Premi, says that we are all eating the fruit of our actions in previous births. According to her *sanskaras*, my dry-as-a-date holy spinster Aunt Alice must have been born again somewhere. For all you know, she may have been born as a fish in a river of Bengal and is now lying on this plate before me. So how can I eat my poor Aunt Alice?"

He placed his hand affectionately on Taggart's. Mrs. Sen looked away. Dick continued, "Mrs. Sen, I love Chris so much that we may even get married some day."

Speeches continued in the Hall about the greatness of the late Madame Yasmin Belmont. Deepali said hastily, "Okay, goodnight. I must make a move."

Dick repeated: "So how do we know this deep-fried fish is not Miss Alice Barlow? Even my great-aunt Mabel might have been cooked on a sizzler. Shhh.... All of us are being cooked on a sizzler. You and I, all of us. If my Bengal Civilian imperialist ancestors—great-great-grandfather, Sir Edward

Barlow, and my uncle, Wing Commander Richard Barlow, and soul-saver ladies, Misses Matilda, Maud, Mabel and Alice Barlow, if they come to know that a son of Charles Barlow, ICS, is gay, and his grandson has become a Hindu swami—they won't merely turn in their graves, they will stand up in their shrouds and howl till Kingdom Come.

"Mrs. Sen, please do not be shocked. We of the Now Generation gloat in our frankness. Hypocrisy was the hallmark of your times. When my forefathers studied in Merry England's public schools...Oh, well, I am sorry that I have embarrassed you, Mrs. Sen, but you are an old friend of the family."

She had already said a hurried goodbye and gone back to the Banquet Hall.

44
The Weavers

THE airliner of Bangladesh Biman landed at Dum Dum airport. Deepali went straight to the railway station and bought a ticket for Bolpur. She was travelling second-class, for she wanted to see India's common people after thirty years of independence.

The train came out of suburban Calcutta, leaving behind gray Shaivite monasteries and mossy John Company bungalows. An old Hindu widow squatted on the compartment floor. She had covered her shaven head with her sari of rough white cotton. She was peeling watermelon seeds with great concentration. A tall and sturdy labourer from Eastern U.P. sat by a window. His four-year old daughter was playing in his lap. She was his married daughter as she wore red sindoor in the parting of her hair. The sight shocked Deepali. Child marriage still existed in India! Three students were absorbed in a feverish political discussion. Soon all three got bored and yawned in unison. A Marwari woman crouched in the corner opposite. She had covered her face with the end of her gold-work, red nylon sari. A blind Vaishnav beggar came in. He strummed his two-stringed lute and sang the mystic Madhavacharya's hymn to Lord Krishna. Some passengers gave him five-paise bits. He waited, expecting more. The crowd remained indifferent. Disappointed, he groped his way back to the corridor.

The train stopped at a country station. Two Muslim farmers climbed up. They wore broad-brimmed straw hats and blue sarongs. Both of them had identical goatee beards, one had Bugs Bunny teeth. They were carrying a sackful of rice. The train moved again.

There were paddy fields on either side. Cranes stood meditating in the watery furrows. Flat, uninteresting landscape, so different from the gorgeous scenery of her own Bangladesh. That used to be my homeland, she thought with a pang, that used to be my country. East Bengal, which has no duplicate in the world. The most beautiful country on earth. And I am an exile.

Burdwan was left behind. The train reached Bolpur.

She stepped out onto the platform and was confronted by a gleaming showcase. It displayed Santiniketan and Balucher saris. The old craft had been revived and Balucher's traditional master, Ustad Abdul Basit Khan of Murshidabad, had been given a national award by the President of the Republic of India. Deepali had once stolen her mother's Baluchers for the Party. That's how it all began, the sad, sad story of her life. Had it now come full circle? She gazed at the saris for some minutes, then went out.

Cycle-rickshaws swarmed outside the railway station. An emaciated, grinning rickshaw-puller peddled enthusiastically towards her. There was the same bazaar in front, the Islamia Hotel, the mosque...the old familiar sights of Bolpur.

"Where to, Didi?" the rickshaw-boy asked. She told him. The usual conversation followed.

"What is your name, son?" she asked.

"Ali Hussain."

"Ali Hussain," she repeated.

This famished rickshaw-wallah, Ali Hussain, was present in India as well as in Bangladesh. Nothing had changed for him.

Santiniketan was closed for the vacations.

She reached the guest-house and inquired about her old professors. Many had died, including Prof. Murtaza Hussain, on whose insistence she had joined Tagore's university. She booked a room, went in and threw herself on a spring-bed. Mosquitoes buzzed around her head.

Desolate. All was so desolate.

Cut out Delhi and rush back home. She visualised her fancy, luxurious bedroom. What must old Lalit be doing at this moment? What would be the time there? Oh, why should I tax my brain working out the time difference between India and Trinidad?

She went to the colourless dining-hall, ate bad food. The people around her looked old and sad. For the first time since she had come to the subcontinent, she realised that having spent twenty-eight years in the western hemisphere, she was a stranger to this place. At the same time she felt she had been suffocated by the affluence and impersonal efficiency of the West. The formal behaviour of Westerners had turned her into a loner. She was treated as part of Oriental exotica. She was sick of explaining her culture. She winced when her music and her literature were referred to as "ethnic". Here she was, back at last in her own Santiniketan, in her own Bengal, and she was feeling out of place... Was this the fate of all first-generation expatriates?

The next morning the sun was hot and piercing as she visited her alma mater. Colourless, drab, ordinary. In her youth it had been like a dreamland. The romance of Santiniketan! The cradle of all learning, all art. She went around Tagore's villa, returned to the guest-house, had her dinner, went to sleep. Everything seemed to have lost its shine. It must be different when term begins, she thought hopefully.

In the evening she went to the campus again. The place seemed unfamiliar. She crossed over to the sprawling "Tree of Peace" under which she used to study; where Rehan had arrived disguised as a Vaishnav monk; and where more than a century ago, Maharishi Debendranath Tagore had suddenly achieved enlightenment.

The comfort of my spirit.
The bliss of my heart.
The peace of my soul...

Corny.

A few girl-students sat on the other side of the tree's thick trunk, discussing the matinee idols, Amitabh Bachchan and Dharmendra. Movie magazines called *Filmfare, Stardust* and *Star & Style* were lying around them, along with a transistor.

The subcontinent is a vacuum in which young people hang in mid-air, listening to film music on their transistors. Nasira Najmus Sahar and people like her would soon be considered stark raving mad in all three countries—India, Bangladesh and Pakistan. *The Revolution is over, baby.*

Deepali looked at her wrist-watch and pressed her kneecaps. Perhaps the beginning of arthritis, she thought with alarm and stood up. As she passed by the Art College she saw the black clay statue of the Buddha. *Its feet were of clay, too.*

Dusk fell. The sickle-carrying peasants of Santhal Pargana walked by on the Sal Avenue.

The moon rose.

He vanished like the rainbow. The moon was extinguished.

The following day she visited the handloom factory of Bolpur; she wanted to buy a few Balucher saris and take them home. That was the real touristy thing to do. Bearded weavers were busy weaving their superfine textile. Their forefathers had woven the superfine muslin of Dacca and the gorgeous silks of Murshidabad. Sarojini Debi, whose poetry had fascinated her, chased her down to the workshop...

> *Weavers, weaving at the fall of night,*
> *Why do you weave a garment so bright?*
> *Like the plumes of a peacock, purple and green,*
> *We weave the marriage-veils of a queen.*
> *Weavers weaving solemn and still,*
> *What do you weave in the moonlight chill?*
> *Light as a feather and white as a cloud,*
> *We weave a dead man's funeral shroud.*

Under the mosque in front of Bolpur railway station a blind beggar woman was calling out to Allah.

The clutter of cycle-rickshaws again. This inhuman mode of transport depressed her. The smiling, tubercular Ali Hussain had brought her from her guest-house.

"Didi, when will you come again?" he asked cheerily.

"Don't know."

The beggar woman under the minaret is listening hopefully to the footfalls of passersby....

45
The Kite-Flier

Sitting on a rocking-chair in her Alipur Road bungalow, Kumari Uma Roy looked exactly like her mother, the late Lady Pritish Roy. The same imperious manner. Snow-white hair. Same wrinkles. A huge emerald ring on a finger. Pashmina shawl. Like a dowager Maharani. A Raj Mata. Queen Mother. She used to be fat. Illness had made her thin and bony.

She was feeding her poodles. A few half-naked, thin and dark Purbi urchins worked in the garden outside. Woodland, Ramna, Dacca, had presented an identical scene forty years earlier. Who says the world has changed or that there has been a 'quiet revolution' or the Naxalite movement? The same autocratic Uma Debi. Hail to thee, O goddess Kali of Kalikatta...

"Nomashkar, Uma Debi."

"Oh, hello! You have turned up again!" She had become cranky, too. Deepali told her the reason for visiting India and Bangladesh.

"You know, my brother Nirmalendu drank himself to death and Rehan went away to Bangladesh."

Her life had been such a tragedy because of Rehan. Deepali felt again that she was a mere bystander; yet felt strangely light and unconcerned.

"Rehan returned to his roots, Uma Didi," she answered dispassionately. "There comes a time when a person realises that instead of facing a subtle undercurrent of culture-clash, one should return to one's roots."

"If he had married you or me, would he have faced a culture-clash?"

"Not in the beginning. Later. When one approaches old age one feels the need for one's own cradle. A man looks about for his mother's culture."

"Is Arjumand Manzil his cradle?" Uma flared up. She began to tremble and cough by turn.

"Perhaps, to an extent Arjumand Manzil as well as his wife, Zohra," Deepali replied, undaunted by Uma's fury. She had been scared of her ever since she was a teenager. Why should she fear her now?

She can't harm me. My hair has turned gray, too. There is no Rehan Ahmed between us, no Dr. Benoy Chandra Sarkar, and I am richer than her now. So why should she continue to bully me?

Should we forgive those who tresspass against us? Had Yasmin forgiven them? Shiva...Shiva...

"I saw Rehan in every situation and remained his loyal friend," Uma began between coughs. "The student in pre-war London. The underground revolutionary, disguised as a Baul fakir in Dacca. Idealist. Romantic. Down-and-out in post-Partition Calcutta. A Minister in the provincial cabinet. Now you have met him as the new tycoon of Bangladesh. He does not write to me. Some months back his pacifist-poet son, Furqan, had come to Calcutta. I saw him on television. He never even rang me up." Suddenly she changed her tone and said, "Deepali, you are very lucky. You always won."

"Do you think so, Uma-di?" she asked sweetly. It looked like two ladies were discussing the teams of Mohammedan Sporting Club and Mohan Bagan after the football match was over.

Grief arrived like a huge black bird. It spread and gathered its wings, bent its head, and sat down near the two women.

"Miss Saheb, motor ready," a servant announced in such a tone as though the coach-and-four were ready for Lady Elijah Impey.

"Come along, come with me," Uma said to her guest.

The Kapalik Yogi of Time has adorned himself with a garland of skulls. There are bells and flags tied to his staff. He stalks ahead of us.

"Bengal Club?"
"No, temple...Mother's temple."
Uma Roy used to be an atheist. She belonged to a Brahmo family which shunned idol worship. Now she was going to venerate the grotesque statue of a stone goddess. How much difference did life leave between her and Bhavtarni Debi?
"Kali Ghat, Miss Saheb?" the chauffeur asked.
"No, Belur."

Evening puja was being performed in front of the huge image of Durga in a marble hall of Belur Math. A number of European and American sanyasis stood about with folded hands. They looked very intense.

Uma and Deepali took part in the puja and came out. Monkeys played about in the trees. A yogini sat under a banyan tree. She had made a side-bun of her thick, glossy hair and looked rather stagey. Her eyes were closed and she was apparently in deep meditation.

Vangali or Bangali is an ancient melody of Bengal. Like all modes and melodies, apart from its image of sound, its psychic form is visualised as a yogini of Lord Shiva. She sits on a deerskin in front of her hut in a forest. There are monkeys on the trees above, and a lion by her side on the deerskin...

The Bengali ascetic woman in Belur Math was no "Bangali Ragini"! She was perhaps an old maid, or a widow, or a tired housewife who had called it a day, or maybe she was a genuine mystic. You never can tell, Deepali pondered, as she accompanied Uma to the adjoining courtyard.

The grey quadrangle resounded with silence. They sat down on a low parapet. Uma Roy dropped her sandals. They fell with a thud on the cement floor. Uma crossed her legs and assumed the position of meditation. Deepali kicked off her shoes. The two pairs looked absurd as they lay scattered on the ground. Deepali raised her eyes and looked above. A baboon was studying her with playful concentration.

"Kal Ratri...Black Night!" she exclaimed, laughing.

"Who...?" Uma was taken aback. The baboon disappeared.

"Nobody in particular," Deepali answered viciously. "Kal Ratri, a goblin who belongs to the household of Lord Shiva. Appeared in the form of a baboon. Wished to say something to you. Vanished."

The empty cells of departed monks looked eerie. Through their barred, open doors Deepali could see the dead ascetics' wooden sandals. They were placed on empty cots.

We leave our footwear behind in the world.

His memory would turn into a fragrance and reach the raintree grove thousands of miles away.

O Rower of the Painted Boat. You came neither with the ebb, nor with the flow. Koels sang in the honey-month of Chait. Fishermen went out with their nets under the winter moon. Ladybirds buzzed among the summer flowers.

"The crazy boat of love sails on the sands as well."

Bloody nonsense.

One was murdered. One committed suicide. One is an exile.

Uma Roy squats coughing under a banyan tree.

Terrible Kali. Terrible Compassionate Great Mother.

No deities exist.

Alone with her poodles and her servants and her wealth, Uma Roy is coughing out the world.

Suddenly Uma looked up and said agitatedly, "Give me some good news. I have very few glad tidings in my life..."

"Nor have I, Uma-di, nor have I," Deepali replied with relish. They were two old cats, their claws out, poised for a confrontation under an ancient tree. After a few moments Deepali said, "With her entire family Jehan Ara perished in the Bangladesh war."

"I know. Tell me some more."

"Earlier, Jehan Ara's younger sisters died in a plane crash. The airliner fell down in the Alps. Their bodies could not be found." Like a ghoulish, sadistic supervisor in a morgue she went into the gory details. "When Jehan Ara was gunned down her room became a pool of red blood. Her brains were spattered on the walls. Nawab Qamrul Zaman was cut into teeny-weeny bits. His son, daughter-in-law and grandson..."

"More..."

"My father, your former handsome fiancé, Dr. Benoy Chandra Sarkar, died of lung cancer. Gave up the ghost in horrible pain. One could not bear to see his tormented face. A couple of years earlier my aunt, Bhavtarni Debi, lost her eyesight. Her blood pressure had shot up to high heaven. She was shrieking like a demented woman when she went to meet her Maker, whoever He or She is..."

"More..."

"See, in front of you, the vampires are spitting fire. Thin-lipped goblins are waiting to devour you and me. Time crushes the arrogant and the mighty."

"You have appeared before me as Kali..." Uma Roy said in a frightened voice.

"Whoever we are, we are about to burn out our present incarnations. The sun will grow cold, too. I immersed my father's and my aunt's ashes in the young Ganga at Hardwar. That is the end of the road. Listen, Uma Debi, to what the sanyasins of Belur Math sing... Mother sits in the marketplace of the world, flying her kites. She cuts off one of the millions of her strings and when the unattached kite floats up, it reaches cosmic space. Mother claps her hands and laughs..."

46
Old Ganga

THE Boeing jet shot through the night like a giant's arrow. Soon its bright lights were swallowed up by the midnight sky. Shut inside a capsule of steel, surrounded by many hundred strangers, an unimportant, meaningless Deepali Sen groped in her handbag for the unimportant Yasmin Belmont's meaningless diary. Her fingers touched the notebook with satisfaction. I have brought it back. Who shall I give it to? Nobody is its claimant. Even I have no inheritors. We are our own beginning and our own end. But... Perhaps Yasmin has a successor. Nasira Najmus Sahar...Perhaps...

Tokyo-Honolulu-Los Angeles-Port of Spain. It's a long journey. The inner and outer journey of time. And beyond that the voyage of ashes and bones floating down the Ganga. And the underground trail of the graves' worms. Rehan was so bloody right. I'm thankful that so many in the world have died, but I'm still living. Weary and tired like Old Ganga at Narayan Gunj, but not dead. Living.

The young American sitting next to her asked pleasantly, "Indian...?"

"Overseas Indian. West Indies."

"Jamaica?"

"Trinidad."

Joyfully she recalled her beautiful house surrounded by her own parkland. She thought fondly of Mistress Saraswati and Mistress Khairun. They, too, had become crotchety old women. Her loyal servants and her faithful, dependable, uninteresting husband, Lalit Mohan Sen. Her comfortable world. Good food. Music. Holidays in the States. She grew frightened again. Wind, my father. Earth, my mother. Fire, my friend. Water, my cousin. Sky, my brother. One is born through you. In the last moments of my life I send you my greetings, Bengal's Sanskrit poet, Yogeshwar, said a thousand years ago.

I hope these are not *my* last moments. She pressed her nose against the window-pane and looked out into the pitch dark night. After a few minutes the darkness lessened. The jet black sea became visible, and the dark sky above. The first night of creation... The notes of the awesome Raga Bhairav. Slowly the first light appeared on the horizon. Now I meditate on the psychic form of Raga Bhairav, Shiva's melody visualised in his own image. She closed her eyes. Auspicious. White garments. Crescent moon on the head. A garland round his neck. Poison in his throat. Red eyes. Bright earrings. The Raga sung by gods at first light.

Dawn was breaking. The conch-blowing pure Bhairav Raga was the whole universe. She began humming the notes of the various modes of Bhairav... Shiva, Bangala, Anand. She dozed, floating on the waves of the early morning melody. Then she looked out at the milky white horizon. I ought to worship Shiva, Cosmic Time, through Bhairav Raga. She began to hum a Bengali hymn to Shankar and looked out at the sparkling expanse of sky and water. Closed her eyes again. What should I meditate on? Can't concentrate on gods. Have they failed? Broken down? There are many hidden pictures inside me. Which one shall I concentrate on? Which melody shall I sing? There are so many secret melodies inside.

The waves of the South China Sea glimmered like liquid silver. Morning light fanned out far and wide. With his golden Noh mask on, the Sun God was slowly appearing over the misty islands of Japan.

For millions of years the sun has been rising and going down and rising again and going down again and rising...

ENG-34

ALSO BY QURRATULAIN HYDER IN WOMEN
UNLIMITED AND SPEAKING TIGER

MY TEMPLES, TOO
A Novel

Transcreated by the author
From the original Urdu
Mere Bhi Sanamkhane

Partition, independence, democracy. This book tells the tale of the birth of two new nations, experienced in the lives and deaths of its young citizens. Set in Lucknow of the 1940s, Qurratulain Hyder's masterly early novel is a story of kinship, intimate friendships and love in a context of political upheaval. Rakshanda, Peechu, Kiran, Salim, Christabel—the youthful protagonists—are idealistic and enthusiastic, fighting for a brave new world. With the turbulence of Partition and Independence, the quiet rhythms of domesticity are brutally disrupted. New animosities replace old loyalties, and the merry 'Gang' of Lucknow is torn apart as the old order begins to fragment.

'In a subcontinent that is still grappling with problems of identity and belonging, *My Temples, Too*…[the transcreation of] *Mere Bhi Sanamkhane* (1949), is an important literary event…a literary milestone for every English-language reader, hitherto shut out by 'the emotional and psychological block' against Urdu.'
—*The Hindu*

PAGE EXTENT: 184 pp   PRICE ₹ 299   ISBN: 978-81-88965-13-7

women
UNLIMITED
an associate of
kali for women

SPEAKING
TIGER